PRAISE FOR AMANDA BROOKFIELD

WALLS OF GLASS
'A perceptive – and very readable – account of the strains of marital breakdown'

The Times

'The story is told in pithy slices using excellent dialogue ... Amanda Brookfield could lead the woman's novel a few steps further out of its cultural ghetto'

Sunday Telegraph

A CAST OF SMILES
'Continues in the same vein of amused perception which characterised her debut ... What is refreshing here is the author's conspicuous sanity and her sharp line in defence of reason. It could be sentimental, but it isn't'

Robert Nye, *Guardian*

ALICE ALONE
'Amanda Brookfield's assurance and intelligence make *Alice Alone* stand out ... a strong sense of humour, a natural narrative gift and controlled, understated characterisation signify a promising debut'

Evening Standard

MARRIAGE GAMES
'Brookfield is spot on with characterisation'

Image

'Amanda Brookfield has an easy, readable style'

Dorchester Guardian

Also by Amanda Brookfield

Walls of Glass
A Summer Affair
Alice Alone
A Cast of Smiles
The Godmother
Marriage Games

About the author

Amanda Brookfield gained a First Class
Honours Degree from Oxford before
working in an advertising agency for
several years. She wrote her first novel
while living in Buenos Aires with her
diplomat husband, and her second while
in Washington, D.C. She has two young
sons and now lives in London and divides
her time between writing fiction and
looking after her family.

Single Lives

Amanda Brookfield

FLAME
Hodder & Stoughton

First published in Great Britain in 1999 by Hodder and Stoughton
First published in paperback in 1999 by Hodder and Stoughton
A division of Hodder Headline PLC

A Flame Paperback

10 9 8 7 6 5 4 3 2 1

ISBN 0340 71266 X

Printed and bound in Great Britain by
Clays Ltd, St Ives plc.

Hodder and Stoughton
A division of Hodder Headline PLC
338 Euston Road
London NW1 3BH

For Ben and Ali

ACKNOWLEDGEMENTS

With much gratitude to Christa d' Souza, Joanna
Simon and Dr Given-Wilson for their invaluable
guidance in areas beyond my expertise, and
especially tender thanks to my husband,
Mark, for endless, unqualified support.

Chapter One

———◆◆◆———

Catching the eye of a tall attractive man in a silk navy jacket, Annie felt some of her interest in the party rekindled. It was rare for her to identify someone so instantly attractive, let alone one who showed a flicker of reciprocative interest. He was talking animatedly to a blonde-haired girl in a plastic miniskirt, stabbing the air with his cigarette and running his free hand through elegant tresses of chestnut hair. Wriggling her toes, suffering in the cramped triangular points of her new stilettos, Annie tried a second glance, only to find that the man had turned his back and moved away.

Aware that she was committing the unforgivable social crime of standing alone, she spun round in search of new distractions. As she did so her left elbow caught on a display board, knocking it into a vast plate of dismembered salmon. The board, whose caption – *RoundUp, A New Journal for a New World* – summed up the rationale for the presence of so many bodies in one room, was already showing signs of wear and tear. A red wine stain, like a cartoon of a fat spider's web, had somehow found its way into the bottom right-hand corner, defacing pearls of critical wisdom from a literary editor about the new publication's chances of success

'Whoops-a-daisy.' Stephen Garr, an eager young political hack who had already spent the best part of an hour treating Annie to a garlicky diatribe on the unparalleled merits of the Internet, reappeared at her side. 'Did I mention that I've got a disk offering fifty hours of free access, which I'd be more than happy to lend, if you'd like to experiment before logging on officially?' He reached across her to straighten the board. 'Like I said, being a journalist and so on, you'd find it invaluable.'

'I'm sure you're right.' Annie smiled at him, wondering for by no means the first time in her thirty-three years why it was that the males most obviously attracted to her tended to be the ones she found the least appealing. Stephen Garr's eager speckled face and springy hair reminded her of the unattractive creature to whom she had entrusted the solemn chore of exchanging a first proper kiss. Shocked at the unpleasant tunnelling of a wet tongue round her teeth and tonsils, it had taken some determination to see the challenge through; a determination born partly out of peer pressure to indulge in such activities, and less easily defined anxieties connected to the discovery that her parents were committing the unmentionable – and unmentioned – sin of sleeping in separate bedrooms. The need to grow up had felt urgent, Annie remembered, smiling at Stephen and wishing she had the courage to be unkind.

'That is a very generous offer . . . very generous,' she faltered, 'but I'm afraid that I don't want to surf – or do backstroke for that matter – on invisible waves of any sort. I've only just managed to graduate from a typewriter to something that plugs into a wall and which bleeps at me when I'm trying to fall asleep.' She drained the last drops of her warm white wine, eyeing her young companion over the rim of her glass and reminding herself that being generous and gentle to such creatures was unlikely to offer any solutions to the deficiencies in her private life.

'You've got a great turn of phrase Annie, really great.' He shook his head happily. 'But then I guess that's why you're such a good columnist.'

The compliment, touching as it did on a subject about which Annie had been feeling increasingly vulnerable in recent weeks, lifted her spirits in an instant. Her face broke into the first natural smile of the evening, showing off the slightly overcrowded mouth of which she had always been unnecessarily shy and the two natural cheek-dimples that insisted on accompanying it. 'I thought politics was your scene. I had no idea that your weekly reading extended to tabloid Saturday reviews.'

'Oh no, it doesn't – I mean, I've seen your column, obviously, but I don't exactly read it because . . . well . . . I've always assumed it's really for women and so on . . . because it's all about . . . clothes and feelings and stuff . . . isn't it?'

'Clothes and feelings and stuff?' Annie laughed defensively, some of her gratitude shrivelling inside. 'Yes, I suppose it is.' She picked up one of the numerous copies of *RoundUp* stacked on the table beside them and began a hurried, unseeing flick through its pages to hide her dismay. 'But things like that are important,' she concluded lamely, telling herself that it would be both foolhardy and pointless to blurt out to a comparative stranger that, instead of proving the refreshing career departure she had imagined, adopting a lighthearted persona for a weekly column was proving to be one of the most arduous challenges of her journalistic career; that, six months into it, she was scratching for ideas with a desperation that made her afraid.

'And you don't look a bit like your photograph – much prettier, if I may say so,' continued Stephen, misreading her hesitation as modesty.

'You certainly may,' quipped Annie, managing a good-humoured scowl at this reference to the cropped mugshot heading her column. Due to space restrictions, a potentially interesting pose had been reduced to an unflattering close-up of what looked like a failed attempt at sultriness, made even worse by the unflattering and curiously asymmetric shapes into which the photographer had insisted on combing her hair. 'It's horrible, isn't it,' she admitted with a rueful smile. 'I look as if I've just been ejected from a wind tunnel—' Stephen burst into appreciative guffaws, drawing looks of sympathetic curiosity from several nearby guests. Including the good-looking man, who had somehow drifted back to within a few feet of her, and was deep in conversation with a willowy redhead with thick, wind-charm earrings that tugged alarmingly at the lobes of her ears. He had another cigarette in his hand, Annie noticed, slotted carelessly between his fingers with the ease of the habitual smoker. Seized with sudden inspiration and courage, she fumbled in her bag for her own cigarettes – the packet of ten low tar which, like many predecessors, she had vowed would be her last – and then looked enquiringly in his direction for a light.

The response was gratifyingly instantaneous, almost as if he had been waiting for just such an opportunity himself. Quickly reaching into his jacket pocket, he produced a slim gold lighter and signalled her to approach.

'But you've got a lighter,' remarked Stephen, tapping her bag, 'I'm sure you have. I saw you use it a moment ago.'

'It's not working,' Annie murmured, sidling past the redhead and tilting the end of her cigarette towards the flame cupped between the man's hands. Long slim hands, she noticed, with perfect white crescents for cuticles and trimmed nails. 'Thank you so much.' She inhaled deeply, ignoring the unpleasant burning which tended to strike during the course of a second packet, and blew a stylish plume of smoke at the ceiling.

'So how do you rate *RoundUp*, then?' she asked quickly, wanting to capitalise on this promising turn of events but taking care to include the flame-haired woman within the frame of enquiry.

'How do *you* rate it?' he countered, tapping ash into his empty glass and inviting her to do the same. He had striking brown eyes, though with such wide pupils that they looked almost black. Like his face, they were constantly animated, giving the impression of eagerness but of restlessness too, as if constantly in search of something to captivate his interest. He looked to be in his early thirties and with enough swarthiness in his complexion to suggest something mediterranean in his ancestry. 'And not a word from you, Moira, please,' he warned the woman standing between them, 'you're biassed.' His left hand performed a flourish of an invitation for Annie to give her response. A hand that contained no gold ring, she noticed, despising herself for the dogged nature of such observations, but feeling an absurd stab of encouragement nonetheless.

'Not too highly, I'm afraid.' Annie flexed her eyebrows in a show of thoughtfulness for a subject which she had barely considered at all. 'Mainly because I can't help thinking it's essentially such a dull concept, printing articles that have already appeared in the news that week. I can't believe it will really catch on. People will have read half of them, and even if they haven't, the subject matter will be so familiar that they won't really be bothered—'

She was interrupted by a nervous laugh from Stephen Garr, who had remained irritatingly glued to her elbow throughout these introductions. 'Annie, I . . . er . . . think perhaps you should—'

'So you think it's a waste of valuable rain forest?' pressed the man smoothly, exchanging a look with Moira and stubbing out his cigarette in his empty wine glass.

Aware of a slight tension in the air, Annie hesitated, giving Stephen the chance to speak first. 'This is Greg Berkley, Annie, one of the co-editors of *RoundUp*—'

She gulped air and smoke. 'What I mean is . . . it has a chance of doing really well – because there's a really big market for this kind of stuff – for this kind of well-written, well-edited, intellectual overview of what really makes the world tick . . .'

Greg Berkley threw back his head and laughed with confident abandon. 'Wow, that's what I call back-pedalling on a grand scale . . . most impressive . . . I'm almost flattered.'

Annie managed to laugh too, but only because to have failed to do so would have revealed the extent of her mortification. 'In with both feet, as usual,' she apologised, once the general amusement had subsided. 'I'd make a lousy politician.'

'I'm pleased to hear it. Politicians are my least favourite brand of people. And you may be right about our fledgling enterprise. Only time will tell, not to mention a little patience from our bank managers. Perhaps we should keep in touch so you can see for yourself how things turn out . . . Oh Christ, Moira, there's Tony Newton – we really ought to have a word.' He placed his hand on his companion's shoulder and began steering her back towards the throng of people by the window. 'One of our backers,' he explained, with a parting shrug of what looked like genuine apology.

'I hope I'm wrong,' Annie called after him, twirling her empty glass by way of a farewell salute and then quickly excusing herself in order to avoid any follow-up commentary from Stephen, who stood gazing after her with furtive longing, musing upon the rare and happy combination of a woman who was both funny and clever without being a show-off about either. Not even the *faux-pas* with Berkley had seemed like a big deal, he reflected incredulously, thinking how similar circumstances would have caused him to faint with shame.

Once in the darkened safety of a spare bedroom, Annie tugged on her coat and scarf with a series of heavy sighs. Though relieved to be out of the mêlée of guests, she was already struggling with the sense of failure which she knew would shadow her home. Not just because of her recent social ineptitude with the most attractive man to cross her path in a decade, but because of the unwritten *FlatLife* column, looming as it always did over the latter half of the week.

Two heated exchanges with taxi drivers looking for rides down towards the river did nothing to lighten her mood. Hobbling because of a blister on her right heel, she crossed the road and took up a new look-out position on a traffic island.

'Are you young free and single, darling?' shouted a supine figure in a dark doorway a few yards up the street.

'Yes, and happy with it,' Annie retorted, not without a certain ironical sense that this was far from the case; that, in spite of the wretched example set by her own parents, any youthful determination not to risk repeating their failures had long since faded to the pitiful point where she could not be introduced to a male without assessing his potential as a life-partner. Wanting a man was so unfashionable and undignified, Annie reflected with a sigh, particularly for a woman who had worked hard to craft an image of self-sufficiency and with a reputation for laughing such tribulations into insignificance.

To take her mind off such matters, she fished out the only

remaining cigarette in her now crumpled packet of ten, and spent several frustrating minutes trying to persuade her lighter to cooperate in the face of a blustering wind. Having succeeded at last, she leant back against the railings and let her thoughts drift to the halcyon days of her youth, when taxis appeared at all hours of the night, begging for rides instead of finding excuses not to give them, when vices like smoking had been a source of pleasure rather than guilt. Days when a close circle of friends, a comfortable flat and a good career seemed like luxuries as opposed to props for survival.

A parked car hooted for attention across the street. For one brief, brilliant moment Annie thought it was Greg Berkley, signalling that all was forgiven, that he loved feisty women with tactless opinions, that a whirlwind romance could begin after all. But it was Stephen Garr, with his lumpy red nose and stiff brush of hair.

'I'll give you a lift if you like,' he shouted. 'You look frozen.'

'I live miles away.'

'Where?'

'Off the Finchley Road – the seedy bit of St John's Wood.'

'I didn't know there was a seedy bit. Come on, get in – I'm blocking the road.'

'But you live in Tooting Bec or somewhere, don't you?'

'Balham. Get in.'

'But—'

'I love driving. Really I do. Please?'

Scolding herself for taking advantage, for nurturing seeds of hope where none could possibly flourish, Annie at last succumbed and clambered into the seat beside him.

'I hope you like Al Stewart.'

'Oh, yes,' she lied, sinking into her coat, grateful for any pretext not to make conversation.

'Good party?' Marina was sitting on the sofa watching television and eating from a large bag of apple chips. Balanced somewhat precariously on a cushion beside her was a full glass of red wine.

Seeing her like that, in her crimson silk dressing-gown, her hair glossy from the shower, her long legs crossed yoga-style in front of her, Annie was struck afresh by the effortless glamour of her flatmate. An effect all the more remarkable given the contents of Marina's one and only photo album, which housed a teenaged version of the same creature, sporting buck-teeth, a beanbag of a body and a scalp-yanking ponytail showing off pink, protruberant ears. Bedtime braces and a good haircut could work wonders, Marina had joked, so clearly at ease with these early attempts to pass for a human being, that Annie, aware of the way her own youthful profile still clung to her, had felt a surge of jealousy and admiration. For months afterwards she had glared with extra ferocity in the mirror each morning, wishing her own body could have performed some comparable meta-morphic miracle to ease the troubled passage into adulthood and middle age.

'No – even worse than expected.'

'Why did you go, then?' replied Marina mildly, keeping her eyes on the screen.

'Because it was the one solitary possibility of a social engage-ment in my entire week, and I thought it might give me some ideas for the column.'

'You make the column up,' Marina reminded her through a mouthful of chips, 'fiction, literary persona – all that sort of clever stuff.' She noisily licked each finger and returned her attention to the screen.

'Yes, I do . . . but even the best fiction needs an idea or two to trigger it off . . .' faltered Annie, revealing some of her own bafflement as to why something which had started out so effort-lessly had lately grown so hard. 'I thought you weren't going to drink this week,' she teased, in a bid to lift her own spirits rather than because she felt the remotest impulse to offer a reprimand. In fifteen years of flat-sharing, Marina was far and away the best, most amicable, companionable, inoffensive person she had met, living her own life with easy independence but offering a solid fall-back of friendship and solace whenever it was needed.

'Red wine's too medicinal to count. Do you want one of these?' She crackled her bag of chips.

Annie shook her head. 'What are you watching?'

'The guy in the black hat has probably killed someone – at least his wife thinks so. She's having an affair with the man in jeans, which is making the teenage girl jealous. Oh, and there was a flashback to a scene in a swimming pool when someone almost drowned – Jake's coming over, by the way.'

'Jake? Oh no, Marina, not tonight . . . I was going to make a start on my column.'

'No you weren't,' Marina corrected her, her mouth full of apple chip, 'it's far too late and you never start it till Wednesday anyway. Tell me more about this awful party.'

Annie kicked off her shoes and pulled a cushion to her chest. 'I found the man of my dreams,' she murmured, flexing her stiff toes, 'Daniel Day Lewis meets Liam Neeson.'

Marina raised an eyebrow. 'Sounds interesting.'

'You haven't heard the best of it.'

'Go on.' For the first time Marina gave Annie her full attention, her big brown eyes already twinkling with expectation. One of the reasons an intended short-term occupation of a bedroom on such an absurd tube-route to work had extended to almost three years was that Annie Jordan made her laugh, that when it came to the business of reporting personal disaster for the purposes of entertainment, her flatmate's abilities were unparalleled. The other was that Annie, unlike any other friend she had ever had, was not interested in the business of passing judgements. She lived moment by moment, coping with life's ups and downs with all the endearing unreadiness of a novice in the front seat of a rollercoaster.

'Things began well,' continued Annie, sensing Marina's pleasure and rising to the occasion. 'Our eyes caught across a crowded room – literally—'

'What the hell are you looking so long-faced about, then?' shrieked Marina who, at thirty-two, claimed to be on a similar quest for romantic fulfilment as her friend, but who was capable of ploughing through as many lovers in a month as Annie had managed in a lifetime.

'Wait, I haven't finished. When I finally managed to engineer a meeting – no mean feat I can tell you, the place was packed – I tried to dazzle him with some sharp criticism of the magazine we were all supposed to be toasting only to find he was one of the bloody editors.'

'Oh no, Annie.' Marina was laughing so much she had to put her chips and wine on the coffee table for safe-keeping. 'Did he guess you liked him?'

'I think so.'

'Worse and worse.'

'Marina,' Annie interrupted urgently, 'do you ever feel that you've got two versions of yourself? The one inside and the one on the outside that everybody knows or thinks they know—?'

She was cut off by the sound of the doorbell. 'What possessed you to invite Jake round?'

'Jake invited Jake round, you know what he's like.' Marina folded away her bag of chips and wiped her mouth with the back of her hand.

'I sometimes think resting actors should mix with their own kind,' muttered Annie, going to answer the door, 'especially after ten-thirty on a Tuesday night.'

'I'm sorry, Annie,' began Marina, now feeling some dismay herself at the lateness of the hour. 'He said his agent hasn't called for weeks and he's nursing a broken heart—'

'What, again?' Annie interjected dryly, going to push the button that released the main door downstairs. While Jake shared few details of his liaisons with either of them, it had always been perfectly clear to her that he wreaked far more damage than he ever suffered himself.

'He's a worse flirt than me,' agreed Marina cheerfully, who had once tried and failed – like many women before her – to convert Jake Harding to the delights of heterosexual relationships, with no satisfactory results whatsoever. Acceptance of this defeat had bred a warm friendship. Although he remained primarily Annie's friend, stumbled upon through her early days as a hack for a South London newspaper. Originally he had shared the flat too, during the era when all three bedrooms were let, when the now-exiled Pete Rutherford had been around as well, with his washing-up timetables and rotas for scrubbing under the rim of the loo.

Contrary to Marina's report, Jake seemed in fine spirits. He bounded into the sitting room, the panels of his greatcoat flapping, brandishing a bottle of champagne and a large punnet of strawberries. 'They're to be eaten with black pepper. I know it sounds odd, but honestly, it's the only way. I brought my own,' he continued gleefully, reaching into his pocket and pulling out a large wooden pepper mill, 'because I knew you hopeless girls would only have sawdust.'

'We're not girls, we're middle-aged women,' grunted Annie, 'who desperately need their beauty sleep in order to appear like unironed napkins in the morning.'

'Speak for yourself.' Marina sidled up to Jake and reached up to ruffle the freshly bleached spikes of his hair. 'Did you bring ciggies too?' She began playfully frisking his pockets. 'Annie's trying to cut down which means she's never got any.'

'For God's sake, you two.' Annie rolled her eyes in despair, though inside she could feel herself relenting. Perhaps a laugh with good friends was all she needed to shake the emptiness away and bring her normal self back into being. 'But I have got a packet as it happens,' she volunteered coyly, provoking howls of approval from Marina, who had the most infuriating capacity for puffing like an addict one minute and then not touching a cigarette for weeks on end. 'My back-up reserves. They're hidden in my top drawer, under a pair of lacy knickers that look ravishing but itch like hell.'

'Good girl,' said Marina. 'I'll find some clean glasses.'

sharpen the imaginative powers on which she habitually relied for the column. A concerted intake of carbohydrate – a large bar of chocolate, two bowls of mashed banana and five pieces of toast and blueberry jam – consumed at a steady pace throughout the day, had left her feeling full of sleepiness and self-recrimination. Apart from two blueberry seeds lodging themselves in the fissures of an ancient filling and providing a welcome spell of distraction with a cocktail stick and a hand mirror, the hours had crawled by with maddening inexorability and little progress.

By three o'clock, with the same execrable sentences on the screen in front of her, a mild panic began to push into the pit of Annie's stomach. Fighting the urge to tread the well-worn path to the kitchen, she wandered round the flat for a few minutes, taking deep breaths and reminding herself that she was a humorous, witty grown-up with a degree in media studies and over ten years of journalistic experience under her belt. That what she was suffering from was not writer's block so much as a hangover, induced by the ill-timed festivities of well-intentioned friends.

A little calmer, she padded into her bedroom to scrutinise the wreckage of her body and face, wanting to check that it was as irretrievably shambolic as she remembered it and finding that it was. Her hair, in spite of its newly acquired burgundy highlights, lay flat and helmet-like around the pallid circle of her face. Her eyes, which could, with a little enhancement, appear almond shaped and of an interesting greeny-grey, looked washed out and small. Though concealed beneath a generous sweatshirt, Annie could feel her stomach cutting into the top of her jeans, reminding her not only of that day's sugar cravings but also of the grim news on the bathroom scales that morning. Nine stone and eight pounds. Only a whisper away from her highest weight ever, a terrifying ten stone, recorded during the weeks immediately after her split from Pete, when she had binged standing at the door of the fridge like a crazed and starving animal. Fortunately for both her self-esteem and her wardrobe, this low point had been followed by a period of reactive abstinence, when she floated round on a diet of cigarettes and mineral water, feeling like a film star in her defining role. The ten-stone mark obligingly moved out of the frame, but never far enough for Annie to feel that it might not take centre-stage again.

Having made herself a strong cup of black coffee, she deferred a reunion with her computer, by seeking solace from the telephone. Finding Marina's line engaged, she tried Jake instead, who sounded dispiritingly perky. His agent had phoned that morning about an audition for a commercial; yoghurt in a Caribbean setting. But they wanted someone dark, so he was busy trying to get rid of the bleach. When Annie moaned about her headache and her deadline, he said her writing was marvellous, that she was marvellous, but that he couldn't talk for long because a bowl of glutinous hair colourant was solidifying in the bathroom.

'Try a slug of whisky in your coffee – might do wonders for the little grey cells.'

'Haven't got any,' she muttered.

'Scotch or grey cells?' he quipped, but Annie hadn't laughed.

'Neither. And anyway, we drink too much.'

'My, we are feeling joyful this afternoon.'

'Do you drink to make the most of your feelings or to escape them?'

'Bloody hell, Annie, where's all this coming from? I drink in a concerted effort to destroy my liver, as you well know. Look, if things are really that bad, why don't you fax me your piece and I'll send it back with lots of helpful red squiggles in the margin.'

'Don't worry, I expect I'll pull something out of the hat in the end,' she mumbled, knowing both that he was trying to be kind and that she had struck a nerve which experience should have taught her to leave alone. Jake's predilection for seeking pleasurable detours round life's problems as opposed to actually confronting them was well known and one of the reasons she had been drawn to him in the first place. Times were hard for him too, she reminded herself, since the financial luxury of a grandfather's trust fund could do nothing to camouflage the fact that, at the ripe age of thirty-five, most of his earnings were still coming from bit parts and low-budget commercials.

'Do you want me to play editorial assistant or not?'

'Like in the old days, you mean?' They laughed, both momentarily swept back to Annie's grim and penurious days as a journalist for *Looking South*, when Jake, then trying his hand at modelling and often with nothing to do for weeks on end, would accompany her on assignments, bringing hilarity into the bleakest and most mundane scenarios.

'Go back to your basin, I'll be fine.'

She tried Marina again, who, like Jake, sounded full of unnatural health and vigour.

'Why do I have the headache,' wailed Annie, 'when compared to you two I barely drank at all?'

'Probably because you're moping around the flat thinking about it.'

'I'm starting a new regime tomorrow. Fitness and fibre. In a week or two you won't recognise me.'

Marina laughed. 'Well, I've got other plans.' She lowered her voice. 'Do you remember that strategist I mentioned, the one in corporate finance? The one with the bald patch.'

'Bald patch?' echoed Annie, too inured to the shenanigans in her flatmate's love life to feel any real interest.

'I think he might be about to make a move. He's really very sweet.'

'Sweet?' She began a grunt of distaste which got foreshortened by a yawn. 'What about Donald?' she asked sleepily, referring to Marina's most recent escort, a tall blond Adonis of a man who worked as a fund manager at the bank from where Marina had recently moved. For a woman with no career agenda beyond the desire to have a good time, Marina had somehow done remarkably well. This latest job not only came with an impressive salary increase, but had also elevated her to a status that shelved the title of 'secretary' altogether in favour of something described as a 'senior personal assistant'. Though her duties still included feeding the occasional parking metre and having conversations with recalcitrant dry cleaning companies, she had also been promised occasional trips abroad – not to the dull European spots that some of Annie's more intrepid features had once led her, but to genuinely exotic places like Hawaii and San Francisco. Most enviable of all, as far as Annie was concerned, was that Marina's career course continued to allow her limited work responsibilities to remain behind an office door, instead of spilling out at home.

'Dear Donald.' Marina sighed heavily. 'He's out of the picture, didn't I tell you? I've got to break the news this afternoon.' The resigned but firm tone of voice was an indication of the strict codes that underlined Marina's colourful social habits. As well as married men and immediate employers being strictly out of bounds, there was never any overlap between conquests. Her turnover might have been high, but never at the price of honesty. 'I'm afraid Donald was getting horribly soppy.'

'I'd love someone to get horribly soppy.'

'No you wouldn't, at least not if it was Donald. Cheer up girl, you sound rotten.'

'I can't think what to write. Nothing happens for me to write about.'

'Make it up as usual, silly.'

'I'm trying. I've written about six lines. They're diabolical. I'll probably get the sack.'

'You're on a contract, remember? You passed the three-month probation. The dreaded Amy Marsden would never have signed you up if she hadn't liked what you do. I've found a fab party for us, by the way,' she continued, jumping subjects with typical illogicality, 'not this Saturday but next. Our first Christmas thrash. The theme is cowboys.'

'How very festive.'

'You'll love it.'

Annie groaned. 'I don't think I'll live that long.'

'Well you bloody well better last until Friday – I'm not playing hostess on my own.'

'Why, what's happening on Friday?'

'Susie and George – if they're back on speaking terms – and Jake.'

'Oh God, I'd forgotten – and I'm out on Saturday too. Zoë and Richard—' She groaned.

'I don't understand you, Annie. One minute you're complaining that your social life is a desert and the next you're moaning about going out.'

'Ignore me,' said Annie lightly, in no mood to confess that she did not understand herself either, beyond a dim and un-settling sensation that two elements of her personality had started to pull in opposite and irreconcilable directions. 'It's just been one of those weeks. I'll get better soon, I promise.'

'Why not write about that nice-looking guy you were so rude to last night? I bet it would make you feel better.'

'Maybe—' Remembering the dark intensity of Greg Berkley's eyes, Annie doubted her capacity to compose anything coherent.

'I might be late tonight, by the way.'

'Oh yes? Because of our new bald friend or lovelorn Donald?'

'Depends how things go, but you won't want me around if you're working anyway.'

Before returning for what she knew would inevitably be a long haul at the computer, Annie ventured out to the overpriced Olympia supermarket near St John's Wood High Street, where she and Marina ended up doing most of their shopping. Feeling fractionally better and determined to get her health drive off to a flying start, she purchased a loaf of wholemeal rye bread packed with poppy seeds, a small jar of low-fat mayonnaise, an iceberg lettuce, a packet of salami, a can of fizzy diet apple juice and a bag of oranges. Only as the cashier was on the point of sliding her switch card through the machine, did she add a bottle of white wine and ten low tar cigarettes, telling herself that few human feats were achieved without incentives.

Outside the main entrance of the flats, Annie found herself being politely accosted by a dark-skinned man requesting to use her telephone. Seeing that he was not from either of the varied entourages that inhabited the other two floors in the building, her first instinct was to refuse.

'But both them boxes down the road are cards only and my car's broken down and I need to call a cab,' he persisted miserably.

Remembering the existence of her mobile phone and telling herself that it was, on the face of it, a perfectly reasonable request; and one that, had the initiator been handsomely dressed and in polished shoes, might well have caused her not to hesitate at all, Annie put down her shopping and opened her handbag.

'I'll pay you,' he said eagerly, reaching into his pocket and pulling out some change. 'It's just that I'm in a hurry – I mean I really need a cab. I'm sorry to bother you, man.'

By the time it became clear that the battery on her mobile was flat, Annie felt too far advanced upon the path of friendly cooperation to back down; a path made somehow more compelling by her determination not to show any discrimination because of the colour of his skin. Telling herself to have faith in human nature, that the majority of human beings were well-adjusted miserable sods like herself, Annie led the way up the stairs in order to see the favour through. Despising herself for appearing distrusting, she nonetheless took the precaution of standing with her foot in the door while he used the hall telephone, her arms folded in a show of nonchalance while her heart pummelled inside.

The moment he had finished her apprehensions seemed so laughable that she endeavoured to make up for them by chatting brightly all the way back down the stairs. Once in the street, they shook hands like old friends. As Annie turned back inside she felt a curious sense of empowerment. She had trusted her instincts and survived. She had helped a neighbour in his hour of need; a forbidding-looking neighbour, twice her height with shifty eyes.

In the jaws of the letterbox was a thin yellow leaflet entitled, *Hypnotherapy – The answer to everyday anxieties. Low self-esteem, smoking, weight-loss – Instant results guaranteed*. But not as effective as a simple old-fashioned dose of human goodwill, Annie mused, grateful and marvelling at her change in mood. She took the leaflet upstairs and stuck it onto the fridge, between an old postcard of bare bottoms that Jake had sent from a holiday in Morocco and a blurred photograph of some of the debauchery at his thirty-fifth the previous spring.

Returning to work with renewed faith in her abilities, Annie spent half an hour or so trying to write about the incident with the telephone man, wanting to find some expression for the curious uplift it had given to her spirits. But after a while she was forced to accept that it wouldn't work, that such a burst of sincerity about an episode in her own life simply did not fit with the jaunty, humorous tone in which she usually wrote the column. Instead, she reverted her attentions to the party the evening before, racking her brains for ways to distort the events into something appropriately frivolous and amusing.

Whether it was indeed the shoes, or the chic new 'gamin' haircut I've lately acquired, (please ignore the photo at the top of this column and refer all insults and jokes to my editor), I was minding my own business at one of the many media events clogging my social calendar when a dreamy, black-eyed Heathcliff of a man caught my eye across a crowded room, his dark arched eyebrows suggesting he knew and shared every nuance of my most erotic thoughts. Grateful that I was a) unmarried, b) relatively sober, c) wearing respectable underwear, I succumbed willingly to what felt like the pull of Fate. Without even trying, the partying crowd seemed to jostle us closer and closer together until at last we were within wine-spitting distance of each other's bodies. On being introduced he took my hand and bent to kiss it. Preparing to faint with ecstasy, I was disappointed to find myself made giddy instead by the unmistakable and overpowering aroma of full-blown halitosis . . .

. . . telling myself that life is full of these little disappointments, I nonetheless took the precaution of stopping at the late-night chemist to buy fresh stocks of minty floss and fluoride mouthwash for my bathroom shelf. If no one had told him, how do I know that I'm not afflicted with the same condition? Do you tell your best friend or lover when his/her breath smells . . . ?

Some three hours later, with a first draft that was adequate, if not remotely brilliant, Annie crawled from the spare room in which she worked to her bed. She was on the point of falling asleep when she heard Marina's key in the door. There followed a giggle and the sound of a soft male voice. Annie sighed and turned over on her side, hugging her pillow round her head like a giant ear-muff. Fearful that her sleepiness might slip away, she embarked on a slow and detailed calorie calculation for the day, a tried and trusted alternative to sheep-counting, which had seen her through many a night of Marina's fraternising in the past.

Chapter Three

Marina Hammond awoke before her lover and peered through the crook of her arm at the hairless circle on the head next to hers, challenging herself to be repulsed. Instead, she remembered the unflinching stare of his grey eyes as they made love and felt a shiver of retrospective pleasure. Tentatively, she put a finger to his scalp and traced it round the remaining circle of hair.

Aware of the sound of Annie already running taps and opening doors, she started to slide out of bed, but felt a hand slip round her waist. 'And where do you think you're going?'

She pressed the curve of her body back into his. 'Nowhere.'

'I'm going to take you out to breakfast. I know a lovely truckers' cafe. Greasy eggs and bacon on fried bread.'

'Hmm.' She nibbled his shoulder, loving the moment, but hating the knowledge that it would not last, that sooner or later, as always, something would happen. Some weakness would reveal itself, bringing the whole fragile, deliciously flirtatious structure tumbling down. Not hair-loss maybe, nor the fact of his absurdly awful name – Bernard Ramsbotham was a burden for any man to bear – but some detail of demeanour or character that would ultimately become the stumbling block to something lasting or worthwhile. With Donald, as with many of his predecessors, it had been the glimpses of doey-eyed devotion, the lovesick look of total sacrifice which had begun as a flicker and turned into a permanent facial expression. In Marina's experience it was impossible to have a laugh with someone so brimful of indiscriminating emotion, impossible to feel any respect for them at all.

She ran into Annie twenty minutes later in the corridor beside the kitchen. She was dressed in trainers, grey Lycra tights and a voluminous sweatshirt. Tied round the reddish jumble of her hair was a green hanky, over which sat the headphones of her Walkman.

'I'm going on a run.'

'I'd never have guessed.'

'I told you, I'm turning over a new leaf. Healthy people don't get nearly so depressed, everybody says so. I've even bought bran flakes.' She held out the large cereal box she had been clutching to her chest and shook it by way of confirmation of her commitment. 'I got fresh orange juice too. It's on the table.'

'I'm going to have bacon and eggs,' Marina declared, idly scratching her right thigh and sauntering into the sitting room.

Annie stood still for a moment, hugging her cereal box, aware of the scent of whoever Marina had slept with hanging in the air between them. On looking up, her speculations were answered by the rather portly man, clad only in boxer shorts, appearing from Marina's bedroom. He looked thirty-seven or eight. Maybe even forty, it was hard to tell. As he got closer she saw that the boxer shorts were covered in red hearts. The scent she had detected on Marina grew stronger.

'Hello,' he said, holding out his hand, 'Bernard Ramsbotham.'

Annie transferred her breakfast to her left hand in order to respond to the formality of the greeting. 'Annie Jordan. Flatmate.'

'Is the lavatory that way?'

'Yup, absolutely, down the hall, third on the right. Nice to meet you.'

'And a pleasure to meet you. By the way, are you going or have you been?'

For a moment Annie thought he was referring to the progress of her morning ablutions. 'I beg your pardon?'

'On your jog. Have you been?'

'Oh heavens no, I'm going to have breakfast first.'

He shook his head solemnly. 'Better not. You'll feel sick.' And having imparted this helpful advice, he proceeded on his way, leaving Annie staring after him with her mouth open, convinced that in affairs of the heart at least, Marina had finally and truly lost her way.

Bernard was right, though. After an initial industrious spurt to the bus stop at the bottom of her road, Annie grew uncomfortably aware of milky mush slopping against the walls of her stomach. Having originally intended to head for Primrose Hill, she set herself the revised and more realistic target of the nearest entrance to Regent's Park, where she flopped onto a bench by a shuttered ice-cream kiosk. The stomach cramps had been superseded by a horrible tightness in her lungs, like the suppression of a hundred unexploded coughing fits.

Having recovered a little, Annie abandoned her seat and strolled into the park. As the heat of exertion gradually died away, she could feel the cut of the wintry air through her sweat-dampened clothes. Only three weeks to Christmas. The realisation brought an absurd, childish reflex of anticipation before she remembered that for her the annual season of good-will meant enduring forty-eight hours of her mother in a draughty Welsh cottage together with a congenitally hostile younger brother and an unpromising creature called Hermione to whom he had recently got engaged. Her father, whom she had always found the easiest member of her family to adore, would be in Portugal as usual, in the barbed and protective embrace of the woman whose tenacity had finally succeeded in persuading him that twenty years of unhappy domesticity with one woman was no reason not to sign on for a few more decades of similar compromises with another.

Annie walked down the path that ran alongside London Zoo, craning her neck through the fencing for a glimpse of exotic fauna, but seeing only three tired crows and a goat-like creature with a long beard and ragged tail. Feeling suddenly very chilled, she rewound her tape – a compilation of ancient

favourites that Jake had put together for a party the year before
– and began a sedate trot back in the direction she had come.
Apart from a willowy woman with an Afghan hound and a
cyclist attending to a flat tyre, the path was empty. The cyclist
was not of the Lycra-clad variety, but a businessman attired in a
thinning suit with bicycle clips pinching his ankles. A flat brown
briefcase was pinned under the metal bar of the luggage rack
behind his seat. As Annie approached, he paused to watch her
pass, so intently that she felt compelled to introduce an added
spring to her stride, wanting suddenly to appear as someone who
jogged miles every morning, someone for whom health meant
pleasure as opposed to pain. A few yards further on, after a quick
glance back to check that her audience had lost interest, Annie
stumbled off the pathway to lean against a tree, dropping her
head towards her knees in a bid to calm her pulse rate. As she
straightened, a grey-haired man with a large moustache stepped
out from behind a nearby bush, his face fixed in a friendly grin.
Annie was on the point of smiling back when she realised that
he was fumbling with the front zip of his trousers.

'Why me?' she snapped, much to her own – and the would-
be flasher's – evident surprise. His hand froze over the gap in his
flies, looking suddenly as if it had been placed there out of
modesty, rather than from any intention to reveal the contents
of his underpants. 'Hangers-on, perverts – everybody's picking
on me at the moment and I'm fed up with it.' She glowered at
him. 'Now bugger off.'

Without a word, the man obediently bolted back behind his
bush. He came into view a few moments later, scurrying across
the wide stretch of grass that led in the direction of the boating
lake. Annie laughed out loud and shouted 'nutter'. While inside
she experienced a tremor of relief, and of anger too, hating the
way the incident had cast a shadow over the new resolve with
which she had launched herself at the day. Was the world more
threatening, or had she merely reached the age when it was
starting to appear so? she wondered, recalling her unnecessary
fear with the telephone man the evening before. During the
course of a decade in London she had handled far more

genuinely intimidating episodes with a much cooler head. She had even been flashed before, not as an adult but while waiting for a bus with her mother on one of their rare excursions to London. A slight, curly-headed man standing next to them had suddenly yanked down his jeans and begun cavorting round the bus shelter. He had looked so comical that Annie's only reaction had been a paroxysm of schoolgirl giggles. But her mother had gripped her elbow and tugged her away at a half-run up the street. Annie could still remember the fear in the grip, and the way she had despised it.

Back at the flat, Bernard's flowery aftershave still lingered in the air. Having showered and changed, Annie sat down to perform a quick final edit on her column, only to find herself attempting to write about the flasher instead. If she could make it funny it might work, she told herself, typing fast and keeping one eye on the face of her wristwatch. Submitting bad articles was one thing; submitting them late was quite another. With half an hour to go, she accepted defeat and pressed the delete button. Not just because it was unpolished and ringing with the discomfort she had aimed to hide, but also because of renewed distrust at all her recent urges to slip from behind the safe mask of her wonderfully banal persona and write about herself. No such impulses had clouded her debut efforts, Annie reflected with some bewilderment, thinking back to the pieces about holiday romances and body-piercing which had persuaded Amy Marsden to take her on six months before. She remembered again what a golden opportunity the column had seemed – a let-out from the treadmill of freelancing in the already oversub-scribed female sector, some financial security, not to mention all the high hopes of establishing herself as a household name. The very idea now made Annie laugh out loud. Mirroring the slump in her inspirational powers, the early trickle of fan mail had dwindled in recent weeks to nothing at all.

And who could expect a response from such drivel anyway? Annie asked herself, scowling at that week's effort and punching out the numbers on her fax machine. The paper began to roll through and then stopped. Seeing the words *line error* flashing on the screen, Annie embarked on a frantic search for the instruction manual only to find that none of its troubleshooting tactics had any effect at all. Stonewalled by busy telephone lines, it was well after her one o'clock deadline when she at last succeeded in getting a call through to a copytaker temping in the editorial department. Speaking with considerably more self-confidence than she felt, Annie then embarked on the laborious task of dictating her five hundred words into the telephone.

'Do you think any of it's funny?' she blurted finally. 'I mean, does it sound OK?'

The girl sounded genuinely surprised. 'Uh . . . yeah. It's killing. Great stuff.'

An hour or so later Annie's fax machine whirred back into life of its own accord.

> *Thanks for this week's FlatLife piece.*
> *Editorial meeting on Thur 6 Dec 9.30 a.m. Hope you can*
> *attend. See you then.*
> *Yours Amy*
> *(Is there something wrong with your phone? Have not been*
> *able to get through this a.m.)*

Chapter Four

On Saturday morning, buoyed, as always, by the sight of her column in print – somehow looking so much more competent and convincing than the copy filed from the mayhem of the spare room – Annie continued her bid for physical self-improvement by treating herself to a face mask. Having smeared her face and neck with a gritty green substance, squeezed from a sachet promising 'instant and visible revitalisation', she then submerged herself in a deep bath, where she lay for a long time, fiddling with the drip on the cold tap with her big toe and trying to think of something original to bring to the editorial meeting the coming week. All her promises to generate a regular supply of features in tandem with the column had come to nothing; the incentive for such matters having been somewhat overridden by the generous terms of Amy's contract. Annie flexed her face against the clench of the mask, hoping it would perform a small herbal miracle against the sinister red lump lurking half a centimetre to the left of her nose.

'Can I come in?' Marina called, knocking and coming in. She was wearing purple crushed velvet trousers, black suede ankle boots and a black velvet jacket, tailored to show off her trim waistline. 'Just read your piece. It's lovely.' She flashed Annie a brilliant smile, before turning to the basin mirror and starting to clean her teeth. 'I can't think what you were so worried about,' she continued, her mouth full of toothbrush. 'It's really funny.'

Annie offered a grunt of gratitude, pointing at her cheeks to indicate she wasn't up to conversation.

The previous evening's dinner party had been cancelled at the last minute, to the barely concealed relief of all. Jake laid claim to a stomach upset, while a telephone message left by Susie and George had rambled at length about work crises, thereby confirming suspicions that yet another setback had occurred in the arena of domestic compatibility. Annie and Marina had spent the night in front of the telly instead, feasting on fromage frais dips and the expensive oil painting of a fruit flan which they had purchased, at some considerable expense, from a patisserie in St John's Wood High Street. The main course, breadcrumbed chicken breasts, stuffed with cheese and spinach, remained in cellophane beside the microwave, never looking alluring enough to receive the five minutes' worth of attention required to make it edible. Though the television remained on, the two women spent most of the time ignoring the screen and talking to each other, revisiting old and favourite topics with all the fearless abandonment that characterises the closest female intimacy. Having begun with the fatefully mismatched Susie and George, they moved on to the old chestnut of long-term commitments and the challenge of finding suitable lifelong partners themselves.

'But not just yet, thank you very much,' sighed Marina, 'I'm having far too much of a good time.'

'So I'd noticed.'

'You're just too bloody fussy, that's your trouble, Annie Jordan.'

'No I am not,' replied Annie mildly. 'I just don't meet anybody. And when I do, I scare them away.'

'Perhaps you give up too easily—'

'I do not. And anyway, trying too hard's just as bad.' She threw the TV console onto the table and reached for a cigarette. 'It either looks too eager or it leads to the sort of mess I got into with Pete, when I tried for months after I should have packed it in.' She waved a cigarette at Marina, who shook her head and closed her eyes. 'God, do you remember how he used to come in here and start tidying – stacking magazines and folding clothes, plugging in the hoover—'

'Pete had other problems too, if I recall,' put in Marina dryly, briefly opening her eyes and closing them again.

'I know, I know.' Annie sighed. 'But sometimes I still think I *ought* to have liked him more . . . that there's this massive gap between what it would be sensible to look for in a man and what I actually find attractive.'

'You mean you can only love men who don't hoover,' Marina teased sleepily.

Annie laughed and threw a cushion at her. 'Better than your problem.'

'Which is?' The green eyes flicked wide open in a flash, alerting Annie to the fact that she had stumbled onto dangerous ground. Offering judgements on each other's lifestyles was a practice they usually took care to avoid.

'Only that you fall for people until they fall back,' she said lightly. 'Then you get fed up and move on.'

Marina relaxed and smiled. 'Too true, too true.' She stood up and stretched by way of an indication that she was ready to go to bed. 'I say, perhaps there'll be a nice cowboy for you at the party next weekend.'

'Who says I'm going?'

'Of course you are – Bernard's told me of this great party shop in Holborn where I can get us all some costumes and props—'

'You're taking him?'

'I've got to – he's the one who got us invited.'

'You never said that till now.' Having envisaged the evening in rather different terms, Annie found it hard to hide her dismay. 'But he's got a silly name and wears boxer shorts with hearts on,' she wailed. At which Marina had only shrieked with laughter, slapping her thigh and saying, 'I know, isn't it crazy?'

Recollecting this conversation from the steamy sanctity of the bathroom, Annie raised an eyebrow at the evident care with which her flatmate was applying her make-up in the misting reflection of the bathroom mirror. Wanting to recapture her powers of speech, she dipped her face several times in and out of the bath water and rubbed furiously at the green doughy substance on her cheeks.

'I thought you said you weren't doing anything today,' she said at last, squinting through half-closed eyes in an attempt to locate a flannel.

Marina frowned, obligingly placing a hand towel in Annie's groping hands. 'I'm meeting Donald in a sandwich bar in the Gloucester Road. Yet another showdown. He begged me,' she added morosely, taking up a perch on the edge of the bath and trailing three fingers in the water. 'He's refusing to accept the situation.' She whirled her fingers in small circles, undeterred by the unsightly film of grey scum left by the residue of Annie's face mask.

Though Annie didn't say so, it occurred to her that Marina was looking particularly attractive. She had thrust her long dark hair up into a scruffy bun from where it tumbled down in corkscrew wisps that curled into the nape of her neck. It was a coiffure Annie herself had tried and failed to emulate a couple of times in the past, during the days when her uncooperative tresses reached down to her collar bone as opposed to her ears. What actually created the subtle but yawning gulf between Marina's elegant dishevelment and a badly assembled hair knot? she wondered now, squeezing out the flannel and flexing the muscles in her face to check they had been restored to full mobility.

'I put out that tape you wanted, by the way,' Marina said, shaking the drops of water off her hand and standing up. 'Though why you suddenly want to start doing all this extra exercise when you look perfectly fine as you are, is a mystery to me.'

'Because I wobble. And because all my life I've wanted to be nine stone.'

'We all wobble, darling,' murmured Marina, 'women are supposed to – it goes with the territory.'

'Only in some places,' retorted Annie, thinking but managing not to say that her flatmate's naturally slim, boyish figure meant she had no concept of the subject under discussion.

Sensing that the conversation could go nowhere conclusive or satisfactory, Marina opened the bathroom door. 'Be a good girl at the Spencers' tonight.'

'I fear there's little danger of being anything else,' quipped Annie, sinking back under the warm water and trying not to feel bleak at the prospect of an entire day alone.

Having draped herself in a towel, she trailed into the sitting room to offer a parting thumbs-up sign from the window. As Marina waved and strode away, her purple flares flapping round the ankles of her boots, a large white van reversed into the parking space behind Annie's green Fiat, only just missing her rear bumper. 'Watch it,' she muttered, rubbing away the window steam with a corner of the towel. A dark, stocky man in paint-splattered overalls clambered out of the driving seat and went to open up the back of the vehicle, where he was joined by a taller, much slimmer man with sandy hair. Having pulled down a ramp, they then paused to chat, beating their gloved hands against the cold. Finding the short one glancing up in her direction, Annie quickly retreated into the kitchen, where she ate a bowl of bran flakes smothered in sweetened Greek yoghurt, and contemplated the chore of exercise.

Annie suspected that some of her eagerness to try out an old eighties fitness tape of Marina's instead of running in the park, stemmed not from the bitterness of the weather, as she had claimed, but from the incident with the flasher. An incident which she had laughed at uproariously enough when relaying to Marina, but which she knew had contributed to her mounting sense of unease about herself and life in general. Perhaps investing in a guard dog was the answer, she reflected grimly, blowing the dust off the video jacket cover, which was emblazoned with the words, *Body Perfect: Callisthenics made easy*, and scowling at the angular, lip-glossed woman posing underneath.

Some ten minutes later Annie was nursing feelings of violent hatred towards the same image, now moving on the television screen in front of her, clad only in a leopard-skin leotard and breathing instructions through a rigid portcullis of a smile. A smile that had to be the product of facial surgery, Annie decided, scanning the woman's ears for signs of tucks in a bid to distract herself from the pain the simplest movements seemed to be inflicting on her limbs. To follow any command from such an absurd-looking creature seemed questionable. She gritted her teeth through another torturous five minutes before switching the tape off and flopping back onto the carpet to recover.

With the television off, the room felt very quiet. She lay without moving for several minutes, enjoying the stillness and the dim sense of virtue generated by the throbbing in her muscles. She was almost asleep when a thump from down the corridor reminded her of the developments taking place in the flat overhead. Whoever the new residents were, they were still being moved in. Tiptoeing to the window, she saw the sandy-haired man emerge from the front door below and disappear inside the back of the van. He reappeared a few moments later carrying a standard lamp in one hand and a large box in the other. An electrical flex hung out of one corner of the box, trailing behind him like an empty lead. Curious in spite of herself, Annie set up the ironing board next to the window so that she could keep an eye on proceedings while reducing the mountain of crumpled garments that habitually resided in the armchair next to the television.

An hour later, her arm aching, she unplugged the iron and rewarded herself with her first cigarette of the day, inhaling all the more keenly at the recollection that the Spencer household was traditionally a no-smoking zone. She remembered in the same instant and with equal dismay that Zoë and Richard had recently moved from their lovely flat in Fulham to a four-bedroomed house on the edge of Barnes, compelled to do so by the increasing pyramid of baby equipment occupying the space in their sitting room and hall.

She had just embarked on a hunt for their change of address card, when there was a knock at the door. Expecting some visitation connected to the removals van, Annie was disconcerted to find herself confronting the man who had wheedled his way into using her telephone a few days before.

'Sorry to bother you, man—' He seemed more edgy than before, bouncing on the soles of enormous, very white trainers, lightly punching his fists into his palms as if limbering up for a fight. 'The door was open . . . I was just wondering if I could use your phone—'

'Again?' In spite of her misgivings, Annie was incredulous.

'Sorry man . . . I ain't got no card for the boxes . . . I need a cab.'

'Again?' she repeated, more feebly.

He shrugged. 'Hey lady – please?'

'Really, I—'

'Last time, I swear.' He ran his finger across his throat and smiled in a way that reminded her of the fortress teeth of the callisthenics queen on Marina's tape.

'I guess so,' she muttered, pulling open the door.

The call only took a few moments. As on the previous occasion, Annie hovered in her doorway, but this time with a show of foot-tapping impatience which she hoped would deter him from coming again.

'Nice place,' he said, replacing the receiver and giving an approving nod to what he could see of her flat.

'Thanks, but no more calls, OK? There's a box that takes coins by the post office—'

'Sure, man, sure. I'm out of here.' He strolled past her, rolling easily on his big rubber soles. 'Thank you for your time and patience.'

'No problem,' she murmured, relenting a little under the blaze of the smile which suddenly illuminated his face.

Along the passageway the two removals men appeared from the stairwell, grunting and cursing over two ends of a long book-case. Without another word her visitor sped off past them and down the stairs, his trainers squeaking on the linoleum.

'Has the lift ever worked?' called the one with sandy hair, just as she was about to shut the door. He looked older than Annie had first judged, probably in his early thirties.

'Not for a hundred years or so,' she called back, 'the land-lord of this block makes Scrooge look like a philanthropist.'

Both men roared with laughter. She wondered whether to warn them about not leaving the main door open, but decided it would appear too fussy, adding instead, 'Perhaps I better warn the new tenants before they move in.'

'Probably a bit late for that,' said the tall one, winking at his companion as he bent down to clasp his end of the shelves.

'I guess so,' Annie agreed, smiling to herself as she shut the door and marvelling again at how meaningless exchanges with strangers could cast shafts of light into a day.

A concerted search eventually unearthed Zoë's change of address card from under a phone book. Dinner with old friends would be lovely, Annie told herself. Just what she needed, in fact. Richard would be his usual reticent self, while she and Zoë could catch up on scandals and the whereabouts of old acquaintances from their days as aspiring hacks on *Looking South*, prior to Zoë's move to the more rarified world of women's magazines.

Map-reading her way from north London to the leafy suburbs of Barnes put Annie in a slightly less positive frame of mind. During the final couple of miles through a grid of narrow, steeply bumped roads, she found herself hissing oaths to cultivate friends on a geographical basis alone. By the time she found a parking space she was very late. Retrieving the warm and frothing bottle of white wine from the floor in front of the passenger seat, she set off at a trot up the street, squinting in the dark for house numbers. A faint rustling in her pocket reminded her of the inspirational last-minute purchase of some baby gifts from a late-night chemist. After a hasty check for price stickers, she tied the handles of the thin plastic bag into a small bow, wanting to compensate for the absence of gift tags and pretty paper.

Chapter Five

Zoë and Richard were rather pleased at Annie's lack of punctuality. It conformed to the chaotically attractive picture they had been painting of her, for the benefit of the guests already seated in their newly painted sitting room, between flutes of kir royal and bowls of Bombay mix. Annie Jordan was funny and unpredictable, Zoë had promised, exaggerating just a little for the purposes of being interesting and casting a special glance or two at the far corner of her elegant four-seater sofa, where her artfully conjured single white male was propped, crunching nuts and nudging cushions. David Portman was a single parent from the day care centre where Zoë had recently started leaving her six-month-old daughter, Cordelia, for three mornings a week, thereby granting herself the time to enjoy some recuperative yoga sessions and at least one stress-free bout of grocery shopping. A man coping on his own with a young child was instantly endearing, Zoë had decided, catching David's eye amongst the all-female clan gathered at the centre's main door and throwing him a warming smile. When preliminary enquiries produced the information that this single parent status arose from his partner having died of a brain tumour, Zoë's compassion for him and his two-year-old son Joshua had soared to new heights, reinforcing her intention that they should all become better acquainted. Even though Cordelia was still too young to socialise with anything more interactive than a squeaky toy, she had subsequently issued a series of invitations to tea, gently pressing the friendship to the point where an invitation to dinner had felt like the most natural thing in the world.

Such cultivation had paid off handsomely, Zoë reflected, making eyes at Richard to fill David's glass and thinking how pleasing it would be if she could one day consider herself the architect of a true love-match. Annie was so clever and funny – pretty too in an unobvious sort of way – that it seemed nothing short of a crime that she should still be so glaringly single. These days Annie never referred to the matter herself and it wasn't a subject that Zoë felt able to raise for her. Partly because their friendship had cooled with time; and partly because women of thirty-three were not so easily interrogated about such things. But Zoë could recall enough shared confidences from their early working days – when the notion of finding the right man had seemed like an inevitable part of life's unravelling plot – to feel that she was justified in offering whatever help she could.

When the doorbell rang, she slipped from the room with a squawk of satisfaction.

'Annie, how lovely to see you.'

Annie was feeling unattractively windswept, and a little chilled, after the hike from the only available parking space in the entire road. As the door opened she was immediately heartened, both at the sight of Zoë, looking remarkably like her old self in spite of the interruption of childbirth, and at the enticing aromas wafting from the kitchen into the hall.

'Sorry to be late, Zo.' They exchanged kisses. 'I brought this for you and this for baby.' Annie held out her bottle of wine, relieved to see that it was looking somewhat less effervescent, and the bag, which contained a plastic monkey rattle and a pair of impossibly tiny yellow socks.

'You sweetie, Annie. Come in and meet everyone. Love the hair, by the way – just great.'

'Cool house,' whispered Annie, tweaking her miniskirt to a less flamboyant distance from her knees and following her hostess through into the sitting room. Subjected to a roll-call of christian names which she knew she would forget, she nodded brightly, all the while absorbing the obvious but awkward fact that the man on the sofa was to be her designated escort for the evening. Though recent years had seen an increase in such well-intentioned actions from married, or partnered, friends, Annie had still to master the art of feeling at ease when dealing with them.

'I've kept everyone waiting, I know,' she gabbled, 'my excuse is I've come from another planet called North London – anyone ever heard of it?' She allowed her gaze to shift from the man's shoulder blades to his eyes, which were a handsome, if rather sombre, brown. His hair was mousey with an air of neglectful as opposed to attractive dishevelment. 'I don't suppose you've got any inspirational ideas for cutting an hour or two off my route home, have you, David? North Circular, M25, John o'Groats – I'm game for anything.'

David, clearly a little nervous himself, laughed quickly and shook his head. 'I'm local I'm afraid – barely go into London these days.'

'Lucky old you,' replied Annie, thinking in the same instant that she herself would be lost without London, that she loved its chaotic seediness and grandeur far too much to ever contemplate sacrificing them for an earnest male with bushy hair, even if he turned out to be a cultural power house with concealed depths of passion and wit.

After a few more polite exchanges, Annie slipped from the room on the pretext of keeping Zoë company in the kitchen. On the way she took a detour past the hall mirror, where she checked her face for smudges and gave a disconsolate poke at her fringe.

'Babe asleep is she?' she asked, plucking a grape off the cheeseboard as she stepped through into the kitchen.

An alarmingly dreamy look came into Zoë's eye. She stopped, a tureen of vivid green soup in hand, and glanced wistfully up at the ceiling. 'Yes . . . yes she is. Honestly Annie, I can't tell you what it's . . . I mean the whole motherhood thing, it's just—'

'Wonderful?' Annie suggested, feeling an unforgivable bubble of impatience and adding, 'You certainly look wonderful,' to make up for it.

Zoë put the bowl down and began dishing out soup, her actions having – rather to Annie's relief – resumed their normal speed. 'I've still got a tummy, but my weight's back down. The really weird thing,' she continued, 'is that I don't feel in any rush to get back to work. I've renegotiated my leave until the spring, but I'm dreading it already—' She paused, absently running her finger round a trickle of soup on the ladle. 'Before – right through the pregnancy – I was so scared of everything. But now . . . I can't explain . . . take breastfeeding for example – it's just the most amazing thing. Did you know, the uterus actually contracts while a baby suckles?' She put down the ladle and patted her stomach with both hands. 'I mean you can *feel* it happening.' She clenched and unclenched her fist by way of a demonstration.

'Wow,' replied Annie, wondering if her lack of interest meant she was jealous or merely cold-hearted, 'so God isn't a total misogynist after all.'

'He certainly isn't.' Zoë began a circuit of the table, carefully scattering minutely chopped sprigs of parsley into the bowls of soup and adjusting the position of wine glasses and napkins. 'But there is just one thing I have *got* to say, Annie – you know me – I need to get things out in the open—'

Alerted by the sudden switch in her friend's tone of voice, knowing from past experience that it could be the prelude to some quite unexpected and devastatingly personal revelation, Annie braced herself, nervously tipping her glass to her lips only to find that it was empty. 'Fire away. What have I done?'

'You? No – heavens – no. It's me. Us. Richard and I. Not asking you to be Cordelia's godmother – you must have wondered—'

'What? I mean, no—' stammered Annie, to whom such a concept had never occurred.

'God, you're sweet.' Zoë came over and kissed her cheek. 'And entirely wonderful. You were on my shortlist, but Richard insisted we had one of his sisters and then we had to have Susie who was at primary school with me, as you know, and because she's having *such* a hard time at the moment—'

'Honestly, Zoë, don't give it a second thought. I'd be hopeless anyway – an atheist with a bad memory – the very worst combination.' Annie gave her a hug, inwardly marvelling at the chasm separating the preoccupations of her existence and that of someone whom she had once counted amongst her closest friends.

'I know you're going to like David, by the way,' said Zoë, breaking a secret promise not to make any special mention of him to Annie. 'He lectures in engineering at Kingston University. A scientist. His wife *died*,' she went on in a whisper, 'and he's been so amazingly brave.'

'Bloody hell. What of?' Annie couldn't help being a little impressed.

There was just time for Zoë to touch her temple and mouth the word 'tumour' before the bereaved hero himself appeared in the doorway, asking if he might phone his babysitter. 'Josh had a bit of a temperature – didn't enjoy his bath,' he explained, triggering an eye-roll of admiration from Zoë the moment his back was turned.

A few minutes later, directed by Richard, who had drawn up a neat seating plan in honour of the occasion, they took their places round the table. David Portman finished his phone call in time to leap across the kitchen and pull back Annie's chair before she sat down. He then proceeded to bombard her with a barrage of attentions concerning bread rolls and condiments. He's only trying, Annie told herself, doing her best to feel gratitude as opposed to discomfort and conjuring up heartrending images of the trials of single fatherhood.

It took until the middle of the main course for someone to ask about the column, by which time Annie had been so inundated with anecdotes about the eating habits and hectic social whirl of a two-year-old that she was more than happy to escape into the limelight of dinner party conversation.

'Watch your tongues everybody, these columnists are vultures,' said the jovial man in the pinstripe suit, who was either Tom or Tim – she could not remember which – and who worked in the same firm of solicitors as Richard. 'What's the thing called? *Get A Life*, did you say?' He laughed loudly.

'*FlatLife*,' corrected Annie quietly, 'and I believe I am safe in saying that I share few character traits with a vulture or any other bird of prey. Anyway, I bet you lot all read *The Times* or the *Guardian*—'

'*Telegraph*, actually,' put in the Tom person, before being interrupted by his wife, who said that she had read Annie's column by mistake once at the doctor's and thought it very amusing.

'All about a holiday romance with a Spanish body-builder, if I remember correctly . . . very funny—'

'That was several months back,' murmured Annie, wishing she could feel flattered, but managing only the familiar stomach flutter of worry about the week ahead.

'Did it really happen?'

'Good heavens no. I mean I've been on holiday to Spain, but that's about it. I have to make up all the funny bits. My real life is far too dull to warrant more than a line or two in a Christmas card.' Beneath the flap of the table cloth Annie's hands gripped her napkin, twisting it round her fingers until the blood throbbed. A terrible urge to confess to unhappiness pulsed inside; an urge which she knew to be both inappropriate and socially unacceptable. Instead, she twisted the napkin tighter still, while volleys of appreciative laughter burst around the table. Rescue was provided by an ear-splitting wail from the Spencers' baby intercom receiver, perched between a bowl of fruit salad and a large white triangle of cheese.

'She'll probably settle if you leave her,' volunteered the woman on the other side of Richard, using the faintly superior tone of one with a vast experience of such matters. 'Petra used to howl for hours, didn't she Charles?' Her husband nodded grimly, while the wailing rose to a crescendo that could have well done without any amplification at all.

'Oh, bring her down,' she pleaded, as Zoë scurried out of the kitchen, 'we'd so love to meet her properly.'

A few moments later the crying stopped. They heard Zoë's voice instead, magnified courtesy of the kitchen receiver, crooning nonsense in a way that suggested she had forgotten the possibility of being overheard. Richard quickly got up and switched the machine off, just as Zoë reappeared cradling their daughter amongst a jumble of pink bed linen. Observing that the child was also wearing a pink bedsuit, Annie began to worry for the fate of her yellow socks.

While grateful that these interruptions had given her time to collect herself, the arrival of little Cordelia and the unbuttoning of Zoë's shirt to silence her did little to alleviate Annie's sense of alienation. Not because she would have liked a baby – broodiness, fortunately, was one burden she did not yet bear – but because David and the assembled females promptly embarked on a graphic exchange of information about their experiences of childbirth. Richard and his two colleagues, meanwhile, formed an intense boys-only sort of huddle down the far end of the table, flexing their eyebrows and swirling their wine in a way that made Annie feel neither welcome nor eager to be made so. Instead, she found her thoughts straying to the packet of cigarettes lurking under the flap of her handbag and the hollow feeling at the back of her throat.

When the craving grew too strong to ignore, she slipped away to the sanctuary of the front doorstep, where she smoked two cigarettes in a row, puffing so quickly and deeply that by the time she finished she felt quite sick and had to steady herself against Zoë and Richard's front wall. She swallowed several gulps of the icy night air, pressing her forehead against the cold stone, nursing the dim sensation that if she could only push hard enough she might squeeze her troubles away.

Back in the kitchen, no one paid much attention to her return. Disinclined to receive further enlightenment on the subjects of enemas and orifices, Annie did not go back to her seat, but busied herself instead with stacking dirty plates and assembling the wherewithal to make coffee. She was leaning against the fridge, waiting for the kettle to boil and idly wondering whether it would be kind or merely embarrassing to go through the charade of asking David Portman for his telephone number, when her attention was arrested by a scene unfolding around Zoë. While his two female neighbours were enjoying a lively, private debate of their own, David himself was observing his hostess as she transferred Cordelia from her left nipple to her right. Observing, so it seemed to Annie, not with the detached interest of a fellow parent, so much as the ogling intensity of something far more base and complicated. 'Got you', she thought, just as the switch on the kettle popped beside her and Richard broke the moment by leaping to his feet to insist on helping with the coffee.

The incident put the seal on a difficult and disappointing evening which, instead of lifting Annie's spirits as she had hoped, merely confirmed the fear that she was losing the power to participate in life; that whatever carapace had protected her in the past was worn almost to the bone.

It was a relief to slide into the cold emptiness of the car, to let the smile of sociability slip and yawn freely. Driving home, Annie kept a watchful eye out both for police vehicles and the sometimes eccentric pendulum swings of her speedometer. As sleepiness began to take hold, she wound down her window and flicked on the radio, catching the tail end of a sincere testament about the miseries of hair loss. She was on the point of changing channels when her attention was caught by the opening chords of a familiar song. Annie paused, letting the music wash over her, sweeping her back as only music could, to the night of her first embrace with Pete Rutherford. To eager, uncomplicated embraces between a sea of swaying bodies and a tilting Christmas tree. Three years and a lifetime before.

Knowing her current mood made her vulnerable to such sentiments did nothing to help press the surge of emotions away. Stupid, she told herself. Stupid, how a tune could do this, how its trickery could literally transplant one to a time and a place and a feeling. Even though the feeling had died. And had good reason to die, Annie reminded herself, trying to focus on all the subsequent and eventually unignorable incompatibilities, but remembering instead the lustre of romance, the way it illuminated and empowered the most dismal of lives.

Nostalgia was such an irritatingly uncontrollable emotion,

she reflected wryly, flicking off the radio and inwardly scolding herself at the illogicality of being able to miss something that had turned out not to exist at all. All her early, positive perceptions of Pete Rutherford had proved to be an illusion, born on a tide of hope rather than evidence or common-sense. Realising that they were incompatible had been a long and torturous haul.

By the time she reached the doorstep to Shrewsbury Mansions, Annie was longing for Marina to be home. To remind her that Pete didn't matter, to listen to funny tales of the woeful David Portman so she could laugh the sourness of the evening away.

But the emptiness of the flat was palpable. Pinned under the hall telephone was a brief note.

Came back for a few things, must have just missed you. Donald under control. Am staying with Boxer Shorts tonight. Back tomorrow morning. Hugs, M. PS There is a NEW person (male) upstairs – came by to borrow milk. Quite sweet so didn't refuse. Will buy more tomorrow.

In a defiant bid not to feel abandoned, Annie sat up for another hour, drinking coffee and watching television. Finding her head nodding onto her chest and feeling not only abandoned but irretrievably old, she scribbled, '*Grateful for silence – long morning lie-in required,*' in red felt tip across Marina's note and slipped it back under the phone. Having jabbed at her teeth in a desultory fashion she then fell into bed, telling herself that make-up-smeared pillows and panda-eyes were of no consequence to women who slept alone.

Chapter Six

————◇◆◇————

Marina sucked the last noisy squirt out of her tropical juice box and threw it with fluent and practised ease into a waste paper bin a few yards away. Towering over the bin was one of several large yucca plants, positioned at discreet intervals between desks in a bid to enhance employees' sense of contact with the natural world; something of a challenge in an office space that not only lacked windows, but which reflected the current culture to have city workers of all levels and abilities wedged elbow to elbow between computer screens and filing cabinets. Though her own square of carpet was quite orderly, Marina sometimes marvelled that any coherent thoughts ever emerged from such a noisy jungle of paper and machinery. Without the emotional protection afforded by individual office walls, the mood swings of the bank were so infectious and tangible, that even a novice like herself, whose rôle involved typing decisions rather than making them, could tell almost at once whether the markets were being docile or misbehaving. The emptiness of the room that lunch hour bore testimony to the fact that it was the fourth day of a slow, indifferent week, particularly for Marina whose immediate employer was attending a conference in Zurich.

'Good shot,' grunted a nearby salesman, his mouth full of sandwich. 'Impressive arm movement,' he added, leaning on top of his computer and giving her a provocative gaze.

'Thank you.' Marina reached into her bottom drawer for her handbag, slotted her stockinged feet back into her shoes and pulled on her jacket. 'I had a good games mistress.' She grinned at him, years of such attentions having taught her to enjoy rather than resist them. 'Goal Attack for my house netball team. It never quite goes away.'

He groaned. 'Don't tell me, pigtails, games skirts—'

'The works.' Marina laughed as she headed towards the swing doors leading to the lifts. 'And it was a convent too,' she called over her shoulder, 'white knee socks and lace-up shoes.' Still smiling to herself, she pressed the button that served all four lifts and leant against one of the large landing windows to wait. In the street down below, hundreds of dark-suited men and women scurried along the pavements, streaming between the high walls of shimmering glass and ancient stone. Like rodents running the proverbial race, she mused, absently brushing her hand across the wide lapel of her yellow coat, as if to seek some reassurance of her own individuality.

The view was one of the few in London that reminded Marina of New York, the city where she had spent most of her school holidays, thanks to an American mother and a father whose consultancy business had made a successful transition to the opposite side of the Atlantic. Though both parents remained committed, and slightly snobbish, anglophiles, they had recently retired to Florida where they were enjoying a faintly surreal existence amongst luxury condominiums and air-conditioned shopping malls. They always kept in regular contact, but Marina, inured to independence through many largely enjoyable years of boarding school, found it hard to miss them very much. She felt so detached sometimes it made her guilty. Unlike Annie, who claimed not to need any member of her family but who could still astonish Marina with her capacity for tying herself in knots over their colourful malfunctions and deficiencies.

The first lift to arrive was the glass-sided box that ran up and down one of the outer corners of the bank's recently refurbished wing. Holding the barrier to steady herself, Marina gazed out over the tops of the buildings as she descended, enjoying the faint giddiness in her head and stomach. As the ground approached, the scurrying figures assumed features and attitudes that made her less wary of stepping amongst them. Eagerly, she pushed through the bank's swing doors and strode out into the fresh air. It was remarkably mild for December; a day of harmless breezes and tufty white clouds, as if the elements had suddenly lost the heart for the seasonal extremes expected of them.

Marina walked quickly, calculating that if she hurried there was just time to take the tube to the party shop in Holborn and be back at her desk by half past two. As she strode along the street, her dark hair streaming behind her, her long legs emerging at intervals from amongst the broad flaps of her bright coat, several heads turned to stare, drawn not just by her looks but by a rarer quality, an inner confidence – an aura of self-sufficiency – that gave an invisible edge to her attraction. With her mind on Stetsons and holsters, and whether Annie's reluctance about the party was serious or put on, Marina was barely aware of the stir she caused. When a hand reached out and tapped her on the shoulder, just a couple of yards short of the entrance to the Underground, she caught her breath and put her hand to her throat in surprise.

'Marina Hammond. How the hell are you?'

'Phillip – hello. I'm fine. In a bit of a rush though.'

'Going down here?' He nodded towards the flight of stairs behind them.

'Yes, as a matter of fact—'

'Great – so am I. I want to hear all about that errant sister of mine. Still nobody to replace the grisly Peter? – Christ she does pick them. But then she always was a disaster when it came to men. Scared a few mates of mine away, I can tell you – schoolgirl crushes and so on – overdoing things, as is dear Annie's way—'

He queued behind her for a ticket and then continued talking as they dodged a chalked 'Out of Order' sign and walked down the escalator.

'—Never see the girl these days . . . What's she writing in that column of hers? Anything I should worry about?'

'I don't think there's any danger of Annie writing about you, Phillip, if that's what you mean,' murmured Marina, leading the way onto the platform and trying not to feel disappointed to find Annie's younger brother following suit.

'Got a late lunch in Chancery Lane,' he explained cheerfully, 'reunion with a few old mates from my days broking at Horsmans. Thank God I got out when I did. Bloody war zone now. Very nasty. Laying people off all over the place. Can't tell you how many friends have come knocking at my door, literally begging for work.'

Anyone else might have managed to deliver such information in a way that suggested an iota or two of compassion, reflected Marina, nodding politely and willing the train to come. But for Phillip Jordan it somehow sounded, like most of his topics of conversation, like a soap-box from which to boast his own contrasting good fortune and virtue.

'Hey – I'm getting married. Did Annie tell you?'

'Oh yes . . . she did mention it. Congratulations.' Feeling the small rush of wind through her hair, Marina turned to face the dark mouth of the tunnel. 'Till death do you part,' she said, not looking at him, her brown eyes gleaming.

'Absolutely,' Phillip agreed, feeling, as he always did with Marina, that he wasn't quite getting through to her. Having at one stage entertained certain intimate hopes with regard to his sister's flatmate, it was a sensation that he confronted with some regret and a momentary flurry of panic about his recent decision to tie the matrimonial knot. He had always imagined he would have slept with a lot more women before settling down; women just like Marina Hammond, with their glorious bodies and challenging stares. Not having done so sometimes made him doubt his feelings for Hermione, or, worse still, his capacity to remain faithful to her should any more glamorous opportunities present themselves. 'My fiancée's called Hermione,' he declared, in a bid to brush such doubts away. 'She's in the film business,' he added, as they stepped onto the train.

'An actress – how wonderful,' said Marina, who knew from Annie that Phillip's girlfriend had surrendered all thespian aspirations in favour of the more regular employment offered by a filing cabinet.

'She . . . er . . . dabbles in acting. Has a day job too.' Seeing his stop approach, Phillip debated whether a parting kiss would be in order, but decided against it. 'Give my love to Annie, won't you? Tell her we'll see her at Christmas. Hermione is going down a day early to help with the cooking.'

'How kind.' As the doors slid shut and the train moved away, Marina gave a little wave, inwardly marvelling that such a creature could be any blood relation to someone as warm and likeable as Annie. Physically they were very different too, Phillip being tall and bony and with a gingery tint to the light brown hair that Annie periodically tried to disguise. The only obvious physical similarity was in their mouths, which were attractively full and broad, lending an impression of generosity to Annie's face, but looking merely greedy on that of her younger brother.

A little shocked by the prices in the party shop, Marina tried to call the flat on her mobile. On hearing the clipped tones of Annie's voice on their answering machine, she remembered the rare event of a summons by the editorial department and Annie's frantic hair-drying earlier that morning.

'. . . if you would like to send a fax, start now, or please leave a message after the long tone . . .'

'This is Marina in the fancy dress shop. They've got some great costumes to hire but they're quite expensive, so I'm just going to get you a hat, and a holster because you can borrow my boots and you've got that black waistcoat. It's fifteen quid, but the hat's really nice, with little silver studs round the band and a great turn-up to the brim. I'm going to rent a squaw costume, so you can borrow my John Wayne shirt too. Hope the dreaded Amy wasn't too dreadful. Bumped into Phillip, by the way, who seemed fine. Talk to you later.'

As things turned out, however, this last promise was foiled by Bernard, who appeared in her department at five o'clock waving two tickets for a performance at The Old Vic that evening. Afterwards, vehemently discussing the play, which had been modern and unintelligible, they strolled to a Spanish tapas bar a few yards down the road. Over saucers of garlic prawns and bite-sized tortillas, Bernard then surprised her for the second time that day by issuing a formal invitation to spend the Christmas break skiing with him in Colorado.

'Skiing – bloody hell Bernard.'

'Is that pleasure or horror? Hang on a minute, you've got something on your cheek.' He leant forward and gently brushed a crumb of something away with his napkin. 'There, restored to full beauty once more.'

Disarmed, as she so often seemed to be in his presence, Marina shook her head gravely. 'It's a lovely idea, but far too soon.'

'Too soon for what?' he asked mildly, dabbing a bit of bread in the prawn sauce and popping it in his mouth.

'For . . . us, for . . . the relationship.'

'Ah yes, the relationship.' He rolled his tongue round the word, frowning. 'Relationship. It sounds so complicated, don't you think? Full of contortions, like "negotiate" or "extrapolate". You just know there's going to be trouble. Whereas I don't feel any of that with us. Do you mind if I have the last piece of bread?'

Marina laughed. 'Go ahead.'

'I'll order some more.'

'Not for me thanks.' She patted her stomach. 'I'm full.'

'I love the way you eat,' he announced matter-of-factly, 'I love your appetite. It reminds me of the way you make love.'

'Shut up, for God's sake,' she hissed, glancing at neighbouring tables for eavesdroppers, but having to put a hand up to hide her smile.

'If you want to come skiing with me Marina, you should do so. By the new year we could all be dead, gunned down by a madman or swept away in a flash flood.'

She giggled. 'From the Thames, I take it?'

'Stuff happens.'

'So I must come skiing with you this month in case I've been annihilated by January,' she quipped, inwardly struggling with the cause of her reluctance and realising that it stemmed not from any clever concerns about the relationship, but from far more mundane and quite separate worries to do with money and Annie. She flicked the crumpled ball of her paper napkin at her glass, thinking guiltily of the meagre state of their holiday fund, supposedly started for a girls-only trip to Barbados the following summer.

'The chalet belongs to a friend of mine and will cost us nothing,' said Bernard, studying her expression.

'Nothing?'

'And I've another friend in the airline business who always gets me the most wonderfully cheap seats.'

'What a lucky boy to have so many useful friends.'

'And I would like any other expenses to be my Christmas gift to you.'

'Oh dear.'

'If it's the thought of being snowbound with only me for company for fourteen days and nights, I would much prefer to know it, Marina – I could handle it – I would prefer to handle it than be fobbed off—'

'God no – it's nothing like that at all. In fact, I can't think of anything nicer than being snowbound with you,' she confessed, reaching out to touch his hand, 'I really can't.'

He beamed, catching the waiter's eye for the bill. 'Good. So that's settled then.'

'I suppose it is,' she said faintly.

'And we could take a detour via your parents *en route* back home, if you like.'

'Now you are being forward,' she teased, feigning outrage, but in fact rather relishing the idea of Bernard working some of his more sickly charms on her mother and switching into full businessman mode for her father. He would manage them beautifully. 'But Florida's one hell of a detour—'

'We could top up our tans. Get rid of the goggle marks.'

'You're mad.'

'Maybe a little.'

Outside in the street he pulled her into the crook of his arm. 'A holiday with you will be good.'

'I know,' she whispered.

'Although I ought to warn you, I'm rather impressive on the piste, so you'll have to watch your back.'

She giggled and poked his midriff. 'Impressive on the piste, eh? I don't believe it.'

'You just better, my girl.' He nuzzled the top of her head. 'I may be a little on the rotund side, but on skis I'm a—'

'You're not rotund,' she declared, leaping to his defence and then faltering. 'You're . . . well . . . a little bit round maybe . . . but in perfect proportion.'

He laughed out loud. 'Now I know you're lying. But I assure you *I* am not. I'm a devil on a mountain – so watch out.' He suddenly stopped and swung her round and against him, kissing her so hard she had to struggle for breath. A minute later she was released and being told about constellations and the star patterns sailors looked for before longitude came to their rescue.

Marina listened, surprised both by his knowledge and the fact that she was interested. 'You know so much,' she murmured.

'I know I love you,' he said, squeezing her hand.

She squeezed it back, too shocked by such boldness to formulate a reply.

Chapter Seven

Venturing into the office, even during Annie's early, more care-free, freelancing days, had always felt like something of a mixed blessing. It reminded her that she was neither fish nor foul, in a more advantageous position than her routine-bound associates perhaps, but more vulnerable too. It also reminded her that on most days she was lucky to have a conversation with anything more articulate than a wilting pot plant and that the one thing she truly missed as a freelance was the unavoidable contact with other members of the human race.

In a bid to suggest the opposite of these and other festering troubles, Annie dressed with particular extravagance for the Thursday meeting, going for the girl-about-town look as opposed to the shapeless-granny-cardigan mode in which she had spent most of the week. A red wool dress with black tights and high-heeled red shoes had been her final selection, by which time the entire contents of her wardrobe lay strewn about the room, their range of sizes and styles depicting a jumbled and disheartening history of the last five years of their owner's exist-ence. She shopped not with a view to what suited her, Annie realised helplessly, hurling a pair of hideous tartan leggings at the bin, but in order to conform to the image of herself that she was attempting to develop at the time.

'How's it going, Annie?' called a familiar voice as Annie strolled past some desks.

'Great thanks, Shona. How about you?'

'Really good – I'm counting the days. Getting married in January. We're going to live in the Bahamas. Rupert's uncle runs a scuba diving business out there. We're buying into the partnership with some money left to me by my grandfather.'

'They don't need anyone to run the gift shop do they? I could be out on the next available flight—'

Shona, who had a lustrous sweep of auburn hair and perfect teeth, shrieked with laughter. 'Oh, good one, I like that Annie – the next flight . . . that's great.'

Marvelling at the good fortune of someone already burdened with the advantages of being young and supremely beautiful, Annie moved off in search of the editorial clan, gathering, so she had been informed, in something called Conference Room A, which turned out to be the old Managing Editor's office with a new plaque on its door. Exchanging a couple more greetings with half-familiar faces did little to lighten the sense of not belonging, which had recently been trailing her like an unwanted shadow. With Marina away so much, even the flat was beginning to feel like hostile territory, full of demands and objects that grated against her nerves instead of soothing them.

'Welcome aboard, Annie,' declared Amy Marsden in her usual clipped and unwelcoming tones. As editor of the *Saturday Review* she assumed the seat of authority at the head of the table from where she was already controlling proceedings like a puppeteer with a string. 'You know everyone I think.' She waved at the assembled group, 'Apart from Derek Forbes, our new motoring expert' – a man with fair curly hair and spectacles nodded his head in greeting – and Yvonne Moore who – I am *extremely* happy to say – has agreed contractual terms with us just this morning. Yvonne joins us from Paris where she has been working as a freelance and doing those *wonderful* 'Letters from Abroad' for *Femme* magazine.'

Annie smiled the special smile she reserved for people towards whom she felt an instant distrust. Yvonne, who looked no more than twenty-five and who had immaculately coiffed blonde silky hair and blue eyes the size of saucers, leant across the table to shake Annie's hand. 'So good to meet you,' she said, revealing a hint of an Antipodean twang, 'I'm a great admirer of your work.'

Humbled but still suspicious, Annie shook the hand, not liking its limpness and the way the fingers slid from her grasp the moment their palms touched. As she leant back in her chair, she patted her briefcase, as if to reassure herself of the five hundred words contained inside, finished – thanks to this rare editorial summons – at the ungodly hour of two o'clock that morning. Her immediate neighbour, a woman called Joy, whose barrel-shaped physique and blotchy complexion had somehow not impeded her from rising to the giddy heights of Health and Fitness Editor, patted Annie's arm in greeting and told her she was looking marvellous.

'Thanks,' Annie whispered back with real gratitude, 'and how are you?'

'Teething problems with the new nanny, but otherwise fine.'

'And how is little . . . the little one?' Annie responded, wanting badly to say the right thing but struggling to recall either the sex or name of the child.

'Great thanks – hard work but—'

'If everyone has their coffee cups and brains in working order,' interrupted Amy, with a pointed look at Joy, 'may we begin?'

While each subject editor took it in turns to summarise plans for the next issue, Annie found her thoughts returning to the previous evening's toil at the computer, made no easier by the embarrassment of a run-in with the new resident upstairs. With Marina having telephoned to say she would be stopping at Bernard's, Annie had been looking forward to an uninterrupted spell of work. In a bid to bolster her spirits, flagging as always at the approach of the weekly deadline, she had sacrificed her health regime for a large bag of tortilla chips and a pot of avocado dip. One mouthful for every sentence, she promised herself, until blankness and panic had blasted every last flutter of self-discipline away. Grease from the chips made her fingers slide unpleasantly on the keys, adding to the sensation that the words themselves were slithering from her grasp, that even the miracle of a solitary good idea would vanish the moment she tried to articulate it.

After a despondent and unproductive flick for inspiration through a pile of old magazines, Annie found her thoughts straying back to the previous Saturday's social adventure in Barnes. A witty diatribe on the pitfalls of parenthood – a subject rife with opportunities to be brash and irreverent – would suit her *FlatLife* persona perfectly, she realised excitedly, licking the last of the dip out of the bowl with her finger and wiping both hands clean on her jeans.

Any woman looking for ways to drown the ticking of the proverbial biological clock should try an ancient, tried and trusted therapy called Meeting The Babies Of Friends, preferably in the company of other smitten parents. Hearing that the faeces of a newborn progresses from a black, sticky coagulum to a yellow substance resembling a piccalilli sauce – just one of many delightful topics of conversation bound to crop up in such company – is a most persuasive argument for remaining content with the less colourful preoccupations of the non-parent . . .

Annie paused, aware that the contents of nappies had come up in conversation at Zoë's and wondering if it mattered. It was already half past ten. Unless she got something down soon she would be working all night – not a fertile part of the day for her imagination at the best of times. She was poised thus, tussling with various conflicting and mostly unliterary impulses, when the silence of the spare room was invaded by the sound of piano-playing overhead.

She punched the space bar several times in annoyance. The sound continued unabated, a musical rippling that was no less irksome for being unquestionably accomplished. After attempting to work through it, Annie trudged to the bathroom and stuffed generous wads of cotton wool in her ears; only to find that a muffled version of her neighbour's piano practice was then contending with an unpleasant buzzing noise between her temples. Seriously irritated, she next resorted to the pugilistic counter-tactic of playing Tina Turner at full throttle on Marina's ghetto-blaster, lowering the volume between sentences to check on developments upstairs.

Perhaps not surprisingly, such distractions did little to alleviate the crisis taking place on-screen, where her musings seemed bent upon straying further and further into the prohibited zone of real life. With only a skin of feeble humour for camouflage, Annie had found herself moving from baby talk to breastfeeding, to ill-conceived blind dates organised by well-intentioned but misguided friends. Aware that she was blatantly drawing on personal experience in a way that she had always despised and publicly vowed to avoid, Annie struggled to wrench the narrative voice back to the detached tracks on which the column had been founded. Back to the chatty, devil-may-care voice of the girl drawn to body-piercing and one-night stands with Spanish tour operators. She was supposed to be composing a professional column, she reminded herself, an amusing counterpoint on topical themes – not a diary of the measly events in her own existence. Meanwhile the music continued to flow overhead, until it felt like a mocking commentary on the dramatic failures taking place in Annie's imagination.

At eleven-thirty Annie seized a large hardback from the shelf next to her and hurled it at the ceiling. The book, a faintly amusing tome of Jake's entitled, *How to Find Your Mate*, caught the edge of a standard lamp on its return journey, knocking it sideways onto the futon, where it rolled back and forth for a few moments, like a body seeking a position conducive to sleep. An unsightly dark smudge marked the point where the book had made contact with the ceiling. Upstairs, there was a brief hiccough of a pause, followed by the sound of fast and furious scales.

'OK you bugger, that's *it*,' hissed Annie, snatching her keys from the hall table. Only at the door of the new tenant's flat did she hesitate, steeling herself for the distasteful business of confrontation. Inside, the scales were still raging. Taking a deep breath she knocked twice, very loudly. There followed a silence, then the sound of slow, heavy footsteps. The door was flung open so violently that Annie took a step backwards.

'I'm sorry to bother you,' she began, somewhat disconcerted to find herself staring into the face of a man she had assumed to be the employee of a removals company. 'Oh . . . so you live here?'

He made a show of looking over his shoulder. 'I believe so.' His tone was sneering.

'I'm from the flat downstairs.'

'I know.' He folded his arms and leant against the doorframe. He wore faded jeans and a black T-shirt. His face was unshaven and dark across his cheeks and jaw-line, contrasting rather curiously with the streaky golden brown of his hair.

'It's just that – the piano – I'm trying to work – I write this newspaper column—'

'I'm trying to relax – a legal activity, I believe.' He massaged the back of his neck with one hand and yawned. 'Tina Turner was a big help, I must say,' he added, a shade less aggressively.

'Er . . . yes . . . sorry . . . but I can't work with background music of any kind you see—'

'Except Tina Turner, apparently.'

'No – that was . . . er revenge.'

There ensued an awkward silence, which he showed no inclination to break.

'Don't get me wrong – I love the piano – Chopin, Mozart and all that—'

'I was playing Debussy—'

'Him too. Great stuff. It's just that I have a deadline and it's . . . very distracting,' she ended lamely.

'If you want me to shut the fuck up . . . why don't you just say it?'

'Well, I wouldn't necessarily have put it like that,' Annie murmured, alarmed both by the curtness in his voice and the unashamed intensity of the way he was staring at her. 'I mean . . . perhaps you could move the piano to another—'

To her consternation he burst into scornful laughter. 'Oh sure, great idea . . . I had to pay three men to lug the bloody thing up here in the first place. I got them to put it in the back room,' he added in an aggrieved tone, 'to minimise sound-carrying problems—'

'But that's the room I work in—'

'So it would seem.' Suddenly he appeared to lose patience with the conversation. 'Message received. Over and out. All quiet on the western front – for tonight anyway. Scout's honour.'

'And you'll think about moving it . . . maybe . . . soon . . . please?' Annie had persisted, concerned that she had made no progress at all in preventing a recurrence of the situation, 'When you get the chance—'

'Yeah, surely.' There was a look of schoolboy insolence in his blue eyes. 'I might do a few press-ups in preparation, maybe—' He flexed his arms, which seemed to contain plenty of muscles already and closed the door.

Annie had retreated downstairs with a gloomy heart, cursing herself for diplomatic ineptitude and Marina for giving away milk to such an unlikable creature.

'Annie?' The sound of Amy's voice brought her back to the meeting with a jolt. 'Any ideas you'd like to throw into the ring?'

Embarrassed at appearing so obviously inattentive and feeling the after-effects of her late night, Annie clapped her hands together in a show of enthusiasm. 'How much time have you all got?' she began, willing the whirr in her brain to clear. 'I . . . I did have this idea for a piece on noisy neighbours—'

'It's only a couple of weeks since we ran that *Neighbours From Hell* feature,' interrupted Amy, stabbing the point of her pencil into her pad. 'Not sure we're ready for anything so similar just yet. Bear it in mind, though. OK?'

Knowing that the 'OK' represented both a dismissal of her first suggestion and a cue for the next, Annie prompted guffaws of appreciative laughter by informing the assembled group that she would shortly be attending a party dressed as a cowgirl with a view to initiating some research into any pockets of Wild West culture that might be flourishing in the British Isles. Their leader had to raise her arms to restore peace. 'Great stuff for the column, Annie, keep it up.'

'I've heard about this amazing new health place in Fulham,' ventured Yvonne, rolling her baby blue eyes. 'Very discreet. No communal workout rooms at all. Just one-to-one with an instructor who not only helps you with body toning, but also talks you through dietary issues, health and so on. It seems to be the way fitness clubs are going – the new holistic approach to self-improvement.'

'I like it,' said Joy.

'So do I.' Amy rolled her pencil between her palms. 'Let's schedule it in for January – catch all that post-Christmas guilt. Yvonne, we'll leave that with you.' She took a deep breath. 'Now then, Annie. We've got a great assignment up our sleeves – one of the reasons we called you in – if you can fit it in with your weekly commitment, of course.'

'I can't wait,' said Annie in an attempt to sound cheerful, but quailing at so clearly being the last person to be let in on a secret that required her cooperation.

'We've been approached by a company called Foreign Relations who organise package holidays in Europe for single people. They're inviting a representative from the paper to go along too—'

'A singles holiday?' Annie looked in dismay at the wall of gleeful acquiescence round the table.

'A free holiday—'

'You'd be perfect for it—'

'Thirty-somethings cavorting round beaches and nightclubs – just your cup of tea—'

The Ulrika Jonsson look-alike was beaming hardest of all. 'Oh God, yes, Annie would be great at that.'

'You're all sadists,' said Annie, laughing to hide the sadness pushing up inside.

'You might meet the man of your dreams,' piped someone else.

'I'd like you to do it,' concluded Amy firmly, standing up to show the meeting was at an end. 'It wouldn't be until the spring, so don't worry, we don't have to decide anything right this minute.'

'I'm honoured to have been asked, of course,' Annie reassured her quickly, joining the drift towards the door.

'Do you have a moment?' One of Amy's impressively delineated eyebrows arched upwards to emphasise the importance of receiving an answer in the affirmative.

'If it's about this week's *FlatLife*, I've got it here—' Annie began, delving into her briefcase.

'Marvellous.' Amy took it and skim-read the first page.

Annie watched, feeling like a schoolgirl with a dodgy report card, hawk-eyed for the slightest lip-twitch of appreciation. 'Everything OK?'

'Absolutely.'

The vehemence of the denial confirmed Annie's apprehensions.

'I mean, this looks great – as per usual—' Amy tapped the top page with the back of her long red fingernails. 'You've got a real gift.'

Annie smiled and said thank you, knowing that the shot had yet to be fired.

'The only thing I would say – would ask – is whether you could perhaps be a little more . . . confrontational? The humour is fab – you do it *so* well – but it would be nice to increase the mail-bag just a little.' She touched Annie's arm, displaying the American style of man-management techniques in which she had been schooled. 'A column like yours really should have a bit more feedback from the readers. Like we had in the beginning, remember? I'm not trying to change you or what you do, Annie,' she added earnestly, 'it's simply part of my job to try and make things even better than they are already.'

'No problem.' I'm thirty-three and going nowhere, she thought, smiling at her employer with shining eyes.

'Are you OK with this Annie?'

'Fine. Absolutely. No problem. Confrontation.' She raised a fist. 'You got it.'

'Good, good. And thanks for this.' She waved Annie's double-printed pages, the last one smudged because the printer had been playing up, by way of a farewell salute.

Annie stared after her editor's receding back with gridlocked teeth, fighting the urge to weep out loud. Something radical had to change, she realised miserably, shutting her briefcase and pushing up the sleeves of her woollen dress, which had proved far too hot for the tropical temperatures of the office. Something that went beyond bran flakes and sit-ups.

In the toilets she took a long hard look at herself in the mirror, hating the unladylike crimson of her cheeks and the limp wispy look of her hair, suffering as always from the effects of static electricity partying round the walls and carpets. As she stared, it struck her that her face was in two distinct halves; the left side a comically drooping version of the right, as if it were bent upon winning the race to old age. It was like looking at two people, Annie decided, holding one hand up as a barrier in line with her nose, intrigued by how much smaller her left eye suddenly appeared compared to the right. Behind her a lavatory flushed and Shona the would-be scuba diver appeared at the neighbouring basin.

'Not gone yet, then?'

'No, not gone yet,' echoed Annie brightly, leaning towards the mirror and pretending to wipe a smudge of something from her nose.

Chapter Eight

———◆◆◆———

Annie blew a bubble of smoke at the ceiling and took another sip of cappuccino, dusted, at her request, with extra shavings of chocolate. There had to be some calorific compensations for having only one glass of white wine and a salad of unchewable plants. She was sitting opposite Jake in the rear, airy, glass-roofed section of an Italian restaurant near Swiss Cottage, surrounded by other Friday lunchers, taking time out from offices or the rigours of Christmas shopping.

'So write about people starving on your doorstep,' suggested Jake, 'or better still, why not "come out" as an official lesbian – that would give you months and months of mileage and be wildly controversial. Your Amy friend would be thrilled.'

'Hmm, it's a thought.' Annie stubbed out her cigarette and pushed the ashtray away. 'But a move like that would take a certain amount of courage and right now I'm feeling about as courageous as a squashed flea.' She hesitated, wanting to continue talking about herself but wary of taking advantage of Jake's patience; his reluctance to face up to his own problems never having limited his toleration for offering what assistance he could to others. He was in a particularly generous mood that day thanks to the news that he had landed not only the yoghurt commercial but a small part in a film as well. He had arrived at the restaurant bursting with pleasure, looking more boyish and hopeful than Annie could remember in a long time.

'Jake, I'm sorry to keep going on about myself all the time –

I mean I am truly excited about you going to Spain and so on—'

'Will you fly down and visit? We're scheduled to start straight after Christmas and won't be finished until the end of March.' He reached for Annie's packet of cigarettes and helped himself.

'I doubt I'll be able to.'

'Probably just as well – awfully boring business most of the time,' he conceded happily, his expression revealing the fact that this film, like several predecessors, had already assumed the status of the possible 'big break' for which he had been waiting.

'The thing is,' continued Annie cautiously, 'I've got two teeny favours to ask you.'

He pretended to look appalled. 'I've already agreed to spend a priceless Saturday night being Clint Eastwood in order to size up this unpromising Bernard creature of Marina's—'

'Would *you* write me a fan letter?' She blushed even though Jake was the least shockable person she knew. 'Something to suggest I've been . . . controversial.'

'That Amy woman's a silly bitch, you shouldn't listen to her,' he interjected angrily, revealing a hint of the true extent of his concerns at seeing Annie in such a state and focusing on the most likely reason behind it.

'I have to, Jake,' she wailed, 'I'll have no job otherwise. Will you write something? Please?'

His face broke into a grin, his pale blue eyes flashing at the prospect of some harmless subversive fun. 'Sure. No problem. "Dear Annie, I think you're the sexiest, most entertaining, original and controversial writer since . . . er . . . Germaine Greer . . . signed, A Secret Admirer."'

'I'd prefer Naomi Wolfe.' Annie patted his hand. 'But that's the sort of thing – and preferably referring to something I've actually said.'

'Why don't you just go back to writing features for a living?' he asked carefully, picking up his dessert spoon and polishing it with a clean corner of his napkin.

'I don't want to. I don't get ideas any more. Anyway it would feel like going backwards. I want . . . oh hell . . . I guess I feel I need to change but I don't know how or in what direction—'

'Is this why you've been eating rabbit food?'

She managed a weak smile. 'I want a new life, Jake, I'm fed up with this one.'

'You've got a lovely life,' he replied stoutly, 'loads of people would want it.' He held up the spoon like a hand mirror, squinting for a view of his new dark-headed reflection. The commercial wasn't until the summer, but he thought he'd keep the colour anyway.

'Like who exactly?'

'Every other single woman I know.'

Annie laughed gratefully, reassured as always by the obstinacy of his commitment to her.

'What's this other favour, then?' Jake pulled out a wad of notes from his trouser pocket, batting away Annie's offer of a credit card.

She cleared her throat. 'Are you busy this afternoon, by any chance?'

Jake eyed her suspiciously. 'Too right I am . . . lines to learn, phone calls to make—'

'Take the rest of the day off,' Annie pleaded. 'You don't *need* to work now you've got this Spanish film—'

'English film. Spanish location,' he corrected her. 'Anyway, I work to improve my soul, as you well know.' He stroked his silky jet head and let out a theatrical sigh. 'Out with it then. What are you after now?'

'A dog,' declared Annie meekly. 'And you to come with me to choose one.'

'A dog? Bloody hell – whatever for?' Jake slapped the table with both hands, looking almost as horrified as Marina had upon receiving the same news the night before. An 'imprudent and unnecessary commitment', Marina had called it, in a most un-Marina like way, before issuing several warnings to the effect that she would not be volunteering to empty bladders or rectums of even the most adorable of domestic pets at any hour of the day or night. To which Annie had rather snidely retorted that the current frequency of her presence in the flat made such personal involvement extremely unlikely.

'This hasn't got anything to do with the pervert in the park or the telephone pest, has it? Because, if it has, forget it. You just had a weird week. Next time go and put some money in a charity box instead of trying to tackle inner city poverty on your own doorstep. Your trouble is you trust people too easily.'

'I want a dog as a Christmas present to myself. I've been thinking about it on and off for weeks. Since I seem unlikely to strike any major blows for the happiness of mankind, I might as well do some charitable good in the animal kingdom.'

Jake burst out laughing. 'Oh come on, Annie, if you're going through with this insanity, at least be honest . . .'

'OK, OK.' She smiled meekly. 'But it is true that lately my life has seemed so . . . single and . . . selfish. I want something to think about other than myself. And yes, the idea of having something to keep me company during the long winter afternoons does hold considerable appeal, as does an unignorable reason to go out for fresh air and exercise. Not to mention the attraction of owning something that will love me without answering back.'

'Darling, if that's what you're after, wouldn't a Japanese microchip do instead? No mess and an "off" switch?'

'I do know about animals you know,' she replied testily, 'my mother has a border collie.'

'Your mother, forgive me for reminding you, resides in the Welsh countryside, as opposed to a three-bedroomed London flat with a four-inch stone balcony for a garden. A puppy may take some time to learn that it has to cross its back paws until its mistress has consumed three mugs of strong black coffee and twenty fags before morning walkies.'

'Who said anything about a puppy? I shall be getting a dog. Something abandoned but housetrained. It's not just Battersea, you know – there are homes for strays all over the place. There's one in north Finchley – last year's discarded Christmas presents.' Annie threw her napkin onto her sideplate. 'I'm going there this afternoon – on my own if I have to.' Her voice faltered. 'And there was me thinking you would be supportive—'

Seeing the distinct tremor in her bottom lip and having observed enough during the course of lunch to conclude that

Annie was immersed in one of the blackest and most volatile patches of their fifteen-year acquaintance, Jake quickly changed tack. 'And so I shall be. What are we waiting for? Lead me to a hostelry for stray hounds this instant.' He threw a few coins onto the table by way of a tip and barked loudly, causing several other diners to look round in alarm.

As they proceeded through to the front part of the restaurant, which was larger and even busier than the conservatory extension in which they had eaten, Annie's eye was caught by a familiar, sandy-haired figure standing at a table in the far corner of the room. She swung round and hissed at Jake out of the corner of her mouth. 'Hurry up with that coat ticket – I'm in danger of being recognised.'

'Really? How delightful,' replied Jake in a loud voice, looking about for the possible source of Annie's embarrassment.

'Jake,' she warned, 'I mean it, please—'

'Just tell me where to look and we'll be out of here in nanoseconds.'

Annie seized the ticket from his hands and thrust it at the girl hovering behind the reception desk. 'Back corner to your left,' she muttered, keeping her head averted. 'The tall waiter with the streaky brown hair – dishing out wine to the old man with the ponytail and the floozy in the orange dress.'

'So succinct,' murmured Jake, taking a surreptitious look and then emitting a low groan of appreciation. 'But he's gorgeous. Golden copper curls. A veritable Adonis—'

'Behave, Jake. We're leaving this instant,' whispered Annie, shaking her head in amused despair and leading the way back out into the street. 'He's my new neighbour upstairs,' she explained once they were outside. 'All I knew about him till now is that he plays the bloody piano at the most unsociable hours of the night—'

'Well?'

'I beg your pardon?'

'Does he play well?'

'I don't know – I mean yes, I think so – though I hardly see the relevance—'

'Sensibilities,' replied Jake haughtily. 'A man who plays music with feeling has an admirable – not to say desirable – capacity for complex emotions.'

Annie rolled her eyes heavenward. 'Sorry to shatter your illusions, but he was also decidedly rude—'

'Rude? Really?' Jake rubbed his palms together. 'Better and better—'

'Don't be a tart, Jake,' she scolded fondly, linking her arm through his and increasing her stride to keep up with him. 'Shall we go back and get my car? It's not far – I looked it up in the A–Z – twenty minutes through the glories of north Finchley—'

'There are no glories in north Finchley,' he growled, raising his free arm at a black cab.

'And you're an extravagant sod.'

'Better than letting money rot in the bank,' he countered, exhibiting the same attitude which two years previously had caused him to move from Shrewsbury Mansions and start pouring his inheritance into large rental payments on an unnecessarily vast and somewhat dilapidated house in Camden Town.

'I say,' remarked Jake slyly, once they were seated side by side on the worn black upholstery of the cab, 'you don't think this new neighbour of yours would like to come with us to this cowboy thrash tomorrow night, do you?'

'No way, Jake,' Annie warned. 'Don't even think about it.'

They continued their journey in an amicable silence, Annie's mind filling with calendar images of loveable pets, while Jake's thoughts drifted on rather more extravagantly romantic currents connected to the new resident in Annie's building. On either side of them the smeared windows of the taxi revealed fleeting and refracted images of the tawdry Christmas glamour outside, already glittering beneath the darkening belt of grey December cloud.

When they reached their destination Jake put out a hand to stop Annie opening her purse. 'You'll have another mouth to feed soon, my dear, not to mention the prohibitive costs of kennels and rabies vaccinations.'

Annie pretended to acquiesce, but when he wasn't looking she folded a ten-pound note and slipped it into the pocket of his coat.

Chapter Nine

One glance at the price of the tickets told Annie that Bernard's cowboy party was to be in a league far beyond her wildest imaginings. They were given to him free of charge by the friend organising the event, he assured them, issuing a similar excuse for the presence of the chauffeur-driven Mercedes waiting with its hazard lights flashing in the street outside.

'But why cowboys?' Annie asked incredulously, scanning the queues of denim-clad guests lined up along the pavement outside the south London nightclub hired as the venue for the occasion.

'Why not?' Bernard had replied mildly, before adding that the acquaintance in question specialised in themed parties and had staged a very successful Arabian Nights event in a stately home the year before. 'These friendly people are to check for illegal accoutrements – weapons and tablets and so forth,' he explained, indicating the tank-sized creatures guarding the entrance, and holding up a section of chain-fencing so his guests could duck underneath.

'Shouldn't we wait in line?' ventured Annie, a little perturbed by the looks of hostility amongst the waiting crowd.

'Not for a moment,' declared Bernard, embarking on an intense consultation with the most physically striking of the bouncers, a chisel-faced Titan, sporting a tattoo of a cockerel on his forehead and with four gold rings hooked through his nostrils and eyebrows. After a couple of minutes they were ushered

79

inside, together with a group from the front section of the queue.

As soon as she had taken off her coat it became evident that Marina, as always, would be the focus of considerable attention. Not just because of the vibrant gold and red stitching bordering her dress and the matching gold and red band round her head, but because of the copious quantities of body glitter she had applied to her cheeks and forearms. The way it shimmered in the beams of the ceiling lights gave the impression she had been doused in a shower of gold-dust. Beside her, Bernard, dressed all in black apart from a polished silver sheriff's badge, looked fractionally more dashing than Annie remembered him; although even with Marina in her heelless squaw slippers he barely reached her cheekbones. Annie seized Jake's hand as they walked down the subterranean hallway towards the throb of noise and music. A few moments later they were in an enormous, strobe-lit, high-ceilinged space, ringed with archwayed escapes to rooms containing refreshments and doses of cooler air. On a stage on the opposite side of the room a band was playing a pulsing concoction of Wild West disco, to the accompaniment of 'yeeha' screeches and the thunderous stamp of feet.

'God, this is weird,' shouted Annie.

'I know, isn't it great?' Marina agreed, clapping her hands and swinging her hips. The row about the dog – like any disagreement between them – had been quickly consigned to the past. Marina had even wailed regrets that the chosen animal – a hairy knee-high hybrid called Bonnie – was not to be collected until the start of the following week. Thanks to some work crisis of Bernard's, the two women had spent a thoroughly enjoyable Friday night at the Swiss Cottage cinema complex with Jake, watching Tom Cruise in some unlikely entanglement with the nuclear arms industry and then eating three large stringy pizzas. Just like the good old days, Annie had mused, both relieved and happy to feel some of the week's worries recede at the prospect of a busy weekend.

When the line dancing started Annie's first reaction was to clutch her bottle of beer to her chest and shrink back against the wall. While Jake, who had been befriended by a young man in a heavily tassled shirt emblazoned with the words, 'A Lonesome Cowboy', began jigging on the balls of his feet. 'Oh come on Annie, it's fun. Communal dancing at its best.' Behind them, Bernard and Marina were already stepping in one of the several lines of people forming across the room. A man in a checked shirt, his hair plastered to his forehead with sweat, was bellowing instructions into a microphone, while enacting a demonstration of each move himself. Jake's companion, a creature of few words but with an engaging smile, began tugging on both Annie's and Jake's arms in a bid to persuade them to join in the fray.

'You two go on. I'll come in a minute.'

'Promise?' Jake eyed her doubtfully.

'Promise.' She held up her bottle. 'Finish this first.' Annie leant back against the wall and tipped the last of the beer, already unpleasantly warm from its brief contact in such a humid atmosphere, down her throat. From under the safety of her hat, she began to study the antics on the dance floor, marvelling at the frenzied enthusiasm of some of the participants and wondering how many energy-enhancing substances had slipped through the frisking of the heavy-duty gang at the door. It was the synchronicity that was impressive, she decided, watching with increasing fascination; the steps themselves were simple. Still reluctant to join the fray herself – in spite of mad signalling from Jake – she reached into the breast pocket of Marina's denim shirt for her cigarettes.

'A light for the pretty lady?' The question, delivered in an exaggerated American drawl, came from a tall figure wearing a broader-brimmed Stetson than her own and with a handkerchief mask across his face and nose. All Annie could see were his eyes, which were deep brown and rimmed with long dark lashes.

'How kind,' she replied, in her best southern belle accent, feeling her pulse quicken and her eyes grow wide.

It was the lighter she recognised first. Slim and gold, with smooth corners and a pretty silver hinge. An image of the handsome editor in the navy silk jacket took a few seconds to merge with the figure in front of her. 'I'm afraid we've met before,' she apologised, resorting to her own voice and blushing. 'I was rude and looked an idiot.'

'I know exactly who you are,' replied Greg Berkley, pulling down his handkerchief to reveal a smug but attractive smile. 'Annie Jordan, columnist and critic of news journals.' He laughed easily. 'No hard feelings at all.' He held out his hand, which Annie shook, feeling somewhat bewildered.

'What on earth are you doing here?'

'An ex-colleague helped organise it. These kind of things are a laugh, I find. What about you?'

'Friend of a friend, sort of thing.' Competing against the rising blast of music behind them left few possibilities for elaborate conversation. 'Are you with a group then?' she asked, looking over his shoulder.

'Yes, but I've deserted,' he confided, taking a step closer. 'Shall we join the line?'

Annie's courage faltered. 'Oh God, I'd be hopeless—'

'No you won't.' He took her cigarette from between her fingers and dropped it into her empty beer bottle. 'Follow me,' he commanded, taking her hand.

After an uncertain start, Annie picked up the steps easily. Greg looked as if he had been having line dancing lessons all his life, adding hip-thrusting flourishes of his own which would have been comical had they not been so rhythmically accomplished. After a few minutes he shuffled closer to her and began to shadow his body movements round hers. A little later she felt his hands on her hips, gently steering her in and out of the steps. Glancing up, she caught Jake's eye a few yards away in a column parallel to theirs. He winked and did a thumbs-up sign which Annie pretended to ignore, biting her lower lip to hide her smile. Beyond him she got the occasional glimpse of a limb belonging to Marina and Bernard, conducting their own, somewhat idiosyncratic, interpretation of the steps down the furthest end of the same line. I am enjoying myself at a party, she realised with some surprise, embracing the sensation like a long-lost friend. Releasing her lower lip, she let the smile arrive, revelling both in the joyous coincidence that had brought Greg Berkley back into her life and the even more wondrous fact that the attraction had been mutual after all. She placed her arms along his where they circled her waist, feeling quite literally as if she had spent the last few weeks falling towards this moment, waiting to be caught and held safe.

When at last the line broke up, Bernard steered all of them down a maze of corridors to a small room containing comfortable chairs, buckets of chilled champagne and several plates of smoked salmon sandwiches. A large screen relayed the activity taking place in the main arena, where a more conventional dancing free-for-all had resumed, aided by a disc jockey who had jumped on-stage to relieve the band.

'Won't your friends be missing you?' ventured Annie, once they had all collapsed into chairs, enjoying the fruits of Bernard's impressive sociability and mysterious influence.

Greg waved one hand to compensate for the couple of seconds it took to dispatch a large mouthful of sandwich. 'I doubt it. Anyway, how could I drag myself away from such charming company?'

'Hear, hear,' chimed Marina tipsily, raising a glass at Greg and then snuggling deeper into Bernard's lap. She had been briefed on the background of Annie's companion during a prolonged excursion in the ladies' loo, when she had also – somewhat slyly – seized a long-postponed opportunity of mentioning Colorado and skiing.

'What a pair of lovebirds you are,' Annie had teased, too full of adrenalin and excitement to muster any uncharitable reactions at all. She borrowed Marina's compact to powder the shine from her forehead and then set about pushing some air back into her hair with her fingers.

Faintly alarmed by the lighthouse glow of happiness transforming Annie's face, Marina could not resist a word or two of caution. 'Go easy, won't you?' she said quietly. 'This Greg person looks divine but—'

'He is divine.' Annie pouted her freshly reddened lips at her reflection. 'And only the other night you were telling me off for being too fussy.'

'I know, I know . . . I'm just saying go in with your eyes wide open—'

'I intend to.' Annie snapped her lipstick shut. 'And to have a good time while I'm at it. He says he's been meaning to get in touch with me ever since that horrible launch party anyway.' She lowered her voice. 'I tell you, Marina, it's not only mutual but *chemical* – like a . . . steam train . . . nothing could stop it—'

'Steam trains aren't chemical.'

'Whatever.' Annie shrugged happily.

'I'm only saying be careful—'

'Back off, can't you?' Annie tried to keep her tone light-hearted, but a hint of real indignation broke through. 'I'm a grown-up too, remember? Just because I haven't had sex for centuries doesn't mean I've lost my judgement completely.' Several other women using the facilities round them exchanged looks and giggles, but Annie was too exultant to mind. 'I can look after myself. And I know when something is right.'

'Of course you do. I'm sorry.' Marina folded her arms and smiled at Annie's reflection in the mirror. 'And I'm *so* pleased for you, really I am. To be with someone you like so much is . . . wonderful.'

'I say, Marina, do you think I'm lopsided?'

She laughed. 'Whatever do you mean?'

'My face. Look at it. It's in two halves that don't match.'

'Don't be ridiculous—'

'You're not looking properly,' persisted Annie, leaning nearer the glass. 'I am seriously unbalanced.'

'Everybody's like that.'

'You're not.'

'Yes I am. Look.' Marina made a face at the mirror.

'Not nearly as much as me.'

'It's a sign of character. Now come along or Romeo might have buggered off.'

The two of them linked arms and rejoined the men, waiting with some impatience in the crowded corridor outside.

Once all the champagne bottles were empty, Jake and his tasselled friend murmured excuses and slipped from the room. Annie and Marina amused themselves trying to spot them amongst the throng of dancing bodies being relayed on the wide

TV screen, while Greg and Bernard sat apart, meandering through a conversation about various tenuous acquaintances they had in common. In a bid for further entertainment the indefatigable Bernard then insisted on leading them all through a torturous exercise designed to strengthen the thigh and knee muscles most vital to the smooth enactment of a parallel turn. Standing with their backs to the wall, each took it in turns to attempt to slide up and down it without collapsing in contortions of pain. Annie, who abhorred the idea of skiing almost as much as she did bridge and home counties tennis clubs, joined in with a show of gusto, before falling onto her knees with a groan.

'I want to make love to you,' Greg whispered, bending down to help her to her feet. 'I want to now, so badly Annie.'

Though out of earshot, Bernard and Marina chose this timely moment to excuse themselves, impelled, they claimed, by a desire for mineral water and more aerobic exercise on the dance floor.

'Come home with me tonight,' Greg murmured, once the door had closed behind them, 'it will be so good.'

'Tonight . . . ?' She hesitated.

'Got a headache?' he teased, pressing her back against the wall and moving his left hand to the front of her shirt, where it encountered a safety pin employed in place of a crucial missing button. 'Fort bloody Knox,' he growled, moving the hand lower down.

'Greg . . . I want to, of course, but—'

'I'll still respect you, if that's what you're worried about.'

'I'm not worried at all,' Annie murmured, 'in fact I can't remember when I felt less worried in my life.'

'I say—' he pressed harder against her, '—does this mean I'm going to make an appearance in that column of yours?'

'Not if you're a good boy,' she whispered, knowing already that no amount of writer's block would ever bring her to risk debasing or shattering the miracle enfolding around her by trying to incorporate it in the weekly chaos of her column. 'Besides, I've got far more interesting things to write about—'

She prised enough space between them to enable her to draw the gun from her holster – where it had been cutting uncomfortably into her hip-bone – and pointed it at his nose. 'You'll have to do exactly as I say now.'

'A cowgirl with attitude, eh? I like that. I like that a lot.' He snatched the gun from her hands and clamped his mouth on hers. His skin, dark with stubble, felt like sandpaper.

These intimacies were brought to something of an abrupt conclusion by Jake, who burst in announcing he was going home.

'You bugger off then,' drawled Greg, barely glancing round, not reading Jake's pale face as Annie did. 'We're still a little . . . involved here, mate, as you can probably see.' He brushed Annie's shoulder with his lips and gave her a conspiratorial smile.

'Christ, Jake, what's going on?' It was impossible to keep the irritation out of her voice. But at the same time she could see he was in a bad way. 'Has something happened?'

'Nothing . . . nothing.' Jake hung his head. 'S'fine . . . get a cab . . . later alligator.' Turning back towards the door, he staggered and fell against the wall.

'I've got to help him – he's completely out of it.' If Greg's evident disappointment was hard, it was nothing to match her own. Yet it was equally clear to Annie where her priorities had to lie. While Jake huddled behind the door, moaning gently to himself, they hurriedly exchanged phone numbers, each writing them with a leaky Biro on the palm of the other's hand.

Feeling thwarted but more than a little noble, Annie looped her arm through Jake's and helped him to his feet. 'You'll explain to Marina for me won't you?' she said, rolling her eyes in despair as her charge swayed in an effort to apply himself to the mislaid art of placing one foot in front of the other.

'Do you want a hand?'

'No, we'll be fine. Get back to your deserted friends,' she commanded, thinking that she had never performed the art of playing hard to get with such panache.

'I guess I might. But I'll be in touch,' Greg reassured her, tapping the numbers on the palm of his hand.

Chapter Ten

Not even grey Sunday morning drizzle and a headache could dampen Annie's post-party euphoria. Having checked that Jake – in a foetal clench on the futon – was still breathing, she skipped back to bed with a mug of coffee and two ancient Danish pastries revitalised by a spell in the microwave. She ate slowly, humming as she chewed, ignoring the stale crumbs cascading onto the bedclothes. According to the bathroom scales, her body had performed the unprecedented feat of losing five pounds overnight, a joyous milestone in a generally joyous twenty-four hours, and one that confirmed Annie's long-held suspicion that weight was almost entirely a matter of psychology as opposed to diet.

Charged with that peculiar zest for life inspired by the possibility of romance, she then took the revolutionary step of cleaning the flat. Although a resting actress friend of Jake's, called Chloë, was theoretically in charge of such matters, the girl's mysterious propensity for illness meant that the place was invariably in a state of sore neglect. A fictionalised, fifty-year-old Irish version of Chloë had put in several early cameo performances in the column, providing much-needed comic backing to tirades against feather dusters and imploding hoover bags. A character of far more practical use than the real thing in fact, mused Annie, prising a loose flap of carpet from the mouth of the hoover extension and thinking how naive she had been to imagine that she could sustain a year's contract as a columnist without some recourse to her own life as source material. But one had to draw certain boundaries, she told herself, aware that her recent predilection for allowing work and real life to get so hopelessly interfused showed that she had been in danger of losing her grip on both.

It wasn't until well into the afternoon, when her appearance and surroundings had reached a fever pitch of perfection and orderliness, that Annie acknowledged the disheartening fact that she was on tenterhooks for the trill of the telephone. By four o'clock, with Marina still not returned and no grunts emanating from the spare room, she was daring herself to commit the invariably fatal crime of over-enthusiasm by calling Greg Berkley herself. 'Hey there cowboy, it's the cowgirl with attitude calling—' Annie scowled at the sentences as they unfolded inside her head, knowing her capacity for wit or nonchalance in such circumstances to be remote. Tempted nonetheless, she turned over the palm of her hand only to find that all that remained of Greg's phone number was a faint five and something that could have been a one or a seven, the remaining digits having been obliterated through subjection to scour cream cleaners and sandalwood aromatherapy bubblebath.

Furious at herself, Annie resorted to a stab at a Christmas shopping list by way of distraction, followed by a summary of what she needed to purchase from a pet shop. *Basket, bowl, brush, food (biscuits?), collar, lead, (TOYS?).* Staring at these achievements, Annie caught herself wondering whether it might be rather fun – and faintly original – to write her Christmas column in the form of a list.

'*Handy-sized vodka bottle for dressing-gown pocket on Boxing Day morning – add to orange juice at breakfast for guaranteed results . . .*'

Feeling the dim and ever-elusive stirrings of literary inspiration, she tiptoed into the spare room to assess her chances of gaining access to the computer. Jake had changed position and was spreadeagled on his back, as if inviting himself for crucifixion. His mouth hung open, giving an uncharacteristically gormless look to the small neat features of his face. At the roots of his hair, sticking out like the spikes of a leafless bush, Annie could see patches of peroxide pushing into the black.

'Jake,' she whispered, 'I'm just going to—'

A piano flurry overhead stopped her mid-sentence. 'Perhaps not,' she muttered, glaring at the ceiling.

'Am I dead?' croaked Jake, moving only his lips, which were cracked and rimmed with flakes of white.

'I'll never walk again.'

'Coffee?'

'Drugs – please – I'll take anything—'

Annie disappeared and came back with three extra-strong analgesics and a glass of water. 'What happened last night, anyway?' she asked more gently, kneeling on the floor beside him and stroking his forehead.

'I died.'

'Your lonesome friend – where did he get to?'

Jake moaned and rolled away.

'Come on, take these while Aunty Annie makes you a nice cup of tea.'

'I'm afraid I was sick a couple of times during the night,' he confessed on her return. Screwing up his face, he managed a noisy sip from the mug. 'I hope I cleared up all right—'

'Really? – I'd never have known – didn't hear – didn't notice a thing,' Annie lied, part of her cleaning programme having involved the immediate vicinity of the lavatory. 'What were you on, anyway, to cause such grief?'

He shrugged. 'Just one tablet . . . he said it was sound—' Jake clutched his head as if the pain contained inside it had intensified at the memory. 'Felt great for a bit . . . then it was like being smashed with a sledgehammer . . . Does this guy ever stop?' he added, by way of reference to the music still trickling through the floorboards upstairs.

'I thought a love of the piano was supposed to be evidence of deep feelings,' Annie couldn't resist reminding him, 'sensibilities and all that crap. Remember?'

But Jake was in too feeble a state to retaliate. 'I want my brain back,' he mumbled, handing her the mug, still full of tea, and shrinking back down into his sleeping bag.

Annie was about to offer more sympathy when the telephone rang. Wanting to take it in privacy, she raced to the hall, slopping tea down her clean shirt. On getting there, she managed, with a Herculean effort of will, to wait for two more rings before slowly picking up the receiver.

'Hello, Annie Jordan speaking,' she said, in her lowest, most Marlene Dietrich tones.

'It's me,' came Marina's voice. There followed a muffled giggle and hissed reprimands in the background. 'Sorry, Bernard's misbehaving. We're still in bed. Wasn't it great last night? We stayed until half past five. Where the hell did you get to?'

'Didn't Greg tell you?'

'We didn't see him – assumed you two had sneaked off to more private premises—'

'Well you assumed wrong,' Annie snapped, without meaning to, suddenly feeling very unsure about every aspect of the events of the preceding evening. 'That creepy cowboy with tassles gave Jake a bad pill. I had to bring him home. He's still here, groaning on the futon. We're through the vomiting phase I think,' she added, letting slip a small bid for sympathy.

'How foul. Poor Jake. And poor you – what a star for taking care of him.'

'When are you coming back?' asked Annie, slightly mollified.

'I've got spare kit here, so I thought I'd stay on. Probably see you tomorrow evening, or maybe Tuesday. Bernard's got a boys' bridge thing on that night.'

'Great.'

'Good luck collecting the dog.'

'The dog? Oh sure, thanks.'

Annie caught part of a muffled shriek before the line went dead.

She spent the rest of the evening smoking and watching television, gloomily pondering why other people's love affairs were so tedious and repellent compared to one's own, and debating how long it would be before Bernard and his ridiculous boxer shorts were told to take the proverbial hike. The longest Annie had ever known Marina stick with anyone was six months, a record set by an itinerant Italian banker with soulful eyes and a hiatus hernia that sometimes incapacitated him for weeks at a time. Far more incapacitating as far as Marina was concerned had been the emergence of a wife living in Milan, with one small child and another just a couple of months from arrival.

The phone didn't ring again until ten o'clock. Telling herself it wasn't Greg, but believing it had to be, Annie once again made herself wait for several rings before picking up the receiver.

'It's Zoë.'

Annie checked her disappointment in an instant. 'Zoë, hi – thanks so much for dinner the other night, I've been meaning to write only—'

'To write, eh?'

'Pardon?'

'You've got a bloody cheek, Annie. A bloody cheek. We're not just friends any more, are we? We're part of your research. If you think things like that you should bloody well come out and say so. All that bollocks you spouted last weekend about despising writers who plunder their own lives because they lack the imagination to do anything else . . . Well, I'm on to you now. I've found you out. So cut the pretence. Use our real names next time, why don't you? David was particularly upset – after all his efforts to be friendly and sociable – what kind of thanks is that? How did you put it now – "the sex-starved look peculiar to the lone, unattractive male?" Very nice, I must say.'

'None of it was true,' countered Annie weakly.

'You must think me very stupid. And poor David—'

'Poor David wants to shag you silly.' The accusation slipped out before she could stop it.

'What did you say?'

There seemed nothing for it but to continue. 'While you were breastfeeding Flopsy he was eyeing your tits like a crazed bull. So count yourself lucky I didn't put that in the column as well.'

'That is an outrageous allegation.' Zoë's voice quivered. 'If you carry on like this Annie, you won't have any friends left at all. And my daughter's name is Cordelia,' she added imperiously, slamming down the phone.

When it rang again, just a couple of instants later, Annie assumed it was Zoë, wanting to add something to her tirade. She snatched up the receiver, ready with the razor-sharp attack of the truly defensive. Only to hear the low, soothing growl of Greg Berkley.

'How are you doing Annie?'

'Oh, Greg – I – how great – to hear you – to talk – after all this time—'

'Only a day, babe. Are you missing me that much?'

'Certainly not. I've been far too busy playing nursemaid.'

'I hope you'd play nursemaid for me if I got sick.'

'I expect so.' Clutching the telephone in both hands, she slid down the wall, aware as she did so of several twingeing thigh muscles from Bernard's ridiculous skiing exercises the night before.

'Sorry it's so late.'

'That's OK.'

'What are you wearing?'

'Wearing? I – only—' Annie surveyed her stained shirt, jeans and slouch socks with some dismay, doubting their ability to satisfy the impulse behind the question. 'My nightie, of course. It's bedtime isn't it?' She hardly dared breathe, the silence on the other end of the phone was so intense.

'Jesus, Annie, Jesus.'

'I've got some little white socks on too, to keep my toes warm.'

'Nothing else?'

'Nothing at all.'

'I've got to see you.'

She lowered her voice. 'Jake's still here.' She looked up to see Jake himself framed in the doorway, rubbing his knuckles in his eyes and blinking at the hall light. He was still wearing most of his outfit from the night before, but his shirt was untucked, hanging almost to the knees of his jeans and his feet were bare.

He had slim, hairless toes, arched in a perfect gradation of size.

'Can't that guy look after himself?' Greg burst out, his voice edged with genuine irritation, before adding more softly, 'I was hoping to see you tonight.'

'Tonight . . . ?'

'Though I guess it is a bit late.'

'I guess it is,' echoed Annie, who would have agreed to anything. 'How about tomorrow?'

'I'm busy.'

'Tuesday?'

'I'm tied up all week. The earliest I can make is Friday.'

'Friday sounds good.'

'I'll pick you up at . . . shall we say eight o'clock?'

'Eight o'clock it is.' As Annie slowly replaced the receiver, she could feel all the unexplained misery of the last few weeks slipping away. At last her life had a purpose, a plot, the focus for which she had been longing. Nothing seemed awful any more, not Zoë, not the column; not even the looming horror of a family Christmas.

Jake had retreated to the kitchen where he was drinking from a tall glass of milk and rummaging ineffectually in the fridge. 'God, you women are hopeless,' he moaned when Annie came in. 'Mouldy cheese and a box of cheap Chablis – it just won't do, I tell you—'

'Feeling better then?' she murmured, the smile on her face trumpeting her feelings with all the subtlety of a brass band. She put a packet of digestives on the table and began carving the green edging off the cheese.

'I suppose that was Greg the Lionheart,' said Jake, licking the milk moustache from his upper lip.

'You suppose right. We're going out on Friday. Oh Jake, I'm so—'

'Happy?' He finished for her. 'And I'm really pleased for you.' He leant across the table and patted her arm. 'Really. Good-looking bastard too.' He managed a grin, his first of the day. 'Got any cornflakes?'

'Stale bran flakes. But no milk. You just finished off the last lot.' Annie looked at her watch. 'And the corner shop shut four minutes ago.'

'Bugger.' Jake hunched his shoulders and sulked for a few moments before suddenly brightening. 'We'll just have to intrude on one of your neighbours then, won't we? Preferably the waiter with the piano,' he added with a wink.

'You're incorrigible. Though, come to think of it, he does owe us milk.' Jake leapt to his feet but she grabbed his arm. 'It's so late, Jake, he might be asleep—'

'I'll knock quietly.'

'I'm coming too.'

'No need.'

'There's every need. For one thing, he doesn't know who you are, and for another I might just take the perfect opportunity to further our dialogue on acoustics.'

'How do I look?'

'Terrible.'

Jake insisted on being given time to comb his hair and brush his teeth before leading the mission to the next floor.

'What I want to know is, how can you be so sure about this guy?' she asked, tucking in a stray flap of shirt as she followed him up the stairs. 'You only caught a glimpse of him, after all.'

'Vibrations,' he replied gravely. 'I get them all the time.'

Chapter Eleven

Bonnie didn't like the car. After trying to keep a hold of her on the back seat, Jake gave up and clambered through to the front. The dog, whimpering, tried to follow suit, slipping on the hand-brake and nearly causing Annie to collide with a cyclist hovering by her left wing mirror. Eventually the animal curled up in the small space at Jake's feet, panting heavily and probing her nose under the soles of his shoes.

'Hasn't some of the need to require a canine companion been somewhat superceded by recent events?' he ventured, hoping he sounded friendly as opposed to critical. Agreeing to spend half his Monday morning chasing between pet shops and dog homes had been the best way he could think of to make up for the excesses of the weekend. 'I mean, the way things are looking, the long winter evenings you mentioned might not be quite so lonely after all.'

'It would have been tempting fate to change my mind,' declared Annie stoutly, having given the same matter some thought herself. 'From the moment I chose the dog everything began to get better.'

Defeated by such superstitious logic, Jake laughed and shook his head. Glancing sideways, he felt a stab of protective affection at the familiar profile. The hair short and wild; the face soft but determined, her eyes shining. She was wearing small, brilliantly coloured earrings; lilac peacocks specked with dots of silver. It needed someone very special to take her on, he thought fondly, someone who could see beyond all the chatter and show of superficial confidence to the warm and generous woman inside, a woman whose hunger for the right love was matched only by her determination for that hunger not to show. The thought of exactly what role a smooth operator like Greg Berkley might have to play in answering such needs filled Jake with concern which he knew better than to express out loud. His own record for caution in comparable matters was woefully poor. All one ever had to go on at the beginning of any relationship was instinct and first appearances, he reflected, smiling to himself as an image of Annie's neighbour formed in his mind. Having decided that his attraction for the man was a serious one, he was rather regretting having been so childish and obvious about it to Annie.

'Anyway, a dog will be a good subject for *FlatLife*,' she remarked, reaching past the gear stick in an effort to stroke some portion of the fur, which looked soft but felt curiously wiry to the touch.

'Which raises an interesting question—'

'Oh yes, and what's that?'

'Whether, as a seasoned columnist, you live to write or write to live.'

Annie laughed quickly, thinking of her new determination about keeping boundaries. 'I write to earn money.'

'I thought that after Zoë's recent tantrum you had vowed to creep back inside the all-weather protection of your fictional shell.'

'I have,' she interjected hastily, still feeling unequal to the task of explaining that it was harder than it sounded, that writing about Zoë's horrible dinner party was something that had happened because of a state of mind rather than out of any deliberate intention. 'Bonnie doesn't count. Since she can't read, I can't offend her, can I?'

'I suppose not,' Jake conceded, eyeing the dribble on his black leather ankle boots and trying to shift his feet away from the dog's mouth. 'That place said they'd have her back if it didn't work out, didn't they?'

'I'm sure there won't be any question of that,' replied Annie archly. 'They also said she's got a sweet temperament – a real family pet—'

'But you haven't got a family,' put in Jake gloomily. 'You've got a canine-hating flatmate and neighbours to whom you're extremely rude.'

'Neighbour. The people downstairs are never there. Anyway, I wasn't rude. Just firm. And Marina's now totally OK about Bonnie.'

They had reached Finchley Road tube station, where a set of roadworks was slowing the traffic to a crawl. Outside the blue skies of early morning had been gashed with slits of grey. Up ahead a black bulge of cloud was skulking somewhere over Lord's. 'The poor guy was quite right – we hadn't a hope of shifting his bloody piano without gouging holes in the floor-boards.'

'He was being deliberately unhelpful. And he didn't have any bloody milk.'

'That was hardly his fault.'

'My God, you do fancy him.'

'Only mildly,' lied Jake, his reluctance to confess to a serious infatuation deepening at Annie's evident antipathy towards the man.

Bonnie, perhaps reacting to the slight rise in tensions between the humans with whom she was being forced to share her new cramped and confusing existence, began growling quietly.

Once Annie had parked, all three occupants tumbled from the car with some relief, particularly the dog, who pulled so hard that it was all Annie could do to keep a hold of the lead.

'I think she wants a walk,' she said, quailing inwardly as something of the magnitude of her new commitment began to dawn. 'Perhaps I'd better do that before introducing her to her new home.'

'You won't mind if I pass and return to my own life?'

'No of course not. You've been marvellous—'

'So have you. Sorry for messing up like that on Saturday.'

Jake kissed her fondly on both cheeks and waved at Bonnie, who had slumped into a disconsolate heap by a lamppost. 'Looks like she might have changed her mind. Better take her though, to avoid accidents indoors and so on—'

'Go away,' she commanded, detecting a smirk in his tone. 'I'll be fine.'

Once Jake was safely round the corner, Annie reached into her pocket for the packet of small, multicoloured, bone-shaped dog biscuits she had brought with her in case of emergencies. At least animals could be bribed for love, she mused, as Bonnie, alerted by the promising crackle of food packaging, came trotting over to investigate.

Though Annie had set off with the intention of introducing her new charge to the delights of Regent's Park, the darkening sky prompted her to veer off into a small enclosed park and playground at the bottom of St John's Wood High Street instead. As well as being much closer to home, it was attractively empty, thereby minimising the chance of encounters with other hounds, several of whom had already been lunged at in a most unpromising fashion on their short journey through the streets.

As they passed through the high black iron gates, the only other walker in sight was an old lady with a chihuahua, both tottering so feebly that a flock of crumb-scouring pigeons barely bothered to glance up as they passed. Annie set off at a brisk pace in the opposite direction, following a narrow tarmacked path that led round to the left of the park, away from the playground and towards a long stretch of shrubbery. Tempting though it was, she knew it might be foolhardy to let Bonnie off the lead until their relationship had become more firmly established. Besides which, the large central square of green, mowed to an impressively immaculate and vivid precision for midwinter, was covered in signs saying '*Keep off the grass.*'

Encouraged by the pace of the dog, Annie broke into a gentle jog. Not only would she be even thinner, by Friday, she told herself, she would be more finely toned too. The thought of the now imminent likelihood of being seen – possibly even scrutinised – by a desirable male without the flattering protection of clothes was disconcerting. As the possibility drew nearer, Annie was beginning to experience schoolgirl terror at what Greg Berkley might think – even if he did not say – of the unsylphlike proportions of her body. She was so out of practice at such situations, she reflected helplessly. No thanks to Pete, who had always lunged for the light switch long before it crossed her mind. Even in the privacy of the dark his awkwardness remained, making her wonder sometimes whether he did not suffer from a fundamental distaste of the sexual act itself, despising it as an embarrassing reflex, something to be endured rather than enjoyed. Looking back she marvelled that she put up with the situation for so long, especially during the prolonged, painful mess of the last few months, when stone figures on a tomb could have shown more evidence of libido.

When Bonnie disappeared under the legs of a park bench, Annie took the opportunity to sit down. The woman and the chihuahua had reached a set of swings rooted in concrete on the far side of the grass. A man in a long black coat was on one of the swings, soaring so high that Annie feared he might go right over the top. While she watched, he suddenly flew off the seat as it swung forward, landing like a dark graceful bird on the edge of the tarmac path. The chihuahua broke into a frenzied yapping, bringing Bonnie out from under the bench, her frizzy ears pricked to attention. She barked twice, as if to assert her authority over the situation and then shot back under the seat. It was only then that Annie noticed that the man in the black coat was heading in their direction, taking great strides across the forbidden carpet of green. Something in the evident purposefulness of the approach alerted her even before she recognised him.

'Time to go, my friend,' she murmured, leaping to her feet and tugging ineffectually on the lead.

'We meet again,' said her neighbour. Under the coat was a dark blue polo-neck jumper and white paint-splashed jeans. In the daylight of a wintry afternoon his skin looked very pale. There were faint freckles that she hadn't noticed before, sprinkled across his cheek bones and the bridge of his nose. 'I didn't know you had a dog.' He squatted down and made a clicking noise with his tongue. As he bent his legs, a slit appeared in the knee of his jeans, revealing a segment of hard pale flesh. Bonnie, much to Annie's dismay, trotted out at once, not only allowing herself to be patted, but even going so far as to lie on her back, paws flopped against the sky.

'I've only just got her.'

He carried on scratching while Bonnie blinked up at him.

'Sorry to have bothered you last night by the way—' Annie continued, compelled by his silence to speak, and feeling that Jake's and her intrusion probably ought to be mentioned. 'It was a bit of a cheek.'

'No worries. I'm seldom in bed before one.' He paused before adding, 'It's allowed then, is it?'

'What?' Annie was already turning her attention to the path ahead, keen to be on her way.

'Dogs in the flat. Are they allowed?' He made a face. 'I mean, you wouldn't want someone in the block to report you to the landlord or anything, would you?'

'Animals come in and out of other flats in the row all the time,' she began.

His expression remained grave, but his eyes were filled with mockery. 'Ah, but they all have different landlords, each one with his own agenda of dos and don'ts.'

Annie hated him. 'Are you threatening me? Because, if you are, I might just take this opportunity to raise the matter of noise pollution—'

'Noise pollution, eh?' He whistled quietly. 'My skills as a musician have received many descriptions over the years, but never one quite so flattering as that.'

'There's a whole department at the council devoted to such things,' Annie pressed on, determined to keep him on the defensive. 'If I contact them they'll give me a notebook to jot down every time I'm disturbed and then after three months—'

'I guess I'll need to find a new career then,' he said, when she had finished.

'A new . . . ? I thought you were a—' She had been on the point of saying waiter, but bit her lip instead.

'You don't know anything about me,' he said quietly. 'And for your information the piano is being moved this afternoon.' With that, he turned on his heel and strode away, back towards the main gates.

'Well he can bugger off, can't he?' Annie looked down to see not a dog, but an empty collar. A quick, panic-stricken scan of the path ahead revealed Bonnie's wiry brush of a tail disappearing through a gap in the shrubbery a few yards further on. A game of hide and seek ensued, until Annie found herself in a warren of gravestones, masked on all sides by thickets of holly bushes and laurels.

'OK dog, I've had enough. You can die here for all I care. I'm going home.'

'She doesn't like the lead.'

Annie literally jumped with shock. 'Bloody hell, where did you spring from?'

'I didn't mean to scare you. I saw she'd run off so I thought—'

'I can manage perfectly well thank you.'

Her neighbour shrugged. 'Suit yourself.' He had turned the collar of his coat up to his ears, where it was ruffling the sides of his hair. His eyes, she noticed, were now red-rimmed and watering with cold. 'Try hiding the lead,' he muttered, before turning and walking away.

After he had gone, nothing stirred but the wind through the dry leaves and the dog, scurrying irreverently round stone-carved testimonies to human love. Annie put the lead in her pocket and crouched down, holding out a biscuit. Bonnie bounced over to her at once, behaving as if there had never been an issue over the matter in the first place. Annie could feel the dog's sharp teeth scrape her fingers as the morsel was snatched and swallowed whole. Seizing her chance, she refastened the collar two notches further down and wound the lead twice round her hand.

'At this rate we'll have a weight problem in common if nothing else, my girl,' she muttered, using her free arm to shield her face as they tunnelled back through the undergrowth to the trimmed safety of the path.

Chapter Twelve

The lustre of romance and an effortless maintenance of her recent weight loss cast wonderful beams of light into what Annie found to be an unexpectedly taxing week. Not for once because of work, or the silence of the telephone – Greg called every night – but because of Bonnie. In contrast to her mother's collie, who seemed to spend most of her life asleep on the kitchen floor, the animal was never still, not even after one of their innumerable walks to the little park at the bottom of St John's Wood High Street. While her mistress flopped on the sofa amidst a recuperative fog of coffee steam and cigarette smoke, Bonnie would immediately resume her vigil by the front door, often lying with her nose slotted into the crack underneath it, as if seeking a whiff of freedom for the consolation of not being allowed to experience it. Apart from exercise, the only highlights of the creature's existence were breakfast and dinner; the combined time of each lasting (Annie timed it) for an average of ten seconds. The instant the bowl was empty, the dog scoured the kitchen floor for missed scraps, before returning, tail down, for some final frantic licking of her empty bowl. The first time this trick was played, Annie took pity and served seconds; only to find the same, innately pathetic ritual being pursued again. Nothing is enough, she thought bleakly, watching her pet collapse dejectedly beside the beautiful wicker basket which she sniffed at but resolutely refused to inhabit.

'God, a psychiatrist would have a field day,' she complained to Marina, who finally appeared with dark circles under her eyes and a bag full of dirty clothes on Tuesday night.

'She's clearly insecure,' declared Marina wisely, 'traumatised childhood and so on.'

'Well, we've all had one of those,' laughed Annie, pushing Bonnie's snout away from her bag of crisps and tutting as Marina opened out her own packet to be licked clean. 'She's already demolished three stale digestives from behind the fridge. She'll get fat.'

'Well she looks skinny enough to me. And you've lost weight,' she remarked, eyeing Annie over the top of the TV guide

'I know, it's weird because I've stopped trying to—' Annie could not contain her pleasure at Marina having noticed. 'I gave up on your tape after the first attempt. I'd rather die of obesity than look like that woman.'

'Must be all this dog walking then,' observed Marina dryly, 'or maybe line dancing?'

'Funnily enough—'

'So it's all happening – between you and Greg, I mean? That's great. I'm really pleased for you.' She hoped her tone betrayed no hint of reserve. The re-emergence of her flatmate's habitual good spirits was too important to start questioning the solidity of the cause. 'Now, sorry to be dull, but I'm going to have a bath and go to bed. Hope you don't mind – I know I've hardly seen you.'

'I don't mind at all,' Annie reassured her, minding a little, but telling herself she had no right to.

Although Bonnie had not protested at being locked in the hall on her first night, she put up a dreadful whimpering protest when Annie tried it a second time. Aware not only of Marina, trying for an evidently much needed early night, but also of the tender and pertinent issue of neighbours and noise, Annie relented and flung open the sitting-room door.

Her reward for such compassion the next morning was dog hair on every inch of upholstery and a pungent brown mess on the door mat. Having narrowly avoided stepping on it, Marina

– handbag and piece of toast in hand – shrieked until Annie appeared to offer some sort of rescue. Even when the mess had been cleared away, Marina made a point of stepping gingerly over the mat, placing one high heel out of the door and sliding the rest of her body after it.

By way of compensation for these trials, managing the Thursday lunchtime deadline that week presented none of its customary problems. Spurred on by the certainty that, while not remotely controversial, the subject of Bonnie was potentially amusing and gloriously inoffensive, Annie wrote the entire piece in one attempt.

The unimaginable has happened: your irresponsible columnist, she who kills spider plants and all other known species of plant life at one watering, has undertaken the massive responsibility of acquiring a pet. A dog called Bonnie, whose hairy face stared at me so pleadingly from behind the cages of her North London dog home, that I chose her on the spot. We have a lot in common, which is fortunate since we spend a good deal of time in each other's company. The state of Bonnie's hair is almost as bad as mine (see above photo), though she draws the blood of anyone who tries to tame it, while I tend to contain myself to mere growling. She is a compulsive eater too, a condition for which I feel some empathy, as well as no small measure of exasperation. Even the fruit bowl now has to live under the protection of a saucepan lid, since, on the rare occasion that it contains anything more nourishing than twiggy grape stems, Bonnie feels at liberty to help herself. (She eats twiggy grape stems too.) Though as keen as the next pet owner to foster healthy eating habits, I have discovered that the consumption of such products has an unfortunately liquidising effect on the contents of Bonnie's stomach. My collection of cleaning equipment has quadrupled in consequence, taking up all the space in the cupboard under the sink, which we have to keep permanently closed because it is otherwise regarded as a source of chewable amusements . . .

Continuing in a similar vein for five hundred words proved even easier than Annie had dared hope. Her only slight dissatisfaction upon finishing stemmed from the knowledge that the hearty, humorous tone of the piece belied the very real problems with which she was grappling. Problems connected not just to the odour left by dog turds and the scratch marks being carved into the panel on the door, but also to the absence of the very affection to which she had been so looking forward. Bonnie was not the pooch by the fireside type she had imagined. The animal tolerated displays of affection, but never invited them. Even having her stomach scratched – a trick which Annie had shamelessly copied from her encounter in the park with her neighbour – was something she endured only for a few seconds at a time. Afterwards she would leap to her feet and give her body an enormous shake, as if trying to brush the memory of such attentions away. Her breath smelt of rotten fish and if approached with a grooming tool she bared her teeth and flattened her ears until her assailant had backed away. In fact, Annie decided, watching her jolly sentences roll through the jaws of her fax machine on their journey into print, the experience was proving to be pretty unrewarding all round.

To admit, only three days into the first week, that she had made a mistake, was hard. Especially given all the cautions she had received from friends. Not to mention her mother, who had taken the news that Bonnie was to be accompanying her mistress to Wales over Christmas with a marked lack of enthusiasm.

'Try and do something endearing, OK?' she muttered on Thursday evening, after Bonnie had spent at least two hours whimpering from her draught-exclusion position along the bottom of the front door. 'Or it could be back to the Finchley Retirement Clinic after all.' Misinterpreting these communications as the possible prelude to exercise, Bonnie leapt to her feet, wagging her tail so hard that the entire rear half of her body swung from side to side. 'For God's sake, we've been out *four* times today.' Annie held up her fingers at the dog. 'That's more than I usually manage in a month.' Bonnie sat down, continuing her tail swishing, but more doubtfully. 'And now, if you'll excuse me, I need to devote some time to making myself beautiful.' She headed down the hallway to the bathroom, making a mental note that talking out loud to the creature was a habit she should do her utmost to avoid.

Though she was alone, Annie locked the door and proceeded to exfoliate and wax herself to a state of marbled, if rather pink, perfection. 'I'll be nice to touch anyway,' she muttered, rubbing palmfuls of moisturiser over her anatomy and trying, to convince herself that sex might not be an issue on a first date anyway. Before leaving the bathroom, she turned back for a last glance at herself, wondering if she was looking a little less lopsided or whether mounting excitement was merely playing tricks with her eyes.

Drinking a litre of water by way of supper, Annie forsook the television for an early night. With Marina at Bernard's until the weekend, there were no other distractions to keep her up any longer. She put the light out at once, stretching one arm up under the pillow and the other round the curve of her stomach, bulging slightly from its uncharacteristic encounter with so much fluid. Sleep might not be in such ready supply the next night, she reminded herself, relishing the growing heaviness in her limbs and adjusting her position slightly to accommodate it.

But while Annie's body was ready to shut down, her mind had other plans. For a few hours she watched, feeling like a ringside spectator, as muddled scenarios involving Greg and pianos and dogs continued to block her path to sleep, to the increasingly loud background accompaniment of growls from her stomach. At three o'clock she flung herself out of bed and stamped into the kitchen in search of food.

Three wedges of bread and butter and a cup of tea later, she felt calmer, but even more wide awake. 'Basket,' she instructed Bonnie, who gave her a mournful look and continued trawling round the table legs for crumbs. She tried patting her, but the animal slunk out of reach. Could pets and people have person-ality clashes? she wondered. Could they be as irretrievably ill-matched as humans? This train of thought was interrupted by a faint tinkle of piano keys overhead, so faint that she knew at once that the offending instrument had at last been moved. But what a tortured soul to be awake at such an unseemly time of night, she mused, before realising that a similar accusation could be levelled against herself.

She was on the point of returning to bed when it occurred to her that Shrewsbury Mansions having a no–dogs policy would provide a perfect solution to her dilemma. She could feign sadness and return Bonnie to Finchley without losing face at all. Even the thought of how the man upstairs might scoff was bearable. Wanting to act immediately, Annie scribbled a letter by hand, addressing it not to the landlord, whom she had never met, but to Messrs Butler and Beaucroft, the property agents who acted on his behalf. Half amused at her own eccentricity, she then pulled a coat over her dressing gown and stepped into her leather boots, still muddy from the excursions in the park that afternoon.

'Your days could be numbered, my girl,' she warned, waving the letter and almost losing her balance as the dog tugged her to the front door. Out in the empty dark of the street, with the cold air whipping round her bare knees, Annie felt less amused and even a little afraid. As they passed the deserted forecourt of the garage, she glimpsed a shadowy figure dodging between flag poles before disappearing behind a wall. It was a relief to reach the main road, where the occasional car and scurrying figure made her feel less alone.

Once the letter had been released, Bonnie retaliated with a long pee against the postbox.

'It'll probably come to nothing,' Annie apologised, pitying the creature suddenly and acknowledging her own impetuous culpability in taking her on. 'Now let's bugger off home.' She walked so fast that for once Bonnie had to struggle to keep up. With each step Annie's bare feet slid uncomfortably inside her boots; while behind her lay a trail of dried mud specks, working their way free from the crevices in her soles.

Chapter Thirteen

The next morning Marina called Annie insisting that she take a break from Christmas shopping in order to meet for lunch in the City. To Marina's relief her flatmate arrived laden with carrier bags, and full of smiles. Though the frequency of her recent absences from the flat had received only a couple of snide comments, she suspected that it was a subject about which Annie probably minded very deeply. Marina minded it too. Living out of a carrier bag, borrowing Bernard's toothbrush and deodorant, never knowing where her next clean bra was coming from, was horribly unsettling, and never what she intended. But Bernard could be so very persuasive. As could the glorious environs in which he lived, a spacious penthouse on the top floor of a converted warehouse on Butler's Wharf. Whenever she was there time seemed to slip by unnoticed, taking with it any sense of duty or responsibility for the outside world.

'Darling, it's so good to see you,' she exclaimed with a rush of pleasure and remorse, hugging Annie and the shopping bags in a great sweep of her arms. 'I'm just all over the place at the moment – so tired – so busy – so sorry.' She released her grip and tried to seize some of the bags from Annie, who resisted. 'Lunch is on me,' she continued, linking arms, 'early Christmas present. It's all going to change, by the way . . . Once this skiing holiday is out of the way I'll be able to get my life back into some sort of shape, back to normal—'

'Don't worry, Marina,' said Annie quietly, grateful for these

reassurances but bristling at the implication that she was something that had to be worried about and accommodated. 'You
don't have to apologise for anything. You're in the early manic
bonking phase – it'll wear off—'

'Cheeky sod.' Marina ducked through an archway under a
sign saying *Il Carito* and down some steps. 'You're a fine one to
talk,' she added, elegantly peeling off her gloves while they
waited to be shown to a table. 'What with tonight's big date on
the horizon.'

'I don't want to talk about it . . . it's all too . . . imminent.'

The place was buzzing with Friday lunchers and office
Christmas parties. A large group in a far corner, wearing flimsy
paper crowns and silly noses, were firing party poppers over each
other's heads. Frilly webs of coloured paper were landing every-
where, subsiding into glasses of wine and plates of half-eaten
food.

They were shown to a small circular table at the back of the
restaurant. Every second or two, waiters burst through the pair
of swing doors beside them, revealing snapshots of stainless steel
and steam from the kitchens behind.

'Bernard tells me he's got a busy period coming up in the
New Year, so he's bound to be less demanding—'

'Marina, you don't have to look after me you know—'

'I wouldn't dream of it,' she put in hastily, thinking that what
she felt towards Annie was in fact much more complicated than
responsibility or protection. Something so complicated that it
had been the subject of the first serious row with Bernard.

'Where does all this guilt about Annie Jordan come from?'
he had exploded the previous evening, after Marina had spent
the entire time it took for him to eat a Chinese takeaway
explaining how bad she felt at spending yet another night away
from the flat. 'She's a grown woman, for Christ's sake. You
share her accommodation. You help pay the rent. You are not
her guardian angel – I mean she's got a fucking dog, for Christ's
sake—'

'Precisely.'

'Precisely? What's that supposed to mean?'

'Annie is not the dog type. She should not have a dog. The fact that she has acquired one is symptomatic of her fragile state of mind.'

'Bollocks.' Bernard, who had insisted they eat with chopsticks, neatly fielded the last two remaining rice grains from his plate and threw himself back in his chair.

Marina, whose own plate was still covered with food, threw down one chopstick and began viciously lancing pieces of chicken with the other. 'It's a girls' thing, Bernard,' she declared. 'I know Annie very well. I know that . . . well, you've no idea how unhappy she's been recently—'

'What the hell has she got to be unhappy about? She's got a good – a great – job, an income, a pretty face, armfuls of friends—' he spread his own arms wide to demonstrate the point.

'But no man—'

'What about Greg Berkley, for God's sake?'

'Precisely.'

'Do you think you could stop using that word? It's beginning to annoy me.'

Marina managed a short sulky silence before bursting out, 'You said yourself he was probably bad news—'

'No I didn't. I said he was extremely intelligent with something of a reputation when it came to the fairer sex. Perhaps he is as smitten with Annie as you say she is with him. Everyone's entitled to fall in love no matter how badly they've behaved in the past.'

Marina cast him a wary glance. She had only managed to be completely honest about the colourful nature of her own past out of the belief that her new lover was not the type to make her pay for it.

'Some sex will certainly do her good,' Bernard muttered, quickly changing tack.

Marina threw down her chopstick. 'Now that's just plain nasty.'

'Come on, it's true. Loosen her up a bit. Give the girl some confidence – a little fire in those pretty dimpled cheeks—'

'You're utterly horrible.'

'I know.' He looked at her, crestfallen. 'Sorry. It's just jealousy. Ignore me.'

'Jealousy?'

'Of course.' He began clearing away the cartons and tinfoil covers, dropping them into the carrier bag in which they had arrived. 'I am more jealous of Annie Jordan than I have ever been of anyone or anything in my life. Not simply of the time she gets to spend with you, but of the space she occupies in your head. Your . . . loyalty to her.' He smiled wryly. 'There, so now you know.'

'Oh Bernard, you twit.'

'Go on, spend a night in your own home if you want to.' He tied a knot in the bag and placed it tidily beside the waste bin next to the sink. 'Christ knows, you've every right to.' He spoke with such uncalculated sincerity that Marina immediately flung her arms around his neck and announced that she had no wish to go anywhere but the kingsize double bed in the next room. As he picked her up, she wrapped her legs around his waist, locking her ankles together and squeezing hard.

'We could always both spend the night at your place, I suppose.'

'We could,' she murmured, undoing the second and third buttons of his shirt.

'On the other hand, I see no immediate reason to leave.'

'You've bewitched me,' she whispered, as he carried her across the threshold of the bedroom, where the wall of un-shuttered windows revealed a panoramic view of the wharf and the river, with the surreal illuminated beauty of Tower Bridge rising like a phoenix behind.

Annie clicked her fingers. 'Tired or merely bored?'

'Exhausted, since you ask,' Marina admitted ruefully. 'And starving. They're taking forever.' She caught a waiter's eye and tapped her watch. 'How's Bonnie, by the way?'

'Great,' Annie lied, having no desire to confess to any mad notions about pet personality clashes or dawn expeditions to the postbox. Seeing the fixed eagerness on her flatmate's face it crossed her mind that Marina's invitation to lunch probably stemmed from a need to assuage her own guilt rather than any genuine desire to familiarise herself with Annie's state of mind. 'Life has turned the proverbial corner,' she continued cheerfully, wanting to make up for such suspicions. 'Even work's looking up. Take a peek at this.' She reached for her handbag and pulled out an envelope. 'It arrived with a couple of others this morning, forwarded by the mafia at work, who pretend not to open anything, but who most certainly do. My first fan mail in months. I know Amy won't have been able to keep her fingers off it.' She sat back with a grin of satisfaction while Marina studied the letter.

'Is this in response to the piece that Zoë got so uptight about?'

Annie made a face. 'I've written and said sorry. But I doubt she'll ever forgive me.'

'A secret admirer, eh?' Marina chuckled as her eyes reached the bottom of the page.

Annie burst out laughing. 'It's from Jake.'

'You're joking.'

'No, really. I asked him to write – something really special and eulogistic. Something to get Amy off my back.' Annie snatched the letter back. 'Sweet of him to be so nice about the photo – he knows how I hate it.'

'He's excelled himself,' agreed Marina, laughing. 'You wicked things.' She clapped her hands, partly in congratulation and partly at the arrival of her steak and chips. Annie had ordered a Caesar salad, which arrived with fat shavings of parmesan and nuggets of stilton cheese. 'What if someone finds out?'

'There's nothing to find out. It's just a letter. Anyway, I've heard some columnists write their own fan mail, for God's sake. At least I haven't sunk that low. Not yet, anyway.' She began scouring her lettuce leaves for evidence of dressing, murmuring, 'Eat too much of that and you'll become a mad cow,' by way of revenge at the relish with which Marina was tucking into her meat.

'I've been one of those for a long time,' quipped Marina, spooning mustard onto her plate and signalling at the waiter to bring a second glass of wine. 'Now then,' she continued, her mouth full of food, 'time for serious business. What are you wearing tonight?'

A few hours later, when a mere forty-five minutes remained until her tryst with Greg Berkley, Annie was still considering the same question. It was a long time since she had felt so sartorially challenged. How to look young-ish, sexy, but effortlessly beautiful seemed to sum up a central and unresolved problem of her life. Any clothes attaining towards a realisation of such lofty hopes felt like a lie; while those that didn't, felt like failure. Depressingly, the sectors of her body most affected by her recent calorific triumphs were not necessarily those she would have chosen herself. The only real cause for celebration was a flatter stomach. Of more dubious worth was the increased definition of her jaw-line and the slight shrinkage in her breasts; something she would have traded any day for a reduction in the obstinate ebullience of her bottom. It would take radical surgery to balance out such imperfections, Annie reflected glumly, staring at her semi-naked self in Marina's full-length mirror and trying yet again to imagine what emotions would strike Greg on being confronted with the same apparition.

At ten to eight, flushed and tousled from so many tussles with clothes, Annie finally settled on the black dress she had worn to the *RoundUp* party, having convinced herself that the risks of being marked down for wearing the same thing twice were far outweighed by the fact that Greg must have found something either memorable or attractive about her appearance that night. In a bid to atone for this repetition, she threw a turquoise chiffon scarf round her neck and treated herself to one of two pairs of glittery stockings she had purchased for Marina during her shopping spree that morning. Not being a devotee of such things, she had to rummage through Marina's underwear drawer for a suspender belt. As she clipped the stockings in place and appraised their effect in the mirror, Annie felt not only wicked but fraudulent. It took some strong red lipstick to bolster such anxieties, together with the now not-so-new stilettos, whose comfort had been greatly improved by the addition of some cushioning insoles.

By five past eight, Annie was as ready as she could be. Bonnie, sensing an imminent departure, began a celebratory bounce between her mistress's legs and the front door. Fearing for the safety of her stockings, and concerned that she would end up smelling more strongly of dog odours than of Chanel Number 5, Annie retreated to the safety of the bathroom for a hefty respray of her neck and wrists. As an afterthought, she directed a sharp jet of perfume into her cleavage and another up under the hem of her dress.

At eight-fifteen she poured herself a glass of water and watched the second half of a programme about the reproductive travails of the Emperor Penguin. At eight-thirty she left a message on Jake's answering machine thanking him for his inspired contribution to her fan mail. At nine o'clock she re-applied lipstick and eyeliner and put four extra daubs of powder on the red blotch by her nose, which while not developing into anything so demeaning as a spot, seemed to have taken up permanent residence on her face. At nine-fifteen she poured herself a glass of wine and shared a packet of cheese and onion crisps with the dog. At nine twenty-eight, just as she was starting to chip holes in her nail varnish and to contemplate the suicidal options of a coward bent upon escaping humiliation as well as a broken heart, the telephone rang.

There was the unmistakable crackle of an ill-positioned mobile. Through it she heard Greg's voice, tender with remorse. 'Annie – so sorry – hellish meeting – only just broken free – forgive me?'

'Don't worry about it. I'm barely ready myself,' she lied, running her tongue round her crisp-clogged teeth and making a mental note to counteract the smell of onions with mouthwash as well as toothpaste before setting foot outside the flat. 'Are you on your way over?'

'It's got so late . . . I thought we could meet—'

'Where?'

The line was so broken she could hardly hear him. '—Restaurant . . . El Greco . . . Kilburn High . . . in ten minutes . . . see you there—'

Telling herself that she should feel cross but managing only to feel relieved, Annie slowly replaced the phone and shuffled back into the bathroom for a final assault on her appearance.

As she was leaving the flat she heard footsteps behind her on the stairs. She turned to see her neighbour crossing the landing. He was wearing what looked like a black silk shirt, collarless and hanging loosely over the top of black jeans. Slung over one shoulder was a weathered black leather jacket. His hair was wet and swept sleekly back from his forehead and temples. Annie returned her attentions to her keyhole, fiddling unnecessarily in order to give him time to disappear. In spite of these precautions she found herself catching up with him on the last flight of stairs.

'Going out?' she enquired, out of a lifetime's preference for inanity as opposed to silence.

He nodded. 'I work in a club most Fridays.'

'Waiting at tables?'

He laughed and ran one hand up an imaginary keyboard. 'Christ no – as a pianist. What about you?'

'Me?' She pulled her coat more tightly about her, suddenly uncomfortably self-conscious of her dressy appearance. 'Oh just—'

'Got your war-paint on, anyway.'

'My—?' She touched her cheek and laughed uncertainly. 'Never without it.'

'Did you catch your dog?' he added, reaching the front door first and pushing through it.

'Yes . . . thanks, I did . . . by hiding the lead,' she confessed. 'Oh and I've written to the agents just to make sure I'm not breaking any of the landlord's house-rules, she added hurriedly.

He paused for a second. 'The landlord's house-rules, eh? Good for you.'

By the time Annie had stepped outside he had passed the bus stop and was almost at the end of the road. She watched until he disappeared; then turned up the lapels of her coat and headed off in the opposite direction in search of a taxi.

A few minutes later she was speeding westwards towards Kilburn, alternately smoking furiously and taking deep breaths out of the taxi windows to quell her nerves. You are a self-contained, mature and desirable female, she told herself, half amused at her own trepidation and half despairing. She had forgotten how draining romantic excitement could be, how horribly threatening to one's confidence and self-esteem. As the taxi pulled up outside a neon-lit sign saying *El Greco* she was tempted to tap the window and order the cabbie to drive on. Entering the restaurant took a disheartening amount of courage, as if she were stepping not merely across the threshold of a building, but past a milestone in her life.

'Over here, Annie,' came Greg's voice from the back of the room. It took several seconds for Annie to locate its origin, and to absorb the fact that she was not the only one who would be enjoying his company over dinner that night. Greg was seated at the far end of a table crowded with unfamiliar figures, all looking merry and relaxed, all wearing the most casual of clothes. Grinning hard to hide her disappointment, Annie edged her way towards them, squeezing in her stomach in order to slide between the mêlée of furniture and people blocking her way.

Place settings had to be reshuffled in order to accommodate her, in a cramped space between a woman with a frizzy perm and a fat man with a smiling face. Annie, feeling overdressed and out of place, was sliding miserably out of her coat when Greg hollered, 'But I want her up here. Come up here, Annie, and tell me you don't mind sharing our date with these oafs.' Relief flooded through her. 'I suppose not,' she murmured demurely, flinging her chiffon scarf over her shoulder and working her way to his end of the table. 'So long as we can give them the boot later on.' There was a burst of approving laughter.

'We've ordered moussaka and salads all round,' Greg explained, standing up and seizing her hand to help her to her seat. As she sat down he nuzzled her ear, murmuring that she looked ravishing and they would leave as soon as they could.

Such reassurances helped Annie not only to relax but also

Chapter Fourteen

Jake, dozing late that Friday night on a sofa with an open script on his chest, asked himself whether it was a sign of middle age that he was beginning to fantasise about the homely delights of a regular partner as opposed to the sharper, more erotic pleasures of one-night stands. Was it lack of youthful energy or loss of courage? he wondered, recalling his grim experiences at the hands of the doe-eyed cowboy in the nightclub and pulling himself upright with a sigh. Annie hadn't known the half of it. Far worse than the escapade with the tablet had been a sordid tussle in a corridor behind the men's toilets, when a couple of his companion's thuggish acquaintances had appeared from nowhere, brandishing flick knives and propositions that made even Jake's liberal sensibilities shy away in horror. For someone who relished a reputation for living dangerously, owning up to such miscalculations was hard. Almost as hard as admitting that after two decades of spirited cynicism on the matter, one mad chance encounter with a handsome face seemed to have turned his imagination to all the monogamous securities he had once vowed to avoid.

Jake put down the script, which contained the twenty or so lines he would be called upon to deliver in southern Spain, and helped himself to a generous top-up of Scotch. He held the drink up to the light and admired its watery gold hues for a few moments before taking a long sip. Swallowing slowly, he set the glass down on the carpet, next to a screwdriver and the entrails of his answering machine, which had suddenly taken to chewing up messages as opposed to delivering them.

The script was not as good as he had first thought. He turned to a new page, knitting his brows together in a fresh effort to concentrate. The lead, an implausible villain with a heart of gold and a penchant for brilliant disguises, had all the best lines. Jake closed his eyes to imagine himself in the part, but found the now-familiar image of Annie's blue-eyed, sandy-haired neighbour drifting into his mind instead. His attraction for the man had increased to an intensity that was almost frightening. He went to sleep following him in his dreams, woke to the thought of him in the mornings. Jake had been the victim of sexual obsession before, countless times. It was, he knew, an integral part of the addictive nature of his personality. All or nothing, every time. Once, he had memorised eight hundred lines of Racine, simply for the chance to breathe the same air as a Frenchman with a head of floppy golden curls and a mouth like a cherry. But something about his attraction in this instance felt different. Something perhaps triggered by the guarded darkness of the man's brilliant eyes. As a frequent companion to loneliness, Jake had no trouble recognising it in other people. This creature had looked so wary and vulnerable, so deliberately insouciant of his beauty, that Jake, sensing deep damage of some kind, had felt his heart go out to him. With Annie so twitchy and hostile on the night of their quest for milk, it had not been hard to appear contrastingly friendly and sympathetic, to elicit a few grateful smiles. By the end of the encounter, Jake had felt as if the pair of them were in secret league, even though they had barely exchanged a word.

Since playing down the matter to Annie on Monday, he had returned to the Italian restaurant in which she had first pointed him out in order to conduct some stealthy research. There he discovered that her fellow tenant was called Michael Derwent; that, far from being a regular waiter, he had been working as sommelier to help out the friend who owned the establishment; and – most promising of all as far as Jake was concerned – that he sometimes played the piano in Louie's Jazz Club on a Friday night.

The chance to engineer a meeting away from Shrewsbury Mansions was particularly attractive. He did not want Annie or Marina finding out anything. Not just because of Annie's hostility, but because he liked the look of the man too much to risk pursuing the relationship in the glare of any critical scrutiny. With the two of them currently so wrapped up in the machinations of their own love lives the only challenge about this minor subterfuge was the limited timescale in which he had to act. Before his now imminent departure for Spain, he had to spend a couple of days at least with his elderly parents in Eastbourne over Christmas; a harmless, usually very restive annual chore which alleviated some of his guilt at seeing so little of them the rest of the year.

It would be nice to go abroad with something to look forward to on his return, reflected Jake, consoling himself with an image of the striking features of Michael Derwent as he surveyed the squalor of his own surroundings. Although it was over two years since his move to Camden, he still hadn't done anything to improve the place. While still elegant on the outside – immaculate grey London brick with white framed windows – much of the interior was bubbling with damp and decorative neglect. As a result, Jake really only inhabited three rooms. The rest were empty or strewn with junk, ideal for wild parties – of which there had been several during his residency – but a sorry reflection on the organisational abilities of their owner. Living in such conditions was, he knew, something he should have grown out of; something to which he sometimes thought he clung as if it represented some lifeline to his youth. A time when the seeds of obsession and laziness had been endearing character traits as opposed to stumbling blocks to achieving anything worthwhile.

Seeing that it was already ten o'clock, Jake abandoned his reading, drained the last of his drink and went into his bedroom in search of a clean shirt. He ran a comb through his freshly dyed black sweep of hair and smiled in the mirror at the result. Grabbing his favourite brown suede jacket from off the back of a chair he bounded out of the house, humming a loud and tuneless rendition of 'In The Mood'. Jazz wasn't really his thing, but he could learn, he reasoned happily, singing with more confidence as he strode down the street. Recalling the Frenchman with the cherry mouth, Jake began to chuckle and then frowned. Ten years on and here he was still lunging after something that never quite seemed to materialise. Lust, fulfilment, whatever it was, dissolving like mirages the moment he got too close.

At the sight of the neon light advertising the entrance to Louie's Jazz club, some of Jake's natural resilience reasserted itself. Feeling like a character in a Raymond Chandler novel, he chose a small table set well back from the tiny stage and ordered a bottle of red wine. A girl with a white face and long black hair, hanging in heavy rods down her temples and back, was halfway through a song. Her voice was low and sonorous, curiously at odds with the painful thinness of her body. A body that confirmed every aspect of Jake's faith in his own sexual proclivities; the arms protruding like bleached twigs, the long tight dress revealing hip bones that jutted far enough for a coat hanger to be suspended from each. With every word her wide lips stretched threateningly round the head of the microphone. Allowing himself a small shiver of physical repulsion, Jake paused from watching in order to catch the attention of a passing waiter and enquire which artist would be performing next. He received little more than a shoulder-shrug in return. Friday was usually a mixture of regulars and newcomers, he was told; only the manager knew who was on and when.

The girl dropped her chin to her chest to acknowledge a smattering of applause. Two men, sitting almost on the stage itself, wolf whistled loudly. The saxophonist who had accompanied her stepped forward for a brief bow. The girl then spread her arms, opened her cavernous mouth and began again, more of a blues number this time, pushing her voice towards higher octaves in a way that – even to Jake's undiscerning ear – suggested more optimism than good sense. He lit a cigarette and closed his eyes, wondering how long he would have to wait for the empty piano stool to be filled by the lean, pale-faced figure of Michael Derwent. While he waited he smoked deeply and steadily, adopting a casual sprawling pose that belied the nervousness he felt inside, the fear and hope as to how the evening might yet unfold.

Annie awoke when it was still dark. Outside she could hear the faint twitter of an as yet unenthusiastic dawn chorus. Her left arm, trapped beneath Greg's broad torso, was throbbing with the numbness and pain subsequent upon a prolonged restriction of its usual blood supply. Badly wanting to release it, yet fearful of waking her lover, she gave a timid tug. Greg grunted and rolled even closer, pinning her arm more firmly to the mattress. Annie lay blinking up at the hazy whiteness of the ceiling, torn between appearing unloving and the desire to remedy her discomfort.

The evening, much to her relief, had developed from its unpromising beginning into an unqualified success. Greg had proved a busy and eager lover. So much so that at times Annie had felt positively swamped by his ardour. Such reactions only confirmed her belief that she was badly out of practice and that the best way of making up for the deficiency was to swamp him with attention in return. If the ecstatic reactions of her body were a little manufactured, the pleasure in her mind was not. Even lying there beside him, Annie had to keep blinking to make sure it wasn't just a dream. He was everything she had always wanted: darkly handsome, witty, popular, accomplished – and mad about her. She knew because he had told her, not once, but many times during the course of the night, hinting at a belief in a future which had seemed to her to be wildly premature but which made her tingle with hope nonetheless.

One bold hard yank and her arm at last was free. Greg oblig-ingly rolled back over onto his side of the bed and threw an arm round his pillow instead. On seeing from her watch that it was still only five o'clock Annie forced herself to doze for a little while longer. But her mind, still dizzy with post-coital euphoria, refused to cooperate. After a while she found herself channelling some of her happiness into thinking up witticisms for her approaching Christmas column. She decided to take the words *Happy Christmas* and use each letter in turn to create her list.

H is for the happiness we must all demonstrate on being presented with Aunt Agatha's home-made purple mittens.

A is for aunts, with which we are all encumbered, especially at Christmas, and of whom we are all secretly rather fond.

P is for party-hats, which serve no useful purpose other than to make grown-ups look foolish. (Helpful hint: can be rolled into a taper and used to light cigarettes from gas-hobs.)

P is also for praying to Jesus, which I used to do a lot of as a little girl, but gradually abandoned as an inefficient method of fulfilling my desires. Being impossible was far more effective.

Y is for Yuletide, because I can't think of anything else appropriate.

C is for Christmas cards, which yet again I will probably fail to send, since they contribute nothing to the friendships I care about and only generate guilt about the ones I've neglected.

H is for hair. The coming year will be a good one for my coiffure. It couldn't really get much worse (first-time readers please refer to above photograph).

R is for romance. If it enters your lives cling onto it with all the tenacity of a dog with a bone. (Talking of which, my poor, loveable pooch is under threat from unfriendly neighbours seeking an eviction order.)

I is for . . .

Having got so far with relative ease, and knowing from previous bitter experience that the infrequency of good thoughts was no guarantee for being able to summon them back at will, Annie resolved to desert the bed in search of the wherewithal to make a few notes. She moved with all the caution of a thief, wanting neither to disrupt her lover's beauty sleep, nor to have her clotheless body examined in the unsympathetic light of dawn. Observing her underwear looped a little mysteriously over each of the end bedposts, she opted instead for Greg's dressing-gown, a Noël Coward-style green silk affair, and tiptoed out of the bedroom.

Before finding a pen and paper, she went to the bathroom to clear her face of sleep grit and make-up smears, and to carve some order out of the chaos of her hair. Morning ugliness was such a hazard when it came to romance, she reflected grimly, grimacing at herself as she recalled the infinitely more pleasing image which had set off for the restaurant the night before. With similar self-deprecating thoughts, she gave her teeth a good going over with Greg's toothbrush, scowling at the fierce peppermint of the toothpaste and vowing never to purchase the same brand herself.

She was sitting cross-legged with a pad of paper on the large black leather sofa on which they had spent a considerable and energetic portion of the previous night, when Greg appeared in the doorway.

'What are you doing?'

She looked up, startled. 'Just scribbling down a few thoughts—'

'Not about me, I hope.' He sounded genuinely concerned.

'God no. Have a look if you like.' She held out the pad. 'It's silly stuff, for the Christmas list idea I told you about—'

'Nah, I'm not bothered.' He dropped his shoulders and leant against the door frame, studying her intently. 'I can think of something else I'd rather do.'

'Oh yes?' she murmured, gripping the pad to hide the tremble in her hands.

'And it involves reclaiming that dressing-gown, of which I'm rather fond.' He patted the hand towel wrapped around his hips. 'You can have this instead.'

Aware that in more fictional circumstances such a moment might be the cue for Kim Basinger to step out of the gown and reveal her glories in a purposeful stroll across the room, Annie instead found herself fiddling nervously with the end of her Biro. She felt far too unsure of herself to be so bold. She still hardly knew him. In the brief time they had spent alone together, they had barely talked at all.

'I want my dressing-gown back,' he said, a trace of excited impatience now in his voice, 'are you going to make me fight you for it?'

Aware both that her reticence was in danger of being misinterpreted, and that to express a desire for conversation and coffee would almost certainly be taken as a put-down, Annie made a dash for the bedroom door and dived under the bedclothes. Greg slung his towel over his shoulder and strolled after her, oblivious to her shyness, thinking only that they were playing a lovers' game. Annie, safe from scrutiny under cover of the duvet, tossed the dressing-gown at him as he approached.

'That's no way to treat my things,' he said softly, 'just wait till I get my hands on you.'

Wanting to make up for all her inner awkwardness, Annie held her arms out to welcome him back into the bed. As she did so she noticed that the Biro had left ugly black ink smudges on her fingers. 'Feel free,' she whispered, curling her hands into fists so that he wouldn't see the marks.

'*I is for insufferably inept, imperfect woman*,' chanted a voice inside her head, while her more competent outer self began to writhe with pleasure long before she really felt it. For if Annie's chequered and unsatisfactory love life had taught her anything, it was that a show of ardour was the best compliment one could offer a lover, the best investment one could make towards any guarantee of being wanted again.

problems, without providing her mother with additional fuel for doubt about the general worth of her eldest child. From the moment of birth, Phillip had been earmarked as the steadier, more reliable infant, leaving Annie cast in the role of the un-cooperative one, forgiven only by her father, whose broad lap often seemed to offer the only sanctuary in the house.

The wind was so strong that as Annie crossed the Severn Bridge she clung to the steering wheel in a bid to prevent the car being buffeted into the railings lining the edge of the road. By the time she crossed the border into East Glamorgan, hefty white crumbs of snow were slanting at the windscreen, filling the view ahead as fast as the wipers could clear it. Annie slowed the Fiat to a crawl, while Bonnie at last curled up in the position Jake had found so threatening to his leather boots.

Faintly thrilled in spite of herself at such a dramatic and festive turn in the weather, Annie tuned into a radio station playing Christmas hits, and allowed her thoughts to drift back over the hectic ten days that had followed her first overnight stay at Greg's. Enjoyable though it had been, it was something of a relief to step out of the fray and be given the chance to reflect on some of its high points. She had never before met anyone so in demand, both socially and at work. When they were at his flat the phone never stopped ringing. Although they ended up spending every evening together, it always involved going to at least one function in the process. Flattered both at Greg's eager assumption that she would accompany him to such parties, and at the public profile it gave their relationship, Annie had been more than willing to go with the flow. With her Christmas list idea virtually written a week in advance, the only gruelling aspect of this social flurry had been rushing between Kilburn and Swiss Cottage to see to the needs of Bonnie. Though Greg kept saying they would take a turn sleeping at her place, it never quite happened; and seeing how frantically busy he was, Annie had been reluctant to push the matter too hard. Such reciprocity of effort would come, she told herself, once the relationship had been given time to settle into some sort of routine; once they found a breathing space to begin the proper business of getting to know each other, instead of spinning round like dervishes in such a mad pre-Christmas whirl.

Somewhere in the midst of these activities she had found time to see Marina off on a train to Gatwick. They had hugged with unusual vehemence, as if each felt the edge of a deeper separation inside.

'Break a leg or whatever.'

'Bloody hope not. And you take care of yourself, especially in the Wild West. Don't let that family of yours get you down.'

'I'll be fine. It's only a couple of days. Greg's promised to come and stay at the flat for a bit when I get back. He's got some great New Year thing all sorted.'

'I'm so pleased for you,' Marina blurted, her eyes glassy with emotion. 'I'll admit I wasn't sure about him, but I've never seen you so happy.'

'Yeah, well, it's good for a girl to have a fling now and then,' replied Annie, her exultation shining in her smile. Talk of the New Year brought home to her how quickly and how radically her life had changed. It was a long time since the prospect of twelve more months had filled her with anything like as much enthusiasm. 'Wait till I unleash the full force of my endearing personality on him,' she quipped, 'then he'll probably run a mile.' In truth, Greg seemed amazingly accepting – almost to the point of being incurious – of her character. Even after such an intense beginning, there had been none of the probing conversations and intimate confessionals that Annie associated with the start of a new relationship. While part of her was pleased to have been absorbed so smoothly into the slipstream of his life, another part remained impatient for the chance to push their intimacy to a deeper, more satisfying, level.

'Now hurry up or you'll miss the train and Bernard will get on the plane without you.'

'He would too. I've never seen him so excited,' Marina said, giggling and then grimacing at the weight of her bulging suit-case as she staggered into the carriage. Annie waited on the platform until her silky dark head appeared at one of the small sliding windows, and then waved hard as the train pulled away.

Annie's sole regret of the week had been not managing to catch up with Jake, who had scuttled off to his parents before they had a chance to meet. He had phoned once, announcing the defunct state of his answering service and promising to call again soon. She had heard nothing since, though there had been another of his fan letters, printed in the same elegant typeface as the first, and expressing such implausibly eulogistic emotions that Annie began to fear Amy and her spies might smell a rat after all. The last couple of lines, about envying the physical attention she was giving the dog, were particularly warped, even for Jake, whose sense of humour could be quite off the wall. There had been two letters from genuine dog-lovers too, which she had slipped into her bag during the last minute dash of packing for Wales, thinking they might trigger appreciation from her mother, whose interest in her career usually seemed to falter after a sentence or two. As far as Annie could make out, she didn't even read the column, hiding behind the excuse that the Sunday papers provided sufficient reading material for the entire week.

For the final part of the drive Annie had to concentrate hard, since the snow was falling thickly and none of the roads were wide enough to accommodate more than one vehicle at a time. In the dim evening light the countryside seemed to glow with a fluorescence emanating from within the snow itself. Branches and bushes heaved under the weight of this new and splendid burden, their masked curves like giant creatures crouched in hiding from the elements raging outside. As Annie gingerly wound her way down through the valley towards the sparse and remote village in which her mother had lived for the sixteen years since the divorce, it struck her with fresh force quite how buried the place was; how leaving Surrey had not been a house-move so much as a fleeing, a tunnelling away from everything associated with a relationship that had fallen apart long before the formalities of signatures on a page. The image provoked a rare stab of pity, which Annie feared, even as she experienced it, would evaporate the moment they came face to face. The mere sight of each other stirred memories and tensions too ancient and entrenched for either to fully understand their origins. Though Annie guessed that on her side jealousy of Phillip had been the start of it, far more complicated threads of disharmony – most of them to do with her father – had tightened the knot later on. Knowing that he was unfaithful, knowing that he had thereby played an integral part in creating the ugly lines of embitterment on her mother's face, could not quite erase Annie's sympathy towards him for wanting to get away. She had felt the same urgency herself, leaving for her first term at college several weeks before she had to, seizing any pretext to get ahead in the race to leave her childhood behind. More specifically, she had wanted to leave her mother, to escape the guilty residue of blame she felt towards her, for not being beautiful or forgiving or loving enough to make her father want to stay.

One left nothing behind in the end, Annie reflected with a sigh, flicking off the radio, which had developed a maddening tremor of interference and changing down into second gear to crawl round a steep bend. Especially not from a childhood scarred by the unedifying business of being used as pawns in an ugly adult game. Marina said Annie's lucidity about such matters was remarkable, that such objectivity was in itself a sign that she had moved on. But Annie knew that it was more complicated; that realising one was the product of a dysfunctional family offered no obvious remedies for dealing with the consequences. Other than a desperate determination not to make the same mistakes herself. The thought prompted a furtive attempt at imagining a future with Greg. Their dearth of confessional exchanges had not prevented him from hinting at such a concept, not once, but many times during the course of the previous week. He too had never felt such an instant pulse of attraction, he said, never been so sure of the rightness of a relationship in his life.

This happy train of thought was interrupted by a sudden, rather graceful gliding sensation as the car wheels lost their grip and swerved towards a bank of snow masking a low stone wall. For a few seconds Annie fought the turn, pulling the steering wheel right as hard as she could. Then, some dim and distant instruction about driving into skids instead of working against them floated into her mind. She spun the wheel left. The car straightened, but not in time to avoid the side of the road. Bracing herself for contact with the wall, Annie was badly jolted by an abrupt nosedive into a ditch that lay concealed a yard or so in front of it. So this is whiplash she thought, as her body was flung forwards and back again, caught by the tightening jerk of her seat belt. Bonnie, without similar protection, let out a yelp of dismay, before scrambling onto the seat and barking frantically at the bleak and unfamiliar scene outside. The snow, less harried by the wind now that they were almost at the bottom of the valley, was floating down in delicate swirls, gently but no less efficiently layering itself upon the objects in its path.

'And a happy bloody Christmas to you too, Lord,' muttered Annie, glowering at the heavens and rubbing the back of her neck. She made several attempts to reverse out of the ditch, clenching her teeth while the engine roared in frustration and the wheels spun hopelessly against snow and air.

'Bollocks.' She slammed the steering wheel and reached for Bonnie's lead. 'Your luck's in old girl. Walkies time again.'

Ignorant of any negative aspect to their situation, Bonnie bounded off down the hill, tugging so hard that Annie slipped and slithered in an effort to keep up. In spite of this, and her neck, which she could feel stiffening further in the cold, Annie could not help feeling faintly elated by this unforeseen adventure. She even stopped at the bridge on the floor of the valley to admire what she could make out of the river and the sweeping, snow-laden branches of the trees reaching into it.

Ten minutes later she was in the porch of her mother's cottage, swinging her bag from her shoulder and stamping the snow from her shoes. Inside she could hear Kit, the collie, barking furiously. The noise receded and there was a burst of light and warmth as Christine Jordan flung open the door. Her face fell at the sight of Annie's unkempt appearance and pale face.

'Has something happened?'

'A bit of an accident. The Fiat got stuck in the ditch up the road. It just spun out of control, but I think it's fine. Gave my neck a twist, but nothing serious. This is Bonnie, by the way.'

Mother and daughter briefly kissed each other's cheek. Annie caught the familiar musky smell of her skin, mingled with the scent of shampoo. After the embrace there was a moment of awkwardness when they both spoke at once.

'Your poor neck – I'll get some aspirin—'

'I'm fine—'

'You don't look fine, you look a sight—'

'That's not the accident, Mum, that's just me—' Annie laughed quickly, to take the edge off the remark.

Christine turned her attention to the dog. 'And this is Bonnie, is it?' She held out her hand for the animal to sniff. 'I've locked Kit in the shed for the time being. I'll let him out when things have calmed down. Shall we have some tea?'

She was trying to be nice, Annie could tell. Brimming with festive *bonhomie* and the goodwill generated by absence. It was months since her last visit. Her mother made a point of never going to London, nor indeed to any town if she could help it.

'Hermione's upstairs having a rest. She came by train this morning and has been an absolute treasure in the kitchen. I can't remember when I was last so organised for Christmas Day. Potatoes, carrots, sprouts – we've prepared the lot. She even made an extra batch of mince pies, just to be sure we're not defeated by Phillip's appetite – where that boy puts his food I'll never know. And still so slim. It's remarkable—' Annie followed her mother through the narrow, low-beamed passageway into the kitchen, happy to let her talk and glad to be granted a small, unexpected respite before having to tackle Phillip's fiancée, a woman who put so much effort into the business of being nice that Annie found herself wanting to be unforgivably rude in return. '—I expect the dogs will be fine together – though it is just as well she's a bitch, Kit's not nearly so good with his own sex. I'll get the kettle on and then give Terry – Mr Grayson – who runs the farm up the road – a call about your car – he's bound to be able to help – get the tractor down there I expect—'

They took their tea through into the sitting room which

adjoined the kitchen and where a small, sparsely decorated Christmas tree stood on a table in the corner beside the hearth. Remembering the enormous trees of her childhood, over-burdened with baubles and tinsel by her and Phillip, Annie felt a twinge of sadness and looked away. A few cards on the windowsills, a sprig of holly on the top frame of the picture above the fireplace and that was it. But her mother seemed happy enough, happier indeed than Annie could remember or had anticipated. Her face looked weathered but healthy, and her hair had grown since the summer from its usual brusque crop to some-thing resembling a bob. Though completely grey for many years now, it had a softness which the shorter style had never appreci-ated. As the hot tea snaked down inside her and her mother continued to talk, Annie found it was very pleasant not to have to do or say anything; not to worry about how she looked or what impression she was creating. And getting warm again had done wonders for her stiff neck. Staring at the fire, and Bonnie, splayed with ridiculous abandonment in front of it, she felt a delicious sleepiness creeping over her. When her mother came to retrieve her empty mug, she realised she had been dozing.

'If you tell me where your car keys are I'll ring Terry now.' She tutted loudly. 'You look washed out. Why not go upstairs for a rest like Hermione?' Though the command was kind, a deep defensive reflex made Annie protest her eagerness to do something useful instead.

'There's nothing to do,' retorted her mother. 'Go upstairs and take something for that neck. You're in your usual room and there's an electric blanket on the bed. If this weather carries on you might be in for quite a stay. I do hope Phillip arrives safely,' she added, in a much gentler tone of voice and wringing her hands as she stared across at a window where snowflakes continued to slide down the pane.

'He'll be fine, Mum,' murmured Annie, while echoes of ancient feelings stirred inside, reminding her yet again that the past would always be there, casting its complicated shadow over the simplest things.

Chapter Sixteen

Annie was woken early on Christmas morning by the sound of barking. Remembering Bonnie, she was on the point of dragging herself out of bed when she heard her mother's voice in the garden below her window, calling both dogs by name. The muffled stamp of footsteps receding down the garden path was followed by the squeak of the gate latch and then a delighted yelping, as the animals were released into the field beyond.

The air in her bedroom was still chilly, its small radiator being the last in the house to respond to the demands of the boiler. Annie pulled the padded edge of the duvet up under her chin, enjoying the snugness of being inside. Rolling her eyes round the overcrowded contents of the room, she was struck by the haphazard links they offered to the past, like a jigsaw with all its pieces pressed into the wrong places. Propped on top of a set of shelves above her bed was an old teddy bear of Phillip's, its left ear torn and one button eye dangling rather gruesomely by a single thread. The eyes had always been loose, she remembered, thanks to her brother's fondness for swinging the creature by its eyeballs before releasing it – with alarming speed and accuracy – across the room. Usually at her. Hailing from an era as yet unrestrained by the notion of toy safety standards, the bear had metal wires in its ears which could scratch badly if caught at the wrong angle; while the head, stuffed with something that felt like concrete, made a formidable missile.

Stacked on the shelf below were several piles of folders from

Annie's sixth form days. A sheaf of torn and dogeared papers had worked their way out of their bindings, revealing some samples of the slanting and careless squirls that had been a source of endless frustration and complaint to her teachers.

Next to the shelves was a small antique desk – hated for ever for irrevocable associations with the pain of studying for exams – on which sat a photograph of her standing between her parents after receiving her degree. They were all smiling at the command of Phillip, who had failed to bring an overcoat and spent the entire afternoon moaning about the cold. By the end of the day Annie, who had at first been touched that her usually hostile brother should take time out from the delights of political studies and punting to attend the ceremony, found herself wondering why he had bothered. The puzzle was answered towards the end of the day by the materialisation of a slight, bony-kneed girl who ended up joining the four of them for dinner in the hotel. Phillip maintained that they had bumped into each other in the street, but Annie, catching glances exchanged over the rims of glasses and between candlesticks, guessed otherwise.

A knock on her door produced Phillip himself, with the improbable accompaniment of a cup of tea.

'Morning sis. Happy Christmas and all that.' He handed her the mug.

'Wow – thanks.' Annie struggled up to a sitting position. 'So you got here safely in the end? Mum was worrying . . . I left her to it I'm afraid – couldn't keep my eyes open—'

'Had a good run down, apart from the last bit. Bad luck about the accident, by the way. Mind you, it serves you right for having a crappy car.' Chuckling to himself, he shoved his hands into his dressing-gown pockets and strolled over to the window. 'Stinking weather, isn't it?'

Annie took a sip of tea. 'I think it's rather lovely.' She stared beyond him at the enticing slice of white scenery revealed between the ill-fitting bedroom curtains, tailored for a previous tour of duty at another, much broader window in Surrey. 'Thank you for this.' She took a generous swig of the tea, which tasted rather stewed. 'I was just looking at that bloody bear of yours and remembering how you used to throw it at me. Christ it hurt.'

'You usually deserved it,' Phillip replied mildly, not turning from his position at the window. 'I've a favour to ask,' he continued, in much the same tone of voice. 'Hermione and I've got a bit of news-breaking to do with Mum later on and would appreciate your support.'

'News-breaking?' Annie echoed, acknowledging with a stab of resigned disappointment that the tea had not been an unqualified gift after all, but a typical Phillip-style move in something far more calculated. 'Is the engagement off?'

He shook his head, scowling.

'Postponed? Hermione's mother needs longer to find a suitable hat – one that will suggest her stature as a woman and yet not block the view of more than three people standing in the pew behind—'

'Annie, for Christ's sake – do you have to make a joke of everything? Can't you be serious for just one minute?'

'Well get on with it then,' she urged, managing to check her impatience. With two full days still ahead of them it was important to get off to the right start.

'Hermione is expecting.'

For a moment Annie found herself waiting for the second half of the sentence, for clarification of the exact direction in which her future sister-in-law's hopes might lie.

'It's fine, of course,' Phillip continued hastily. 'I mean, it doesn't change anything, but . . . I'm just not sure how Mum is going to take it. Being an old-fashioned witch and so on—'

Annie could not help bristling at his tone. It had always seemed wrong that Christine Jordan's evident and unqualified devotion to her son should never be regarded by him as grounds for being particularly kind or loyal in return. Behind her back he was always far ruder than Annie herself would ever have dreamed.

'—So fucking stuck in her ways it would take dynamite to blast her out of them.' He cleared his throat. 'Anyway, the point is, it would be nice for Hermione to know that she had your support.'

'For Hermione . . . of course,' Annie murmured, staring at her tea. 'Babies out of wedlock are hardly a big deal these days—'

'Not out of wedlock,' he snapped, tightening the cord of his dressing-gown and turning to face her. 'It will mean bringing the wedding forward, that's all. Before she gets too large.'

Annie felt an uncharacteristic stab of pity for Hermione. If such early signs were anything to go by, her brother was not going to make the most empathetic of birthing partners.

'I take it this . . . turn of events was not planned?' she ventured.

'What kind of dumb question is that?' He rolled his eyes in despair. 'Of course it wasn't bloody well planned. Hermione had bought one of those new predictor things that tells you when you can and when you can't. We got the all-clear. I'm seriously thinking of suing the manufacturers.'

In the end compassion won out against all other less charitable reactions doing battle inside Annie's heart. He was her brother after all. And he was right, her mother might find it hard. 'Don't worry, I'll back you up all the way – you and Hermione. It will be fine, you'll see. Though—' she hesitated, knowing from previous bitter experience that her sibling did not take kindly to advice of any kind, especially not from her '—if I were you I'd wait until after lunch and presents and so on. When we're all full of wine and goodwill.'

'Right you are. Er . . . and thanks, Annie – knew I could rely on you.'

As he left the room Annie heard Bonnie's familiar yelp outside. She got out of bed in time to catch sight of her mother grappling with the garden gate, tugging with both hands to persuade it through the mounds of snow swamping the lower slats. She wore a padded navy anorak and a large dark blue head-scarf, from which wisps of hair protruded round the edges. On her feet was a rather curious pair of green shin-length boots trimmed round the top with brown fur. The two dogs trotted in front of her, playfully nudging each other like two old friends sharing a private joke.

On impulse Annie decided to open the window. The catch, stiff with lack of use, resisted her efforts before bursting open so suddenly that she half lost her balance and found her entire upper body launched into the cold morning air.

'Happy Christmas – and thanks for walking Bonnie,' she shouted, catching her breath in shock at the cold.

Her mother stopped and looked up, putting her gloved hand to her forehead to shield her eyes from the glare of the sun, rising over the roof above Annie's head. 'Had to be done. Are you dressed yet? You can feed them while I see to the turkey.'

Annie pulled the window shut and struggled into her clothes. Had her mother's tone of voice been intended as a put-down, she wondered, or had years of expecting such responses made her incapable of interpreting a comment in any other terms?

With the sun to warm it, the top layer of snow glistened with light and moisture. Annie brushed her hair, staring at the picture postcard prettiness of the view, now safely back behind the frame of a closed window. Something of the wildness of the country-side had been lost, she reflected, softened by the huge folds of white, draped over winter's spiky edges like a giant's mantel. Stretching through the garden and across the pristine blanket of the field beyond, she could make out the criss-crossing channel of footprints left by her mother and the dogs. Annie forced her eyes to follow the trail as far into the distance as she could, for a moment enjoying the simple poignancy of the imprint of life on land.

A few hours later it was all over. The presents, the food, the Queen making stiff and irrelevant pronouncements about the Commonwealth – even the washing up, thanks to the tireless industry of Hermione, who shooed them all out of the kitchen with rubber gloves and sang loud, warbly carols to while away her self-imposed exile at the sink. Not even the announcement about the pregnancy, made by Phillip over port and mince-pies, had caused much of a stir. Annie was almost disappointed.

'We wanted children anyway,' put in Hermione a little breathlessly. 'Now we're over the shock, we're actually rather pleased.'

Apart from a beat of a pause before responding, Christine Jordan's reaction gave little away. 'Of course, you must be – how very exciting for you both.'

'Hermione has already told her parents. They are OK about it too.' Phillip helped himself to two more mince-pies and several dollops of cream and brandy butter. 'Looks like the wedding will be in April instead of August.'

'Just so long as you're happy.' The statement, though clearly addressed to Phillip, was rather wasted on him, Annie decided, observing how casually her brother glanced up from his food, and guessing that beneath her mother's glassy gaze lay emotions of an altogether more fervent kind.

'Well, what I say is congratulations to the pair of you,' Annie burst out, wanting to keep her promise. 'Babies are always great news.' She raised her wine glass in toast. 'And weddings, too, for that matter. Well done Hermione and Phil,' she concluded, her voice tailing off slightly out of concern that she might have sounded a little too hearty to be true.

Later on, mellowing out in front of a roaring fire and Judy Garland, trilling her way through 'Over the Rainbow', Annie turned to study the profile of her mother, silent in the armchair beside her. Did she mind about Hermione's baby? Did she mind growing older, becoming a grandmother? Fuelled with curiosity and wine, Annie toyed with the bold idea of probing such thoughts out loud, of confiding that the lack of maternal pressure – endured by so many of her acquaintances – to get married and produce infants herself was something for which she was very grateful. But some aspect of the rigid set of the elder woman's face made Annie look away instead, surrendering to the realisation that the yard between their chairs belied a distance of a far more unbridgeable kind.

If Christine was aware of her daughter's scrutiny she gave no indication of it, continuing instead to stare fixedly at the television, her strong jaw clenched firmly, the rounded chin thrust out slightly as if in preparation for defiance should the need arise. Across the room the almost identical jaw-line of her son had sagged into the pull of sleep. He was propped rather endearingly against Hermione, their heads bent together, as if they had dozed off in mid-conversation.

The lion was stammering through his application for a dose of courage when the telephone sounded in the kitchen.

'That will be your father,' said Christine, not taking her eyes from the screen. 'He'll want to talk to you.'

Taking her glass of wine with her, Annie left the room.

'Dad, how are you? How's Portugal?'

'Hello mouse. It's raining and the telly's broken.'

'We're on the last bottle of wine and the bloody *Wizard Of Oz*. And of course it's a smoke-free zone as per usual.'

He groaned sympathetically. 'Torture. How's your mother?'

'Fine. Good, actually—'

'And Phillip?'

'He's asleep, but OK . . . though there is a bit of news on that front. Are you sitting down?'

'Why, what's happened?'

'Only that Hermione's discovered she's pregnant, so they're getting married in the spring instead of the summer.' There was a humph down the other end of the line. 'Anyone would think family planning hadn't been invented.'

'They seem fine about it, really they do.'

'Well that's the main thing I suppose.'

'Any qualms about becoming a grandfather?'

He laughed loudly. 'It's happened too often for any niceties like that – every time our backs are turned one of Eileen's daughters produces another damn baby. Cath, her eldest, has got four.'

'Would you like a word with Phil? He's asleep but I'm sure he wouldn't mind—'

'No, no leave him be.'

'Do you want to talk to Mum?' she blurted, knowing the

answer but feeling the question had to be asked anyway.

'Better not – I've got to go anyway.'

'Already?'

'I'm being summoned . . . but you're all right are you, mouse?'

'Great. I'm still being paid to write nonsense and I've even got a boyfriend who's almost respectable—'

'Splendid . . . got to run. Be in touch when we return to the UK. Happy Christmas. God bless—'

Annie put the receiver down with an all too familiar feeling of disappointment. Ever since she could remember, there had never quite been enough of him. Even when they were all still living under the same roof, her father had always seemed to be on the point of going somewhere, flinging affection at her in hurried farewells that never quite led to anything else. It occurred to her in the same instant that he was the one who had run away, the one who had been trying to run away all his life.

To buoy her spirits she smoked two cigarettes at speed, standing on the back door mat, and then dialled the number Greg had given her during the course of their farewells the previous morning. He was to spend Christmas exiled from London, he had complained, surrounded by hordes of distant cousins and venomous children in a large country house of a horsey sister in Hertfordshire. The phone would be his lifeline, he assured her, his reassurance that the real world awaited his return.

A woman with a strong home counties twang, whom Annie assumed to be the sister in question, answered the phone, to the accompaniment of muffled shrieks of merriment in the background.

'Don't worry if you're all too busy—' Annie faltered, aware of the contrastingly dull hum of the television coming through the doorway behind her.

'I'm just not sure whether he's here. Some of them have gone out. Hang on – I'll check. We've got such a crowd – I hardly know whether I'm coming or going—' After a few minutes the woman returned to report that Greg was indeed absent from the house. 'They've left all the children with me, the sods.'

'You don't know when they'll be returning, I suppose?'

'Dread to think. They've gone shooting and then there's a drinks thing afterwards . . . Who shall I say called?'

'Er . . . just Annie. Thanks.'

'Just Annie – right you are then.'

Telling herself that there was no reason on earth why the sister should have been briefed about her existence, Annie returned to the sitting room to find that her mother and both dogs had gone out for an afternoon walk. Though still asleep, Phillip and Hermione had shifted apart. His head was now flung back along the top edge of the sofa, while his fiancée had turned away from him, her legs curled up under her, one arm protectively round her stomach. She was so slim and petite Annie couldn't imagine her having a baby. With her tousled hair, specks of mascara under her eyes and traces of pink lipstick at the corners of her mouth, she looked no older than a little girl who had been at her mother's make-up box.

Annie switched off the television and went upstairs in search of analgesics; more because she could feel the early throb of a headache, than for her neck, which was much better. She was about to return downstairs when she found herself tempted by the idea of a long soak in the bath. Having sat for so long near the fire, the contrasting cold of the rest of the cottage struck her more keenly than usual. The whole place was falling apart, she thought irritably, tapping the landing radiator for evidence of heat and finding it stone cold. While frequently complaining about the idiosyncracies of the boiler, not to mention the draughts round the windows and doors, her mother never did anything about them. If quizzed on the subject, she said she couldn't afford it, which Annie knew for a fact wasn't true. In her meaner moments Annie even speculated that Christine relished these minor physical deprivations, as if they evinced the irretrievable injustices she had suffered as a wife.

There was nothing wrong with the hot water system though, mused Annie, sinking deep into her bath and smiling to herself at the sheer pleasure of being wet and warm. When she felt almost too hot for comfort, she sat up and began soaping herself, making as much lather as she could and remembering how as a child she had spent hours trying to blow bubbles through her fingers. She could feel her hair, dampened by steam and perspiration, sticking to the back of her neck and forehead. After a few minutes she sank back down into the water, crossing her arms on her chest and closing her eyes. As she did so, the fingers of her right hand encountered something unfamiliar; a small, hard lump on the undercurve of her left breast.

For a long time Annie lay there without moving, feeling the bubbles of water in her ears and the strangeness under her left hand. When finally she climbed out of the bath, the water had grown so tepid she was shivering with cold.

Chapter Seventeen

———◆∘◆∘◆———

Lying next to Bernard along the wooden bench of the sauna adjoining their ensuite bathroom, Marina wondered dreamily whether it was entirely permissible to feel so happy. 'I think I like you because you're rich,' she had told him over dinner the night before, 'because you spoil me to bits and don't seem to want anything in return. It must be that, mustn't it? I mean, what the hell else could it be?'

'My chiselled features, my lissome body?'

'Lissome?' Marina giggled and stretched her stockinged foot out under the table and up between his thighs. 'You're built like a tank, darling. A beautiful tank.'

'Watch it,' he warned, squeezing her toes under cover of his napkin with one hand and endeavouring to continue eating with the other. 'What about my brain,' he teased, 'how does that score on the Marina Hammond Richter scale of male perfection?'

She made a big show of frowning, shaking her head at her plate, which contained two empty halves of an entire lobster and a few stray curls of lettuce. 'That's a tough one. If I'm too insulting you might put your cheque book away and if I'm too generous you might get complacent. And we couldn't have that, could we?' She wiggled her toes, confident that she communicated enough of her real feelings for Bernard to know that all her talk about his wealth was merely teasing – merely a way of coping with it, in fact. He was far far better off than she had imagined, thanks not only to a decade of city bonuses, but also to a sizeable personal income of his own. 'Let me see now, seven and a half out of ten – eight on a good day maybe—'

'I'm flattered.' Smiling at her, he put down his fork and reached into the pocket of his jacket. 'So flattered that I feel emboldened—'

'—Emboldened? What sort of a word is that?'

'Don't interrupt. Where was I?'

'Emboldened.'

'Ah yes . . . that I feel sufficiently emboldened to present you with this small – but I hope you'll agree singularly beautiful – token of my affection, and to ask you – hang on a minute—' He gently lifted her foot off his lap, pushed back his chair and came round to her side of the table. 'Miss Marina Hammond, I want you to marry me.' He went down on one knee and placed a small red leather ring box on her side plate. 'Please will you marry me.'

Marina was dimly aware that they had acquired something of an audience. Several other diners, realising what was happening, were murmuring and smiling behind their hands. A couple of waiters, less bashful about their curiosity, had taken up front row positions beside a nearby pillar.

'Bloody hell, Bernard,' she whispered.

'Is that your answer?' He smiled up at her, only the wideness of his eyes betraying the intensity of his emotion. 'You haven't opened the box.'

With trembling fingers she prised open the lid. Inside was a large solitaire diamond, set between claws of gold. 'Bloody hell, Bernard,' she whispered again, more quietly.

'Do you think you could give me an indication as to how much longer this is going to take? I hate to rush you but my knees are beginning to protest.'

'Shh.' She put her finger to her lips and then pressed the palms of both hands on either side of his face. 'I love this moment. I love it. I don't want it to stop.'

'Does that mean I can put the ring on?'

'No – there's just one thing—' More people had gathered to

watch by now. A couple at a nearby table had even turned their chairs round for a better view.

'If this goes on much longer I'll never walk – let alone ski – again,' he murmured, frowning hard in a bid to hide the serious misgivings stirring inside.

'It's about your—' she lowered her voice '—your being so rich. You know that's not what it's about for me really, don't you?'

'Of course.' He blinked at her slowly. 'I'll gamble it all away if you like, if it would make this easier for you.'

She pretended to think hard about this proposition for a few moments, but then shook her head gravely. 'No, I think I can manage as things are.'

'You mean—?'

'I mean yes.' She raised her voice. 'Yes, I will marry you. Now quickly put the damn ring on before I change my mind.'

The two waiters began a timid clapping, which gradually gathered volume until a resounding applause filled the entire restaurant. The *maître d'hôtel* presented them with a free bottle of champagne, while the couple who had turned their chairs round left their table to shake Bernard and Marina by the hand.

'We've been married twenty-three years and four months to this day,' declared the man in a strong southern drawl, 'and we're even happier now than the day we started out.'

Marina had drifted through the rest of the evening in a daze, telling herself to savour every moment in case the magic wore away. But it remained, even at five in the morning, when the after-effects of the champagne awoke her with a stabbing headache and a dry mouth. She had lain with her eyes open, her hands tucked under one cheek, staring across the wide bed at the sleeping figure lying beside her; thinking what an unlikely package he was for a perfect husband and how very fortunate she was to have stumbled across him.

Seeing now that her lover had performed the improbable feat of falling asleep in the sauna, Marina sat up and gently nudged him awake.

'I'd like to call Annie. Is that all right?'

'Of course,' he replied lazily, wiping the sweat from his eyes. 'Give the number to reception and they'll put you through. Say Happy Christmas from me too.'

On hearing Annie's voice, Marina sang two verses of 'We Wish You A Merry Christmas' very fast at the top of her voice.

'If this is a singing telegram, I think you should consider looking for a new career.'

'Oh Annie, it's so good to hear you. How are things? Have you survived? Has Bonnie mauled any sheep?'

'Everything's great. What about you?'

'The most amazing thing has happened.' Having planned to be cool, to bide her time and reveal her enormous news with tact and dignity, Marina found that when the moment came, control lost out to elation. 'I've agreed to marry Bernard,' she shrieked, 'he asked me last night – in a restaurant of all places, surrounded by people – down on bended knee – had the ring all ready – beautiful whopping great diamond – the whole bloody resort was watching – it was just – fantastic—'

'Wow. I mean, congratulations.'

'Are you pleased for me?' urged Marina, detecting a trace of reluctance in Annie's tone.

'Of course – oh, of course I am,' insisted Annie hastily, with a wry passing thought for Bernard's heart-studded underpants and the unfathomable mysteries of human attraction.

'I – we – want you to be bridesmaid.'

Annie swallowed. 'Bridesmaid?'

'And we want to get married really quickly – we both think engagements are a waste of time – oh, Annie I'm so happy I could die. I just never thought it was possible – not for me anyway – to feel all this . . . stuff.'

'So it's true love, is it?' she pressed gently.

'God knows – I suppose so – I can't describe it. I just want to be with him all the time; I feel better when he's in the room; every time the phone goes I want it to be him; I feel as if we've known each other for ever but also just for a few minutes—'

'Yup. Sounds a pretty clear-cut case of love to me,' interjected Annie, assuming the tone of a doctor pronouncing the diagnosis of an acute disease.

'Oh it is, it is—'

While Marina persisted in her attempt to describe the indescribable, Annie fiddled with the curly flex of her mother's kitchen telephone, wondering whether it was intrinsic selfishness, not hearing from Greg, or being the proud owner of a breast lump that was making it so hard to be spontaneously empathetic. During the six hours since its discovery, the knowledge of the lump had taken up residence at the back of her mind, like a defendant awaiting trial. For long periods she did not think about it at all; and then suddenly, for no reason, the memory of its presence would sweep through her consciousness, leaving her quaking with imaginative speculations as to what ghastliness the future might hold. Marina was the obvious person with whom to share such worries. Yet the longer the conversation continued, the more impossible the raising of such a subject became. It would have contrasted too ludicrously with her good news. Worse still, it might have made her feel guilty for being so happy – a consequence which Annie, acutely aware of the limitations of her own responses so far, was most anxious to avoid.

'But isn't there an age limit on bridesmaids?' she countered, once some of Marina's romantic exuberance had subsided. 'I've got eye-bags and chin bristles for God's sake—'

'Chin bristles? Since when?'

'Well I haven't yet – but I will soon.'

'What do you think tweezers were invented for, woman? Oh, Annie, please say yes – I so want everything to be perfect.'

'I had no idea you were such a traditional princess at heart.'

'Neither did I. But now the moment's come I've realised I want it all – six-tier dresses and wedding cakes, a jungle of flower arrangements, a hysterical mother—'

'Are your parents pleased?'

'We haven't told them yet. We're saving it for New Year when we visit *en route* back to London. But I know they'll be over the moon, especially because Bernard's so disgustingly rich. He sends his love, by the way.' Anxious not to be overheard by her future husband, whom she could now hear making splashing noises in the bathroom, Marina lowered her voice. 'He's very concerned not to come between us, you know, Annie. He respects our friendship tremendously. So you see, nothing's going to change – between you and me, I mean. We'll still have girls' nights out and so on – maybe not quite so often, but that just means we'll enjoy them even more.'

'Of course nothing's going to change,' agreed Annie, suspecting otherwise, and guessing that deep in her heart Marina probably did too.

'I've said I'll move in with him straight away,' Marina blurted, having kept the most awkward aspect of these developments till last. 'To check out the goods, so to speak. I mean, you never really know until you've watched each other floss and squeeze blackheads—'

'No one,' cut in Annie firmly, 'lifelong partner or passing fancy, will *ever* see me do that.'

Marina burst out laughing. 'Oh Annie, I love you. Never change, will you?'

'I bloody hope so—'

'Better stop now. Have a wonderfully wicked time with Greg, won't you? And by the way, I'll pay rent till you find someone else.'

'Don't be silly,' murmured Annie, inwardly quailing at the prospect of revisiting the crude and impossible process of advertising for a soul-mate. 'Scrounging smokers with senses of humour are two-a-penny in North London – I'll have applicants queuing all the way to Paddington. Now don't go losing that precious rock in a snowdrift, will you? And I suppose I'll agree to be your blooming bridesmaid on the condition that you absolutely promise to put me in a dress that's so elegant and chic that Greg might even feel a twinge of pride at being acquainted with the oldest bridesmaid in the world—'

'Deal. We'll go shopping for it together.'

'She was fine about it – thrilled to bits—' declared Marina delightedly, slamming down the phone and racing to greet

Bernard as he emerged from the shower. 'And she's even agreed to follow me down the aisle.'

'I'm so pleased, darling,' he murmured, hugging her and inwardly allowing himself a twinge or two of relief. In spite of what he had told her, he sensed that Marina still had no idea quite what a daunting adversary her best friend made. Befriending prospective parents-in-law would be a breeze in comparison to winning the respect and trust of a woman like Annie Jordan; a woman whom he believed he could grow to like enormously but whose aggressive defence mechanisms left men in his delicate position quivering in their socks.

Chapter Eighteen

———◆◆◆◆◆———

Lying in bed later that night, her senses assailed by a mysterious variety of screeches and howls emanating from the darkness outside, Annie found herself longing for the simple drone of passing cars. The celebrated peace of the countryside was a fallacy, she decided, pulling her pillow round her ears in a vain attempt to ease herself into sleep. Instead, the silence thickened into something that felt threatening; a sense of movement in the dark; tiny scuffles and rustles until she began to feel as if the cottage was under secret siege. Or maybe the snow itself was creaking, she mused, shuffling to the window with her duvet clutched round her shoulders and seeing nothing beyond the grey mist of her own breath.

Knowing that she had overtaken the point where sleep would come without a distracting interlude of some kind, Annie decided to go downstairs to make a hot drink and to search for the tray-sized chocolate bar which Phillip had given her for Christmas. An inspired gift, she had to admit, and one that almost made up for the book that had accompanied it – a slim paperback, entitled *Ten Easy Steps To Becoming A Successful Human Being*. It was a hilarious satire, Phillip assured her, though, as ever, Annie suspected other agendas lurking behind his words. Her brother, as she knew only too well, had long since decided she was A Hopeless Case, partly as a reaction to their differences in personality and partly because it amused him to entertain such opinions. Refraining from the attempt to shift such views was one of the major achievements of her adult life.

As always, the taste of chocolate had a wonderfully soothing effect on her nerves. By the fourth mouthful Annie began to feel almost serene. There had to be some compensations for a woman at death's door, she reasoned, continuing to eat steadily and contentedly while stirring a saucepan of milk over the stove. Half closing her eyes, she imagined a deathbed scene of Hollywood perfection and poignancy: friends and enemies marvelling at her bravery and selflessness; a forlorn family clan regretting having taken her so much for granted; Greg pronouncing on eternal love at her funeral, reciting a bit of Auden perhaps, in the clipped moving tones of the delicious actor in *Four Weddings*, who had made her weep so profusely that Pete had hunched down into his seat in shame.

Scolding herself for failing to broach her newly discovered problem with anything like the realism or maturity it demanded and knowing that this was probably because she was still in shock, Annie blew ripples into her mug of Ovaltine and tried to reassemble her thoughts. She would consult her GP the moment she got back to London. She would buy a library's worth of books on women's health. She would confide in no one but Greg. The thought of him brought two quick pulses of hope and disappointment followed by a redoubling of hunger – almost like a burning pain – for confectionery. She broke off another row of chunks from the enormous bar, telling herself that since her lover had allowed the milestone of Christmas Day to pass without making contact, she had every right to retrace a few steps back down the well-worn path towards obesity and self-revulsion.

'Annie, is that you?'

'God – Mum, you made me jump.'

'Couldn't sleep?' Christine Jordan reached for the kettle and began filling it noisily from the tap, which had a disconcerting habit of spurting as much air as water. She opened a cupboard and got out a miniature blue teapot in which Annie could remember learning to make her first brew of tea, standing on a stool, full of seven-year-old eagerness to learn and the belief that acquiring such skills would provide a key to the mysteries of adult happiness and power. 'Chocolate won't help.'

'Chocolate always helps.'

'Not insomnia.'

'Who says I've got insomnia?' Annie muttered, licking the last of the sweetness from between her teeth and thinking that already the taste was soured by the fact of no longer being alone, by the almost tangible sense of disapproval.

'Are you worried about something?' Delivered with all the gentleness of a gunshot, the question provoked no desire in Annie to answer honestly, although a part of her longed to. 'Just thinking about Marina,' she lied, 'about her getting married and so on – I'll need to find someone else to share the flat . . . help pay the rent.'

'Might be nice to have a change. A new face about the place.'

'Yes,' she replied without conviction.

'I thought the day went well,' Christine continued briskly, setting the teapot down on a table mat, followed by a small jug of milk, a teaspoon and a cup and saucer. 'Very smooth indeed,' she added, as if reflecting upon the successful evasion of a crisis. She stirred the tea, three times one way and three times the other, before putting the lid back on and pulling out a chair opposite her daughter. She then sat back and folded her arms across her chest with a deep sigh. 'Though I'm worried about Phillip, obviously.'

'Phillip?'

Christine poured a splash of milk into her teacup and reached for the teapot. 'The situation is hardly . . . ideal.' She shook her head and stared mournfully into her tea.

'Few situations are,' Annie murmured. 'But Phil has proved on countless occasions in the past that he is quite capable of looking out for himself. They were getting married anyway—'

'I married your father because I was pregnant,' Christine said quietly. She picked up her cup, made as if to drink from it, but put it down untouched. 'I miscarried three weeks after the wedding. It's all right,' she continued quickly, seeing the look of sympathetic horror on her daughter's face, 'I'm not saying it would have changed anything either way. I just wanted you to understand why shot-gun marriages are a subject on which I'm rather sensitive.' She gave a short laugh. 'It took a long time to get pregnant after that . . . a long time before you came along.' She cleared her throat. 'I just don't want Phillip to be trapped into something that's not right.'

'No, of course not,' Annie muttered, adding, 'love is blind,' because it was all she could think of to say.

'Love is a state of mind,' retorted Christine, disposing of her tea in three gulps. 'Just like sleeplessness. Not a condition that afflicts members of the animal kingdom,' she added, her face softening at the sight of the two dogs, wedged head to toe in the dog basket by the back door.

Annie readily seized on the distraction. 'They've had a good Christmas anyway . . . thank you for taking charge of Bonnie.'

'I'll keep her if you like.'

'Keep her?' Annie's first instinct was defensive. She opened her mouth to refuse the offer, but admitted instead, 'I was thinking of taking her back to the dog home, it . . . wasn't working out quite as I had planned.'

'That was obvious,' remarked Christine, getting up to rinse out her mug and dashing most of Annie's gratitude in the same instant. 'She's taken ten years off Kit – he's like a puppy again. Makes my life easier, having him so entertained.'

'But I'm not sure, maybe—'

'Nonsense. We'll call it settled. You can see her whenever you want – best of both worlds for the pair of you.'

'Thanks Mum, I—'

But Christine had turned her back and was busily tipping away a bowl of washing-up water. She dried up her teacup and returned it to its hook on the dresser. 'Bed, I think. Unless there was something you wanted to get off your chest?'

Annie looked at her for a moment before blinking and shaking her head. On the way upstairs she placed her bare feet where Christine's slippers left faint imprints on the carpet, and pondered the confused signals of kindness and criticism which had characterised their communion in the kitchen. It was ever thus, she realised sadly, ever since she could remember.

They parted on the landing. 'Say nothing of my concerns to Phillip, of course,' murmured Christine, briefly brushing her lips across her daughter's forehead.

'Of course,' Annie echoed, already retreating to her room. She sat on the edge of her bed listening not to the countryside now but to the confused clamour inside her head. Other daughters would have shared intimate secrets, she thought wistfully, groping in her jacket pocket for her cigarettes and dragging a chair to the window. Strange lumps and neglectful boyfriends would have formed just a small part of a host of confidences spilled in such circumstances. She inhaled deeply, steeling herself for the usual flood of anger, invariably invoked by the consideration of Christine's maternal shortcomings. But for once none came. She thought instead of her mother's miscarriage, of how complicated the truth was, of how bitterness could make people so unloveable that patterns of rejection repeated like breaking waves.

The smoke from her cigarette curled out of the open window before teasingly drifting back inside, much as it had at other windows throughout her teenage years. The sense of not having moved on was both familiar and unwelcome. Yet things were different now, Annie reminded herself, clinging to the thought of Greg and absently sliding her cold fingers into the front of her nightie. For a moment she thought the lump had gone and her heart soared. But it was half an inch further down than she remembered. Or had it moved? Were moving lumps good or bad? Sensing suddenly that she was being watched, she pulled her hand free and spun round. But no one was there, apart from Phillip's teddy bear staring its lopsided stare from the shelf above her bed.

Chapter Nineteen

———◦◦◦◦———

Annie stepped into her flat to find a modest stack of mail inside her postbox and her answering machine bleeping for attention upstairs. Thanks to the freezing weather she had spent two extra unscheduled days in the country, mostly trying to avoid other members of the household and almost dying of boredom at the alternatives. The small scattering of yellow cigarette butts behind the tool shed had swelled to mountainous proportions; so ugly amongst all the white that she eventually felt obliged to chisel a hole in the hard ground and bury them in a mass grave. It wasn't until the afternoon following Boxing Day that the thaw had begun in earnest, converting treacherous ice to friendly puddles and banks of dulux snow to gritty sludge.

Like a broken promise, Annie had thought, surveying the scenery on her drive back out of the valley. Though pleased to be leaving, she quailed at the prospect of getting back behind the helm of real life. The focus of her apprehensions kept shifting between the continuing silence from Greg and the question of what, if anything, to do about the lump in her breast. As time passed, she felt a growing temptation to do nothing at all; to wait and see if it grew or moved or disappeared back into the mysterious space from which it had emerged. Any more definitive course of action would constitute a level of concern for which she still felt wholly unequipped.

Trailing clouds of cigarette smoke round the flat for the sheer joy of being at liberty to do so, Annie made herself a cup of coffee and broke off two of the remaining three rows of Phillip's bar of chocolate by way of lunch. On hearing Greg's voice leading the queue on her answering machine, she let out a small yelp of relief and punched the air.

'Annie, darling, you must have wondered what I was up to. You're not going to believe this but I managed to lose your number in Wales. I tried Directories of course, but without the address they couldn't – or wouldn't – help. Sorry old girl. Phoebe said you'd called and I felt a real brute not being able to get back to you. I don't know exactly when you'll get this message but I just wanted to tell you I'm missing you badly and can't wait to pick up where we left off. My plans have changed slightly on that front, thanks to a last-minute invite to make up numbers on a skiing trip. Verbier and no rent. Sorry Annie, I know it means spending New Year apart, but I just couldn't say no. I'll be back in town on the Monday after and will call you right away. I'll make it up to you, I promise.'

Annie's fist weakened and flopped to her side. 'Bloody marvellous,' she muttered, cheered by the communication, but lamenting the inherent difficulties of falling for someone so perpetually in demand by other circles. The next message was from Amy.

'We need to talk dates for your singles holiday – the sooner the better as far as I'm concerned – I feel it could be a real departure for you—' Annie glowered at the machine, partly because the appeal of the Foreign Relations assignment had not increased with time and partly because she thought she detected a certain desperation in her editor's tone. She could at least have mentioned the Christmas list contribution, out of courtesy if nothing else.

'—and while I'm on, can I put another date in your diary? January 18th – cocktails and Peruvian pipe music – Miles and I thought we'd blow away some of those post-Christmas winter blues. Love you to come – with or without a partner, of course.'

The last message was from Jake, sounding curiously formal and subdued.

Just a quick call from the family estate. I fly to Málaga tomorrow. Look, Annie, I'm sorry but I never got round to that fan letter business.

I feel bad because I know I promised and I really did want to help. My only excuse is that I'm a shambolic, unreliable sod and I have had a lot of . . . distractions recently. And anyway you shouldn't need stupid letters to know you're marvellous. I'll call soon.'

So he hadn't written after all. And therefore had every right to sound so guilty, Annie decided, pondering the matter as the tape clicked and rewound itself. While impressed at the bizarre coincidence of some stranger unwittingly stepping into the breach of Jake's failure, the mix-up of the letters did not bother her unduly. Having an epistolary admirer hadn't exactly made any difference to Amy anyway, she reflected, recalling the flat tone of her editor's message and rifling through her letters in the hope of some consolation.

Three bills, two tax demands – one of them in red ink – and a Christmas card from Pete, coyly suggesting a trial reunion, did nothing to lighten her mood. Nor did a letter from the property agents informing her that the landlord of Shrewsbury Mansions would be calling at her flat in person at two o'clock that very day in order to discuss the matter of keeping a pet. Realising to her horror that it was already half past one, Annie threw down her letters and embarked on a whirlwind tidy-up of the flat, stuffing items of clothing under the bed, closing drawers and stacking papers into orderly piles. Only the sight of the half-empty water bowl and a mauled plastic bone under a chair in the kitchen made her pause, causing a twist of shame at the alacrity with which she had conceded defeat over Bonnie. For a moment she even felt tempted to call her mother and claim the creature back, to pretend that she hadn't noticed the instant transformation wrought by a large garden, country walks and a companion of her own kind.

Armed with a J-cloth and a bowl of soapy water, Annie began a hasty trawl for any obvious, removable patches of dirt along the walls and skirting boards. Finding that the sections she cleaned only made the rest look worse, she soon gave up and fired copious clouds of air freshener at the furniture instead. Thanks to her recent absence, the kitchen was mercifully presentable, as was the bathroom, though she took the precaution of closing the toilet lid to hide the limescale ridges in the bowl and rearranged the shower curtain to mask the white scuffs in the avocado panel along the bath.

By the time the doorbell rang at just past two o'clock, Annie felt as ready as she ever would be for such an ordeal. In all her four years of residency, she had never once been called upon to confront the landlord of Shrewsbury Mansions in person, the few problems that had arisen having been dealt with by the property agents. After hearing the usual unintelligible fuzz of a reply on the intercom, she pressed the buzzer to open the front door and stepped back for a quick check on her appearance in her hall mirror. Four days without the necessity or incentive for any self-beautifying had left her looking somewhat scruffy, but fractionally refreshed, Annie decided, raking her fingers through her hair and biting her lips to give them a bit of colour. With a last regretful look at Bonnie's claw scrapes in the lower section of the door, she took a deep breath and turned the handle.

After such a build-up it was with considerable dismay – not to say alarm – that Annie found herself confronting the tall, dark-skinned man who had made so free with her telephone a few weeks before. For one wild moment she wondered whether he might indeed be the owner of the building, whether this explained his evident sense of claim over her belongings. But just one proper glance at his appearance put paid to such imaginings. Since their last encounter on her doorstep he had clearly slid considerably further down the lower rungs of society's grimy ladder. His anorak and jeans were stiff and colourless with dirt. His trainers, once so white and new, looked worn and muddied, while his hair, sticking up in solid, unbrushed clumps, was a small private wasteland of neglect. Worst of all was the expression on his face, which had clearly abandoned every effort at niceties of any kind. All Annie's instinct told her in an instant that she had every right to feel concern, not merely for her telephone bill but for her welfare on a wider scale. Her first thought was to try slipping back behind her door, but common sense warned her that this was a manoeuvre she might not manage to complete alone.

'I'm afraid you'll have to leave,' she said, loudly and querulously, shooting an imperious look down the hallway behind him. 'I'm expecting a visitor.'

'You let me in girl,' he said softly, 'and I'm coming in.' He took a step forward and placed his right arm across her body, resting his hand on the door frame. His face was so close that Annie could see the red squirls of broken blood vessels floating in the whites of his eyes. She could smell his breath too; a stale, sour smell, like rotting onions.

'I am expecting my landlord at any moment. So I would leave while you can.'

He shook his head scornfully. 'Your landlord, yeah? Sure, girl, sure. And you've got a boyfriend the size of Arnold Schwarzenegger in your wardrobe, I suppose.' He placed his left hand on the other side of the door, so that Annie was trapped in the space between his arms. 'I watch you, girl. I see you live alone——' He lowered his voice to a whisper and pressed his body so close to hers that Annie felt the zip of his jacket nudging her chest.

At the sound of the front door clanging shut downstairs they both started, and for one, almost comical, moment, gazed into each other's eyes.

'I told you my——' she began, but he clapped his hand over her mouth and began trying to steer her backwards through the open door of her flat, hurrying against the pulse of footsteps coming up the stairs behind them.

'Is everything OK?'

On glimpsing a portion of the dark leather jacket of her neighbour Annie tried to speak, but found her throat too dry to emit a sound. Her assailant had already released her and was backing down the hallway. 'She asked for it,' he growled, pointing and shaking his finger at her. 'She gave me the come-on, invited me up here——'

'It doesn't look like much of an invitation to me,' remarked Michael Derwent, blocking his path. 'Perhaps you would like to——' But the man spun round and barged past him, hurling himself down the stairwell.

Michael set off in pursuit, leaving Annie staring after them in shock and disbelief. A few moments later the front door slammed and her neighbour reappeared at the top of the stairs, profuse with concern and apology. 'He was too fast,' he gasped, coming over to where she stood and then bending over to his knees in a bid to catch his breath. 'You OK?'

Annie nodded. 'Fine . . . no harm done at all . . . thank you very much indeed. He's bothered me before . . . asked to use my phone, but this time things really were getting out of hand, to put it mildly. If the bloody landlord had turned up when he was supposed to it wouldn't have happened at all.'

'Landlord?'

Although having suffered no physical exertion, Annie found that her breath was also coming in gasps. She managed a smile. 'Sorry – perhaps I should have warned you. I've been away. Only got the letter this morning. I'm due for a visitation from the powers on high – about my dog, as you'll no doubt be pleased to hear. The joke is I haven't even got the animal anymore – though perhaps in the light of recent events I should think about getting her back,' she added ruefully, rubbing the spot where her intruder had seized her arm. 'Well, thanks again,' she repeated, overcome with awkwardness now the moment of crisis had passed, 'and don't worry. When and if our dear landlord finally deigns to arrive I won't let slip any comments about musically disruptive neighbours.' She turned to enter her flat, aware that he was still standing watching her.

'Shouldn't you call the police?'

'Er, yes, I guess so. Though I'm not sure what good that will do. He didn't exactly commit a crime. And, as he so sweetly pointed out, I was the one who opened the front door. As I said, I thought it was the land— Never mind . . . Call it a bad day.'

'I would be a witness,' he persisted quietly. 'I do think it would be wrong not to do anything about it at all.'

'I appreciate the advice – I'll think about it. And thanks again for your help. You've been great,' she added meekly, closing the door. Once safely inside, Annie leant back against it with her eyes closed, taking deep breaths to try and quell the trembling in her arms and legs. After a moment or two there was a timid knock behind her.

'Yes?' He was still standing there, shifting awkwardly from foot to foot and rubbing the back of his neck. A recent haircut had left a trim of paler skin round his sideboards and ears, she noticed, giving a boyish look to his face and more prominence to the wide, dark blue eyes. Beneath the jacket were paint splashed jeans and a white T-shirt with some lettering inscribed across the front. 'Are you sure you're OK?'

'Sure. Thank you.' She started to close the door again, but stopped, realising he was struggling to say something else.

'This is really difficult – embarrassing – but – well – I'm afraid it's me.' For the first time his gaze locked onto hers, his face flushing with the guilt of the admission. 'I'm . . . er . . . the powers on high . . . the bloody landlord.'

'You?'

He held up both hands. 'Don't go mad, please. I was going to tell you—'

'So this . . . this appointment—' She could hardly get the words out.

'—Is with me. Yes. I thought it would be a bit of a laugh—'

'A bit of a—?'

'Winding you up about having a dog and so on . . . I love dogs. You can have six if you want to.'

'A bit of a laugh?' she repeated stupidly, still trying to digest what he was telling her, a detached part of her thinking that he didn't look seedy enough for such a rôle.

'And I guess, if I'm honest, I was a bit annoyed about the fuss you made over the piano and so on—'

'I had every bloody right—'

'Don't start that again,' he groaned, pushing up the sleeve of his jacket and holding out his hand. 'Pleased to meet you. I'm Michael Derwent.'

Annie studied the carpet for a moment or two. 'Yes, well I'd worked that much out from your post. You know my name of course.' She barely allowed their palms to touch before snatching her fingers back and folding her arms. 'So, have you been the owner of this property all along?'

'Only since the autumn. My father left it to me. He died in October.'

'Oh dear – sorry.'

'Don't be,' he cut in shortly. He gestured at the hall and landing. 'The best thing he did was leave me this lot—' He stopped abruptly, suddenly looking self-conscious. 'I say . . . you wouldn't like to come up for a cup of tea or something, would you? Or perhaps something stronger,' he ventured, casting a look at her hands, clenched so tightly across her chest that he could see the whites of her knuckles.

'I need cigarettes,' she declared, observing the line of his gaze and quickly dropping her arms to her sides.

'Fine. I'll wait.'

Annie could not help exclaiming in amazement at the transformation that had taken place on the top floor since her brief glimpse of it from behind Jake's shoulder a couple of weeks before. Instead of walls there were a series of archways and open spaces.

'God, I thought you were doing a spot of furniture moving – I had no idea—'

He laughed, looking a little shame-faced. 'I've had a busy Christmas. There's a long way to go yet . . . I can't bear the feeling of being holed up—'

'I can see that.' Annie trod a cautious path across a dust sheet and several piles of tools. 'Wow, it's going to be great.' She looked about her in genuine admiration, thinking of the identical floorspace in her own apartment and how she would never have had the vision, imagination – or whatever it took – to conceive of so contrasting and yet so simple an adaptation herself. 'It's very . . . bold,' she continued, seeing the piano down the furthest end of the room and realising that she was in effect staring from the equivalent of her hall down through to the bathroom.

'The kitchen will be here,' he continued, beckoning her to follow him round a corner into the section of the flat that she used as a sitting room. 'I like cooking so this is going to be a big space, room to lounge as well as stir saucepans and so on. Though it's just a kettle and two rings at the moment. I've decided to build my own cabinets, which will take a bit of time—'

Annie's eyes widened in amazement. 'What the hell *are* you?' She laughed uncertainly. 'I mean, first I think you're a waiter, then a pianist and now this—' she gestured about her, '—carpentry.'

'So you think everyone has to be something in particular, then.' He filled a kettle and dropped a couple of teabags into two brown stained mugs.

'I'm not sure, I—'

'Why not call the police now?' He squeezed the teabags out with a teaspoon and deftly tossed them into a cardboard box full of wallpaper shavings. 'Not 999, just the local police station. The number will be in the little white book behind the toaster. Go on, I really think you should. I mean, what if that guy comes back?'

Annie sighed. 'I suppose you're right. First, I just need a—' she looked about her for something that might serve as an ashtray.

He held out a chipped porcelain saucer and then tapped the telephone. 'Go on. They'll probably be really grateful.'

A few minutes later Annie found herself sitting on a weather-beaten but very comfortable sofa staring out over the rooftops towards Regent's Park. It was amazing how much better the view was one storey up. The police had been impressively inter-ested and sympathetic, asking if she had been hurt and promising to send a couple of constables round within the hour. Michael had then pulled off a series of dust sheets to reveal a table, sitting-room furniture and an improbably small CD player into which he fed a disc of someone called Miles Davis, of whom Annie had never heard. The mellow, teasing sound of a trumpet began to weave its way round the room, easing the pressure for dialogue. Annie sipped her tea and puffed on her cigarette while Michael busied himself punching cushions and wiping the worst of the dust off surfaces with the sleeves of his jacket. Watching him,

Annie found herself wondering whether Jake had been right to entertain any hopes for himself. There was certainly something beautiful about the man, something to do with his slim, fine-boned features and darkly lashed blue eyes, contrasting so markedly with the almost gingery brown of his hair. With it cropped so short he looked no more than thirty at the most. Yet he wasn't obviously feminine, Annie decided, noticing his hands, which looked hard and broad – more the hands of a carpenter than a musician – and seeing how his figure filled his clothes. As he flung his jacket on the back of a chair he turned and caught the tail-end of her stare. Annie flushed and looked quickly away, inwardly chiding herself for allowing her mind to stray down pathways she had no business – nor any desire – to explore.

'So, you're a writer.'

She laughed. 'I always think it sounds so pretentious, put like that . . . but, yes I am. At the moment I write a weekly column called *FlatLife* – trying to be funny about . . . er . . . clothes and feelings.' She made a face. 'Nothing too taxing.'

'It must be bloody hard, thinking of stuff week after week. I used to write the odd piece about wine – took me hours. Not because I didn't know what I wanted to say but because of the problem of how to say it.'

'What *do* you do exactly?' she gasped, realising with some frustration that he still hadn't told her.

He frowned. 'Exactly? Let me see now . . . I suppose you could call me a freelance wine consultant. That's probably the easiest thing. Though it's very much a sideline, to earn a bit of cash and because I like wine. I make sure I don't get too busy because I need time for my music and—'

'Cupboard-making?'

'Absolutely.' He drained the last of his tea and smiled absently into the bottom of his mug. 'I once tried having a proper job – being one thing every day of the week – mostly to please my father, I think, looking back on it.' He sighed. 'But it made me miserable.'

'What were you?' she asked, curious.

The frown deepened. 'A man in a dark suit. I grew very rich,' he added gravely, as if confessing to a sin, 'when I didn't deserve to at all. Moving large sums of money around for other people and taking a cut from the profits – it really shouldn't be allowed.'

'And you chucked it in?' Annie couldn't hide her amazement.

'I'm afraid the old clichés are true; money doesn't make you happy. And in my case I was so fucking busy I never had time to enjoy spending any of it. I saved rather a lot though, which has been useful.'

'And so you're happy now?' From the way his face darkened Annie had the immediate impression that she had trespassed on forbidden ground.

'I survive. More tea?'

'Better not.' She put down her mug. 'I've got my date with the Old Bill, then the small matter of my weekly column, then—' Some of the other details of the life awaiting her downstairs made her break off uncertainly. A longing for Greg welled up inside, a longing for someone who could offer a rather more intimate level of sympathy for all that she had been through, not just that afternoon, but over the question of whether to surrender her left breast to the cold-fingered probing of one of the brisk, overworked doctors at the practice in Gould Road. Aghast at the realisation that she was on the verge of tears, Annie leapt to her feet and almost ran to the door.

'You might be wanting these,' he said quietly, following her and handing over her cigarettes and lighter. 'Would you like me to come down and wait with you for the police?'

'Goodness no. I suspect they'll come up to grill you anyway once they've done with me.' She smiled tightly, avoiding his eyes.

'But if you want to – well, talk about it or anything – sometimes there's a sort of delayed shock thing – you might find you suddenly feel scared—'

'No chance,' she insisted, thinking that if he said one more thing that was remotely kind she would start weeping and never be able to stop.

'Here let me – it's stiff.'

She stepped back to let him get to the door. As she did so she caught sight of something familiar hanging on the coat stand in the corner behind the door, half-hidden by a long black trench coat. It was Jake's white silk scarf, lovingly owned since college days; unmistakable not only for the faint trace of brown staining left by events at a particularly exuberant party, but also for the initials J H, stitched in black silk along the hem of tassels. It was not completely surprising, she told herself, and hardly significant. But for some reason she felt a small measure of disappointment press through her unhappiness.

'Well, it was nice to become acquainted with my landlord,' she stammered, rushing through the open door without looking at him. 'And thanks again for the tea . . . and everything.'

'Don't mention it,' he murmured, frowning to himself as she made her way down the corridor to the stairs.

Chapter Twenty

'*What a start to the year! Never a dull moment at château Jordan!*'

Annie took a large gulp of what might have been her fourth (she had deliberately stopped counting) glass of wine and squinted at this new attempt at an opening sentence through half-closed eyes. She was never sure about exclamation marks: whether their attention-seeking was cleverly sarcastic, or merely a pitifully grasping attempt at being funny.

'*Where to begin?*'

As a punctuational accoutrement, the question mark was an altogether easier, less complicated package, she reflected, tipping her chair back and studying the screen with tipsy satisfaction.

'*With my car accident or the hijack of my dog? With my lover's voluntary exile on the pistes of Europe or my recent physical assault at the hands of a potential rapist?*'

For a few minutes Annie toyed with the appealingly point-less challenge of making every sentence in the entire article end with dramatic punctuation of some kind. If she was going to be trite, she might as well manage it on a grand scale.

Instead, the urge to write about herself reasserted itself with a vengeance. An urge which she had tried to drown in alcohol but which had resurfaced nonetheless, bobbing up on the seas of her consciousness like an obstinate cork. Around her chair were scattered copies of her earliest articles, wrested from the cardboard box that served as a filing cabinet in a vain attempt to remind herself that what had been achieved in the past could be achieved again. That it was just a question of finding the right start, the right tack, the right voice.

She pressed the delete button and stared at the screen, still hearing no voice but her own.

Aware through the fug of alcohol that she was dangerously close to a point of total incoherence, Annie at last began to type, slowly at first and then much faster, spilling out the thoughts as they unfolded inside her head. Just to see where they led. Just as a way of getting rid of them. What harm was there in writing about herself after all? she reasoned. Who could complain if the only person she exposed was herself? Several paragraphs poured out before she could stop them.

> . . . I don't feel like I imagined I would. I mean, in a weird way the lump feels like a part of me, as valid as a tummy button or an eyeball. What right have I to question its existence? Then there's this other part that feels illogically and absurdly safe. Mine must be a mutant lymph gland, a harmless globule of some kind, one that will slowly disappear of its own accord. Life-threatening tumours are for TV documentaries and women's magazines. For other, better columnists who've shown more bravery and insight than I could manage in several lifetimes. I'm only writing this because, just at the moment, I can't think of anything else to say. Because there's nothing else inside my head . . .

And because you've no one else to talk to, Annie thought, but did not write, because there were boundaries after all and she only felt able to take the step she had because it laid no one open to vulnerability but herself. She broke off from typing and tugged her jumper up over her bra. It was still there. If anything, more solid than before. Slowly she returned her fingers to the keys.

'. . . *because sometimes I just can't pretend to be anyone else.*'

Once she had finished, Annie felt curiously elated and quite safe. The relief of expressing some of the feelings that had been churning around inside her for the past few days was immense. As yet it was just words in her computer, she told herself, seeking consolation as doubt welled up inside, and fumbling in her still unpacked bag for her wash things. There was still all the next morning to craft it into something less raw and ready to face the world. Catching sight of the two dog-lover fan letters which had remained in her suitcase throughout her stay in Wales, she rammed them into a wastepaper basket, marvelling that she had once attributed significance to anything so trivial.

Armoured by alcohol, Annie fell into a deep sleep almost at once. She dreamt vividly, too, of fluttering letters that became snowflakes. Looking up she saw a postman lounging amongst the clouds, laughing at her, until his face suddenly darkened and developed a bruise. Then the clouds became mountains of snow and Greg came flying down them on skis, his knees bent, his shoulders hunched, the reflector lenses of his goggles hiding the expression in his eyes. Within the strange logic of the dream Annie watched the speeding figure approach – so fast yet taking for ever – and as it did so she found herself straining for a glimpse of the expression behind the lenses, as if her survival depended on it.

Not many feet above her Michael Derwent was playing the piano, his foot on the soft pedal, a bottle and a glass of wine on a stack of music at his side. Unlike Annie, he was neither drunk nor bent upon being so. A sleepless night was nothing new either, but something he had learnt to respect rather than to fight. He would sleep late the following morning if he needed to, or catnap later in the day. He played his way lazily through some Chopin and Debussy, before moving onto the more tightly ordered synchronicity of Bach. He closed his eyes, only half reading the music, his fingers feeling for the notes, while his mind followed the twists and turns of the tune, turning in on itself but always finding a way out again, like a swimmer coming up for air. As always, Michael had turned to the Preludes and Fugues with a genuine sense of need, relishing the mathematical sureness of the harmony, the stitching of patterns that made sense. Improvising his beloved jazz was something he reserved for an altogether different frame of mind, when it felt thrilling to start a tune and see where it led, when the elusiveness of an ending felt like an adventure rather than a terror. When he was more in the mood for the hazards of real life in fact, Michael reflected wryly, closing the book of music at last and pulling the dust sheet back over the piano.

He moved quietly round the flat, looking for things that needed straightening and pondering his recent failures to lead the cocooned existence at which he had, until recently, so excelled. An existence perfected during his days in the City, and unexpectedly resurrected only a year into his grand bid for freedom, when his emotions had been so mangled by misfortune that he had no longer felt able to deal with them. Maybe the easy scapegoat offered by the rigours of a twenty-hour working day had suited his temperament after all, Michael thought bitterly, picking up a framed photograph of his father and shaking his head. Instead of the simple release for which he had always hoped, the old man's death had prompted a host of complicated and wholly unforeseen regrets, to do with mourning a relationship that had never come into being and waving a last farewell at the possibility of it ever doing so.

Perhaps sifting through the unwanted debris of such re-actions was what had burst the bubble of his self-reliance, Michael mused, noticing Jake's silk scarf had slipped to the floor and bending down to pick it up. He shook the dust off and absently stroked the silk with his fingertips, thinking back to the Friday of Jake's visit – how shocked he had been, and how impressed. To think of the man tracking him to the club like that. Following him home through the dark, rainy streets after-wards. So drunk and full of passion. Prepared to risk everything in a way that Michael had long since surrendered, scarred by consequences for which he had been punishing himself ever since.

Michael started to slide the bolt on his door into place but then decided to go downstairs and check the front door was properly closed first. A precaution he had taken every night since the intruder. As he passed Annie's door he bent down and checked underneath for signs of light. But all was still and dark.

There was no sound on the ground floor either, apart from

the muffled whirr of the occasional passing car in the street outside. The tenants in the garden flat had finally given notice and moved out. The agents promised they could re-let it at once, but Michael had resisted. As with his own accommodation, the place was badly in need of decorative attention, some of which he was sure he could claim on insurance and the rest of which could be financed out of their deposit. He would move onto it once he had finished with his own place, he decided, his spirits rising as always at the thought of having some practical project ahead of the one in hand. He gave the front door a good tug before turning on his heel and retracing his way back upstairs, his mind sufficiently settled at last to bring some likelihood of sleep.

Chapter Twenty-One

The waiting room was very crowded. Annie, slotted between a wide woman with a pink nose and an ashen-faced teenager with a rasping cough, stared hard at a wall chart about head lice. Contrary to popular legend, head lice couldn't jump, she learnt, nor could they survive without a strand of hair on which to cling. There was a rather endearing picture of a small, beetle-like creature demonstrating this fact, hugging what looked like a long pole, its little face set in a stubborn expression of one determined not to be outwitted by adversity.

It had been a bad morning, mainly because there had been so little of it. By the time Annie surfaced from under the bedclothes, clutching her aching head and scowling at the stale metallic taste in her mouth, it was already past midday. Still in her dressing-gown and with a jug of black coffee beside her, she had sat down to attempt some hasty pre-deadline editing of the previous evening's outpourings, only to find that no alternative words would come to mind. At one o'clock she dialled the newspaper and shoved the pages through her fax machine, wanting only to be done with it, past caring what anyone thought or said.

Armed with a cigarette, which tasted foul but with which she persisted nonetheless, in the vain hope that it might start to taste better, she had then plucked up the courage to telephone the Gould Road surgery. Informed by the receptionist that there were no appointments until the end of the following week, she was surprised and appalled to find herself bursting into tears.

'Come along at three then, dear, we'll squeeze you in,' clucked the woman at once, 'I just thought you said it wasn't urgent.'

'It isn't,' wailed Annie, 'I mean, it probably isn't . . . it's a lump—'

'Ooh, well in my view lumps of any kind should be seen and no messing. You come along this afternoon and the doctor will sort you out. All right?'

Having absorbed every detail of the lifecycle of the head louse, Annie rummaged in her handbag for a second look at her post. Marina's postcard from Colorado, showing a dog in ski-goggles on a snowboard, exuded heady happiness. Even the writing – large and loopy – looked somehow breathless. Another language in fact, mused Annie, doing her best to focus on Marina's good fortune, aware that she was in danger of sliding back into a separate twilight world in which she was capable of empathising with nothing but the kaleidoscope of her own disappointments.

> *See you soon – if we survive my parents. Florida is being beaten up by tornados at the moment so we might not! Bernard cracked a rib during a fall, but is being very brave and still skiing like a Trojan. (Did Trojans ski?). Hope all is brilliant with you. Mxxxxx.*
> *PS HAPPY NEW YEAR – going to be the best ever, I just know it!*
> *PPS Back Sunday Jan 1st.*

There had also been another letter from the admirer unwittingly making up for Jake's broken promise with regard to her fan mail. Studying the contents, which were growing increasingly sugges-tive, Annie experienced the first *frisson* of real apprehension. The guy was clearly cracked.

> *. . . I've taken to cutting out your articles and keeping them under my pillow . . . I feel I know you really well, that we're*

*on the same wavelength, that, given the opportunity we could
become really close . . .*

She was allocated to a tubby doctor with small round spectacles,
whom she had seen once before about inflamed tonsils. He had
a pleasant round face with cherubic lips and concerned brown
eyes, magnified behind the lenses of his glasses. As she walked
in she found herself glancing at his hands, in preparation for the
ordeal of being touched. They were small and tidy with deep
dimples along the ridge of his knuckles. A part of her mind withdrew then, as it did when she went to the family planning clinic
to have metal instruments levered between her legs. With her
apprehensions thus locked inside, Annie sat as demurely as an
interviewee for a job, answering questions about periods and the
health of her grandmothers' breasts in a voice so matter-of-fact
that she barely recognised it as her own. When motioned to the
bed behind the curtain, she took off her shirt and bra and lay
down with a wonderful feeling of calm. She rested her hands
together on her stomach and stared at the white squares on the
ceiling, inviting the same blankness to occupy her mind. By
the time he examined her she felt so separate from the experience as to be almost sleepy. When asked to sit up, she could
barely manage it for yawning.

Annie re-emerged from behind the curtain, fully clothed
once more, to find the podgy fingers flying with remarkable
dexterity over the keyboard of his computer. The moment she
sat down, he turned to face her. The brown eyes, peering over
the top of the round silver frames of his glasses, looked kind.

'I don't think there is any cause for alarm.'

Though he was smiling at her encouragingly Annie detected
caution in his tone.

'It feels benign, Miss Jordan, and with a healthy personal
history like yours, I fully expect it to be so.' He paused. 'But I
wouldn't be doing my job if I didn't suggest we get it checked
out more thoroughly. I'm referring you to a specialist breast
clinic where they'll do a couple of tests—'

'What tests?' She eyed him steadily.

'Purely routine – they'll give you an examination, an X-ray, take a sample of breast cells—'

'And how—' Annie's mouth felt so dry she had to pause to swallow, '—how will they do that exactly?'

'With a syringe – but it shouldn't be painful,' he added quickly, 'nothing worse than an injection at the dentist's.'

'I hate the dentist,' she muttered, gathering up her coat and bag and deciding that ignorance would have been preferable after all.

'Really, Miss Jordan, I have every confidence—'

'There was that woman on the telly who was told her breast lump was friendly and it wasn't,' she snapped. 'I saw the documentary. Three times she went to see her GP and three times—'

'That's why I am referring you,' he said quietly. 'Now then, do you have someone at home you can talk to about this? You seem a little—'

Annie's mind flicked through her meagre list of possible confidantes, for the first time fully confronting the fact that the three people she relied on most in the world were all absent from the country. 'Heaps. I've heaps of people to talk to about this. No worries on that score at all. So I wait for a letter, do I?' She was at the door, half out of it.

'You should hear before the end of next week.'

Are victims born or made? Annie wondered, as she trudged out of the surgery and into grey drizzle, more like wet air than real rain. Illogical though it was, she was beginning to experience a dim sense of responsibility for this new turn her life had taken. Not just because of a history of ineptitude over her own health, but also because of something inside her head, some grain of hopelessness which she worried she might somehow have allowed to take root. At thirty-three a woman was supposed to be in her prime, she reflected gloomily, peaking in bedrooms and boardrooms alike, finding self-fulfilment and making her mark. At the back of her mind she had always imagined that such a crescendo would eventually be her reward, that although an unsatisfactory childhood might have got her off to a slow start, she would meet the right person, the right job and get there in the end. Wandering alone in the rain, contemplating ghoulish prognoses for her health, without her lover or a friend at hand to offer comfort, Annie was forced to accept that this might not be the case. That such rites of passage were probably the preserve of the Marinas of the world, who managed to leapfrog ruts of trouble and depression instead of slithering into every one like a helpless lemming.

She got back up to her flat to find a note had been slipped under the door.

Some flowers came for you. I took delivery on your behalf. Come up and collect any time. Michael (aka the bloody landlord).

Annie took the stairs two at a time. Her neighbour answered the door with a mask over his mouth and several large metal implements clutched in his left hand. His hair and eyebrows were thickly crusted with white dust, like some clumsy theatrical attempt at ageing. When he slipped the mask down, there was a marked line where the skin around his mouth met the dusty pallor of the rest of his face. At the sight of her, he smiled broadly and then frowned.

'Are you OK?'

She was momentarily taken aback, both by his appearance and the enquiry. 'Why?' she replied, sounding hostile when she knew there was no real need.

'Sorry . . . I only meant . . . you look a bit . . . pale.'

'Pale?' Given his own ashen-faced appearance Annie found it impossible not to laugh. And once she had started she couldn't stop. Realising the focus of her amusement, Michael tried to pat the dust off his cheeks and then burst out laughing himself.

'Actually, you look a lot better now,' he remarked, recovering and eyeing her a little curiously.

'Bad day,' she gasped, stifling another giggle and biting her cheeks in a bid to press the laughter away. Some of it had felt dangerously close to crying, almost like hysteria. 'Overslept, hangover, deadlines – usual stuff—' She swallowed hard. 'Er . . . the flowers?'

'Flowers, of course. Come in a moment. No don't, on second thoughts.' He retreated amongst the complicated tent of dust sheets behind him and emerged with an enormous bunch of yellow roses. 'Someone must love you very much.'

'Probably from my mum.' She made a face.

'Really?'

'Christ, I hope not.' She laughed again, but more naturally this time. 'Thanks so much for taking them.'

'No problem. They might be a little . . . dusty.' He took a big breath and blew at the crowd of yellow heads, which bobbed prettily in response.

As he withdrew, Annie found herself glancing inside for any sign of Jake's scarf. But the door closed before she could get a proper look. She skipped back downstairs, gently hugging the roses to her chest. Tucked amongst the stems beside a packet of plant-feed was a small envelope containing a card.

To Annie, love Greg.

Annie stared hard at the words, wanting to wrest every last drop of meaning from them and wishing they could have been written in something other than the cautious schoolgirl style of an employee of Interflora. Tenderly, she transferred each stem to a vase. After much drifting from room to room, she placed the vase on her bedside table, finding just enough space between her alarm clock and box of tissues.

Before turning out the light that night, Annie kissed the florist's handwriting and propped the note amongst the flowers. After closing her eyes, she could still see the yellow of the half-open buds, glowing like a lantern in the darkness inside her head.

Chapter Twenty-Two

———◆◆◆◆———

There was a way of looking as if you were listening when you weren't really at all, Annie decided, studying Marina through the screen of coffee steam and cigarette smoke. Her skin looked lustrous, a smooth honeyed brown, save for a faint whiteness around her eyes and the occasional pinprick of a freckle. After pronouncing herself determined never to become a marriage-bore, as she called it, she had spent nearly all of their reunion talking of little else, interleaving details of her forthcoming nuptial plans with anecdotes from the slopes of Colorado. When finally she pushed aside the sugar bowl and leant across the table to say, 'but tell me about you Annie – I want to hear everything about how you've been,' Annie felt something harden inside. It felt too much like being given her slot of time, like confidence on demand, as if all the intimate difficulties of the last two weeks could be poured out at the turn of a tap.

'Nothing to say, really.' She looked round for a waitress, waving a five-pound note to cover the cost of their cappuccinos. They had barely had an hour to themselves. Soon Bernard was scheduled to reappear behind the wheel of a borrowed van to help move Marina and her modest assortment of possessions from the flat. A walnut dressing-table, a Victorian coat stand, a full-length mirror and a tea chest with brass hinges. By the evening, Annie would be alone.

There was bound to be a little awkwardness, Marina reminded herself, noting Annie's reticence, a little jealousy even.

The onus was on Annie to accept the situation, to see that their friendship still did – and always would – matter very deeply. 'There's so little time to try it out,' she explained, 'to try living together, I mean. And here I am with only six weeks till D-day. I must be mad,' she concluded, with a grin of utter confidence in her own sanity.

The wedding was to take place on Valentine's Day. Unaccustomed to associating her flatmate with romantic clichés of any kind, Annie had received this news with some incredulity. While Marina, too euphoric to observe anything very much beyond the state of her own happiness, had continued to gush with other related news. The wedding dress had already been bought – from a designer boutique in Miami – and altered to the exact contours of her figure. It hung now in her mother's spacious walk-in wardrobe, ready to accompany her parents when they flew to London. The wedding was to be at a small seventeenth-century chapel in Southwark, with the reception afterwards at a place Annie had never heard of called the Beaumont Gallery, where the curator was an old friend of the Ramsbotham family. The indefatigable Bernard was organising everything, including buttonholes, flowers for the church and a string quartet to play during the party afterwards. He had got so carried away that Marina had had to remind him that it was traditional for the parents of the bride to feel at least fractionally involved in the proceedings. Marina chuckled at the memory, proudly describing the advice-seeking about nosegays and menus which had followed, the manly sigh of resignation with which Bernard had greeted the sight of Frank Hammond's cheque book.

'I'm a selfish cow, I've been talking too much haven't I?' She threw down her napkin in a show of self-disgust. 'Sorry.'

The waitress came and deposited the bill on a side-plate next to Annie's five-pound note. Marina leant across the table and seized it at once. 'I'll do this.' She folded her arms and gave Annie a hard stare. 'But we're not going until you've told me something about yourself. How's the irresistible Greg Berkley for a start? How was last night—?'

'Last night?'

'New Year's Eve – remember? Was it that good you've forgotten? I must say, I never thought spending it on an airplane could be so much fun—' she raced on, momentarily forgetting that she had intended the subject as a conversational prompt for Annie rather than herself. '—though of course precisely *when* midnight occurs with a five-hour time difference is rather open to debate—' By the time she finished, Annie had given up every hope of having the sort of dialogue for which she had longed, and of which she knew herself to be very much in need.

'I spent New Year's Eve in the company of Clive James, actually,' she declared, rather enjoying Marina's look of horror as the implications of this admission sank in. 'With baked beans on toast and half a bottle of Bulgarian red. Greg is skiing, but he sent me beautiful flowers and is coming back tomorrow, so that's OK. Let's see, what else?' She knitted her brows in a show of concentration. 'Oh yes, I gave up smoking till quarter past twelve when Jake phoned, all tipsy and sad to say he's missing London like hell. I lit up without thinking and haven't looked back since. Oh yes, and it wasn't him who wrote that fan letter after all, but some nutter who goes to sleep with my articles under his pillow.'

Marina shrieked with delight. 'Bloody hell. How weird can you get . . . but sort of flattering too I guess . . . And poor old Jake,' she continued, ignoring Annie's scowl, 'how long is he going to be there?'

'A while yet. Though I'm sure he'll jet back for the wedding,' she added quickly, guessing Marina's train of thought. 'He was thrilled for you – said all the right things—'

'So he's missing London, is he? What a shame – when he was so looking forward to going away.'

'Well, maybe not London exactly, but someone—?'

Marina's face lit up at the scent of romantic intrigue. 'You mean that versatile heart of his has mended itself yet again?'

'God knows – I'm only guessing – you know what Jake's like, he won't admit to anything.' On another occasion Annie might have found it amusing to mention the secret liaison between Jake and her newly identified landlord. His evasiveness on the subject during the phone call had been maddening. But without Marina's proper attention, not even gossip seemed appealing.

'Darling Jake. And darling you.' Marina seized Annie's hand, her large brown eyes misty with emotion. 'I know I'm jetlagged and wired up and self-obsessed, but I just want to say that I am truly happier than I have ever been in my life and I know it must seem tedious to you, but if you could just understand—'

'Oh, I do,' insisted Annie earnestly, 'I'm just not doing a great job of showing it . . . perhaps because I've had a bit of a mixed Christmas—'

'Let's make a date this minute for dress shopping,' Marina interjected, hastily wiping her eyes with the back of her hand and pulling out a slim brown leather diary from her handbag.

'Dress shopping?'

'Your dress, Annie.' She beamed. 'Something truly spectacular, like I promised.'

'Spectacular sounds dodgy. I'll settle for inconspicuous.'

'Money no object. We'll have lunch too. What about next Saturday . . . oh no, hang on, I can't. We're spending the weekend with Bernard's parents. Ten acres, horses, a fucking ornamental lake, for Christ's sake – I'm bound to use the wrong fork and throw wine onto the carpet. *And* he's got a younger sister who's modelled for *Vogue*—'

'You'll be fine.'

For a moment Marina's angular face paled with genuine uncertainty and concern. 'It's the only thing he really tricked me about – the money.' She took a deep breath. 'He's so fucking rich it's scary.'

'I'm sure you'll cope,' remarked Annie dryly.

'The Saturday after that looks OK. Shall we aim for that? Hit Knightsbridge in a big way?' Marina drew a thick line across the page in her diary and wrote, *Annie*, in capital letters.

Annie quickly agreed, inwardly quailing at the notion of having to make an appointment, at being fitted into a life of which she had once felt an integral part.

'We'll see each other before that, of course,' continued Marina easily. 'Catch a movie or something.'

'Of course.'

'Shit, I've only got dollars. Could you pay this time and I'll make it up later? Do you mind? I could use a credit card, but we're so late already and Bernard hates it if I'm late. If he changed his mind on me now, I think I'd die. He says if I'm late at the church he'll—'

Annie left her five-pound note and followed Marina and this fresh flow of Bernard-speak out into the street.

When they got back to Shrewsbury Mansions Bernard was sitting in the van reading a book. He wound the window down to greet them, releasing a blast of something operatic from the van radio. Marina stood on tiptoe and tilted back her head for a kiss. Though the embrace was fairly modest in itself, it was succeeded by a lingering eye-to-eye feast of mutual admiration that eventually prompted Annie to make a tactical withdrawal to the front door.

A few hours later they were gone. Annie waved them off from the sitting-room window, fluttering the generous rent cheque Bernard had given her by way of a valediction. Even though it was too dark outside to see them, she knew that they could see her, framed in the window like a figure on a screen. Mostly she was glad to see the back of them; their evident happiness, their endless touching and looking, had been almost too much to bear. Standing beside their tanned, vibrant faces had only made her feel pale and sickly in comparison, unable either to compete or offer relevance on any level. She had busied herself with helping Marina to pack instead, while Bernard made cups of tea and offered an amusing commentary on the proceedings, leaning in the doorway of the bedroom with his arms folded and wearing a smile which seemed to Annie to be tinged with triumph. Presented with such a scenario, every last ember of a hope for a proper talk with Marina died away. She hadn't told her anything about anything, Annie realised with incredulity and much regret as she stood back to let Marina bounce on the last suitcase in order to force it shut. Not even the relatively trivial fact of the absence of Bonnie had been remarked upon.

As Bernard manoeuvred away from the kerb, Annie waved and smiled hard, not wanting either of them to catch a glimpse of the sense of loss for which no amount of rent money or lunches or shopping dates could compensate. You could advertise for a flat-mate, but not a friend, she thought grimly, turning away at last and pulling the curtain closed.

Only the thought of Greg's imminent return from Europe the following day made the prospect of the approaching week seem bearable. Yet it filled her with a certain trepidation as well. The Annie Jordan who had enjoyed the whirlwind of an early romance in the run-up towards Christmas felt like a distant relative compared to the woman staring back at her from the bathroom mirror that Sunday night. Absence didn't make the heart fonder so much as more doubtful, she mused, grimacing at her reflection as if it were a picture in need of restoration and observing that the lopsidedness seemed to have returned with a vengeance.

Thanks to the sachet of plant food, the roses on her bedside table looked even fresher than they had on arrival. All the buds had opened, revealing the layers of velvety petals inside. Like an intimate secret, thought Annie, as she curled up in bed, her hands folded protectively across her chest.

Chapter Twenty-Three

When the stylist was called to the telephone Annie could not resist reaching for a magazine and flicking to her horoscope. It was full of incomprehensible descriptions of planet movements until the final paragraph.

> Initially facing issues is difficult, but once underway, one thing leads to another and you will be able to capitalise on personally rewarding developments. By the beginning of next week you'll be addressing matters you wouldn't have dared to touch a few days before.

Feeling vaguely reassured, she smiled at the girl who had returned to blast the finishing touches to her fringe. The final effect was outrageously bouffant and smooth; but indisputably glamorous too, Annie decided, nodding her head approvingly as the girl held up a mirror to show off the high curve at the back and the clever way the usually feckless side strands swept smoothly into the overall shape.

'Going somewhere special tonight, then?'

'Just a date with my boyfriend. We haven't seen each other since before Christmas,' she added shyly, feeling a sudden shudder of terror as well as pleasurable anticipation at the prospect of her reunion with Greg. As the moment drew nearer, she was beginning to appreciate just how difficult broaching the subject of vagarious breast tissue over a candlelit dinner might be. That she had already confided the matter to thousands of strangers via that weekend's column offered little consolation. In fact it seemed little short of incredible. She had deliberately not bought a copy of the paper herself and in the intervening two days there had not been so much as a murmur of response from any quarter. In fact, Annie was seriously beginning to wonder if the piece had been used at all. It would be just like Amy to pull the plug on her and never say a word.

Greg had phoned that morning, sounding so harried and with such a background hubbub of phones and voices that Annie had shied away from revealing the full extent of her relief and delight at hearing his voice. There would be a right time for more intimate exchanges, she warned herself, fixing her sights on the approaching evening. Just the two of them, he promised, in the Greek place in Kilburn.

'I'll give it an extra spray, shall I? To keep the shape.' The aerosol was whooshed in a deft figure of eight round Annie's ears before she had time to protest. Back out in the street, she could not help slowing to glance at her reflection in every shopfront, wondering whether her lover would like her looking so spruce. Feeling her new coiffure's stout resistance even to the buffeting of the brisk January wind, she began to worry whether the hairspray had been a precaution too far. Peering at herself in the window of WH Smith in the hope of allaying such fears, her eye was caught by a book in the window entitled *Woman and Breast: A Health Guide*. Spurred on by a dim sense of preordination, Annie stepped inside and bought herself a copy, hastily slipping it inside the carrier bag for fear of arousing any speculative interest from the boy at the till, or the man breathing down her neck in the queue behind.

Back at the flat, there was a gulping, curiously low-voiced message on her answering machine from Amy.

'I just want to say I think you're really brave — that is, we think — all of us here think — you're really brave. If you still want to do the holiday slot, that's fine. If not, just say the word. Don't worry about coming in this week, I'll send the stuff for you to look at — brochures and so on. Christ, Annie, Jesus — I mean, this week's FlatLife *was*

just . . . amazing. I don't know what else to say . . . Call me, or whatever. If you want to, that is.'

Annie listened to the message twice, touched and a little guilty to hear her editor talking in such tones, certain that her predicament deserved nothing so extreme. Picking up the carrier bag, she retreated to an armchair, where she was soon scouring every paragraph for references relevant to her own experience, grimly fascinated by the mysterious and wilful machinations of a part of the body that she realised now she had always taken for granted. At the chapter entitled, *Causes of Breast Disease*, she slowed to read with particular care, a part of her hoping for more answers than had yet been provided by the doctors. Even though she had already been notified of an appointment for a cytology test that Friday, it would be several days after that before she received a definitive diagnosis.

Spurred on by numerous references to the possible links between all her favourite vices and breast disease, Annie was disappointed to find that the conclusions of the chapter were as evasive as the horoscope at the hairdresser's. There were no easy answers, she realised, pausing for a somewhat vengeful lighting of a cigarette and telling herself to leave the rest of the book till later. The doctor had said her growth was almost certainly benign. There was no need to spook herself with worst-case scenarios. A few minutes later she was nevertheless engrossed in the next chapter. Not out of morbid curiosity so much as a dim sense that finding out the worst might somehow armour her against it happening. As the light from the window faded, she absently reached out and switched on the table lamp beside her, casting a dramatic silhouette of her shadow against the wall behind. By the time she had reached the final section – on hospice care and the rights of the dying – she was clutching the arm of the chair as the words swam before her eyes.

> Our choices are as real in the last months as at any other juncture in our lives. We may decide that we want to spend the time quietly with those we love, or we may choose not to have any further treatment. We have so much to learn from each

other at such times. With those who die and those who survive, there is a world of experience to understand and to share.

Annie closed the book with a curious sense of elation, afraid but somehow ennobled. She had read for so long that it was pitch black outside. There was barely time to wax her legs or ponder what to wear. Was vanity merely lack of confidence? she wondered, quickly picking out a short skirt and a grey silk shirt with a pretty collar. Hurriedly dabbing on her make-up, she had the strongest sensation that she was not enhancing her features so much as burying them, painting on a mask for the world's benefit rather than her own.

To her amazement, Greg, who was always late, was already sitting with an open bottle of wine waiting for her. Glimpsing him unawares for a second or two, Annie was surprised to feel a small twist of disappointment at how hunched and gloomy he looked, fiddling with the wax dribbling from the table candle like a bored child. On seeing her, he immediately straightened and smiled, revealing a glorious facial tan and dispelling all her doubts in an instant. For the first half-hour they busied themselves with the menu and an easy exchange of pleasantries about family Christmases and the allure of mountains and snow. When Annie related the episode about the intruder, he was suitably horrified and reached across the table to pat her hand. She was just wondering how to nudge the conversation into even more intimate territory when he sighed and said he had some bad news.

'A work crisis, I suppose you could call it. I'm afraid your earliest predictions for the fate of *RoundUp* are looking uncannily accurate. If we don't start to see an improvement in circulation in the next few months, we'll have to fold.' He carefully balanced his knife and fork on opposite edges of his plate and crossed his arms. 'It will mean seeing less of each other, I'm afraid Annie. A lot less.' He studied her gravely. 'I'm so sorry.'

'Oh dear, Greg, I'm sorry too . . . for you. But it needn't affect us. Not if we don't let it. Seeing each other at weekends for a while is fine by me. The truth is, I've got some bad news of my own, which I wanted to tell you myself, before you heard it from anyone else.' Alerted by the sudden look of intensity that flooded his face, Annie hastened on, pouring out her fears and telling him about the letter she had received summoning her to a breast clinic for tests that Friday. 'So it will all be resolved one way or another soon enough. But I've been slightly on edge about it, as you might imagine, and of course you had to know, you of all people—'

'Do you feel ill?' he asked, sounding not so much sympathetic as appalled.

'No, not in the slightest.' She was relieved to see his expression soften. 'I feel completely normal. I probably *am* completely normal—' she put down her own cutlery '—but suddenly not very hungry. I'm not mad about Greek food,' she confessed, surprised to see that this delayed admission created no discernible reaction at all. 'Would you mind if we left?' she faltered, '—Went back to your flat – I just feel—'

'My flat?' The look of anxiety returned to his face in an instant. 'No – but – let me see now, I was thinking it might make a nice change to stay at your place.'

'My place? But we're in Kilburn now—'

'It doesn't matter. I'll get them to call a cab. My pad is a tip – ski poles and dirty washing – much better not to see it.' He laughed with an uncertainty she did not recognise. 'Unless of course, you'd rather be alone.'

'Alone?' It was Annie's turn to look appalled. 'No,' she stammered, suddenly embarrassed at her need of him, wary that if she revealed too much of it he might shy away. 'I was rather looking forward to becoming reacquainted.' She smiled her most dimpled smile, inwardly dumbfounded.

'Great. Thought I'd better ask.' He hesitated, before adding, 'Just want to do the right thing, Annie.'

She reached across the table and clutched his hand, loving and wanting him with, if anything, even more fervour than before. 'Thank you, Greg, that's sweet. But throughout my extensive research into the subject I have so far found nothing to suggest that sharing a bed is bad for suspect tumours. In fact, if the book I read this afternoon is to be believed, anything that assists in the release of tension is positively good—'

'Would you mind terribly if I made a quick phone call and then finished up here first?' he interjected, gesturing rather sheepishly at his plate of food and the half-bottle of wine. 'You could have a coffee or—'

Annie held up both hands to silence him. 'I'm fine. You eat. I'll watch. I really don't mind at all,' she insisted, minding a little but telling herself it was extremely unreasonable of her to do so. The man had a right to his dinner.

'I'm writing about it in my column, by the way,' she explained, when he had returned from the phone booth, 'you probably ought to know about that too.'

He stopped, a slithering forkful of aubergine halfway to his mouth. 'You're what?'

'My Saturday column. I'm covering this breast lump thing.'

'Why, for God's sake? I thought it was supposed to be funny stuff that you made up.'

'It is – or at least it was . . . Oh Christ, I don't know, it just sort of slipped out last week and now I've started, I think I'll see it through. Some of it's still a bit funny . . . I think.'

'It's up to you, of course.' He had resumed eating, taking large swigs of wine between mouthfuls.

'Yes it is,' she agreed quietly, suddenly longing for a cigarette, but knowing it would be rude to smoke while he was still eating. After his main course he ordered a pudding, coffee and a brandy, seeking her permission first, but in such a way that it felt impossible to refuse. Though genuinely not hungry, Annie found herself accepting a few mouthfuls of dessert – a sweet yoghurty affair which set her teeth on edge – just to make him feel more at ease. By the time they left the restaurant, she could not help noticing that he was visibly unsteady on his feet, which made her wonder if there had been a precursor to the wine and brandy. Within a few minutes of getting into the taxi, his head had lolled sideways onto her shoulder.

The same thing happened when they got into Annie's bed, only this time to the accompaniment of some throaty snores.

Annie cradled his head in her arms, endeavouring to feel loving as opposed to merely deprived. Skiing was an exhausting business, she reasoned, not to mention the pressure of running a floundering news journal. But at the back of her mind she could not help remembering the run of late nights preceeding Christmas, when no amount of alcohol or tiredness had had any detrimental effect on his surges of testosterone. Lying there in the dark, her arms going numb under the dead weight of his head and shoulders, Annie found herself wondering whether her talk of growths and doctors had turned things sour; whether a part of him – maybe even a subconscious part – simply felt too intimidated to touch her in the way he had before.

Chapter Twenty-Four

Jake, sitting at a small wobbly metal table outside an ice-cream parlour facing the sea, with the dregs of some cold coffee and a stack of unwritten postcards beside him, wondered if he was experiencing something similar to the pain Annie liked to moan about, when faced with one of her deadlines. Certainly, the blank spaces on the postcards seemed to demand an exercise of energy and inspiration which he felt thoroughly disinclined to provide. While much of this apathy could be attributed to his enthusiastic exploration of Marbellan nightlife, Jake knew that a greater portion of it derived – in spite of considerable efforts to the contrary – from his failure to have a good time.

It was far worse being unhappy when one had so hoped otherwise. Especially in a holiday resort, surrounded by people hellbent upon indulgence and the pursuit of pleasure. At the table next to him an English couple with strong Manchester accents were sharing a large fluorescent green ice-cream, taking it in turns to lick round the edges and giggling suggestively every time their tongues touched.

Having longed for a day off on his own, away from the tedium of the set, Jake had found himself quite at a loss as to what to do with it. With the vague aim of becoming acquainted with something a little more Hispanic than a continental break-fast and an Irish pub run by a retired Glaswegian footballer, he had hopped on a bus heading east out of Marbella, only to find himself amongst increasingly dense thickets of holiday towers and ugly concrete hotels. Between each building were other half-finished carcasses of holiday accommodation and patches of scrubby wasteland. Even the sea looked less beautiful, bobbing with bits of broken plastic and waves that lapped as much froth as water onto the sand.

Dear Annie, Jake wrote before pausing. Even through the drunken fug of his phone call on New Year's Eve, he had found time to worry about her. No one should spend such times alone, especially not when they had almost been mugged in their own home and when they were as lovely as Annie and deserving of so much more happiness than they ever seemed to get. Jake flinched at the recollection of the absurd mix-up over the letters. He should have written. After all his promises to do so, who could blame her for assuming the epistolary admirer to be him? Having a real crackpot for a fan made her feel like a real colum-nist, she had reassured him. But he had felt ashamed nonetheless, and a little despairing. The episode, trivial though it was, contributed to his overall sense that life was slipping out of his control, that since meeting Michael Derwent he had lost his balance, or whatever it was that had allowed him to be reckless and excessive without falling into misfortune. He couldn't stop thinking about the man. Couldn't stop wanting him. Not even after copious quantities of alcohol or one of the expensive little packets of white powder that were as readily available as cold beer and nicotine.

> *Just a line from your other 'secret admirer', the truly devoted one, who can guarantee no sexual overtones at all. Filming is duller than ever. But next week I get to say my three lines, so things are looking up. Research into local nightlife has been predictable and painful (i.e. sore head). Take care of yourself. Hope your reunion with GB was deliciously worth the wait. Cuddles, Jake.*

Writing to Michael was harder. So much so that Jake ordered a cognac to go with a second coffee and had drained all but the last drop before picking up his Biro again.

Dear Michael,
I hope you have forgiven me.

It was several minutes before he could think of anything satisfactory to add, not for lack of thoughts, so much as fear of expressing them ineptly.

Thank you for keeping an eye on Annie. Like I said, she's frightfully good at having a hard time and not admitting to it. I'd still rather not tell her about us, if that's all right by you.

After that it seemed simplest just to sign his name, which he did with his customary flourish, the line across the top of the J reaching far beyond the end of the last letter. Before posting it, Jake took the precaution of slipping the card into an envelope, to ensure that the contents were for Michael's eyes alone.

Early on the Wednesday of that week, Annie was summoned downstairs to take charge of a fat brown envelope that would not fit through the letterbox. Still in her dressing-gown, self-consciously haggard with sleep, she accepted her package without looking the postman in the eye. Amongst the mail already on the doormat was a postcard of a bullfighter from Jake and a thick, white, beautifully italicised envelope, which she identified at once as being the hand of Marina at her neatest and most elaborate. The wedding invitation, she thought, with a twist of disbelief followed by girlish excitement on Marina's behalf. Pausing to brush some unruly strands of hair from her eyes, her attention was caught by a Spanish stamp on one of Michael Derwent's letters. Of course, Jake would be writing to him too, she mused, bending down to identify the writing and then hurriedly straightening at the sound of footsteps on the stairs.

'Good morning. Anything for me?' He was wearing a pinstripe three-piece suit, over which hung a beautifully tailored long dark overcoat. Slung loosely round its wide lapels was a pale blue cashmere scarf that highlighted the fierce colour of his eyes. Gripped in his left hand was a smooth black leather briefcase, embossed in gold with the letters MD.

Annie tugged self-consciously at the edges of her dressing-gown – a tartan wool one of Pete's which had somehow become a permanent feature of her wardrobe. 'Yes, several. I was just going—'

He quickly knelt down and rifled through the remaining envelopes, before clipping open his briefcase and slipping them inside.

'A wine consultant day today, I take it?' she murmured, stepping past him and heading for the stairs.

He made a sweeping apologetic gesture at his clothes as he stood up. 'Costumes help, don't you find? You look pretty good yourself.'

She blushed and scowled at her dressing-gown. 'It's ghastly, I know, but warm. I keep meaning to throw it out—'

'No further word from the police, I suppose?'

'Nothing . . . not yet anyway.'

'I thought I might change the locks,' he went on, 'have something more solid put on, maybe even a burglar alarm – what do you think?' She was about to answer – to say she wouldn't mind at all – when he burst out, 'Look you're frozen – go back to bed – get dressed – whatever – we can discuss it another time. Haven't you even got slippers, for God's sake?'

Annie laughed uncertainly before scampering up to the landing and out of sight, her mail clutched to her chest.

Much to her astonishment, the large brown envelope contained not only brochures, but fan mail on a scale beyond her most ambitious dreams. Having begun reading ravenously, tearing each letter open, revelling in the intoxicating sense of being appreciated and responded to, Annie soon found her ardour giving way to something rather more complicated. Compared to many of the case histories recounted in the letters, most of them revealed with an agonising lack of fanfare or complaint, her own plight seemed utterly paltry. Soon, the tears filling her eyes were seriously affecting her capacity to continue.

Abandoning her reading, she boiled the kettle, intermittently blowing her nose and trying to take stock of what was happening; to equate the unguarded, wine-induced out-pourings of the previous week with the deluge of sympathy and confessions spread on the table beside her.

For a while she sought distraction amongst the travel brochures which had been forwarded in the same envelope, trying to focus on snapshots of balcony views and lovers entwined round kidney-shaped swimming pools.

Clipped to the one on Italy was a handwritten note from Amy.

> *Annie,*
>   *I've a feeling these letters are just the start of it. Obviously it's exciting for all of us in the Saturday team but, much more importantly, I hope they bring some comfort to you.*
>   *Herewith too a sampling of what Foreign Relations have to offer. They do Germany and France as well but I thought the enclosed looked the most appealing. Like I said, you are free to pull out of the assignment altogether, though could you let me know soonish(?), so we can sort out a replacement. Sorry to rush you. I know you must be going through a pretty rough time right now. Miles and I do hope you will still make the party next weekend.*

The party would be hard, Annie realised, with everybody thinking things they dare not say and speculating madly the moment her back was turned. Yet she knew too that it was something that had to be got through, that the first confronta-tion with acquaintances since the revelation of her gynaecological worries would always be potentially the most awkward. She thought with gratitude of Greg's promise to accompany her, delivered as he flew out of the flat on Tuesday morning. He would be putty in her hands from Saturday after-noon onwards, he had promised, to make up for their enforced exile from each other for the remainder of the week.

Annie pushed the brochures aside and reached for another

letter. A holiday for lust-crazed singletons was the last thing she needed or wanted. Everyone would understand. She would tell Amy to ask the lovely Yvonne instead. Absently, she ran her finger under the seal of the envelope in her hands.

Dearest Annie Jordan,
  The doctor that gets to touch your breasts is a lucky man.
As I write I can smell your skin, feel the softness of you.
God, the very thought of it is making me hard. Now as I
write I'm rubbing my—

Annie stuffed the letter back into its envelope, determined to try and ignore it, not to let it cast a shadow over all the other wonderful correspondence which had given such an unexpectedly uplifting start to the day. Slowly, she gathered up the other letters and retreated to the spare room. She had a proper audience now, she reminded herself, punching the keys to open her *FlatLife* file.

I would like to begin by saying how truly moved—
I cannot describe my feelings on receiving—
To all of you who have written letters to me this week, I
would like to say an enormous—

It took a while for Annie to realise that to be funny was still permissible, that humour could raise the intensity of an emotion as well as lower it. That it could make difficult things palatable, in life as much as on the page.

If I had only known what a potentially life-threatening medical condition would do to my weekly mail bag I would have been tempted to make up something months ago. Such a small lump doesn't seem worthy of such a big response. Happily my GP wasn't impressed with it either (how come a doctor feeling your breast is so completely unlike sex?) and has referred me to more doctors who are going to do things with needles that I prefer not to think about . . . What I hadn't expected was that the process I seem to be going through should prove to be so good for me. Not just because of the postman staggering to my door under the weight of all your lovely letters, but because I have embarked on enough research into the mysteries of the human body to retake my O level Biology (yes, I know it's a GCSE, but what I failed was called an O level) . . .

. . . It's not just breast tissue either on which I have become an expert. While waiting at the doctor's this week I also learnt many fascinating things about the head louse – a friendly unsuspecting creature, judging by the diagrams, and one which deserves a lot more respect than it currently earns. For tenacity under threat of chemical annihilation if nothing else. Contrary to popular opinion, the poor little darlings can't even jump, but have to cling to a hair to sustain themselves. Nit combs *break* their legs. Cruel or what? I have high hopes of learning yet more spellbinding aspects of our human and animal life on the wall charts at the clinic I'm due to attend this Friday. Who knows? I could become the next media expert on women's health, that is if I have time to read anything other than your letters, of which I shall have a whole stack to get through and each one of which reminds me that I am fortunate and being thought about, which is about the most any human can ask for.

Annie sat back with a sigh of satisfaction both at the knowledge that she had produced something acceptable and would not be called upon to do so again for another seven days. Stiff with cold from having sat in her dressing-gown for so long, she decided to run a bath. On the way past Marina's room she could not resist pushing open the door and peering inside. Dusty rectangles marked the spaces where her pictures had hung. Hair grips, rubber bands and fluff balls lined the edges of the carpet. The mattress was stained brown and bulging with a forced re-distribution of its contents. Not only the emptiness, but the ugliness, of it was somehow shocking. As was Annie's subsequent realisation that she felt no particular longing to have

Marina back. Having the flat to herself had begun to feel almost normal. The thought of again having to surrender some of her space to another human being was growing less appealing by the day. But remained an unavoidable necessity, Annie reminded herself, closing the door of the spare room and continuing down the hall. Bernard's cheque would tide her over nicely for a couple of months, but in the longer term she definitely would not be able to manage.

Before taking her clothes off, Annie checked the blinds were fully closed. She stepped into the bath and slipped down until the water level was tickling her earlobes. Taking the soap bar she washed herself with extra care, working her fingers slowly over her body, showing herself a tenderness that felt new. When she had rinsed away the lather she sat up and began to press her fingers under each armpit and across her breasts, feeling the map of her body for any additional contour that should not be there. Closing her eyes, she worked systematically as the book had suggested, using small circular movements with her fingertips. It was a relief to feel that nothing had changed, that there was still just the one lump, so small and discreetly sited that unless you looked hard you would never know it was there.

Annie spent the rest of the day reading and answering letters, working in long hand and writing several pages to each correspondent. By the evening she was barely a third of the way through the pile. Feeling drained, but curiously satisfied, she tumbled into bed without a single qualm at how many hours she had spent in the silence of her own company. Nor did she remember to spare a thought for the now seriously ageing bunch of yellow roses in the vase beside her alarm clock, steadily shedding petals amongst her bedside knick-knacks like a tree in the cut of an autumn breeze.

Chapter Twenty-Five

On seeing that Michael's motorbike was the size of a large pony, all Annie's doubts about involving him resurfaced. The policeman who had phoned early that morning to invite her to view a line-up of twelve suspects in a North London Witness Identity Suite had clearly assumed she would be coming alone. They had a man in custody for a series of burglary charges who fitted the description of her assailant, he explained, and would value her assistance. Though pleased, Annie's mounting apprehensions at undergoing such an experience on her own had eventually driven her to Michael Derwent's door to ask if he would consider coming too.

The sight of him evidently already hard at work, in stiff, paint-daubed jeans and a torn rag of a T-shirt, had almost prompted her to turn on her heel without making any request at all. 'Look, honestly, I can cope perfectly well on my own,' she assured him, having explained the situation. 'You're busy, you're still covered in paint – I shouldn't have asked.'

'I said I'd help out in any way I could, and I meant it,' he insisted. 'Going on the bike will be far quicker. I've got a spare helmet.' As he spoke he peeled off his T-shirt and quickly reached for a clean, long-sleeved shirt hanging on the back of a hall chair. But not so quickly that Annie did not have time to observe his torso, moulded into muscular shapes that she normally associated with male underwear adverts in glossy magazines. The perfect complement to Jake, she mused, who was effortlessly thin, but in the reedy, bony way of a starved girl. Annie felt a surge of impatience to quiz Michael on the subject, to burst the silly bubble of mystery surrounding their acquaintance once and for all. She opened her mouth but closed it again. After the morning's excursion was over, she told herself, looking away as he tucked in the tails of his shirt and making a polite study of a chip in the door frame instead.

'I've even got a spare set of leathers if you want them.' He eyed her skirt doubtfully, sucking in his bottom lip to disguise a smile. 'Though you might want to consider a rethink on your outfit—'

'I am perfectly happy as I am,' retorted Annie, who had spent some considerable time selecting a skirt that was dowdy enough for a visit to a police station and yet smart enough for her to be taken seriously. 'I shall manage perfectly well. I've ridden on motorbikes before,' she added defensively, by way of reference to a brief teenage fling with a would-be hell's angel, whose meagre monthly allowance had enabled the purchase of a small, single-seater moped. With Annie wedged behind him, the lover in question had made up for the shortcomings of his machine by driving with great gusto, screeching yee-has of excitement at every corner, even when they were going slow enough for Annie to hop off and walk alongside.

'So you know all about the art of pillion riding then, and will need no tutoring from me,' said Michael, once they were both out on the kerb.

'None at all.' She pulled on her helmet, which was much too large, and fiddled with the strap, which was much too tight.

'Here, let me. Suck your chin in.'

'That's a physical impossibility.'

'Well try. There we are.'

'I can't talk,' she complained, through clenched jaws.

'You won't need to – I won't be able to hear you anyway.'

A few minutes later they were weaving their way in and out of the bottlenecks of traffic caught at every set of lights up the Finchley Road. In spite of the circumstances, Annie, gripping wedges of leather jacket between her hands, could not help being a little thrilled. A dour, dreadful morning had been suddenly and unexpectedly transformed. It helped that the sun was high in a blue sky, surrounded by ripples of white cloud, no bigger or more threatening than shimmers of waves on a pond. Though still bare of buds or colour, there was a sense of life about the swaying trees and in the occasional snatches of brilliant green grass visible through the slats of garden gates and fences.

Thanks to a close study of the A–Z before they left, Michael drove without stopping once – as Annie knew she would undoubtedly have had to – either to consult a map or to seek advice from pedestrians. Whenever the coast was clear he accelerated, taking detours down pretty, tree-lined streets to avoid the crush of the main roads and swerving expertly round the humps designed to slow the progress of cars.

Contrary to its rather luxurious-sounding title, the Witness Identity Suite turned out to be a grey concrete block round the back of a police station. They were met and chaperoned by a uniformed policeman, introducing himself as the inspector in charge. The whole process was very quick and formal. After filling out a form and then overcoming the initial shock of seeing twelve sullen-faced men staring at her, Annie dared to step closer to the glass for a proper look. The police officer had cautioned her to take her time, but it was only a matter of seconds before she spotted her would-be assailant, four men down the line, his spriggy black hair more matted than ever, his shoe laces trailing and caked with mud. She pointed and whispered her choice, glancing at Michael for support.

He nodded at once. 'Annie got a better look, but I'd swear that was him.'

'So what happens now?' asked Annie, lightheaded with relief both that the harrowing part was over and that it had proved so relatively easy.

'If you'll accompany me back outside, I'll explain—'

The three of them strolled back across the station yard while the officer broke the tiresome news that she now had to return to her local station and see the investigating officer in charge of her case. A further statement was required, he explained, as well as a decision on whether to pursue her charges into the courts.

At the last moment, when Michael was already levering himself back onto the bike, it occurred to Annie to ask about harassing mail and what if anything could be done about it. 'I've even got an example with me,' she explained eagerly, rummaging in the side pocket of her handbag where she had stuffed the latest sample.

'Being bothered in all directions, aren't you?' remarked the policeman, watching her closely.

'Sort of.'

He glanced at the letter before handing it back. 'Your best bet is to show all the correspondence down at your local station and ask them to advise you. Though, for what it's worth, in my experience games like this are usually played by someone you know. My daughter got nasty phone calls for a while – and some hate-mail too. Carried on for weeks. Went ex-directory, changed the locks and everything. Turned out it was her ex-husband out to make trouble.'

'Oh dear. Did he go to jail?'

The officer laughed, revealing a handsome bridge of gold connecting his lower back molars. 'Nah. Once she realised it was him, he gave up and apologised. She withdrew all charges and he fell in love with someone else.' He laughed again, rocking back on his heels. 'That's human nature for you, eh? Him in there,' he gestured at the concrete block behind them, 'has confessed to enough to get ten years without your help,' he added kindly, perhaps responding to the look of perturbation on Annie's face, 'so you can rest easy now on that score, whether you pursue your accusation or not.'

The return journey was less enjoyable. Michael seemed to drive much faster, taking bends at disconcerting angles and sometimes squeezing through such narrow gaps that Annie felt compelled to press her elbows and knees inwards by way of a precaution against losing a limb. The wind felt colder too, cutting in through the cracks in her clothes and making her eyes stream no matter how she positioned her head.

Although she tried to put the matter from her mind, the words of the officer kept coming back to her. What if her warped correspondent wasn't a stranger at all, but someone she knew, winding her up for the hell of it? Not Jake or Marina, certainly, and definitely not Greg. But Bernard possibly? His distrust of her was all too evident. Or maybe someone at work? Annie forced herself to scroll through colleagues whom she might have snubbed or misled over the past year, but could think of nothing more contentious than a jogged elbow and the odd irritating typo. A more obvious suspect was Pete, she decided, perhaps making a last-ditch effort to regain her attention. Maybe the coy Christmas card had just been a smoke-screen for a grander scheme? The notion was so disconcerting that she lost the concentration keeping her pinned to the middle of the pillion seat. The bike lurched left, caught the edge of the kerb and swerved sharply right, before regaining its balance just as a stream of traffic came pouring alongside.

'What the hell happened there?' Michael barked over his shoulder, during a pause at a red light. 'For a minute I thought you were trying to jump off.'

'Sorry,' she shouted back, catching her breath as they took off again, overtaking a van driver who caught her eye and stuck his middle finger in the air by way of a greeting.

Instead of going straight to the police station as they had agreed, Michael brought the bike to a halt outside the coffee shop where Annie had spent her disappointing reunion with Marina.

He pulled his helmet off with a voluble sigh of relief. 'Time for refreshments, don't you agree?'

'I don't know, I'd really rather—'

'They do these great pastries in here – filled with raisins and cinnamon and topped with icing sugar.'

'I know, but I—'

'You've got mascara down to your chin, by the way.'

'Have I? Bollocks.' Annie groped in her bag for a tissue. Using one of his wing-mirrors, she spent a few moments cursing quietly and wiping the worst of the black rivulets off her cheeks. 'Look . . . I think I'll walk home from here if it's all the same to you,' she continued, endeavouring to rake some order into her hair, which one wash – not to mention the confines of a helmet – had restored to its usual wilful mess. 'Though can I just say again that I am *extremely* grateful—'

'Have a coffee, for God's sake – you're dying for one, I know you are. We'll sit in smokers' corner,' he added slyly, taking hold of her arm and pulling her after him. 'And anyway, you can't go home until you've been to the local nick, remember?'

'I'll walk there too,' she began, but they were already inside the café, being greeted by a wonderful smell of coffee beans and a wan waitress in a long dark skirt. A moment later Annie was pretending to scrutinise the menu and wondering how to make the most of such a good opportunity to explore her suspicions.

'You've become friends with Jake, haven't you?' she blurted, once the waitress had strolled away with their order.

There was a visible rush of colour to his cheeks. 'We have . . . got to know each other a bit, yes,' he admitted, picking at a blob of paint on his trousers and looking, for the first time in their sporadic, somewhat bizarre acquaintance, truly at a loss. 'He's . . . um . . . he seems very nice.'

'Yes, he is,' muttered Annie, wishing already that she had left the subject alone. The sight of Michael Derwent squirming was not nearly as enjoyable as she had expected. He and Jake had their right to privacy as much as any couple. Hurriedly she returned to the topic of their morning's adventure, telling him what the policeman had said about the man going to jail anyway, and how she saw little point in taking her own case any further.

While offering all the right commentaries, Annie could not help noticing that Michael grew progressively subdued and preoccupied. Having ordered a sticky Danish studded with raisins, he left half of it uneaten, spending most of the time instead chasing flakes of pastry round the plate with his finger-tips. As they were leaving, he repeated his offer to accompany her to the station, but with none of his original insistence, making it all the easier for her to refuse. Annie set off on her own instead, leaving Michael to roar off on his motorbike, his spare helmet strapped to the seat behind.

Chapter Twenty-Six

Pete Rutherford followed Annie for several yards before daring to catch her up. He couldn't get over how different she looked, how very much slimmer and more . . . He struggled to think of the word. Poised. That was it, she looked poised, as if some invisible inner component had slotted into place. That such a process should have occurred when she was meant to be ill and after, as opposed to during, their two-year relationship was as disheartening as Pete's certain belief that he himself had not fared so well. A brief fling with a secretary at the graphic designers where he used to work had come to nothing and been followed by a six-month trauma of redundancy and job-hunting. Although he had eventually secured a promising position at a reputable firm in Kennington, the experience had left him scarred with an innate sense of insecurity. Seeing Annie reminded him more sharply than ever of the bright days of his early thirties, when self-confidence had been something to take for granted, when a game of squash left him merely stiff as opposed to seized up, when hair grew on all parts of his head. Remembering this relatively new cause for self-consciousness, Pete hesitated for a moment, briefly touching the exposed patch of his scalp, before hurrying to catch Annie up.

'Annie, hi there.' Considerable deliberation on the subject had caused Pete to accept the fact that there was no clever or easy way of announcing his presence.

She stopped, looking amazed. Then flung her arms round

him in a brief sisterly – but nonetheless encouraging – embrace of welcome.

'But Pete this is weird – I was just thinking about you – well, not right now but earlier this morning—' In spite of her earlier broodings, Annie found it hard to feel remotely threatened now that her former boyfriend was actually standing in front of her. On the contrary, it was curiously pleasant to see him. Remembering the icy acrimony that had coloured their final, drawn-out weeks together, she smiled in disbelief. 'How are you?'

'How are you, Annie?' he countered earnestly, peering at her with his soft brown eyes in a way that she recalled as having once found rather endearing.

'Surviving—'

'I know, I know,' he cut in, nodding his head mournfully.

'What do you know?'

'I read your column . . . I always have,' he faltered.

'Bloody hell, do you?' She was appalled, but also a little impressed.

'I'm so sorry you're ill, but you look great,' he added, sounding almost accusing.

'Thanks Pete, but I'm fine, really I am. I'm having some tests tomorrow which will probably prove that it's all been a fuss about nothing.' She waved her arms dismissively, not wanting to discuss her fears. 'But what an amazing coincidence bumping into you—'

'It's not a coincidence,' he declared flatly, pushing his hands into his coat pockets and looking at the pavement.

Annie found herself overtaken by the urge to be kind. 'We could talk and walk for a bit, if you like,' she offered gently, linking her arm through his. 'You're not writing me dodgy letters, by any chance, are you – out of delayed post-relationship revenge or something?'

'No I am not.' He looked sufficiently mortified at the idea for Annie to believe he was telling the truth. 'Unless you're referring to my Christmas card?'

'Of course not.'

'What sort of letters, for God's sake?'

She shrugged. 'Hard to categorise, really. They began as complimentary but are getting progressively twisted. The last one was full of some pretty perverted stuff – all about some sexual fantasy he has – tying me up against a garden trellis, if I understood it correctly – it got a bit complicated towards the end.'

'Have you been to the police?'

'I'm thinking about it.' They walked on in silence for a few moments, until Annie, deterred by the way his fingers were stroking her wrist, pulled her arm free. 'What do you want, Pete?'

'I want to be with you,' he whispered, not looking at her. 'I want to try again.'

For a nanosecond of a moment Annie was astonished to find herself tempted to acquiesce. Pete was a known quantity, something which, however maddening and uninspired, could be relied upon to deliver copious supplies of sympathy and support – emotional items of which she knew herself to be sorely in need. Being with Greg, in contrast, with all his dashing unreliability and vacillating surges of attention, was like flying in the dark. 'Oh Pete, you oaf,' she said softly. 'We were a disaster, from start to finish. I'd be horrible to you – chew you up and spit you out when I'd done.'

'Is it because of . . . him?' he interjected, '. . . The man with the motorbike?'

'The man with the . . . you mean Michael Derwent?' Annie laughed out loud. 'Not because of him, no. He's my neighbour – and landlord, as it turns out. And – apart from anything else,' she continued with a light laugh, 'he's got a thing going with Jake. Remember Jake?' she asked slyly, recalling with pained amusement how badly the two of them had got along.

'Yeah, I remember Jake.' Pete sighed and then spent several moments shaking his head from side to side. Like a forlorn bear, thought Annie, watching him and feeling sad. 'I just can't bear the thought of you being ill, Annie,' he continued bleakly. He extracted a large clean blue handkerchief from his coat pocket into which he blew four trumpeting snorts in quick succession. Annie's nerves jarred at the sound, as they always had. She caught herself remembering the hanky too, how carefully he would iron it and its rainbow of companions, fussing round the corners like an old woman.

'And I forbid you to be so funereal about my health,' she exclaimed, throwing up her hands. They had been standing for several minutes by a Belisha beacon. Passing cars kept slowing to let them cross and giving them curious looks when they made no move towards the zebra crossing. 'I feel fine. And everyone – everyone who knows – is being so kind—' Annie broke off with an uncertain laugh, feeling quite unequal to the task of articulating the spectrum of emotions generated by all the letters of support from her readers. 'Including you. Now please, I think you better go.'

'I think maybe you're right.'

The clench of bravery in his face moved her far more than anything she ever remembered from their past.

'Bugger off then, before I start getting sentimental.'

'I wouldn't mind one bit if you did—'

'But it wouldn't be good . . . not in the end.'

He mouthed a goodbye at her before shuffling to the edge of the road and over the zebra crossing. He lowered his eyes to the ground and kept them there, even when an impatient driver made a big show of screeching his brakes and slamming his palms on his steering wheel.

Annie presented herself at the police station in something of a daze. When she explained her reluctance to subject herself to the rigours of pressing charges, the investigating officer was pleasantly reassuring, reiterating his colleague's view that the man would go down for a good stretch anyway and sympathising with her anxiety to put the incident behind her and get on with her life. Of the letter, she made no mention at all, not out of reticence so much as a sudden revelatory sense as to how trivial it was. They were only words on a page, she told herself, potent only if she allowed them to be, by doing the obliging thing of worrying about them. A few yards outside the police station there was a lime-green public waste bin. She took the most recent offering from her bag and began to tear it into tiny pieces, each large enough to accommodate no more than a single word of this latest crude testimony of adoration: '*Dreams . . . slackening . . . ropes . . . trellis . . . masturbate . . . admirer.*' Separated from each other their meanings were defused, impotent, even amusing, Annie decided, brushing the palms of her hands together with satisfaction as the shreds of paper fluttered down amongst a sticky jumble of empty cans and torn Styrofoam.

Chapter Twenty-Seven

Seated in the waiting room of the Mary Louth Breast Clinic the following morning, all of Annie's bravery – that innate belief in her own invincibility – dissolved. Whoever had designed the room had obviously done so with the precarious mental state of prospective patients in mind, she reflected gloomily, surveying the soft pastel shades and the tasteful framed prints on the walls. Directly opposite her was a faded lilac version of Monet's waterlilies, which she studied with exaggerated concentration, counting brushstrokes of colour as if her life depended on it. Although the room was quite crowded, there was a sense of subdued stoicism in the atmosphere, quite unlike the bored fidgeting and coughing of her regular surgery. Annie found it was impossible to look at any of her fellow patients without speculating as to how sick they were. While another despicable, scared part of her didn't want to acknowledge them at all. As if keeping herself separate was the only way to feel less afflicted.

The door leading to the consulting rooms opened and a young, dark-haired girl appeared, followed by a woman with uncannily similar features and grey bun in place of the girl's tidy bob. The girl looked as if she had been crying. Or maybe her eyes were always like that, Annie reasoned, scolding herself for being melodramatic and trying not to stare as the pair made their way across the room to the water dispenser in the corner. Though the girl was clearly well into her twenties, her mother had charge of coats and bags and was fussing round like an attentive parent with a toddler. She took a paper cup, filled it with water and handed it to the girl, all the while talking quietly and soothingly about getting home and cups of tea and rests. Annie had to fight the urge to put her hands over her ears, not just because it was sad – because of the injustice of the elder being so evidently more robust – but also because it brought home to her quite how alone she was in her own predicament. The only person close to her who knew so far was Greg, whose tentative offer to accompany her she had refused out of hand. Partly because he was clearly so frantic at work, but mainly because she was anxious not to make him any more unnerved by her condition than he clearly was already. Thousands of readers might express sympathy, she thought wryly, but there was still no one available to share a vigil in a waiting room. Least of all a mother who seemed to regard sympathy with all the wariness of a saint encountering an eighth deadly sin.

Annie had just decided that, if squinted at from a certain angle, Monet's waterlilies could look extraordinarily like giant beetles, when her name was called out by the receptionist. A few minutes later she was sitting opposite an angular-faced lady doctor with a piercing stare and a thick ponytail of long black hair. The lump in her breast would be subjected to a triple test, the doctor explained, a standard investigation comprising feeling, needling and imaging.

Annie tried her best to focus, reminding herself of what her book had advised, that with knowledge she could make judgements and demands, control her situation, defuse some of the fear.

The doctor's fingers were cool and deft, her voice soothing. She was starting to go grey, Annie observed; a few strands behind the ears and at her temples . . . 'What I expect we'll find is that you have what's called a fibroadenoma, that is an overgrowth of fibrous and glandular tissue – sometimes known as breast mice – they're usually about one centimetre in width—'

'Breast mice?' Annie laughed nervously, her imagination soaring with images of parasitic rodents. A moment later she was led out of the room and down the corridor to be briefed on the delights awaiting her in the X-ray department.

'Just to show you there's nothing to be afraid of – it will feel cold and a little uncomfortable – here, put your hand in and then you'll get a better idea.'

Gingerly Annie allowed her hand to be sandwiched between two metal plates.

'We do each breast twice – from the sides as well as top and bottom. OK?' The doctor eyed her carefully, perhaps registering the fact that her patient had said practically nothing since the consultation began.

'Fine, no worries.' Annie managed to sound hearty, out of a perverse concern to reassure the doctor, whom she knew was trying hard.

'Good. First I need to take a sample of fluid to send to the cytology lab.'

Annie's mouth went dry. Time for the needle.

'—A cyst is just a hormonal pocket of fluid that has collected in the tissue—'

Once more Annie willed her consciousness to cut loose. She thought of Marina lost amongst yards of wedding lace, of Greg slaving in *RoundUp*'s cramped warren of an office, of Jake, sunburnt and jaded under the strobe light of a Spanish night-club. The images swelled and faded, drifting from her mind like spirits from another life, leaving only the white wall to stare at and the faint smell of the doctor's soap as she bent near Annie's chest.

'—Always easier sitting down . . . You might feel a bit of tenderness – that's a good sign, frankly – and then afterwards there will probably be a bit of bruising . . . Hold still . . . that's it . . . Just enough cells to stain a slide—'

It hurt. Annie clenched her teeth and fists, keeping her eyes fixed on the wall, but seeing only a grey blur. She was on the point of crying out when suddenly it was over. The doctor held up the slide with a smile of triumph.

'I'll send this off today. We should have results by the end of next week.'

After that, having her breasts treated like mounds of kneadable dough was plain sailing. The radiographer, a young girl with a gentle Irish lilt, explained and apologised so much for the discomforts of the process that Annie found herself being contrastingly relaxed and amenable.

She didn't become aware that she was trembling until she was back behind the steering wheel of the car. By which time she was shaking too much even to manage lighting a cigarette. The next moment she was sobbing with dramatic abandonment, not even bothering to shield her face from a bent old man who peered at her curiously through the windscreen. While alert to the fact that she painted something of a desolate picture, Annie was aware too of a wonderful release of tension. The doctor had been nothing but reassuring. Just one more week and the agony of suspense would be at an end. In the meantime she had a weekend with Greg to look forward to, and Amy's Peruvian party, which might even turn out to be fun.

By the time Annie had finished blowing her nose she found that she was already composing how she would write up these latest experiences for the column; seeing in retrospect all the opportunities for humour which were already making the memory of it more bearable.

As I guess those of you who've enjoyed foot stirrups and vaginal hoovers in the interests of procreation know already, maintaining one's sense of dignity amongst the medical fraternity is not always a viable possibility. As a woman who has recently had both breasts play the role of bacon in what I can only describe as a large, unappetising metal sandwich, I speak with some authority . . .

Chapter Twenty-Eight

———◇◇◇———

Marina badly wanted to help herself from the pretty circles of sandwiches arranged around the silver teapot on the table separating her from Bernard's mother. Each one was so small, a tiny crustless triangle of no more than two bites, that the two she had been offered had slipped down without any satiating effect at all. The first had been cucumber, pared to the slimmest slices, layered on a rich bed of butter. The second, soft, moist egg with just a sparse scattering of tiny cress leaves and the occasional crunch of sea salt and fresh pepper. Would it be judged complimentary or rude to ask for more? she wondered, casting an eye at the jowly face of one of Bernard's ancestors strung up above the fireplace and registering a hint of disdain in the heavy-lidded eyes.

The primary cause of Marina's obsession arose from having missed lunch. At Bernard's suggestion she had asked for the afternoon off and driven to the country before the onslaught of the Friday stampede for the M25. Bernard himself was due to catch an early evening train, together with his father, who had been up to town on business. Though the plan made more than enough sense, Marina had found arriving at Stanton House on her own even more of an ordeal than she had expected. Driving up the winding tarmacked drive in her green Volkswagen, she could not help feeling like some poor outsider being forced onto the set of a lavish costume drama in which she could play no part. Whistling the theme tune of *Brideshead* to bolster her spirits, she had parked several yards from the grandly pillared front of the house and then sat for several minutes in the car, taking deep breaths and pondering the suddenly imminent question of whether to kiss Lady Ramsbotham or merely shake her hand. In-laws kissed, surely; but on only the second meeting? In the event, the decision was made for her by her hostess, who simultaneously took her hand and lightly dusted the air near her left ear with her lilac lips. She then conducted Marina to a bedroom, commanding her to freshen up before presenting herself in the drawing room for tea.

Locating the drawing room was the next challenge; though, having done so Marina soon began to wish that she was still loitering in corridors. She had forgotten how worryingly silent Lady Ramsbotham could be, a trait which imposed far more pressures sitting *à deux* in the cavernous Stanton House sitting room than it had during the flurry of their first meeting in London. Marina's sense of ease was not encouraged by the presence of a rotund dachsund, who spent most of the first half hour trying to mate with her left leg and then retreated to a footstool to lick its genitals and cast longing looks at the tea table.

'Of course you'll want to see the rings,' remarked Lady Ramsbotham at length, patently unperturbed either by the distasteful habits of her pet or the clanging silence between her and her future daughter-in-law.

'The rings?' Marina set down her teacup and made a deft swipe for a sandwich before withdrawing between the fortress walls of her armchair. While Lady Ramsbotham appeared politely insouciant − or perhaps ignorant − at this lapse in manners, the dachsund, who was called Oscar, was not so forgiving. He leapt from his perch and took up a new, pleading position at Marina's feet, ignoring her wide-eyed glare of hostility and releasing long spools of dribble onto the carpet. 'The rings?' she repeated faintly.

'The family rings. You are to choose one to celebrate your engagement. It's family tradition. Did Bernard not mention it?' Her thin beige eyebrows arched in surprise.

'Oh he did – yes of course he did. That will be wonderful, I can't wait.'

'They're in the safe, of course. Victor will get them out when he returns. The rubies belonged to Ivy Carvell – that noble gentleman's unwise choice of a wife—' she flicked a disparaging look at the portrait Marina had been scrutinising a moment or two before '—and the emeralds were Alice Archdale's, the finest of the whole bunch.'

'It will be fun choosing,' managed Marina, having considered a range of more ambitious responses, but opting for the simplest.

'Are you entirely ready?' enquired Lady Ramsbotham, placing her own teacup on the tray and pressing her napkin into the creases at the corners of her mouth.

'Ready for—?'

'The wedding, my dear, the wedding.' A hint of impatience escaped in the sigh that followed. Unsure whether she was being questioned with regard to her state of mind or the logistics of organising a gathering of nearly two hundred people at only a few weeks' notice, Marina found yet more pitiful inarticulacy colouring her answer. 'Oh yes, I am . . . that is we are . . . in fact Bernard is taking care of everything.'

Lady Ramsbotham smiled. 'Bernard likes taking care of things. His last fiancée couldn't abide it – too much of an organiser herself.' She folded her napkin into a small tidy square and sighed deeply. 'But she did play a marvellous round of bridge. Do you play?'

'No, no I don't.' Marina, who was beginning to feel she was trapped in some sort of nightmare, stood up. 'I'd like to go on a walk.'

'By all means.' Her hostess waved a careless arm in the direction of the handsome windows overlooking the several acres of family estate surrounding the house. 'Be our guest. Oscar would love a walk, I'm sure. Don't let him near any deer though, he worries them so.'

As soon as she was a few yards from the house, Marina pulled out her telephone from her pocket and dialled Shrewsbury

Mansions. On hearing the click of the answering machine, she swore vehemently and tried Annie's mobile, praying that it was one of the rare days when the batteries as well as the item itself had been accommodated.

Annie was on the point of manoeuvring out of her parking space near the clinic when she heard the bleeping in her handbag.

'Annie . . . thank God . . . Annie . . . help.' The crackling accompanying these dramatic introductions was so intense that Annie quickly got out of the car in search of a better reception. When the line cleared Marina was still talking, loudly and with mounting hysteria.

'I think I might be making the biggest fucking mistake of my life – I mean Christ, his *mother* . . . Annie you have no idea what it is like trying to talk to that woman – she's either a sadist or a lunatic, I can't decide which. Bernard must have known, sending me down here like this, on my own – like bloody Samuel in the lions' den—'

'Daniel. It was Daniel, and the lions didn't—'

'*And* she had the cheek to bring up the subject of the bitch he got engaged to *three years ago*. Bernard broke it off you know – the woman was devastated – hung around his front door at night for weeks and weeks, like some sick daft cow—'

'Marina, calm down. Where are you?'

'I'm strolling round the fucking ornamental pond, accompanied by a demented dachsund who eats reindeer—'

'When's Bernard arriving?'

'Tonight. But I'm not sure I'm going to be here. I'm not sure about anything any more. I don't want to be a part of this, Annie, it's just not what I want.'

Annie hesitated before responding. A few carefully chosen sentences and Marina might even jump into her car and beetle back to London. With a little more artfulness and a good deal of luck, she might even be persuaded to stumble back to all the joys of female interdependency which they had known before Bernard stole the scene: flat-life, girl-talk, muddled intimacy. Annie allowed herself a small sigh of acknowledgement at the temptation, which she knew she should – and would – resist. Not just because Marina's passion for Bernard would bubble back up to the surface, but because, as Annie well knew, it was both impossible to travel backwards and invariably fatal to try.

'Marina, you are not marrying his family,' she said gently.

'But they're *unspeakable*,' she wailed.

'No, only the mother is, so far. You said the dad was quite sweet—'

'I said he flirted with me—'

'Well so what? Better than hating you, isn't it?'

'Suppose so.' There was a short silence. 'This place is so big it's spooky. We've got separate bedrooms, miles apart—'

'Well that's hardly for very much longer is it?'

'Perhaps Bernard will evolve into a male version of his mother.'

Annie couldn't help laughing. 'Have you seen any signs of it?'

'No, not yet . . . though he does play bridge.'

'I can think of worse social crimes. It will be fine. Say you've got a headache and need to lie down for the rest of the day. When Bernard arrives you'll feel quite different, you'll see. Just be yourself, Marina, that's all Bernard wants, for God's sake. It's pretty blazingly obvious the man loves you for . . . well, for you.'

There was a pause. 'Do you really think so?'

'Only a dumbwit would think otherwise.' It was only as the words came out that Annie realised she spoke the truth. If anyone deserved a fair crack at marital bliss it was Bernard and Marina. 'Roll on the bloody nuptials, I say. You're in limbo at the moment, not knowing quite what you are – totally between feelings and phases—'

'For an old spinster you speak remarkably knowledgeably,' teased Marina, sounding much more like her old self. 'Is there something you're not telling me?'

That her ex-flatmate was clearly oblivious to the recent contents of the *FlatLife* column served as a further indicator to Annie of just how far their lives had moved apart. Suppressing the urge to answer Marina's question by explaining how she had spent the morning, she laughed instead. 'I'm loaded with secrets, but I've no intention of telling you any of them – Greg would never forgive me.'

'Bloody hell, I miss you sometimes, Annie,' Marina burst out, 'and I'm so looking forward to our shopping next Saturday—'

By which time she would know whether she was in for minor lump-removing surgery or chemotherapy with all the trimmings. The thought flooded Annie's concentration, for a moment drowning the sound of Marina's voice.

'Annie, are you still there?'

'Reading you loud and clear.'

'I just want to say thanks for – oh bloody hell – there's a deer – a whole fucking herd – I've got to go – going to have to run—'

Annie turned off her telephone and slowly returned to the car, feeling drained of energy but nursing the dim satisfaction that accompanies the knowledge of having done the right thing. Life had got harder, but curiously richer too, she reflected, driving slowly so as to enjoy a view of a pretty hedged park to her left and thinking of the pleasantly quiet afternoon stretching ahead.

Chapter Twenty-Nine

'I've got your mother,' announced Michael, having descended the stairs three at a time in order to catch Annie before she disappeared behind her front door. 'I saw you from the window,' he continued breathlessly, as if this were all the explanation such a statement required.

'I beg your pardon?'

He shrugged his shoulders in the direction of the stairs. 'She's painting my skirting boards. I told her not to, but she insisted.'

Annie smiled incredulously. 'There must be some sort of mistake. My mother never comes to London. And on the rare occasion that she does I get ten warning phone calls and six months' notice.'

'You'd better come up then – she's certainly under the impression that you're closely related . . . You've done that mascara trick again, by the way,' he remarked gently, pointing at her face which was still smudged from her bout of crying in the car.

'Thanks.' Annie wiped furiously at her cheeks.

'Her name is Christine. Does that help?'

Annie slowly pulled her door shut behind her, shaking her head in disbelief. 'Something awful must have happened,' she murmured, her mind racing through a series of ghoulish possibilities involving Phillip or her father.

'She looks quite cheerful. I found her scribbling a note to slip through the door. When she saw me she asked if I knew where you were or when you'd be back. One thing led to another and soon she was—' He let his voice tail away, inwardly marvelling at this new power of other people's lives to intrude on his own. More curious still was the fact that he seemed to be enjoying the experience.

'Painting your skirting boards.'

'Exactly. Are you coming or not?' He bounded back up the stairs, springing on the balls of his feet which were clad in thick grey socks, wearing thin at the heels. In place of the customary paint-splashed denims was a pair of faded black trousers and a loose black T-shirt with a white question mark emblazoned on the back.

'The prodigal daughter returned,' he declared easily, as Annie peered round the open door of his flat. Her mother was on her knees in the hall, wearing a crumpled blue-and-white butcher's apron and wielding a small paintbrush. At her side was a large open tin of silky white paint.

'Hello Annie.' She balanced the brush across the top of the tin and struggled to her feet. 'Couldn't bear not to make myself useful . . . It's going to be lovely isn't it? When Michael's finished.'

Annie could not help gawping. 'Yes . . . lovely . . . er Mum, this is quite a surprise.'

Christine pushed a curl of grey out of her eyes with the back of her hand. 'I know.' She hesitated, looking at a loss for a moment. 'I just thought that if I phoned, you would tell me not to come.'

'Not necessarily—'

They both suddenly became aware of Michael, hovering tactfully by a far window.

'Shall we retreat downstairs then?' suggested Annie, as sweetly as she could, but inwardly cursing the imminent collapse of her weekend. With Greg coming, the last thing she wanted was her mother as a house-guest.

'Perhaps I could just freshen up first?' Christine held out her hands apologetically, revealing several smears of white paint. 'I daren't touch a thing like this.'

'Of course. The kitchen sink is full I'm afraid. You'll have to risk your luck negotiating your way through to the bathroom – there's some white spirit on the windowsill I think—'

'Don't worry, soap and water will do. I'm painting my own house at the moment so I've had plenty of practice at scrubbing clean.'

'Not exactly a rapturous welcome, I see,' remarked Michael dryly, once Christine had disappeared. Kneeling down, he picked up the brush and began stroking paint onto the fresh brown wood of the skirting board.

'No.' Annie folded her arms and set her lips together. 'Not that it's any business of yours.'

'Absolutely not. Wouldn't dream of it. Filial disaffection is one subject on which I'm not at liberty to make any judgements at all . . . though fathers are my main speciality.'

'And mothers?'

'I'm afraid I hold the breed in rather high esteem. Probably because mine had the audacity to die before we could become properly acquainted—' He stopped painting for a moment and carefully extracted a stray brush bristle from a freshly painted section of wood.

Annie cleared her throat. 'I'm sorry . . . but I'm afraid I hold mine in wonderful esteem just so long as she's doing her own thing in the Welsh valleys and not buggering up my weekends.'

'So you had other plans?' He worked the paintbrush with deft flicks of his wrist, smoothing on inches of thick paint at a time.

'To put it mildly.'

'With the man who sends roses, I take it?'

'Yes, yes, with him.' His curiosity made her defensive. 'We've both had a hell of a week. The last thing we need is—'

'Just tell her. Surely she'd—'

Annie sucked in her cheeks. 'You don't know my mother.'

'There we are, that's better,' announced Christine a little too loudly, as if aware of the necessity of heralding her approach. 'So nice to meet you Michael. Last time I was here – a while back now I'll admit – there was some very shady types on this floor

– heaven knows what they got up to. The trouble with land-lords these days is—'

Annie patted her mother's shoulder. 'Come on, Mum, let's go.'

Michael accompanied them to the door. As they turned to leave he said, 'I've got a wine tasting this evening. I know Annie is busy, but if you wanted to come along, Christine, you would be most welcome—'

Annie stared over the top of her mother's head in unabashed amazement. She would not have expected such a sacrifice from Marina, let alone Michael Derwent. She opened her mouth to protest but Christine got there first.

'Why, Michael, that is an *extremely* kind offer—'

'Got to repay all that decorating somehow,' he interjected easily. 'It's one of the less formal ones, guests allowed so long as they behave—' His face creased into a charming smile. 'I expect you'd find it quite interesting.'

'I certainly would.' Annie could tell from the flush in her mother's cheeks that she was genuinely flattered. 'But sadly, I cannot accept. I'm seeing Annie's brother for dinner. I was hoping to persuade Annie to join us – I've arranged to stay the night with Phillip too,' she added, giving her daughter a sharp look, 'just in case you were wondering.' She returned her atten-tion to Michael. 'But thank you *very* much for the invitation, it was most kind.'

Annie, too, murmured her appreciation, while inwardly she caught herself wondering whether Michael Derwent was still playing games, whether behind this extraordinary display of amiability he was laughing at the pair of them, poking fun for his own amusement.

'Such a nice young man,' remarked Christine, while Annie bustled round her small kitchen finding mugs and teaspoons.

'Yeah, well don't go getting any ideas, he's most definitely spoken for.' She slopped boiling water over a teabag and pushed a carton of milk across the table. 'Were you planning to stay in London for the whole weekend?' Having aimed for an anything-is-fine-by-me tone of voice, she was aware that she had failed dismally. Embarrassed at her own transparency, Annie quickly dropped her eyes to her mug, noting two small blobs of cream that had refused to dissolve.

'No, Annie,' Christine replied quietly, 'just long enough to see how you are. I shall go back tomorrow. I can't leave the dogs for long. Terry is kindly coping, but he's very busy. Bonnie is fine, by the way, behaves as if she's never lived anywhere else.'

'To see how I am?' repeated Annie cautiously.

Christine sighed. 'I know you're not well. Phillip told me. Hermione reads your column.'

'How nice of Phillip to be so concerned.'

'He said he wanted to ring you but didn't know what to say. He's going through a hard time himself at the moment. He . . . I think he wants to break up from Hermione.'

'But she's—'

'I know, I know, it's a mess.' Christine pressed her teabag into the palm of her teaspoon and looked round for a bin.

'Under the sink,' Annie muttered, still grappling with the notion that her mother had felt concerned enough about her welfare to get on a train, unsure whether such uncharacteristically extravagant behaviour was something which should evoke gratitude or annoyance.

'Realising that you'd write about yourself in a newspaper before talking to me was quite a shock, I can tell you.'

Annie squirmed in her seat, twisting her legs together under the table. 'Mum, we've never talked about anything. Anyway, I would have told you. I was waiting for the results.'

'What results?'

'I've had some . . . tests – just this morning. X-rays and so on. I should hear before the end of next week. I didn't really intend to write about all this in the paper at all,' she burst out, 'it just sort of happened during a patch of writer's block, and set a ball rolling which has gathered its own momentum. It's been incredible – I've had all these letters—'

Having dispatched her teabag Christine remained leaning against the kitchen sink, blowing and sipping at her mug. 'I've always worried about you more than Phillip,' she said softly.

'Really?' After a lifetime of inferring precisely the opposite, Annie could not conceal her astonishment.

'Because I was scared for you, probably.'

'Scared?' Annie's incredulity leapt to new heights.

'I didn't want you to make the same mistakes I had – to lose your independence—' She drifted back to the table and slowly lowered herself into a chair. 'Annie . . . I know I've—' She reached out a hand. But at the touch of her Annie flinched and pulled her arm away, distrusting the look of pitiful eagerness on her mother's face. It was too easy, too pat, too sentimental.

'Mum, you didn't have to come here or . . . to say anything you didn't want to. I've had a hard time recently but it's been good too in a weird sort of way. Life has sort of slipped into focus . . . I can't describe it. I'm worried of course, but deep down I feel better about myself than I have for years.'

'I thought your generation believed in talking things through – I thought that's what everyone believed in these days. I thought it was supposed to help make everything better.'

'Look, Mum, I don't blame you for anything, OK?'

'That may or may not be true,' she replied quietly, 'but I blame myself.' She paused and swallowed before continuing. 'When you were born, Annie, I was so pleased to have a little girl, and so afraid, and at the same time so . . . jealous.' She raised her head and looked her daughter full in the face. 'You always loved your father more.'

'I did not—'

'You did. And who could blame you? He was more forgiving, more easy-going, more . . . indulgent.'

'Maybe—'

'But I've come to realise that the hardest thing of all, the thing that made me most wretched, was that he loved you more than me.' She let out a short laugh. 'So simple in retrospect. Yet so complicated, so confusing at the time.'

Annie leant back in her chair and crossed her arms over her chest, pressing hard to quell the pounding of her heart. She let out a long slow breath. 'I should be on my deathbed at the very least for us to be having a conversation like this.'

'Annie, don't talk like that—'

'I don't want you to say anything you're going to regret Mum. I don't need to know everything. We've all muddled through somehow. And will no doubt continue to do so—'

'And Phillip.' Christine tightened her mouth till the corners turned downwards. 'I've spoilt him. I've made him into the very thing I always wanted to avoid. He's going to leave that poor girl. He's the worst kind of man, I can see that now – but not as a mother – as a mother I—' She pushed away her tea and buried her face in her hands. 'I couldn't bear it if you were ill.'

'Mum don't, please.' Annie felt panic-stricken. It was literally years since she had seen her mother cry. Decades. Not since . . . She struggled to recall, pushing her memory back through the late-night door-bangs and whispered arguing of her childhood, through all the prolonged, chilling sense that there was a dark adult world of unfathomable truths and terrors. There had been tears then, occasionally as shrill as a raised voice, but usually muffled through the flimsy protection of walls and the pillow that Annie pressed around her ears. Almost worse would be the sight of her mother at breakfast the following morning, silent and puffy-eyed, working kettles and toasters as if her life depended on it. Eventually the disagreements, the resistance, stopped altogether. When, years later, her father finally left, Christine had been resigned and stony-eyed, her face scarred with all the sour unattractive wrath of the wronged.

Annie got up and placed a tentative hand on the heaving back. 'Come on, now, you can't blame yourself for everything. Phillip is as he is. I am as I am. And I'm certainly not ill yet. Please, Mum, stop this now.' Christine dropped her hands from her face and reached up into the sleeve of her cardigan for a tissue, which she dabbed at her eyes without any visible effect on the flow of tears. Annie pulled up a chair next to her and put a firmer arm across her shoulders. 'I command you to stop this or you'll have me going.' She tried to sound scolding, but inside she felt curiously happy and strong.

'Sorry.' Christine grimaced in an effort to suppress her tears.

'That's better.' Briefly Annie touched the steely grey waves of her mother's hair, smoothing them back into place. 'I shall disappoint you all and be given the all clear, just you wait and see.'

Christine sniffed. 'I certainly hope so.'

'Here, drink your tea up.'

'What can I do?'

'Nothing.'

'And Phillip—'

'Phil must live his own life. We all must. If he doesn't stay with Hermione he'll still have to pay for the child. Better apart than marrying when it wouldn't be right,' Annie added gently.

'Oh yes, indeed,' Christine whispered, taking her mug to the sink and rinsing it clean.

Half an hour later she had fallen asleep in an armchair in the sitting room, Annie's book about breast health open on her lap. She was an old woman, Annie reflected sadly, absorbing the fact as if for the first time. Gently she removed the book and placed it on the floor at her feet. For some moments she remained standing, watching the cardiganed chest rise and fall, intensely and poignantly aware of the simple, fragile process by which the body sustained life. In the slackness of sleep her mother's face looked softer. Studying the faint criss-crossing of lines, Annie found herself searching for evidence of the younger woman who had once occupied the same skin. A woman filled with hope for the future, a woman who had buried her own ambitions in the shadow of a man who had betrayed her. And as she watched, Annie felt a dim understanding of the pain that must have been suffered, losing the love of a husband, yet seeing it held so firmly, so effortlessly, in the cup of a daughter's hand.

Chapter Thirty

—◆◆◆◆—

Annie was putting the finishing touches to her lipstick when Greg phoned to say that he would be working so late it really wasn't worth their meeting that night after all.

'By the time I'm finished here I'll be no fun for you or anyone,' he assured her, sounding so miserable that Annie immediately felt it would be churlish to kick up too much of a fuss.

'I don't mind meeting up later on,' she offered, swallowing her disappointment. It was almost an hour since her mother had left, insisting – somewhat ironically, given this new set of circumstances – that she meet Phillip alone.

'You go off on your date and have a lovely time. Is it with someone I've heard of?' Christine had added timidly, sufficiently encouraged by the afternoon's events to venture a curiosity on a matter that she would normally have left well alone.

Annie bristled and then checked herself. 'No . . . he's called Greg Berkley. Tall, dark and handsome. A co-editor on a news magazine thing called *RoundUp*.'

'Sounds frightfully clever.'

'He is,' she agreed with a small smile of pride.

They had parted with an awkward but well-intentioned hug, that highlighted for both of them that there was much still to be done, that genuine intimacy could not be reclaimed like a mislaid item of property, but had to be worked at and nurtured like a wayward child.

'There's still the whole of the weekend left,' Greg reassured her now. 'I might have to pop into the office briefly tomorrow morning, but I'll call as soon as I can.'

Determined not to be too deflated, Annie poured herself a glass of wine and studied the evening's offerings on the telly. Hospital dramas and sports quizzes were taking over the world, she reflected glumly, casting aside the TV guide and consoling herself with a cigarette and a second glass of wine. A few minutes later she kicked off her high heels and slipped her feet into her trainers. She would venture out to WorldVideos, she decided, and browse around for something to lift her spirits.

'Has your mother gone?'

He appeared so quickly and silently on the landing behind her that Annie had the fleeting impression that he had been lying in wait. His face, freshly shaven and smooth, gleamed with cleanliness. His hair, too, looked shiny and sleek, apart from one obstinate wet tuft on the crown of his head.

'Yes. Thanks again, by the way, for . . . fielding her. It really was incredibly kind.' She hesitated. 'Do you make a habit of asking mothers of tenants out on dates?'

He laughed. 'Certainly not. It was quite a gamble, I'll admit. I was sure she'd say no. It was just a way of letting her know you had other plans.'

'Well, it was kind.' Annie looked at him uncertainly.

'Is your date off then?'

'No . . . I mean . . . yes it is, but how did you—?'

'The shoes.' He shook his head gravely. 'They kind of give the game away, if you don't mind my saying so.'

Annie, who did mind, both the acuteness of his powers of observation and his audacity in voicing them, looked down at her feet, absorbing for the first time quite what an absurd accoutrement they made to her sheer black tights and short velvet skirt. 'Right . . . of course. He . . . my boyfriend has a work crisis thing. We've postponed meeting until tomorrow.'

Michael nodded sympathetically. 'Oh yes, I do know a little bit about such things – at least I did once upon a time. Sometimes I used to feel as if my entire life was on hold, waiting for that elusive moment when there were no more meetings or phone calls. Although it's obviously quite different if you love your work,' he concluded hastily, 'as I'm sure your friend does.'

'Yes he does.' Annie stuck her chin out. 'Now if you'll excuse me I've got other plans—'

'Involving a video maybe?' he hazarded, following her down the stairs. 'And before you ask, I saw the card in your hand.'

'Well, aren't we observant?' she retorted dryly. 'My mother ended up insisting on meeting my dear brother alone, if you were wondering about that too.'

He opened the main door and stood back for her to walk through. 'Actually, I was more preoccupied by whether you might prefer a spot of wine tasting to the thin pickings on offer at WorldVideos.' He looked at his watch and frowned. 'This time on a Friday night you'll be lucky to get anything except a reel of Disney cartoons.'

'Oh no, I couldn't.'

'Couldn't or don't want to?'

Annie tried to think of a reason not to accept. 'I'm not very good on wine—' she faltered. 'That is, I drink a lot of it, but mostly anything that costs less than a fiver—'

'You can get some good stuff for a fiver.'

'And I only ever know if it's corked by the headache I get afterwards.'

'That is more serious.' He pretended to ponder the matter deeply, leaning back on the open door, through which she had yet to venture a step. 'But not necessarily irretrievable. You don't have to taste anything at all if you don't want to. The only thing that wouldn't work, I'm afraid, is the . . . er . . . footwear. Otherwise you're splendidly dressed for the occasion.'

'Look, you've been kind enough already—'

He stepped aside and let the door fall shut. 'I really would value some company. Go and put your party shoes on and I'll wait here.'

'I'm not going anywhere near that Harley Davidson contraption of yours,' she warned, backing down the hall.

'Public transport it shall be, I promise.' He did a mock salute, while Annie turned and scurried back up the stairs, inwardly chiding herself for getting roped into something which she should have had the wherewithal to avoid.

'This wasn't quite what I had in mind either,' Annie muttered, once they were seated side by side on a swaying half-empty bus.

'I know.' He smiled.

They were full, beautiful lips, she observed, studying his face in the reflection of the window, as full of life and expression as the eyes. An image of the same lips pressed against Jake's agile mouth flickered in her mind. Michael Derwent would be a passionate lover, she realised. There was a sense of contained energy about him that she could imagine Jake finding very appealing.

'We can always hop off *en route* if you get the urge for nicotine.'

'What? For God's sake, I'm not that bad.'

'Sorry.' He shrugged apologetically. 'I was such a bad-tempered smoker, I expect everyone else to be the same.' He peered out of the window. 'Actually we're almost there . . .'

'Oh, so you've given up smoking as well as the evils of the rat-race, have you? Don't tell me, you woke up one morning and decided to quit. Just like that.'

He laughed. 'If only. Chewing gum, skin patches, hypnosis – I tried the lot.' He nudged her with his elbow and swung out of the seat. 'Next stop is ours.'

'Ex-smokers are always horribly complacent,' she muttered, 'but go on – I know you're dying to tell me how you gave up.' The bus stopped so abruptly that she almost lost her balance, lurching down the gangway and onto the platform. He offered a hand to steady her, but she seized the pole between them instead.

'A godfather of whom I was very fond died of lung cancer. Not a pretty sight. It was like watching someone slowly suffocate to death.' He jumped off the bus almost before it had stopped and stood waiting for her to join him on the pavement.

'Oh dear, how sad,' Annie murmured, berating herself for having inadvertently stumbled on yet another unhappy aspect of his past and vowing to be more careful. He was impossible to make out, an ill-fitting jigsaw of a man, clearly not at ease with himself yet struggling to appear otherwise. The more she saw of him the more she got the impression that he was holding something back; something beyond the evident reticence about his sexuality.

Michael set off up the street without another word, taking such long strides that Annie tottered on her heels to keep up with him. A light rain had started, giving a greasy sheen to the pavements. 'Should I – I mean, should you perhaps tell me a bit about the difference between a Sauvignon and a Sancerre or something? Whether to sniff before I gargle . . . stuff like that?'

He chuckled and slowed his pace to match hers. 'I'd rather leave your mind free for a clear interpretation of your own. Women are supposed to have much better palates than men – scientists have proved it quite conclusively. My only advice would be to try the whites before the reds – not so much tannin in them, you see, so less of an assault on your taste buds. At least, I always prefer to leave the heavier stuff till last. But you must do as you please. One other thing: when using the spittoons it is prudent to keep scarves, jewellery, hair and so on well out of the way—' he peered at her '—you're wearing dark colours, that's good – won't show up too many dribbles.'

'Spittoons?' Annie's sense of inadequacy about the challenge ahead edged up another notch. 'Don't say I've got to go in for all that fancy stuff as well—'

'Not if you don't want to. Here we are.' He dropped her arm and led the way up the wide steps of an entrance to a hotel. The door was opened for them by a young man in a grey top hat and tails. Behind him an elaborate chandelier illuminated a plushly carpeted lobby and a sign with an arrow saying *Mauder & Veale Wine Tasting, Conference Room 1*.

'Can I change my mind?' Annie whispered, as they were overtaken by a loud group of portly, middle-aged men in bow ties.

'Absolutely not. I'm here to do business and would relish your opinions.'

The room was as large as a cinema and filled with milling people and tables of wine. 'A woman of your independent nature would probably find it a strain to follow me around,' Michael remarked wryly, handing her a piece of paper from a stack on a table by the door. 'This is called a tasting sheet. It's got the names of all the wines, see? And a little space underneath so you can jot down your thoughts. I've even got a spare pencil. Feel free to do your own thing. I'll be around if you need me. And no smoking,' he added over his shoulder, throwing her a cautionary but friendly scowl before sauntering off into the mêlée of people.

Annie, feeling somewhat abandoned, but determined not to appear so, strode off in the opposite direction, resolved, now she had got this far, to enjoy herself. After a tentative start at a sparsely attended table advertising spring wines at modest prices, she began to approach some of the other grander and more popular displays. With each tasting, her confidence grew, aided considerably by an empty stomach and the two glasses of wine she had consumed before leaving the flat. Her notes, initially meticulous, began to spread across the print and into the margins. Each time Michael caught her eye and made as if to cross the room, she waved him back, pointing at the papers in her hand to show that she was doing as she had been told.

When, after an hour or so, he tapped his watch and raised an eyebrow to see if she was ready to leave, Annie again shook her head vehemently. Ignoring the faint dizziness pushing in at her temples, she embarked on another round of the tables, avoiding the spittoons altogether now, and exchanging expressions of mutual interest with those around her instead of shyly burying her nose in every glass. While enjoying a generous sample of a spicy Argentinian Malbec, she fell into pleasant banter with three ruddy-cheeked young men introducing themselves as afficionados of something called the Harwich Wine Society. Women were better at it than men, she told them earnestly, remembering what Michael had said. Better at what quipped the one in the middle, who had dark hair slicked back from his fore-head and button brown eyes. His companions roared with approving mirth, exchanging knowing winks and glances. Annie roared too, but only because the men were so silly and didn't realise it.

She drifted back to a table of New World whites that had slipped down with the sweetness and ease of lemonade on a hot day. There she got talking to a man with cherubic blond curls and hard grey eyes. She was assisting a wine consultant friend who valued her palate, she explained, not liking the way the eyes seemed to watch her mouth.

'Oh he does does he?' replied the man, 'And who might this wine consultant be? Perhaps I know him. I know most people on the circuit.'

Annie was on the point of answering when Michael himself appeared at her side.

'Just meeting your new assistant, Michael,' said the man, booming with laughter. 'I expect she's invaluable.'

'She is.'

Feeling the grip of Michael's hand on her elbow, Annie shook herself free. 'What's up? I'm just getting into my stride.'

'Time to go, Annie, or they'll be kicking us out.'

She suddenly became aware that the room was almost empty. 'I took lots of notes.' She waved her pieces of paper in his face. 'New World's my hot tip, especially the Coonawarra—' It took several attempts to get her mouth round the word.

'Would it be the distinctive Terra Rossa soil in that region that gives the wine its flavour, or do you have other theories on the matter my dear?'

'Back off, Geoffrey.' Michael's voice was soft but steely.

The blond-haired man raised his hands in a show of apology. 'Just trying to pick the brains of your charming assistant, Michael. Though I can't help thinking she needs a little more . . . training.'

'As do your manners. Come on, Annie, let's get out of here.'

'I thought you operated alone these days, Michael . . . a solo performer in every regard.'

'I don't think he liked me,' Annie murmured, shaking her head mournfully as Michael propelled her out of the room.

'He doesn't like me either, if it's any consolation. Geoffrey's speciality is making up for his own deficiencies by reminding other people of theirs.'

'And what was all that solo business?' she asked, slumping down on the entrance steps and lighting a cigarette.

Michael looked at her for a few moments, aware of an impulse to talk freely and wondering whether to distrust it. 'I had a bad episode a couple of years ago, with a partner who saw fit to take an overdose because of me . . . because I found someone else and took my time being honest about it. We worked together, which made the whole thing more complicated. Geoffrey was rather fond of the person concerned and has never forgiven me for it.'

'And what happened to the someone else?'

'That got fucked up in the process.'

'Oh dear,' Annie murmured, aware through the blur in her head that what he was telling her went a long way to solving some of the contradictions she had found so puzzling. She guessed that Jake must know the sorry tale already, that it had probably played a large part in persuading him to be so secretive.

Michael left her to wave down a cab, which slowed and then accelerated away.

Realising that the smoke was making her nauseous, Annie dropped her cigarette and ground it out under her heel. 'Bloody hell, I've drunk too much,' she moaned, dropping her head into her hands. 'Was I . . . am I . . . embarrassing?'

'Not remotely. In fact some of these notes are rather fine. I especially like – let's see now—' He held out one of her pieces of paper and squinted at her writing, ' – *stewed apples – tsp of cream* for the McLaren Vale Chardonnay, and the even more imaginative *bonfire – peppery burning – heavy smell – good crap*, or is it *grape*? – for the Walker Bay Pinot Noir. You could have a great future as a vinter. Maybe even a whole new career—'

'Could do with that – and a new body, for that matter,' she

mumbled, staring morosely at the concrete under her feet.

'Annie?' He stepped back from the edge of the pavement and looked at her intently for a moment. 'If you ever want to talk—'

She shook her head, too sleepy suddenly to muster the energy for conversation.

Once inside a taxi, Annie's drowsiness grew worse and was accompanied by a dim sense that she had misbehaved and should give some account of herself. 'Sorry if I've . . . things on my mind. Jake's a—' She meant to say 'lucky man', but her eyes closed before the words completed the journey from her head to her lips.

As the taxi sped through the dark wet streets, Michael could not prevent his thoughts from drifting back to the episode he had described to Annie, and to Jake too, but for rather different reasons. That he was beginning to talk about it was, he knew, a sign that the fear of causing such damage again was fading at last. That his need for other people was really reasserting itself. Bringing all its concomitant problems, he reflected, sighing heavily and shifting his chin so that Annie's head rested more squarely and safely on his shoulder blade.

Chapter Thirty-One

Annie awoke the following morning feeling faintly fragile. On catching sight of the open bottle of white wine – the initiator of her demise the night before – still sitting beside its cork on top of the fridge, she frowned in distaste and tipped the remainder of its contents down the sink. After showering and getting dressed, she composed a careful note to Michael Derwent, thanking him for taking her out and apologising for her somewhat extravagant enjoyment of the evening. Some further explanation seemed called for.

> *I've had quite a week and I think it all caught up with me. Alcohol always goes straight to my head when I'm tired. I do hope I did not disgrace myself – or you! Enclosed is to cover the cost of the taxi home.*
> *From your penitent tenant.*
> *PS. My headache isn't too awful which must mean the wine was rather good (?!)*

Wanting him to know that the extent of her inebriation had not included memory loss, that she had been touched by his confidence and remembered it, she added, *'PPS. I've always thought people who kill themselves are very selfish.'*

Shy of actual confrontation, Annie slipped the envelope under his door and scuttled back downstairs to resume her vigil for Greg.

Four hours later, anticipation had soured to impatience and finally to anger. To vent some of her frustration Annie embarked on an enraged tidy-up of the flat, kicking objects in her path and lamenting the fact that, at aged thirty-three and three quarters, she was still hanging round dormant telephones like a sad teenager. All her life had been spent waiting for something, or someone, she seethed, hurling abandoned clothes in the direction of the laundry basket and punching pillows till their feathers flew. For a woman facing the possible implications of a life-threatening illness, such passivity was particularly pathetic, she reflected darkly, flopping back onto her freshly made bed and glaring at the ceiling.

As the minutes continued to advance towards the evening, the temptation to forego the dubious pleasures of Amy's Peruvian party crept into mind and was frogmarched out again. When Greg still hadn't phoned by half past seven, Annie wrenched herself into some appropriate clothes and stabbed some order into her face and hair, resolved upon going through the ordeal alone.

It was only on the point of leaving that some of her rage melted into uncertainty. Perhaps Greg had been involved in an accident? Perhaps he was gridlocked in conference to save not only *RoundUp* but his entire career? Annie hovered on her door mat, tossing her car keys from one hand to the other, before making a final lunge for the telephone.

She left two identical messages on his office and home machines.

'Greg, it's Annie. I'm setting off for Amy's now. Her address is 14 Egham Crescent. Join me if you can.'

It was something of a relief to find the door opened by the slight, wiry figure of Miles, Amy's partner of the last three years. As well as running his own PR consultancy, he was reported to occupy much of his spare time in the more physically strenuous practice of running marathons. He had the lean, taut look of a man whose body has grown accustomed to deprivation, while his grey hair was so closely cropped to his scalp as to be barely in evidence at all. He must be ten years older than Amy at least, Annie judged, handing over her coat and offering a few witty pleasantries about Saturday night rush hour traffic and the fact that Egham Crescent lay buried under a staple in one of the middle creases of her A–Z.

'Drinks are flying round on trays,' he explained, leading her down the hall towards the back of the house, where a considerable hubbub of partying was already well underway.

'How's the running going?' Annie enquired, in a bid to delay the inevitable moment of being launched into the fray.

'Kind of you to ask.' A lump between his jaw bone and his earlobe moved when he talked. 'I'm training hard these days.'

'For the . . . ?'

'The London Marathon. I'm up to ten miles three times a week. Left knee's playing up which is a bit of a bugger, but my physiotherapist reckons I'll be all right on the night.' If Amy had briefed him as to the dubious state of Annie's health, he gave no indication of it. As they got to the threshold of the sitting room, the doorbell rang. 'I expect you know most of this rabble.' He seized a glass of champagne from a passing waiter and handed it to her. 'Back in a tick.'

Casting a surreptitious glance towards the front door on the slim chance that the new arrival might prove to be Greg, Annie turned back towards the room. There weren't nearly as many familiar faces as she had expected. Having steeled herself for the ordeal of being scrutinised, it was almost disappointing. Instead, she discussed the ethics of fox hunting with an Indian man and then became ensnared in a lament on the demise of TV drama being championed by a blond-haired woman in a sequinned black cocktail dress and gold shoes. Across the room she spotted Derek Forbes and Yvonne Moore from the *Saturday Review* team. Looking somehow intimate, Annie decided, catching Yvonne's eye and smiling a greeting which she hoped was sufficiently diffident not to summon her across the room. Her own group, meanwhile, had progressed to some fervent speculation about the Oscars, when they were interrupted by their hostess and a string of gloomy-faced men in ponchos.

'Sorry, darlings, can you move? We need this place to set up. There's plenty of room next door. When you are ready, OK?' Amy patted one of the band on the shoulder, prompting a brilliant grin of gaps and gold teeth and some vigorous head-nodding.

'Como la señora quiere.'

'Quite, quite, molto bueno,' replied Amy.

A short man with a wooden pipe began playing a bright, breathy tune which was quickly taken up by his fellows. Amy clapped delightedly before spinning round to Annie and seizing her by the elbow. 'I am *so* glad you came. I tried to get over to you before, but one's own parties are such hell when it comes to actually talking to anyone. This lot will keep them amused for a while. Now, follow me,' she instructed, leading her out of the room. At the foot of the stairs they were accosted by Stephen Garr, springing from a doorway only to find himself brusquely ordered aside by their hostess.

'Sorry Stephen, women only,' declared Amy in a tone of voice with which only the bravest would have argued. Once they were halfway up the stairs and out of earshot she hissed, 'Odious man, but he gave me two tickets to the opera once – good thing about a party this size, is one can repay all sorts of social debts with the minimum of pain or fuss.' She steered Annie into what was clearly her and Miles's bedroom and slammed the door. 'Now, my poor poor girl, how *are* you?'

'Really, Amy I'm—'

'You are brave, that's what you are. One of the bravest women I know and one of the cleverest . . . the column is just *fabulous* at the moment.'

She was full of sentiment and champagne, Annie realised, casting a longing glance at the door. 'Really, Amy, there's no need for this . . . I . . . I mean I'm no Ruth Picardie. If the results next week are nasty I'll probably turn tail and run – retire to Wales, reclaim my mother and my dog—'

'Nonsense. You're not the type to run away.' Amy sat down on the large double bed beside them, shattering both the taut perfection of its counterpane and Annie's hopes of an early release. 'Whatever happens, you'll cope beautifully, I know you will. And if there's anything – anything at all that I can – that any of us can—'

'Thank you, that's very kind,' murmured Annie, sidling towards the door.

'And well done over Greg Berkley, by the way.'

'Greg?'

'Giving him the push, not putting up with his games. That man's about as capable of fidelity as a fly is at resisting a dung heap. I shouldn't think Lucy Collins will last long either.'

'Lucy?'

'The one he took skiing. And don't look so surprised at how well informed I am, the grapevine works fast in our business, as you well know. You did well to get out when you did.'

'I just didn't know that you were acquainted . . .' faltered Annie, her mind spinning back to how preoccupied Greg had been after his skiing holiday, how awkwardly he had reacted to her bad news. It dawned on her in the same instant that the meal in the Greek restaurant had been his planned venue for telling her it was all over, that he had never intended for them to go back to his flat – or her flat – at all. That he must have done so out of nothing but cowardly pity.

'Acquainted?' Amy let out a terse laugh, rolled off the bed and went over to inspect her reflection in the mirror of her dressing-table. 'That's one way of putting it.' She picked up a bottle of perfume spray and fired a few quick jets round her earlobes. 'Oh yes, Mr Berkley and I were certainly acquainted at one time, years ago now . . . but I bet his methods are still the same. Keen in the bedroom, but not nearly so avid when it comes to the finer points of a relationship, is he? And sending flowers when he's feeling guilty – I bet the bastard is still doing that.'

Annie swallowed even though her mouth was quite dry. She went to sit where Amy had been on the bed, carefully positioning herself on the section of the bedspread that was still creased. Compared to her own bedroom, the place was as ordered as an art gallery. Tasteful framed nudes hung from the dado rail between pretty tulip-shaped light fittings that cast curvy shadows on the walls.

'Flowers?' she echoed faintly.

Amy was deftly working a powder puff across her cheeks and round her mouth. 'It might be endearing if it wasn't so fucking infantile.' She snapped the powder compact shut and stood up. 'So, as I said, well done. Shall we return to battle?' She held out her arm.

'And how's his business, these days? That *RoundUp* magazine of his—' Annie carefully straightened the bedspread before crossing the room. 'I've rather lost track since Christmas, as you might imagine—'

'Going like a train, I gather. Miles knows more about it than me – he actually buys the thing. There's talk of distribution in Europe.'

'Crisis over then,' murmured Annie, gliding out of the room.

'I beg your pardon?'

'That Foreign Relations assignment.' She turned at the top of the stairs. 'I'm ready for it as soon as you want. This week if you like. Buy the tickets, book the hotel, I'll be there.'

'Annie, you're amazing.'

'Honestly, I'm looking forward to it – I've always enjoyed a challenge.'

Stephen Garr was lying in wait for her in the hall, perched on one of Amy's elegant Georgian hall chairs with all the goggle-eyed patience of a devoted lapdog. Annie, who had her thoughts focused on the front door and how to slip through it as quickly and unobtrusively as possible, continued in a trance-like state down the stairs and past him into the small annexe containing piles of coats and a half-buried door to a small lavatory.

'Can I drive you anywhere?' he enquired cheerily, peering at her from under the overgrown thatch of his fringe. 'Like I did last time, remember?'

Annie cut him off before he could complete the reminiscence, unaware that he had spent many hours since feeding on its every detail, reliving it, elaborating it, bleeding it dry.

'I've got my own car, thank you, Stephen.' She tugged on her coat, deliberately keeping her back to the lavatory door to quell any gentlemanly impulse he might have to offer assistance.

'You don't look ill,' he blurted, 'you look . . . fabulous.' As she side-stepped past him he made a clumsy lunge for her hips.

She jerked free, half laughing with shock and irritation. 'For Christ's sake—'

'What's wrong with me?' he blazed. 'Only good for taxi-driving women like you around, is that it? Good enough to fetch and carry—'

Annie swung her bag over her shoulder and buttoned up her coat with businesslike fingers. 'Don't be silly.'

'Silly?'

'Look . . . this is not a good time.' Annie was aware that whatever reserves of patience she possessed were close to running dry. 'Right now I'd turn down Mel Gibson and Leonardo di Caprio. All my life I've assumed I needed a man to be complete, that somewhere out there was my other, better half, that I required a male counterpart in order to make myself whole. Well tonight I've realised how misguided I've been. Tonight, I officially quit . . . OK?'

During the course of this tirade Stephen had been looking at the ground, tracing the herring-bone lines of Amy's oak floor with the toe of his shoe. When Annie stopped talking he lifted his head, the blankness of his expression conveying that he was neither sympathetic nor consoled.

'Well, goodnight then,' muttered Annie, hurriedly letting herself out of the front door.

Outside, the night was clear and still. A luminous full moon shone like a single spotlight on an empty stage. Annie glared at it as she retraced her steps to her car, unconsciously increasing her stride to keep time with the muted strains of Amy's Inca friends, now beating and blowing all their energies into a haunting threnody on the vagaries of the human heart.

Chapter Thirty-Two

—————◆○◆○◆—————

'Why the hell didn't you tell me?' Marina thrust four more coat hangers of dresses over Annie's outstretched arms and strode across to the next stand of clothes. 'That's what I can't understand. I mean – Christ – what are friends for and all that? But no, I have to go and *read* about it, for Christ's sake, along with half a million other poxy strangers who don't know you or give a shit about you—' Marina stopped abruptly, overcome for by no means the first time that Saturday morning by the sense of injured outrage. 'I mean . . . bloody hell Annie, what were you thinking of?'

Annie blinked at the rainbow array of materials draped across her arms, struggling both with the urge to apologise and the new, disturbing notion that over the past few years this friendship she had so treasured may have held her back as much as it supported her. 'They do give a shit,' she said quietly. 'People have been so amazingly kind—'

'Well, so would I have been if only you'd give me the chance. I mean, it's great and everything that now you say it turns out to be a harmless little filoadenoid, but—'

'A fibroadenoma,' Annie corrected her.

'Whatever. But I'll never forgive you for not telling me.' She seized a buttercup-yellow taffeta cocktail dress and thrust it up to Annie's face.

'Not yellow, please,' pleaded Annie, feeling the first stab of conscious association with their surroundings. 'Yellow drains

me of colour. People will wonder why you've chosen a bridesmaid suffering from a tropical disease.'

'I've got yellow trim on me,' replied Marina stoutly, 'so it
would be nice if there was some on you.'

Annie shrugged her acquiescence, not wanting to generate
more antagonism between them than existed already. That
Marina had managed to take offence over a matter on which she
had expected nothing more complicated than sympathy was
yet further confirmation of the extent to which the small but
potentially serious question mark over her health had affected
her life. The benign diagnosis, indicated by something called a
C2 rating on the cytology lab sheet forwarded to her the day
before, had been a tremendous relief. Every time she thought of
it a shiver of pure joy tiptoed down her spine. But her life had
changed radically anyway, Annie realised, not just at work and
with friends but within the subterranean muddle of her psyche.
After Amy's party, her anger had surprised her by hardening into
something that felt like resolve. She had ended up walking for
almost half an hour before returning to her car, focusing not on
disappointment about Greg so much as a sense of liberation. An
extraordinary lucidity had flooded her mind. A lucidity which
had remained with her ever since and which, after hearing her
cytology results, seemed to lead quite naturally to the decision
to resign from the column.

Amy, whom she had called at home that morning, had been
unashamedly appalled. 'But it's just taking off, Annie, you simply
can't mean it.'

'I'm sure Yvonne will be able to take the reins.'

'Is it . . . is this because there's been some sort of develop-
ment in your . . . condition?'

'Partly, yes. It's been officially diagnosed as a friendly presence after all. Something called a fibroadenoma. A couple of
hours in a day surgery and all I'll have is a tiny scar to remember
it by.'

'Oh Annie what a relief,' she gushed, while a small, despicable part of her experienced a pinprick of disappointment.
Annie's illness had been one of the unparalleled highlights in the

entire career of the *Saturday Review*. It was impossible not to lament its passing.

'But it's not that, Amy. It's more that writing the column hasn't been good for me—' Annie faltered, struggling to articulate something she hardly understood herself. '. . . I sort of . . . lost control over it . . . let it get muddled with my real life, which was never my intention . . . In the end it was more like therapy.'

'I don't care what it was, it was bloody marvellous.'

'Maybe, but not for me. I'm much more comfortable writing facts about other people's lives than my own. There's only a couple of months or so till my contract runs out anyway—'

'But we were banking on renewing it.' Amy lowered her voice. 'We were planning on offering twice the money—'

'You're not listening to me, Amy. *FlatLife*, at least my version of it, is over. I want out.'

'Back to freelancing articles, you mean?'

'I guess. I might look for a proper job. I almost fancy being back in an office again – give myself a reason to get out of bed in the mornings.'

'Annie you're mad. Change your mind this minute, I'm begging you.'

'I'll see out my contract of course, if you insist on it.'

'Well, thank God for small mercies,' Amy had muttered, some genuine annoyance seeping into her tone.

'And, like I said, I'll do the Foreign Relations assignment in Rome. So long as you're not expecting too many romantic interludes. I'm not exactly in the mood to start anything new.'

'And who can blame you, my dear,' Amy murmured. 'I'm just glad you'll still do it. Yvonne is good – very thorough – but she lacks your . . . lightness of touch. Takes life rather too seriously in my view. Clogs up her writing. Anyway, your ticket has been booked. You leave on Monday 16 February. And it's not Rome, it's Venice – apparently they've had to double up two groups due to lack of support.'

'Sounds promising,' Annie remarked dryly.

'An even balance of professional single people all looking for meaningful relationships—' Amy sounded as if she were reading directly from the Foreign Relations brochure, '—getting to know each other amongst gondoliers and sinking museums. My dear girl, you'll have a ball. And even if you don't, I know you'll be hilarious.'

'You're not concentrating,' Marina accused Annie, nudging her arm.

Annie blinked slowly. 'I know, sorry. I was thinking—'

'Do you miss him terribly?' Marina's face crumpled with sympathy.

'Who?'

'What a bastard . . . What a worm, wriggling out of the relationship like that.'

Annie laughed out loud. 'I can honestly say I am not missing Greg at all. In fact, it's a positive relief not to have to think about him. I was always waiting for him, always worrying – about him, about me, what I looked like, what I should wear – Christ, it was so exhausting—'

Marina gave her a long hard stare, unconvinced both by this show of bravura and several other related aspects of the new and alien version of her friend which had been revealed to her during the course of their morning's trawl around Knightsbridge. Unforgivable though it was, she found herself missing the more obviously muddled, emotionally dependent creature she had known before.

'You seem so different Annie,' she said quietly. 'And all this business about giving up the column . . . are you sure you know what you're doing?'

'Not remotely. Do you think I could try on some of these before my arms give out or we're arrested for attempted shoplifting?'

'Bernard's got loads of contacts in the media world if you—'

'I'm sure he has,' Annie interrupted, 'but I don't want to meet any of them. Perhaps I'll fall in love with Italy and become a foreign correspondent—'

'Or fall in love.'

'Absolutely not.' Annie wrenched off her jeans. 'In spite of the curious irony of finding myself about to embark on the first lonely hearts assignment of my career, I have finally accepted the fact that I don't mind being on my own – that I like it, in fact – and I intend to keep things that way.' She peeled off her socks and flung them at Marina. 'You know, one of the things I've realised recently is that you were never looking for a man in quite the way I was.' She reached for the yellow dress.

'Yes, I was.' Marina looked indignant.

'No, you weren't – at least not as a way of . . . of completing yourself, of literally finding your other half. You like yourself, Marina, you always have. It shows. It's part of why you're attractive. Whereas me—' Annie shrugged helplessly '—I've never liked myself, not one measly bit of me.' She turned to look at herself in the mirror. 'My hair, my face, my body – I hated the whole damn lot—'

'You twit – you're gorgeous—'

'Don't interrupt. I'm not gorgeous. I never will be. But I'm all right. I'll do.' She made a funny face at her reflection. 'Lopsided or not, I have at last – I think – accepted myself – both halves of me.' She turned to face Marina with a rueful smile. 'It's only taken thirty-three years and a health crisis.'

Marina, for once at a loss for words, leapt from her perch on the stool and busied herself with the dress zip which had caught on a thread of loose cotton. 'Hold your breath in, that's it – nearly there.' The metal teeth slid together in a sudden easy rush, leaving Annie feeling as if the ridge of each rib was visible through the material. They both stared into the mirror for a few seconds, aware that the conversation hung incomplete between them.

'I knew you were unhappy – I told Bernard – but I didn't know how deeply—'

'You couldn't have helped.' Annie delivered the verdict not as an accusation but a statement of fact. 'Actually, looking back, I can see that in many ways you made it worse—'

'Thanks a bunch.' Marina's tone was light, but Annie saw from the way her eyes glittered that she was genuinely hurt.

'It's nothing personal, Marina. The same could be said of Jake. It was my fault: I let myself get so used to leaning on you two – on being the hopeless one, copping out of facing up to things – it became a habit.' She flung out her arms in exasperation. 'One deep breath and these seams will blow.'

'Nonsense. It's got whalebone in the bodice – tough as concrete.' Marina rapped her knuckles on Annie's ribcage to demonstrate the point. 'I love it.' She pulled a small piece of fabric out of the pocket of her jeans. 'See, it matches the trim on my dress perfectly. Put the jacket on, before you make up your mind.'

'An improvement,' Annie admitted a few moments later, balancing on the balls of her feet in an effort to simulate the accoutrement of high heels and then slumping down on the stool in the corner of the cubicle. 'If it means avoiding that lot—' she waved a despairing arm at the remaining pile of dresses '—I'll agree to anything.'

'Oh no, we've got to see what these look like as well. Then there's the shoes and handbag—'

Annie groaned.

'But you like shopping.'

'No, I don't. It's another revelation I've had, didn't I tell you?'

'Sod your revelations, we've got work to do. Slip that one off and try the blue.'

'And you've lost more weight,' Marina accused, several outfits later, opting for a scolding tone as the only safe tactic for not having the compliment hurled back at her. 'We'll have to have a massive lunch – feed you up a bit. Unless you've had a revelation about food too?'

'Only that it seems to contain more calories when you're sad,' replied Annie thoughtfully, stepping out of a puddle of cream silk. 'Contentment burns energy,' she murmured. 'I'm thinking of researching an article on the subject. But lunch will have to be quick, I'm afraid. I've got someone coming about the spare room and a train to catch.'

'The spare . . . my room, you mean? That was quick.' Marina laughed uncertainly.

'I put a postcard in Mr Patel's window. Last chance to change your mind—' Annie's smile was equally unsure. For a few moments the two women stared at each other, aware that a door was closing behind them for good.

'I'm bad for you, remember,' quipped Marina, reaching for the last dress in the pile, a simple white linen flecked with spots of pink. 'And where's this train going, then?'

'Wales – I'm popping down to see my mother. I want to tell her my good news in person – or at least before it breaks in the paper next week. Like you, she was a bit put out at stumbling upon intimate details of my physical and mental state in the national press.'

Marina opened her mouth to exclaim at this unprecedented show of filial attention, but quickly closed it again, warned off by the fiercely protective expression in Annie's eyes. 'Just so long as you're back for my hen night next week,' she teased, swallowing the fact that Annie's life really was moving on into new territory and that she had no right to disparage it or to try to hold her back.

Michael Derwent stood at his window watching his tenant walk briskly up the street and disappear under the frame of the front door. On the window seat beside him was a newspaper, folded at a page revealing a smudged black-and-white print of Annie's head together with a typically self-deprecating and humorous account of her experiences at the breast clinic the Friday before. At the muffled slam of the front door, he felt the floor beneath his bare feet vibrate slightly. On inspecting his palms, he saw a line of deep pink ridges where his nails had pressed into the skin. Through the glass beside him, heavy clouds moved like armoured ships on a steely sea. Not even the piano had helped that morning. The music inside his head had fragmented at the touch of the keys, while his fingers obstinately defied even the safe rigours of complying to notes on a written page. He had punched the piano in frustration, creating a series of loud, ear-gratingly discordant clashes that seemed to sum up the ineptitude in the wider realm of his personal life, his utter incapacity to live within himself as he had intended and the mess he was making in consequence.

Michael picked up Jake's silk scarf, which he had found amidst a pile of old dust sheets that morning, and twisted it round his knuckles until his fingers turned white. After a few moments he found a large brown envelope, folded the scarf into a fat rectangle and slipped it inside. Seizing a pen and pad, he wrote a hurried message.

> *You left this here the night you came to visit. Of course I*
> *forgive you for what happened, I told you so at the time. I*
> *have kept my promise of making no mention of it to Annie,*
> *but with increasing discomfort. We have seen a fair bit of each*
> *other, what with one thing and another, and I have wanted to*
> *talk to her about it several times. Since she is such a good*
> *friend of yours I feel that nothing can progress naturally*
> *between any of us until I do. I have tried the phone number*
> *on your postcard several times but without success. I hope the*
> *filming is going well.*
> *Yours, Michael Derwent*

After a moment's consideration he decided against slipping the latest *FlatLife* piece between the folds of the scarf. How Annie Jordan broke the news of her medical condition to close friends was hardly something that warranted his involvement. At the thought of her, Michael glanced out of the window again as if some imprint of her recent presence in the street might remain. Why was illness so hard to mention? he wondered desperately, picking up the newspaper and slapping Annie's article with the back of his fingers. Not just during the course of the wine tasting evening, but on several other occasions, he had longed to broach the subject, wanting so badly to express some sort of sympathy, but fearing how it might be received. The woman had such a look about her sometimes, as if she would strike out at anyone who dared to get too close. Or perhaps it was just him, Michael decided glumly. Perhaps it was so long since he had tried to communicate properly with other people, let alone women, that he had simply lost the knack. Her thank-you card had been nice though, he reflected, slipping his note to Jake in next to the scarf and running his tongue along the flap of the envelope. Particularly the second postscript, for which he had been very grateful.

Setting off for the post office, he was accosted on the doorstep by a serious, bespectacled girl who told him she had come about the spare room. For a moment Michael was tempted to sabotage the appointment. The girl didn't look like Annie's sort at all – far too earnest and glum – with lips that turned down at the corners, as if flexed that way in the permanent expectation of bad news.

'You'll be wanting Annie Jordan. First floor.'

The girl started in through the open door, but he put up a hand to stop her. 'Perhaps you'd better use the intercom to let her know you're here? We've had a few . . . shall we say unwelcome visitors recently—'

'Unwelcome visitors?' The girl took a step backwards. 'Whatever do you mean?'

'Nothing.' Michael hastily offered her his most reassuring smile. 'We're just keen on security, that's all.' He patted the box. 'It's a spanking new system – we like to put it to good use.'

'I see,' replied the girl slowly, eyeing him with evident suspicion. 'I'll ring the bell then.'

'You do that. Annie's great – you'll love her.'

Michael set off in the direction of the post office, telling himself that whom Annie Jordan chose to share her rental commitments with could be of no import to him, even as a landlord. But having despatched his parcel to Spain, he had to quell a schoolboy urge to barge into her flat and make disparaging faces behind the room-hunter's back. He could offer to lower her rent, he thought wildly, confess that he knew some of what she was going through and would like to help. For a few yards Michael strode purposefully in the direction of the mansions, but as he reached the Finchley Road his pace slowed once more to an uncertain crawl. In spite of several opportunities, his tenant had never revealed the remotest inclination to return his confessions with confidences of her own. Probably because she had countless friends and lovers to turn to first, Michael reminded himself, turning up the collar of his jacket and veering left towards Regent's Park. By the time he reached the boating lake, he had resolved to keep away from her until he had heard back from Jake; to let their acquaintance evolve naturally or not at all.

Chapter Thirty-Three

If one stayed in the same city for long enough, every place would end up with a jumble of associations attached to it, Annie mused, staring round the high grimy interior of Paddington station and recalling a particularly fond farewell she had enjoyed with Peter in the days when he was still commuting to Bristol. It was on the Sunday evening after they had first met. He had put his tongue in her ear, she remembered, and whispered that his life had changed for ever. Annie shuddered, partly at the recollection of the tongue, which had felt alien and unwelcome, and partly at the hopelessness of wisdom with hindsight. Some inner physical essence of her had shied away at the touch of him, yet she hadn't listened to it – had been too pathetically sure that a male was the one missing vital component of her life to want to listen to it. Similarly with Greg. A part of her had known from the start it wasn't right – that she was working and worrying far too hard for it ever to become right – but a bigger part had felt a terrible reluctance to admit to the possibility of it being preferable to be alone.

'But not any more,' she muttered, striding out across the forecourt towards an attractive mobile caravan-style shop, selling coffee and French pastries.

'One white coffee and a cheese and ham croissant please.' As she was clipping her purse shut, Annie glimpsed a familiar figure wheeling a pushchair towards the noticeboard of departures. In no mood for confrontations of any kind, she made a dash for the open doorway of WH Smith.

She was feeling relatively safe, ensconced between a rack of motoring magazines and a shelf of bestsellers, when Zoë caught up with her a few minutes later.

'Annie, I thought it was you – what a lovely surprise.'

Baffled by this show of sweetness and goodwill, since Zoë had made no response to her letter of apology after the column about the dinner party, Annie smiled brightly, echoing similar effusions of welcome in return.

'You're not catching the 6.17 to Bristol by any chance, are you?' Zoë continued.

'No . . . Cardiff . . . the 6.10.' Annie checked her watch. 'I haven't got long—'

'Oh what a shame.' Zoë bent down to her daughter, screwing up her face in a show of comic despair. 'Mummum can't have her lovely chat with her friend, can she?' Cordelia, still too young to manage a coherent verbal response, tugged off the fetching purple beret covering her hairless scalp and hurled it into the display of magazines.

'Zoë, I really—'

'There, that's better.' Having retrieved the beret, Zoë repositioned it with the help of an elastic strap and stood to admire her handiwork with a sigh of satisfaction. Observing the crimson cheeks of the infant, Annie experienced a mild urge to take Cordelia's part and rip the offending article off herself.

'Annie, I know you're in a rush and this is hardly the place, but there's something I've simply got to tell you—'

Annie braced herself. Of course Zoë would want to talk about what had happened. And quite right too. In fact, she thought despairingly, she should have raised the matter herself – cleared the air – the moment they met. 'It's not for you to say anything Zoë,' she interrupted quickly, 'it was all my fault, the whole business.'

'No, you don't understand.' Zoë's voice was pleading. 'You were right.'

'I was?'

'About David Portman. He was . . . after me.'

'Oh my goodness—'

'Oh Annie, you're so wise,' wailed Zoë, 'I just don't know how you do it.'

'Wise?' The notion was somehow more shocking than Zoë's news. 'I only noticed that he—'

'He made his move the very next time we met.' Zoë folded her arms, shaking her head dolefully at the memory.

'Oh dear, poor you.' Annie sneaked a look at her watch, aware that it would seem unfeeling to excuse herself at such a critical juncture, but fearful of missing her train. There was seven minutes left and she already had her ticket. She could feel the steam rising from her coffee, gently warming the fingers of her left hand where they clutched her paper bag.

'The worst of it was, I responded,' continued Zoë. 'I was flattered, I suppose. I mean . . . well, to be honest, things haven't been too good between Richard and me since Cordelia arrived. Sex and so on—' She frowned. 'I know some women say breast feeding makes them feel alluring, but it's never worked for me. Nor for Richard for that matter.' Zoë let out a short laugh. 'So anyway, things have been . . . tough. We're seeing someone from Relate now to try and get us back on the rails. I only slept with David twice, but its rather thrown things off balance—'

'I can imagine . . .' Annie murmured, inwardly marvelling at the travails of married couples and experiencing a fresh surge of gratitude at the simplicity of living alone.

'Look, you've got to go.' Zoë shook a smile back onto her face. 'I'll walk with you to the platform – I think it's the one next to mine. How are things with you, anyway? I don't read your column these days, I'm afraid – at least not since—'

'It was unforgivable of me to write about your dinner party like that,' Annie blurted, 'I'm so sorry. I tried so hard not to write about real life, but it kept sneaking in. In fact it's because of that – among other things – that I recently took the decision to resign.' Realising that Zoë knew nothing of her recent medical scare, Annie decided it would be simplest to avoid the subject altogether. 'So at least I can go back to living my usual muddle of a life without feeling the awful pressure to write about it.'

'But that's incredible – I mean I've resigned too,' exclaimed Zoë, jogging behind the pushchair to keep pace with Annie as they crossed the forecourt.

'You mean you're not going back after maternity leave?' As they reached the ticket barrier, Cordelia celebrated a successful end to protracted negotiations with the offending chin strap by throwing her hat several feet away onto the platform.

'I'll get it,' volunteered Annie. 'Hang on.'

'I'm going to be a full-time mother,' declared Zoë, when Annie was back at her side. 'I say, you wouldn't be interested in my job, would you? I'd be more than happy to put in a good word. Magazines pay so much more than newspapers – and they're crying out for good people at the moment. The woman who's been covering my maternity leave has been a complete disaster, commissioning all sorts of crap from people that nobody wants to read—'

'But they wouldn't want me, would they?' Behind her, Annie was aware of the guard blowing his whistle, 'I mean, all my experience is as a writer as opposed to an editor.'

'Ideal. Experience from the other side. Send me your CV.'

'Thanks, Zoë, I might just do that.' Annie turned to go and then stepped back again. 'If it's so great, why are you giving it up?'

Zoë patted a small swell of a stomach hitherto concealed beneath her jumper and rolled her eyes at the smeary glass-panelled roof arching over their heads. 'A sibling for Cordelia. Not planned, needless to say. Richard's welcome-back-to-the-marriage present – at least I think it's Richard's.' She made a face. 'That's one of the reasons we're having counselling.'

'Bloody hell, Zoë—' Behind her the guard was starting to slam carriage doors.

'Don't worry, everything will be fine, I just know it. Richard and I will be stronger than ever if we can come through this. Go on, hurry, it's about to leave.'

'I'll call you,' shouted Annie, feeling desperate both about her train and Zoë's extraordinary optimism in the face of such a fraught set of circumstances.

'And I mean it about the job,' Zoë yelled after her, waving her arm in farewell.

It was only as she threw her bag onto the luggage rack that Annie realised that the reviled purple beret was still in her right hand. She began to tug at the window, but then thought of Cordelia's pink face and changed her mind. Seeing that the train was already lurching out of its giant cage towards the chequered suburbs of West London, she placed the beret on an empty seat for someone else to find.

As the taxi swerved round the final bend in the road, just yards past the spot where her Fiat had taken an unscheduled nose-dive into the ditch on Christmas Eve, Annie experienced the first serious pangs of uncertainty as to whether she was doing the right thing – whether a move of such bold spontaneity would cause the chink of understanding between her and her mother to widen or disappear for good. In response to these fears, she instructed the cab driver to stop several yards from the cottage, out of some vague notion that if she changed her mind at the last minute she might be able to tiptoe back up the lane and find a bus stop.

'Are you sure you're all right?' enquired the cabbie, eyeing the darkness outside with evident uncertainty. It was almost nine o'clock – far later than Annie had intended to arrive thanks to an unexplained forty-minute interlude sitting on the tracks outside Cardiff.

'Fine, thanks – it's just around the corner. I want my arrival to be a surprise,' she explained, impelled by the look of bafflement on the man's face to offer further justification for her behaviour.

On turning the final bend in the lane, Annie was surprised to see that all the windows in the cottage were unlit. More surprising still, was that she could make out the ghostly shadow of her mother's white Ford, parked as always between the side of the house and the wood shed. As she approached the porch she was greeted by the sound of muffled barking. Sensing already that it was pointless, Annie nonetheless spent several minutes ringing the bell and calling through the letterbox. She was about to embark on a search for open windows, when she remembered that there was a spare back door key behind a paint pot in the shed. Leaving her bag on the doorstep, Annie stumbled round the side of the house past the car, slipping on loose stones and groping for balance in the dark. By the time her fingers had located the cold metal of the key, the dogs were in such a frenzy of excitement that she was almost scared to open the door.

With the animals bounding round her, she groped for the kitchen light. The walls gleamed with evidence of fresh paint. All was still and ordered: a single cup, saucer and teaspoon on the draining board beside the kitchen sink; a shopping list pinned by a magnet to the side of the fridge saying, *apples, talc, potting compost, fish(?)*. Two paint brushes sat in a large glass jar on the windowsill, next to a large tin of paint. In the sitting room a table lamp was on, casting a lonely light across her mother's favourite armchair. On one arm of the chair lay an open book and a used tissue. The cushioned seat still contained a deep imprint from when it had last been occupied, contributing both to the sense that the room had only recently been abandoned and Annie's mounting intimations of doom. Taking the stairs three at a time, she raced up to the landing and searched the bedrooms, finding only more freshly painted walls and an accompanying sense of order that felt new. In her bedroom all the ornaments and books had been tidied away into cardboard boxes and stacked along the walls, together with several paint rollers and a step ladder.

Upon establishing that the house was completely empty, Annie retreated to the kitchen, her mind whirring with morbid possibilities. A walk would have required her mother to take the dogs. If she had gone into town, she would have used the car. Annie reached into her handbag for her cigarettes, only to remember that she had deliberately refrained from buying any. Pressing a stick of peppermint chewing gum into her mouth instead, she concluded that the most sensible course of action would be to elicit the support of Terry, the farmer who had towed her car out of the ditch at Christmas and whose dilapidated farmhouse was just a mile or so up the road. At the last minute, she clipped Bonnie's lead to her collar and tugged the surprised animal out of the back door after her.

It was a long walk. Bonnie, unable to share in her companion's sense of calamity, insisted on stopping to sniff at every clump of weed and stone lining the edge of the lane. Striding under the high arch of trees, their limbs only dimly visible under the clouded light of the moon, Annie was aware of having to keep a primeval fear in check. She looked straight ahead, not wanting to see the half-formed shapes on either side of her, her nerves jangling at every rustle and snap in the dark.

Their arrival at the farm triggered a wild medley of barking from one of the barns. Seeing only a single light in an upstairs window, Annie's heart sank. But by the time she reached the front door the hall light had been flicked on. A moment later Terry Evans appeared in a short towelling dressing-gown, revealing two white hairy bow legs and a pair of faded tartan slippers. He did not look sleepy, so much as horrified.

'I am so sorry to bother—' Annie faltered. 'I'm Annie Jor—'

'I know who you are. You'd better come in.'

'I know it's late – I'm sorry – it's just that I'm worried about my mother,' she babbled, 'the cottage is locked but a light's on – the car's there and the dogs—' At some point during this bout of incoherence, Annie became aware of a third party, other than Bonnie or the ginger tabby weaving in and out of Terry Evans' thin shins. Looking up the stairs, she saw her mother, clad in her old blue dressing-gown, her face bare of make-up, her short grey hair sticking out at wild angles. She was clutching the lapels of the gown tightly together with both hands, confirming Annie's immediate suspicion that her chest was bare and that her presence in the farmhouse signified rather more than a desire for conversation on a winter's evening.

'Annie.'

For a moment Annie felt a surge of something like anger.

Then she found herself starting to laugh, as relief – coupled with no small measure of wonderment – washed all other emotions away. The two lovers remained motionless, Terry still by the front door, Christine at the top of the flight of stairs, each as flushed and dumbstruck as teenagers caught with their trousers down.

'Oh Mum, I'm so sorry,' Annie gasped at last, 'I came on a whim – planned to surprise you – but not like this – I mean, Christ, I thought you'd been abducted – thank God you're OK.' She wiped the tears from her cheeks with the sleeve of her jacket. 'I won't even begin to tell you some of the horrors that have been going through my mind.'

Slowly Christine began to descend the stairs. 'You mean, you don't mind?' she said quietly.

'Mind?'

'About . . . us?' She went to stand beside Terry, who had been staring anxiously at his tartan slippers.

'Mum – for God's sake – of course I don't mind. How could I possibly? I'm just glad you've not been whisked away by aliens.' They all laughed at that, even Terry, who led the way into the sitting room, stoked up the embers of the fire and suggested a round of nightcaps. While he was fetching glasses Annie whispered that the doctors had given her the all-clear, that the primary reason for a visit had been to tell her so in person. Christine made as if to stand up, but then simply reached across the space separating their chairs and patted Annie's arm. 'Wonderful. That's wonderful.'

Annie nodded happily, still savouring the discovery of a relationship which she would have believed utterly impossible. Though keen to hear the whole story, she did not want to ruin the moment by appearing over-curious.

'We've been friends for years,' began Christine, drying up as Terry reappeared, clutching three sherry glasses and a full decanter of sloe gin.

Annie drank quickly, resisting Christine's offer to return with her to the cottage, eager to leave the two of them alone. On the way back she walked slowly, tugging at leaves on low-slung branches and smiling to herself at the manifest shyness of two lovers both in their sixth decade. That her mother had been so worried about her reaction was also humbling. It revealed a new twist in a vulnerability which Annie realised she was only just beginning to understand. One of the many legacies of her dear father, she reflected, sighing as always at the thought of him. There had been no communication between them since Christmas Day. A solitary effort of hers to call Portugal had been met with brusque reports that he was taking exercise on the golf course.

Demons only existed inside your head after all, Annie mused, brushing the familiar sentiments of disappointment from her mind and tipping up her chin to admire the misty dark of the sky. All her earlier terrors had now been supplanted by a sense of beauty. The moon was a mere brushstroke of a presence behind a veil of cloud. Three or four stars glinted down like needles of sunlight piercing a darkened room. As Annie strolled between the walls of whispering trees, the dog at her side and the warmth of the gin in her belly, a rare rush of pure contentment welled inside; a rush connected to the full absorption of the fact that she was not ill after all, that, barring fateful misfortune, a future of unimagined fulfilment might yet await her.

'Come on Bonnie, let's run.'

After a moment of puzzlement, the dog broke into an excited gallop. Annie, sprinting in her usual ungainly style alongside, nonetheless felt reckless and exciting. She ran till her lungs were bursting, cherishing the realisation that her energy sprang from sheer euphoria, from the new desire to throw herself at life instead of scurrying for cover.

Chapter Thirty-Four

———◆◆◆———

Annie signed for the boxes – four large flat ones – with some dismay. The boy in the shop had said nothing about the work station in the window being self-assembly. 'I don't suppose you'd like to stay for a cup of tea and put the thing together for me?'

The delivery man looked more offended than amused. A reaction that was not helped when Annie absently put his pen in the pot beside the hall telephone instead of his outstretched hand.

Lugging the boxes into the spare bedroom took some time, as did moving the computer and her original desk – a small formica table covered in unattractive brown stains – out of the way first. Impeded by the after-effects of her spell in the day surgery unit a couple of days before, Annie paused for several rests, cursing both her slowness and the unforeseen irritations of a bruised and tender breast.

Inside the largest box was a single, somewhat blurred sheet of pictured instructions, comprising a daunting criss-crossed web of arrows and coded numbers. It was only after Annie had identified all the parts, surrounding herself with tidy rows of different-sized nails and slats of wood, that it became apparent that her meagre tool collection did not stretch to the right kind of screwdriver.

Eager now for the quickest way to complete her task, she decided to call upon the resources of Michael Derwent. Having seen nothing of him since the night of the wine tasting the week before, Annie was beginning to suspect that their curious flurry of a friendship might be over. A fact which left her unexpectedly disappointed, but not entirely surprised. While imagining that her somewhat inelegant behaviour must be partly to blame, she guessed too that the strain of never mentioning Jake was probably beginning to take its toll.

Such speculations caused Annie both to pause outside her landlord's door, and to make a private vow to refuse all offers of assistance beyond the loan of the implement in question. Putting together her new office was to be a practical and a symbolic demonstration of her commitment to a new phase in her life; a phase linked to the elation she had felt in Wales, the belief that she could do whatever she chose without fearing the consequences. She had sent her CV to Zoë, but was seriously thinking of using the impending trip to Venice as an opportunity to try her hand at travel writing as well. Something to which she had always been dimly attracted but had never had the chance to attempt.

Michael had just stepped out of the shower when the buzzer sounded. He hurried out of the bathroom with a towel clutched round his waist, his wet feet skidding slightly on the freshly stripped bare floorboards, which now extended into every corner of the flat.

'Yes?' he called, without opening the door.

'It's only Annie.'

'Hang on. I'm not decent.'

'I can come back,' Annie began.

'No worries . . . one minute.' Michael pulled on a clean T-shirt and knotted the towel more securely round his waist. By the time he opened the door great damp patches had spread through the grey cotton of the shirt where it clung to his skin. His hair was sticking up in dark wet clumps, and dripping down the back of his neck and into his eyebrows.

'Oh dear, you really should have sent me away,' Annie apologised, putting her hand to her mouth at the sight of him.

'I was washing varnish out of my hair – virulent stuff.' He

grinned, shaking his wet head so vigorously that a shower of droplets scattered across her face. 'What can I do?'

Annie hesitated, overcome by the sudden realisation that whatever the sexual predilections of the man standing in front of her, she found him excessively attractive. 'Nothing . . . er . . . that is to say . . . one of these—' She twirled her screwdriver. 'If you've got it. But with a different end. Not the straight across kind, like this, but the round indented kind – for those screws that have the little hole in the middle. I'm building a desk,' she concluded rather grandly, wishing as soon as she had spoken that she had possessed the grace and good sense to remain silent.

'A desk, eh? Wow.' He folded his arms and leant against the doorway. 'That sounds . . . ambitious.'

Annie reddened. 'That is, someone has already built it, but then taken it apart again, so I've got to—'

'Put it together?'

'Exactly. It's very straightforward. I got it from one of those enormous shops where families spend their weekends.'

'Would you like to see my garden?'

'I beg your pardon?'

'I'm building a roof garden.'

'In this weather?'

'It was beautiful earlier this morning. Come on, I'd like you to see it – tell me what you think.'

'I really don't—' she began, but he had already retreated inside on the evident assumption that she would follow.

'Access is via the fire escape, but if you stand on the chest of drawers in my bedroom and look through the skylight you'll see most of it,' he explained eagerly, disappearing into his bathroom where the towel was exchanged for a pair of faded blue cotton shorts.

'On the chest of drawers?' Annie peered into his bedroom. In the far corner stood a large mahogany chest, inlaid with circular patterns of mother-of-pearl and supported by four carved sturdy feet.

'I don't want to bring the ladder in here because it's sticky with paint and general muck and this room is more or less done – apart from the mural.'

'Mural?' Annie stepped inside.

'Something for that far wall and maybe the ceiling. Nothing too erotic.' He snatched a glance for her reaction, but she was busy inspecting patterns on his chest of drawers. 'I sometimes spend long segments of the night awake, I thought it would be a good idea to have something soothing to look at. You don't paint do you, by any chance?'

'Only pin-men and bubble clouds . . . I do a nice line in those.'

He pretended to consider these options seriously for a moment. 'I was thinking of something a little more classic.'

'Are you honestly expecting me to scramble up there to look onto your roof?'

'Step on the bed first. Then the bedstead – like this—' He nimbly demonstrated. 'And once you're up here you get a perfect view. Come on.' He held out a hand. 'I'll help you from the bed.'

'Two of us on that thing? We'll break it.'

'It's very strong. Come on. And then I'll find you a screw-driver – might even give you one for keeps if you're lucky, I've got hundreds of the wretched things lying about the place.'

With some difficulty Annie scrambled up the suggested route and gingerly took up a position in front of him on the chest of drawers. Deliberately not looking down or to the side, she stared steadily out through the slanting window in front of her face, which presented, like a wide, deep TV screen, a perfect view of a space she had never known existed. Even through the blur of rain she could see that it was going to be beautiful: tubs of shrubs, a rock garden, the wooden skeleton of a small pergola housing an elegant stone birdbath and a sun dial.

'It's . . . perfect.' Forgetting her dizziness, she stretched up onto the balls of her feet for a better view. 'I had no idea—'

'There's a lot of work to be done yet. Once spring kicks in I can get some colour up here. I was thinking of investing in a square or two of that fake grass stuff, just to complete the picture.

I've got plans to rig up a hammock too. You'll be able to get to it from your flat by the fire escape outside your bathroom window – use it any time you want—'.

Annie sank back onto the flats of her feet. 'Oh no . . . I mean that's very kind . . . but it looks far too . . . private. I mean, it's the sort of place where you'd want to go with—' Losing courage, she felt all her awkwardness return. 'Could I just . . . get down?' she ventured, sidling back past him as best she could. 'I think I can feel a spot of vertigo coming on.'

'With?' He kept one leg out, blocking her way.

'I beg your pardon?'

'You said, "where you'd want to go with—"?'

'Oh I see . . . yes, I meant, you know, a . . . partner . . . Someone with whom you would want to be . . . Someone like Jake.' The last two words slipped out before she could rein them in, following her train of thought rather than anything related to her intentions.

'Jake?'

'Could I get past please?'

He pressed back against the wall with exaggerated care, giving her ample space to manoeuvre herself back across to the bed and down to the ground.

'Jake?' Michael repeated, staring down at her from the top of the chest of drawers.

Annie slipped her shoes back on, biting her lip and trying not to look upwards, partly because she found the geography of their positions somewhat threatening and partly because of his bare, dark-haired legs which seemed to fall in the natural path of her eyeline. 'I'm sorry if I've offended you by mentioning it. It's just that I know Jake *very* well – it really doesn't bother me either way . . . I say, you couldn't track down that screwdriver for me now, could you? I was rather hoping to have my construction project completed before the millennium.'

'Do you know your trouble?' He was still standing there, arms folded now, eyes blazing down at her. 'You see what you want to see. You judge on first appearances.'

'No I don't,' she retorted, folding her arms and glaring back up at him. 'But I do think it is a bit ridiculous – in this day and age – for two unattached males who like each other to be so ridiculously clandestine about it.'

He threw up his hands and slapped them hard against his thighs. 'Jesus Christ—' He leapt down from the chest of drawers, landing deftly on the balls of his feet. The movement reminded Annie of the way he had flown off the swing a few weeks before. She flinched, but stood her ground, dropping her eyes to the floor. When she looked up again, Michael was crossing the room towards her. Before she could step aside he had cupped her face in his hands and pressed his lips against hers. Caught so completely by surprise, it took a moment to disentangle herself; a moment during which she registered the faint soapy smell of his skin and the warm energy of his mouth.

As she pulled away he made no attempt to hold her, but let his hands drop to his sides. 'I'm not gay, Annie,' he said wearily. 'I've tried most things in my life, but not that. Much as your friend Jake would have had it otherwise.' He ran his fingers through his hair, flattening the damp clumps into a smooth sleek sweep. 'You know, I even suspected this at one point, that maybe you thought—' He let out a brief laugh, shaking his head, 'I mean, I realise I haven't exactly been leading an extravagant social life during the last few months. I thought I'd explained some of the reasons why the other night . . . I thought you understood.' He looked so hostile she took a step backwards. 'I also thought that a sensitive soul like you might pick up on at least some of the right . . . vibrations.' He burst out laughing. 'Oh Jesus, I guess this is bloody insulting.'

'Insulting?' murmured Annie, finding her voice at last. 'Yes, I suppose, it is. I'm so sorry, Michael . . . It's just that, I knew Jake liked you from the start and then . . . well . . . one afternoon I saw his scarf on the back of the door, and I just assumed—' Her voice tailed away under the scrutiny of Michael's recriminatory stare and the pressure of the realisation that she had admitted to the sin of which he had accused her not once, but several times during the course of their acquaintance. 'I suppose I did jump to conclusions—'

'And you didn't think to quiz Jake himself on the matter, I suppose? That would have been too simple, would it?'

'He went away—' she faltered. 'And anyway, I did try and ask him about it and got nowhere.' She was silent for a moment, still trying to assemble her thoughts. 'But you can't deny that the two of you have struck up some sort of secretive friendship. What was I supposed to think? Seeing items of his clothing lying about the flat, letters from Spain—'

'My, my, we have been playing the detective.'

'Look, I'm sorry, obviously you don't have to justify anything to me.'

'No, I don't.' Michael folded his arms and leant against the doorway. 'But I will anyway.' He sighed heavily. 'Jake charmed his way up here one night just before Christmas. I'd been playing late at the club. He came backstage for a bit afterwards and then trailed me home. There followed . . . How shall I put it now? . . . An awkward scene—' He shot her a wry smile. 'I felt very sorry for him. He'd had a lot to drink and was in quite a state. He stayed the night – on a mattress on the floor – and breakfast too. A nice man, I liked him. When he asked if I'd mind keeping the incident to myself, I agreed. It seemed a reasonable request. He was adamant about it – worried, I assume, that you and your ex-flatmate might find the episode amusing.'

'But that's ridiculous—'

Michael sighed heavily. 'I'm only telling you what happened. It really didn't seem such a big deal at the time. I wanted to tell you, more than once. But failing to keep promises is not yet on my list of numerous shortcomings. I've even been trying to make contact with Jake to sort this absurd business out once and for all, but haven't been able to get a response from the man.' He paused, rubbing his hands over his face and drawing Annie's attention to the fact that his usually bright eyes looked lined and tired. 'There we are, I believe that covers most of the essentials.'

'No hard feelings?' she concluded weakly, a little appalled to find herself wondering about the kiss, whether it had been a purely practical and efficient demonstration of his sexual preferences or something dimly connected to his emotions.

'I guess not.' Michael sighed and uncrossed his arms.

'And so . . . the person you mentioned the other night, the one who killed themselves, was a—'

'Female.' He let out a short laugh, shaking his head in despair.

'God, Michael, I'm sorry. I feel such an idiot.'

'I'll dig out that screwdriver then, shall I?' He disappeared through the archway into the kitchen, leaving Annie to embark on a self-conscious stroll around the sitting area, admiring the pinky-brown sheen of the pine floorboards, the scattered rugs and artfully arrayed prints on the walls.

'Can never bloody find anything when you want it—'

'Tell me about it,' she called back, drifting over to the window seat and sitting down, partly for something to do and partly to halt the tremor in her knees. Overcome by an urge to smile, she patted her lips with her fingertips, as if to rub it out of sight before he returned. Lying beside her was a large hard-back book entitled, *Gardening In The City*. Poking out from the pages, presumably by way of a page-marker, was a postcard of a large black bull standing on a hillside, under a banner celebrating the name of a famous brand of Spanish wine. Still smiling, Annie eased out the card.

'. . . *thank you for keeping an eye on Annie . . . She's frightfully good at having a hard time and not admitting to it . . .*'

'Success at last.'

Annie slammed the book shut and stood up. 'Great,' she replied, while inside the new, small and utterly pitiful bubble of hope burst and died. He had been attentive because Jake had requested it. As a favour to a man who had aroused his compassion. 'Back to work,' she declared stiffly, accepting the implement he held out for her with a nod of gratitude. 'Unless there are any other earth-shattering truths with which you wish to acquaint me before I make an even greater fool of myself than I have done already?'

'Only that I know about the lump in your breast,' he replied quietly.

'Oh, do you now? Well, don't worry about it, so do several hundred thousand members of the population. And anyway, as of two days ago it's gone – an ex-lump, flown to the happy hunting grounds provided by hospital incinerators—'

'Annie, if you weren't so hellbent on being amusing about yourself, it might give other people a chance to offer sympathy—'

'Who says I need sympathy?' She waggled both screwdrivers at him. 'I'll have you know, I've had bucketfuls of the stuff – too much in fact – far more than I deserved for something that turned out harmless after all. And anyway, how the hell do you know about the state of my breasts? Not from Jake presumably—'

'I read your column,' he replied simply. 'I started when you told me what you did for a living. I've been a secret admirer for weeks – another thing I've wanted to mention, but wasn't sure how you'd react—'

'Well, now you know. Thank you for your concern. Thank you too for all your other protective surges over the past few weeks—' she continued, undeterred by the look of bafflement on Michael's face '—over intruders, the entertainment of visiting family members and so on. But could I just seize this opportunity to make the formal announcement that I can take care of myself – that I would positively *relish* the opportunity to be *allowed* to take care of myself.' She took a deep breath. 'Thank you in advance for this, too,' she added, gesturing a little sheepishly with the screwdriver. 'I shall return it the moment I have overcome my inherent slothfulness and purchased one for myself—'

'Don't be so bloody silly. Keep the damn thing.' He reached past her and pushed open his door, almost shoving her outside in the same movement. 'I like your writing, by the way,' he snapped, 'you're funny, even if it is a precaution against anybody else being funny first.' And with that he slammed the door, leaving Annie to return to the DIY challenges awaiting her downstairs.

It was only as she was on the verge of sleep that her conscious mind clamped onto the thought that had been gnawing at her throughout the evening's unrewarding tussle with heavy panels of wood and drawer runners that did not run. Michael Derwent had referred to himself as a secret admirer. A chance throwaway remark, or a slip of the tongue? Annie pulled a pillow to her chest and groaned out loud. Being angry about Jake's conniving vigilance did not prevent her from wanting her landlord to be a decent human being. Nor was the recent drying up of the sick letters any consolation for the fact that she had never established who they were from.

Michael Derwent was too nice, she reassured herself, and more significantly perhaps, too uninterested in her. Yet at the same time he had proved himself more than capable of playing games, of dissembling for effect. Fuelled by fatigue and the confusing events of the afternoon, the seed of doubt refused to die, casting long shadows across the paths of Annie's dreams.

Chapter Thirty-Five

———◆◇◆———

The next morning Annie awoke to the news that Jake seemed to have disappeared, not simply from his Marbellan hotel, but from life in general. Marina, who had gleaned the information from a conversation with Jake's agent, seemed more concerned about the incomplete state of her seating plan than for the welfare of their friend.

'Of course I hope he's all right and everything, but I do think it's inconsiderate not to have replied at all. His agent wasn't amused either, I can tell you. Says he's having nothing more to do with him. Apparently he just walked out on the whole shooting match a couple of days ago, checked out of the hotel without so much as a forwarding address. It's sort of childish. The man's thirty-five, for God's sake, he should have grown out of this kind of behaviour by now.'

During the call Annie had kept most of her concerns to herself. But the pulse of worry quickened as the morning passed. If what Michael Derwent had told her was true, Jake's resolute silence about what had occurred between them made Annie wonder whether he had in fact been hurt very deeply; whether some of his flirtatious resilience had run out of steam at last. The temptation to tell Marina the story of misunderstandings had crossed her mind, but only fleetingly. Not just out of a sense of loyalty to Jake himself, but because she still felt too confused to know in quite what terms to tell the tale. Since the extraordinary events of the previous afternoon, she was aware of having lost all sense of perspective about Michael Derwent; had no idea whether he was to be trusted or was following some dubious agenda of his own.

The disturbing news about Jake was depressing confirmation for Annie that whatever grasp of control she managed to acquire over life, there would always be elements of it that slithered out of control. For once it was a pleasing distraction to sit down at her new desk, which had acquired side panels but no working drawers, in order to tackle her weekly deadline. The announcement of the all-clear on her health had to be delivered first, followed by an account of her experiences in the day surgery. Annie worked quickly, driven now by such a firm sense of dialogue with her audience that the sentences seemed to write themselves. She would miss the letters, she realised. The chore of replying to them was immense, but so too was the sense of communication, of having, however briefly, touched and made a difference to other people's lives.

Finding there was still space for another paragraph, Annie decided to conclude with a few lighthearted thoughts on the wedding festivities scheduled for the approaching weekend. As her fingers touched the keyboard she felt the effortless return of the voice of the persona with which she had lost touch, the one that was an imaginative echo of herself as opposed to the real, raw thing. It occurred to Annie in the same instant that everybody had two selves, that it was controlling the balance of them that mattered.

. . . and if you're wondering how I feel about becoming one of the oldest (most tightly packaged) bridesmaids in the world, the answer is . . . marvellous. As everybody knows, weddings, like funerals, are a great place to meet new talent. The bride in question has hordes of delicious ex-boyfriends eager to make the acquaintance of a real live columnist, even one with corns on her toes and an abnormally emotional relationship with her hairdryer. (Talking of which, my hair will be done professionally on the morning of the great day. I've been promised a coronet of fresh flowers and ringlets that would make Shirley Temple turn in her grave, if she's dead, which I suspect she might not be.) Failing that, I have high hopes with regard to the bouquet. If my outfit (not only figure-hugging, but of a shade that will confirm some people's suspicions that I am, after all, terminally ill) permits, I shall be lunging forwards the moment the bride tosses her flowers, elbowing my way through throngs of other hopeful single-tons without regard to politeness or personal safety. Never having been a dab hand on the cricket field, I've been prac-tising round my flat, hurling unlikely objects at awkward angles in the air and diving to retrieve them before they hit the ground. As a result I have become extremely proficient and retain high hopes of making a successful catch (in every sense) on the day.

Annie's fingers flew over the keys, relishing the forgotten pleasure of telling fiction as opposed to fact, of being able to slide the shutter on real life back and forth at will.

Having safely filed her column Annie found herself driving over to Camden in the hope of finding that Jake had simply sneaked back home. The avalanche of envelopes visible through his letterbox told her otherwise, as did the faint but distinct smell of stale air which caught her nostrils as she lifted the flap. Something about the evident neglect of the big empty house made her inordinately sad. She returned to Shrewsbury Mansions more concerned than ever, only to find an unstamped, white envelope waiting for her on the doormat, addressed in the unmistakable type-face of her anonymous admirer. At the re-alisation that the envelope had clearly been deposited without the aid either of her employers or of the Royal Mail, all Annie's apprehensions redoubled. If it wasn't Michael Derwent, then it was certainly someone who knew where she lived. This was new, dangerous territory, she realised, something that could no longer be ignored or fought on her own. With vague notions about evidence and fingerprints, she picked up one corner of the envelope between finger and thumb and held it away from her like a diseased object as she scampered up to the sanctity of her flat. She almost called the police there and then, but even through her fear, it was impossible not to be curious. Carefully she slid a knife under the sealed flap and extracted the single sheet of paper inside.

I suppose you could call this a farewell. You have hurt me too much. I realise now that my affections have been wasted on you. Women like you think men are slaves, to be there at your beck and call, to be summoned and dismissed at will. Well, I'm rejecting you, Annie Jordan. A job opportunity on another continent will take me away for good, away from London, away from females who have the audacity to dismiss devotion like mine as 'silly' . . .

On reaching the word, the identity of the writer was so instantly obvious that Annie let out a small cry of recognition. It dawned on her too that while pretending to maintain his anonymity, Stephen Garr had clearly reached the point where he wished to make himself known, perhaps out of some perverse notion that he might be able to evoke a stab or two of guilt in the process. Relieved and furious, Annie reached for a pen and pad.

Stephen,
　　If you ever write threatening or sordid letters to me again, I will go to the police.

Having addressed the note to the newspaper for which she knew he did most of his work, Annie began pacing round the flat, chewing furiously on a tasteless stick of gum and fighting the urge to run upstairs to issue some sort of apology to Michael Derwent. A ridiculous urge, of course, since the poor man had no idea that he had ever fallen under the shadow of any suspicion. And going to the bother of explaining that he had, would almost certainly confirm his view of her as a half-witted, neurotic female with a remarkable capacity for getting the wrong end of the stick.

Yet the urge for a pretext to go upstairs persisted. She could ask him about Jake, Annie reasoned, on the offchance that he had been in touch. Or maybe even seek assistance over the malfunctioning drawer runners, still lying like segments of toy railtrack all over the floor of her study bedroom.

After such a tortured build-up, it was something of a disappointment to find her door-knocks at Michael's flat unheeded. It was only having trudged back downstairs that Annie remembered the existence of the roof garden. It was a beautiful spring day, she realised, peering properly out of her window for the first time. Although wet, early February had been exceptionally mild. The tree wedged between the paving stones outside the flats was already bursting with buds, while brave crocuses could be seen poking their bright heads out of the window boxes decorating the block next door.

A few minutes later she was pulling on her trainers and a fleece and clambering out of her bathroom window. The staircase outside was so rusted that it left ginger imprints on her hands where she clutched at the side rails. It was steeper than it looked, too, especially if one was imprudent enough to look down. On reaching the top, she carefully hooked her elbows over the low parapet wall and peered out across the roof. Immediately in view was the TV aerial. Beyond that stood the old chimney stack round which Michael had positioned some of the larger plant tubs, one of which was already sprouting with clumps of daffodil stems.

There was such a sense of stillness that it took Annie a few moments to register the presence of Michael himself, sitting in a deep orange-and-red striped deckchair, angled away from her with his knees facing the sun. He wore a honey-coloured sheepskin coat, dark glasses and scuffed black hiking boots. Beside the deckchair was a yellow mug from which small swirls of steam spiralled into the air. Open on his lap was a book. A pair of leather gloves lay on the ground at his feet, alongside a small trowel.

Annie opened her mouth to declare her presence but closed it again, deterred by the firm hunch of his shoulders, the forbidding quietness of the scene and the lack of any real justification on her part to shatter it. It suddenly occurred to her that, in view of what she knew of Michael's past, alarming him with reports of Jake's disappearance would hardly be kind. She descended slowly and with a heavy heart, wondering suddenly whether her landlord might be one of those creatures who lived in the shadow of disaster. Someone who attracted bad luck like a moth to a flame. Though unappealing, Annie clung as tightly to the thought as to the rungs under her hands. Because it was plausible. Because it offered some consolation for the sensation that from the top of the ladder she had stared hard at a turning point and allowed it to pass her by.

At the bathroom window she hesitated, some part of her hoping to see Michael Derwent's pale face peering over the top of the ladder. But there was only blue sky, so blue that after a moment her eyes ached and she had to look away.

A ring of anti-climax circled the rest of the afternoon. Annie returned to the practical challenge of her work station, discovering in the process that all problems with the drawer runners stemmed from their having been screwed into position upside down. She almost forgot to get ready for Marina's hen party, scheduled to take place that night on a boat moored somewhere along the Embankment. She had barely struggled into some appropriate clothes when the minibus organised for the occasion tooted for attention outside.

Before clambering aboard, Annie could not resist turning to look up at the line of dark windows above her flat. There had been nothing but silence for hours. She missed the sound of him, she realised. She even missed the faint tinkling of the piano, of which there had been no evidence for days.

Chapter Thirty-Six

It felt as if the bed were swaying gently from side to side, mimicking the push and pull of the water which had so exacerbated the problems of remaining upright during the latter stages of the night before. Having embarked on the evening with every intention of remaining sober, Annie had been puzzled to find herself succumbing with alarming rapidity to the crazed merriment afflicting most of her companions from the outset. By the time she discovered that the barman had been instructed to lace anything non-alcoholic with vodka, she felt too at ease with the world to register even mild annoyance. A gyrating male floor show seemed a fitting climax to such debauchery, as did the disgraceful howls of disappointment when none of the bulging G-strings were removed. Once the troupe of performers had been shepherded to safety, a shambolic all-female disco rampage ensued, led by Marina and two of her friends from the City. Inspired perhaps by recent disappointment, they began discarding items of their own clothing and shrieking at those guests still standing to do the same. A sea of female nudity was only averted by the timely eruption of all the main lights and the brusque announcement that carriages awaited them on the quay outside. After that, Annie's mind was blank, apart from a disquieting image of herself on her knees on the doorstep of Shrewsbury Mansions, waving at the minibus as it sped away into the night.

The bed was definitely moving, Annie decided, screwing up her eyes in a bid to press the sensation away and recalling in the same instant, like a dim and distant memory of a past life, that the doorstep scenario had culminated in some problem to do with keys. Door keys. Her door keys. How then, had she managed to crawl into bed? She opened her eyes and stared hard at the ceiling, a dazzling white space that looked curiously unfamiliar. Impelled by the throb of pain behind her eyes, she let her lids fall shut and turned on her side, moving slowly out of respect for the tenderness of her head. During the course of this delicate manoeuvre, some part of her conscious self was alerted to the disquieting discovery that instead of a nightshirt she was in her bra and pants.

'How are you feeling?'

At the sound of the voice Annie jolted upright and then collapsed back onto the pillows with a loud groan of horror as well as physical pain. 'Oh, shit.'

'That bad, eh?' Michael Derwent chuckled. 'Sorry to disturb your beauty sleep, but today is one of those days when I have to pretend to be a grown-up. In other words I need to attire myself in a clean shirt, tie, two matching socks, that sort of thing.' He moved around the room as he talked, opening drawers and doors. On observing, through the clenched eyes with which she felt able to confront her surroundings, that her host was wearing nothing but a pair of boxer shorts, Annie slid a little further down inside the bed, racking her dehydrated brain for a couple of images that might give her a clue as to exactly how the evening had progressed.

'Did I . . . undress myself?' she asked in a small voice.

Michael stopped at the end of the bed, a bundle of clothes in his arms. 'No, you did not.' He made as if to leave the room, but turned back again, a look of exaggerated incredulity on his handsome face. 'You mean you don't remember what happened between us?'

'I . . . of course I remember . . . bits—'

'Bits?' He pretended to look hurt. 'Just . . . bits?'

Annie twisted a thread in his duvet cover round her index finger, struggling for an appropriate answer. The thread of cotton snapped. 'It's just that—'

'Don't worry, Annie. Call me old-fashioned, but I've always preferred lovers that were both willing and vaguely conscious. Not that you passed out immediately.' He bent down and scooped up a pair of dusty black leather shoes from under the bed. 'To begin with, you were very talkative.'

'Talkative—?' Annie swallowed. Her throat felt so dry it hurt.

'Oh yes indeed. I learnt all sorts of interesting things—' He frowned. 'Let me see now—' he held out a finger to mark each point, '—you've traded low-tar cigarettes for sugar-free chewing gum, you're to be a bridesmaid on Saturday, you thought I was an epistolary pervert but have changed your mind—'

'Jesus,' Annie clutched her head, 'I can explain—'

'Don't interrupt, please, I've barely started. Since you're so clearly struggling with your own memory bank it seems only fair that I should fill in a few gaps for you – check the facts, as it were. On Monday you leave for a journalistic assignment that will involve fraternising with unattached members of the opposite sex, but if any male, unattached or otherwise, dares to lay a fingertip on you he will pay dearly and gruesomely – you were most insistent on this point – for his pains.' Michael shook his head solemnly. 'Oh yes indeed, your views were most enlightening.' He flexed his dark eyebrows. 'Not having the greatest of night's sleep on my sofa, I've had plenty of time to reflect on your antipathy towards the heterosexual strain of the male species.'

'Look, I'm so sorry—' Annie began to swing her legs out of bed, only to remember her state of undress and whip them back under the covers again. 'If you could just tell me where my clothes are—'

He pointed to the chair, muttering, 'Modesty was hardly a problem last night. In fact, if I recall correctly, you were rather keen to show me your scar . . . I'm delighted about your clean bill of health, by the way,' he added wryly. 'I made mention of the fact last night, but in view of your condition—'

'Show you my scar? I couldn't have – oh God, how awful.

Michael, I just don't know what to say—'

'Say nothing then,' he replied giving her a curious look. 'There's a glass of orange juice and two painkillers on the chest of drawers. Go back to sleep. I've phoned the property agents and asked them to drop round a spare set of keys to replace those lying on the bottom of the Thames.'

'The Thames—?' she echoed faintly.

'That was your hottest theory last night . . . something about performing a can-can on a gangplank. Now, if you'll excuse me, I must get dressed. And since you would clearly be ill at ease if I attempted to do so here, I shall retreat to the bathroom.'

Annie obediently gulped down the juice and pills, before slumping back against the pillows, overcome with mortification and self-disgust.

A few minutes later Michael emerged looking grim-faced and businesslike. He had cut himself shaving Annie noticed, trying not to stare at the bauble of blood on his chin while he wrestled with the knot of his tie and blew the dust off his shoes.

When he spoke, the terseness of his tone did little to alleviate her discomfort. 'I've been meaning to ask how the interviewing for a flatmate is going. The girl with the white face and spectacles, did she make the grade?'

'The girl with the . . . no—' Annie dried up under the glare of his gaze.

'Thank God for that.'

'In fact, I'm rethinking the whole flatmate thing,' she mumbled, 'because I like living alone and—'

'No chance of free rent in return for sexual favours, then.' The remark was followed up by a tight, unfriendly smile. 'Just joking. It's the pervert in me, you know. Help yourself to breakfast.'

As Annie was waiting for the sound of the door to slam he poked his head back into the room. 'And no, Jake has not been in touch. And no, I do not know whether his affections for me would warrant any behaviour that might jeopardise his personal safety.'

Chapter Thirty-Seven

It wasn't until the morning of Marina's wedding, a good twenty-four hours later, that Annie felt wholly recovered from the after-effects of the hen party. Her stay in Michael Derwent's flat had culminated in the sudden recollection of having stowed her keys in a zipped inner pocket of her handbag, for safe-keeping. The realisation that the humiliating events of Thursday evening might so easily have been avoided was quickly superseded by the even more worrying notion that some drunken part of her subconscious might have contrived the situation deliberately. Appalled at herself, Annie had quickly forestalled the impending arrival of spare keys with a phone call to the property agents and then scribbled a note of thanks to her host. Not her first, she realised glumly, remembering the night of the wine tasting and reflecting that the object of her inconvenient obsession would now be perfectly justified in adding the charge of alcoholism to the long list of reasons for finding her company abhorrent.

> *Thank you for taking me in. It won't happen again. Annie.*
> *PS Jake is more than capable of being foolhardy without the trigger of whatever he might feel about you or anything else. If at any stage I suggested otherwise I apologise unreservedly. From what I can gather you have been kinder and fairer to Jake than he could ever realise.*
> *PPS In spite of all evidence to the contrary, I promise I am not alcohol-dependent (not yet anyway).*

After some hesitation Annie decided not to heap more humiliation on herself by mentioning the small muddle over the keys. All that remained was to keep as much out of Michael Derwent's way as possible, and to hope that by the time she got back from Italy, the matter would have blown over sufficiently for regular neighbourly civilities to be restored.

The wedding wasn't until three o'clock. At twelve o'clock she was scheduled to join Marina and her parents in their hotel suite for a light lunch and a session with a hair-stylist. Annie's outfit was hanging on the back of the front door, safely protected from outside hazards by tissue paper and layers of polythene. In a bag at its feet resided silk yellow shoes and a small, matching handbag of a style that Annie associated with fifties film stars.

By ten-thirty she was in her coat, clutching all required props, including a four foot tall giraffe-shaped lamp, which she had chosen in defiance of the tedious domestic items on the wedding list and because she liked the world-weary look on the creature's face. Gripping the animal by the neck, careful not to crush the large ribbon of a collar serving as an alternative to the impossible challenge of wrapping paper, Annie used her elbow to lever the handle on her front door. As it swung open, encouraged to do so by a sharp kick from her left foot, she found herself facing Jake, smiling like an angel, his finger poised over her bell-button.

'You . . . bastard, where the hell have you been?' She dropped all her baggage, including the giraffe, which rocked precariously for a moment before regaining its balance, and flung both arms round his neck. 'I was so worried—'

Jake returned the hug so hard she was lifted a few inches off her feet. After releasing her, he stood back and shrugged apologetically. 'I can't think why, and anyway, what about you? Getting ill and writing about it. Falling out with the divine Mr Berkley – I phoned Marina this morning who told me everything. Can't I leave you for a minute without your entire existence falling apart?'

'But I'm fine, Jake,' interjected Annie earnestly, wanting to convey some of the genuine sense of wellbeing which had grown out of her misfortunes. 'Apart from a mild case of unrequited lust I haven't a care in the world – at least not now you're back, you sod. And looking so dashing.' She emitted a low whistle of approval at his appearance. 'Ready for the nuptials, I see.'

Jake responded with an elaborate pirouette that made the tails of his grey pin-stripe twirl outwards like the panels on a flared skirt. 'Moss Bros special. There's a hat too. And a car. I've hired a Lamborghini for the day – buttercup yellow – so low on the ground my knees are up to my ears—'

Annie laughed delightedly. 'Does it have room for back seat passengers?' She picked up the giraffe and gave it an affectionate pat. 'Because if me and my friend here don't make a move soon, we'll miss our appointment with the curling tongs, upset the bride and throw the whole ship off course before it's launched. They're all at a hotel called The Grand, somewhere between Park Lane and Victoria—'

'I know, Marina told me. I have maps as well as transport. Your destiny is entirely in my hands,' declared Jake grandly, scooping up the rest of Annie's stuff and leading the way down the stairs.

'But how did you get in here anyway?' she asked, puzzling suddenly at the realisation that she had never been called upon to answer the main door.

'The lock down here had jammed open,' replied Jake quickly, not yet ready – if he ever would be – for a post mortem on the visit to Michael Derwent which had preceded his arrival outside Annie's door. Like a dog that prefers whipping to no attention at all, he had been unable to resist an encounter with the person responsible for more longing and frustrated fantasising than he had ever known in his life before. If a part of him had hoped that the cloud of desire blighting his life might dissolve in the face of the reality, he was sorely disappointed. Worse still, there was none of the kind patience from which he had drawn so much consolation. Michael Derwent greeted him with unabashed hostility, ranting about his futile insistence on secrecy, his failure to reply to his note, his thoughtless vanishing act, his selfishness in worrying Annie . . . Annie. The subject of her kept returning, weaving its way through Michael's responses until Jake had wanted to weep out loud.

'You're quite mad,' declared Annie, rolling her eyes at the sight of the long, gleaming yellow vehicle parked outside the front door.

'I know.' Jake fired the alarm decoder with a flourish and flung open the nearside door.

'Whatever did it cost?' she gasped, carefully laying her curious assortment of baggage on the narrow back seat.

'It doesn't matter. It's not every day your best friend plays bridesmaid to her best friend.'

'Oh, Jake, it's so good to see you.' Having settled into the passenger seat, Annie leant across and kissed his cheek. 'But tell me what happened exactly. Where the hell did you go? And why?'

Jake waved one arm dismissively. 'I just couldn't bear it a moment longer – making a crap film in an ugly place – the utter boredom of life on set when you've only got seven words to call your own.'

'So it had nothing to do with . . . anything back home then? Michael Derwent and so on . . . I sort of know most of what happened before you left for Spain,' she confessed. 'And in case you're wondering, I don't think it's funny at all.'

'Don't you? Well I do. Worse than a French farce.' He laughed easily. 'But I can assure you I'm over it now. Just one of those itches that never got scratched.'

'Thank God for that. I don't know why, but when I heard you'd disappeared I kept thinking that—'

'Annie I'm so sorry. I've behaved abominably. I can see now it was unforgivable. And all for a tantrum.' He patted her knee, while an echo of the desperation he had felt in the hotel bedroom a few days before flickered inside. A desperation born not just out of a misguided, irrepressible obsession for the wrong person, for having made a fool of himself, but out of a sudden objective picture of his place in the world: middle-aged, mediocre and alone. Without the talent, tenacity or willpower to change anything. Or to bring anything to a dignified end. He had checked out of his hotel full of whisky and plans to leave his suitcase amongst the cigarette butts and bottle tops on the sand. To swim until he sank. But he hadn't even been able to manage that. Every time his head bobbed down below the surface of the water, his arms and legs had beaten like wings until it was out again. 'It was just a little jaunt,' he went on lightly, 'hitch-hiking up through Spain and France, trying to recapture the freedom of my misspent youth – you know the sort of thing.'

'And did you?'

Jake let out a bitter laugh, for the first time revealing a hint of some of the emotions locked inside. 'In a manner of speaking. Though the mattresses in cheap *pensions* felt uncommonly lumpy. Oh, but I nearly got raped by a lorry driver in Calais,' he added, 'now that *was* a thrill. And such a shock. You'd have thought three decades of sexual promiscuity would have taught me something about how to defend myself in such situations but honestly, my dear, I was as dumbstruck as a young girl—'

Annie relaxed back into her seat, her legs stretched into the small funnel of space in front of her. There was another serious side to Jake's anecdotes, she knew. There always was. It occurred to her in the same instant that his inner and outer life was balanced more finely than hers, that whatever tightrope she had been walking, Jake had probably passed the same route long before.

'But now I want to hear all about you,' he urged. 'Have you got to have your boobs monitored every month for the rest of your life and all that sort of thing?'

Grateful for his frankness, Annie let out a hoot of laughter. 'No, not at all.'

'Women's health is *such* a bugger – there are so many bits of you that can go wrong. Whereas all we boys have really got to worry about in that department is that naughty little gland which has to develop a growth the size of a football before anyone knows it's there, by which time of course it's too late—'

'Do you mind if we change the subject,' interjected Annie, laughing. 'The vagaries of the male prostate are hardly matters I wish to be thinking about as I stalk Marina up the aisle.'

'Talking of stalking, did you ever decipher the mystery of those creepy letters?'

'Just yesterday, as a matter of fact. A twit called Stephen Garr.' Annie scowled at the map open on her lap. 'Fortunately he's leaving the country, otherwise I might be tempted to pursue the matter. Just a mad, sad man—'

'Obsessions can make people do funny things,' murmured Jake, staring hard at the windscreen.

'Hmm, I suppose they can,' agreed Annie, more concerned now with the grid of streets on her knees. 'We ought to think about turning left pretty soon, or we'll get sucked back up to Hyde Park Corner.'

Jake turned so suddenly that the car rode up over the corner section of the pavement, narrowly missing a lamppost. Annie reached back a protective arm to her giraffe lamp.

'It didn't have to be that soon. Jake? Are you sure you're OK?'

'I'm great. Tell me about this case of unrequited lust. Anyone I know?'

Annie squirmed, wondering what had possessed her to mention such a thing. Her problematic attraction for Michael Derwent was not a matter she was yet prepared to discuss with anyone, least of all poor Jake. 'There's nothing to tell. A real non-starter – doomed in every direction. Turn right here.'

'Sounds intriguing,' he murmured, gripping the steering wheel.

'I can assure you it's not.' Annie slammed the map shut with a humph of satisfaction and returned it to the glove compartment. 'The next on the right and we're there.'

'Perhaps you'll meet someone divine on this Venice trip – Marina told me all about it.'

'Oh did she now? Well, I've no intention of doing any such thing. The last few weeks have been full of surprises, not the least of them being a fondness for my own company. Look, here's the hotel and they've even got an underground car park. Oh Jake, I'm so glad you're safe and sound.' She reached an arm across his shoulders and sighed happily. 'What will you do now, do you think?'

Jake hesitated for just a moment. 'Find a new agent and carry on, I suppose.' He made a funny face in case he had sounded too serious. 'I'm good at carrying on,' he added lightly, steering the long nose of the car down into the dark tunnel ahead of them.

Chapter Thirty-Eight

There was a gasp of appreciation as Marina entered the back of the church, a soft swirling vision in cream, yellow and white, sartorially harmonious in every aspect, from the freesias laced into her hair, to the delicate yellow trim on her dress and the intricate little roses embroidered into her silk shoes. To Annie's relief the gown needed no serious attendance either on her part or that of the solemn-faced little pageboy instructed to walk behind her. All that was required was a show of composure during the long parade up the aisle, stomach clenched, resisting the urge to stare at the ground, where her spiky yellow heels were in constant danger of snagging in the decorative grating inlaid into the church floor. Marina floated ahead of her, appearing to glide rather than walk, her arm linked firmly through her father's, her eyes fixed on the pin-striped back of her future husband as if her life depended on it.

Which it probably did, reasoned Annie, trying to invest the scene with at least some sense of reality in order to combat both the fairytale feel to the day and the dangerously hypnotic effect it was having on her. A life of bickering and treading on each other's toenail clippings awaited them, she told herself. Cycles of disagreement and compromise would push through like weeds in a plot of grass. The passion which currently crackled with all the subtlety of an electric storm, would choke, flicker and die, until all that remained was the memory of it and the habits of cohabitation.

In spite of such bids at cynicism, however, the lump of exultant emotion that had arrived in Annie's throat refused to be swallowed away. While the happy couple were exchanging vows, bravely reciting obscure love poems to each other with the light of joy shining in their eyes, she found huge, unblinkable globules of tears forming under her lashes. Fearing for the fate of her mascara, she endeavoured to return her thoughts to the grim realities of domestic strife. Instead, her mind was unexpectedly arrested by the memory of Michael Derwent, smiling and spattered with paint, doing such a good job of being kind. Thinking back, Annie found herself longing for the power to rewrite the script between them, to rewind the clock to a point before the catalogue of misunderstandings had begun; before Jake's casting of her as a hopeless case, requiring vigilance and pity from friends.

As Bernard and Marina kissed, a ripple of murmured appreciation ran through the congregation; an irresistible tide-wave of emotion that blew the last of Annie's critical commentary away. During the slow procession back down the aisle, the open sunlit mouth of the church door beckoned like an entrance to a dream. Annie felt as if she were floating towards it, drifting on the tide of warmth and goodwill emanating from the smiling faces lining the pews.

Afterwards they dined like kings and queens within the panelled splendour of the Beaumont Gallery, served by waiters in white tails and gloves, attending glasses and plates with all the deft flourish of magicians. The seating plan placed Annie on the top table, between Jake and the groom himself, facing the main body of guests, who were seated in lines down the three long rectangular tables filling the rest of the hall. They ate fresh tiger prawns followed by wedges of pink salmon, served with pebble-sized new potatoes and pretty sprigs of green salad. For dessert there were strawberries, decorated with rings of kiwi and topped with miniature melon balls and scoops of vanilla ice-cream.

Not wanting to intrude on any sweet nothings that couples might feel compelled to share in such circumstances, Annie devoted most of her attention to Jake, and the little pageboy next to him, who proved to be a mine of bad jokes and hilarious commentary on some of the less advertised idiosyncracies of the Ramsbotham clan.

At the entrance of a glorious three-tiered cake, crawling with white and yellow roses, the hubbub of conversation shrank to a subdued, appreciative hum. Marina's father stood up and chinked his glass with a breadknife for attention. The pageboy, sensing a spell of impending boredom, yawned hard, stuck two fingers in his mouth and clambered, uninvited onto Jake's lap. Jake rolled his eyes in a show of helpless dismay, but Annie could tell from the tenderness in his smile that he was thrilled.

Marina's father spoke in the relaxed, unhurried drawl of a businessman used to commanding the attention of large audiences. Without actually telling any jokes, he was very amusing, even before he had moved onto the mandatory embarrassing tales of his daughter's childhood. He concluded with an earnest tribute to the virtues of the man with whom Marina had chosen to make a lifelong connection and a heartfelt hope that members of both families would make regular trips across the Atlantic.

In contrast to such a polished performance, Bernard appeared faltering and faintly shambolic. His tie had been knocked askew and stray wisps of hair were sticking at curious angles from the wall of growth ringing the circle of baldness at his crown. Annie, expecting to feel pity, was surprised instead to find herself spellbound. Every impression of bluster and dishevelment was eclipsed by the quiet sincerity of what he said. Marina was the light of his life, his soul-mate, the woman of his dreams. The miracle of their meeting was exceeded only by the miracle of her agreement to marry him. Tears filled his eyes as he talked, until at one point he had to mop them away with his napkin. The effect was so intense, so personal, that, while moved, Annie could also hardly bring herself to watch. It was almost a relief when he moved onto the more practical task of thanking all those involved in the organisational feat of the wedding. A roll-call of names followed, during which Annie found her thoughts straying to the question of what to put in her suitcase for Venice. She was trying to recall the most likely whereabouts of her camera when a fresh turn in Bernard's speech alerted her to the fact that the beam of attention was being cast her way.

'. . . to take this opportunity to say a special thank you to Annie Jordan, not just for being a predictably impeccable brides-maid – the picture of poise and loveliness—'

Annie kept her eyes glued firmly to her knees, feeling neither poised nor lovely.

'—but also for gracefully allowing me to share and then monopolise the acquaintance of a woman whose friendship I know she values very dearly and all at a time when she has endured enormous personal difficulties herself. I know you are hating this, Annie, and I apologise, but I would be failing in my duties if I did not single you out for special praise as a remark-able lady and a remarkable friend. I hope very much that we get to know each other rather better over the coming years. In the meantime, Marina and I would like to express our gratitude and affection by offering you this small gift—'

There was no alternative but to wrest her eyes from her knee-caps. Everybody in the hall was clapping. Bernard slipped his hand under her elbow and pulled her to her feet, before kissing her fondly on both cheeks and handing her a small parcel wrapped in gold paper. There were a few whistles from the crowd. Then some bright spark yelled 'speech', and the cry was taken up by a few other voices scattered round the hall. Horrified, Annie turned to Bernard, who mouthed the words, 'Don't worry,' and pressed her gently back into her seat.

'Annie has performed quite hard enough today without being called upon to exercise her skills in public speaking as well—' And the moment passed.

A few minutes later, while the best man was unveiling a blown-up photograph of Bernard as a naked toddler in a paddling pool, Annie set the gift on her lap and gently peeled off the wrapping paper. Inside was a blue leather box, embossed with the letters A.J. and containing a coral and pearl necklace. The stones were iridescent and very small, each one a different shape from its neighbour.

'Uncultured pearls,' whispered Bernard, from beneath the

napkin he had elected to place over his face by way of remonstration at the humiliations being heaped upon him by his oldest friend. 'Supposed to be much luckier.'

Annie kissed the section of the handkerchief nearest her. 'Thank you, they are exquisite.' She leant forwards and blew a kiss at Marina, who beamed.

Before long, all that remained was for the happy couple to go away. On the cobbled stones that ran past the entrance to the gallery an awaiting horse and carriage painted the final fairytale touch to the day. The wintry afternoon light was fading fast. The guests, gathering on the steps in their finery, huddled together and blew on their hands for warmth. Jake, meanwhile, had gallantly thrown his jacket over Annie's shoulders and was giving the pageboy piggy-back rides round the forecourt.

When Marina and Bernard at last burst through the doors there was an eruption of confetti and camera-flashes. Annie, empty-handed and overcome suddenly at the poignancy of the occasion, took up a position at the bottom of the steps, biting her cheeks to stop the tremble in her jaw.

Bernard, dressed in a white tropical suit and panama hat, was in charge of the suitcases, while Marina, in a strawberry trouser-suit, clutched her handbag, vanity case and wedding bouquet. Their progress down the steps was slow, impeded by innumerable handshakes and hugs from the crowd. Too far back to offer an embrace herself, Annie at last caught Marina's eye and did a thumbs-up sign – a gesture which Marina chose to interpret as the moment to relinquish the bouquet, hurling it with all her might towards her friend. Annie stared in wonder as the missile approached, spinning through the air with the peculiar clarity of slow motion. The wedding party around her appeared to freeze, all eyes tracking the object as it spiralled towards its intended target. As the moment unfurled Annie found many things flashing through her mind, not the least of them being the difficulty of resisting an attempt to catch an object so obviously flying one's way.

It was a good shot too, requiring nothing too inelegant or athletic on the part of the recipient. But at the very last instant

Annie pulled her hands to her side and ducked, with the consequence that the flowers hit Jake instead, catching him square in the chest, where he had no option but to clasp them with both arms.

'They were for Annie,' complained Marina, shouting over her shoulder as Bernard helped her into the carriage.

'My need is greater—' Jake's voice was lost amidst the clamours of farewell. At a quick flick of their driver's whip, the horses picked up their hooves and trotted away, revealing Bernard and Marina's smiling faces and waving hands framed in the rear window of the carriage.

'Will you come to my wedding?' quipped Jake, linking arms with Annie as they walked back up the steps.

'If you can guarantee that I won't be selected as bridesmaid, matron of honour, page-woman, best lady or anything else, yes, I might just consider it.'

'You did well,' he murmured, patting her hand, 'and thoroughly deserve your trinket.' He smiled approvingly at the gift, already in place round her neck.

'It's been lovely.' Annie sighed. 'Not real life, but lovely.'

Inside the hall the tables were already being cleared away, surrounded by guests retrieving coats and hats and bags.

'God, I hate the end of parties,' growled Jake, 'let's go and get drunk very quickly before we start to feel sad.'

Annie hugged him. 'No thanks, I'm tired. And you've got to drive your yellow beast of a car, remember, so it would be unwise—'

'Christ, isn't reality dull.' Jake scowled, feeling the now familiar darkness pushing up inside.

'Not always,' murmured Annie, suddenly longing for the quietness of her flat, the chance for a soak in a bath and a long sleep before the ordeal of clearing up and packing to go away.

They got back to Jake's car only to find that it had been clamped. Ignoring Annie's protestations, he hailed a taxi and pushed her inside. While appearing generous, the truth was he could feel his wall of cheerfulness crumbling and wanted to be rid of her.

'Jake, I've had this great thought.' She wound down the window and thrust her head outside. 'Why don't you come to Venice too?'

He laughed. 'I'd cramp your style—'

'No one need know you were a friend. It would be a laugh – oh, please say yes. Then it would be more like a proper holiday. Foreign Relations are low on numbers, Amy told me so.'

'Darling, I'm hardly ideal material—'

'I know, but they needn't find out. I'm on a 2.30 flight from Gatwick – Monday afternoon – please say you'll think about it.' The taxi driver fiddled pointedly with his fare-recorder.

Jake kissed her on the forehead. 'The man of your dreams could be in the group and he wouldn't want a rival.'

Annie snorted. 'Spoilsport.'

'Trust me, you'll have a wonderful time.'

He stood and watched as the taxi drove away, waving Marina's bouquet in front of his face in a bid to disguise the tears streaming down his cheeks.

Chapter Thirty-Nine

Watching the black streak of runway under the wheel of the accelerating plane, Annie said a short silent prayer to aid its elevation from the ground. Knowing that the laws of aerodynamics contained a logic for the process never prevented the sight of England's receding patchwork quilt of a landscape from making her feel as if she was party to a small miracle. When the view became shrouded by a blanket of dull cloud, she exchanged her chewing gum for a boiled sweet and opened the thriller she had bought in her whistle-stop tour of the airport shops; all hopes of a more leisurely camp-out in the departure lounge having been scuppered by an overturned lorry on the M23.

> Jack Bridges slipped his fingers round the hard curve of the gun. Panting slightly, his handsome chiselled features creased in concentration, he forced himself to count slowly to ten before making his move . . .

The woman sitting next to her was knitting, shaking her head and sighing between rows. Beside her, the man in the aisle seat had got out a laptop and a sheaf of papers covered in graphs and numbers. The screen of his computer shimmered into life, a marine green colour which Annie was sure would have given her a headache. Sensing her staring, the man glanced up. Annie quickly returned her attentions to Jack Bridges, whom she suspected she was going to find rather irritating.

. . . stealthily as a cat, he eased himself out from his seat and tiptoed up towards the front of the plane where he knew the terrorist was sitting. Not the most likely looking terrorist either, mused Jack, recalling the seductive curves of the woman whom he had been trailing for the last three days. A woman with feline green eyes and big breasts which she liked to show off in tight mini-dresses with daring necklines . . .

Annie tipped her head back and closed her eyes, letting her thoughts drift from Jack Bridges' dangerous sexual fascination for his enemy to the more mundane preoccupations of her own life. While undeniably pleasant to be leaving England for a while, it was impossible not to feel some apprehension at the prospect ahead of her. Her position as a journalist was to be public knowledge, but then so was her status as a single, un-attached woman. That she was currently happy with such a status might not be the easiest thing to advertise amongst a group of people who had paid several hundred pounds towards a conflicting objective and whose customary inhibitions were likely to be eradicated by a few pints of Chianti. Annie shud-dered, vowing for by no means the first time to confine herself to the role of observer and to mark out some time for exploring on her own. Arriving on a later flight was a good start, she re-assured herself, pleased that she had held out for the small extra expense in the face of considerable resistance from Amy. The rest of the group had departed at an ungodly hour that morning, and were probably already knee-deep in pigeons and longing for their first espresso.

'It's a sleeve,' remarked the woman next to her, holding up a bedraggled rectangle of purple wool and sighing deeply. 'I can't read, it makes me nauseous,' she added, peering disdain-fully over the top of her half-moon spectacles at Annie's book. The glasses had slipped to the very tip of her nose, where they seemed poised to slide down onto her upper lip. 'And anyway, why read about life when you can live it?'

'To escape it, I suppose,' admitted Annie, reluctant to be drawn into conversation, but unable to let the challenge pass.

Her thoughts drifted to her column, to the difficult but ultimately helpful effect it had had on her own life. 'And perhaps to make reality more bearable . . . more understandable sometimes—'

But the woman had already lost interest. 'I hope they do peanuts,' she said, eyeing the approaching drinks trolley.

Annie returned her attentions to Jack Bridges, whose fictional escapades seemed unlikely to support any of her grandiose literary theories or the point-of-sale hyperbole which had prompted her to make the purchase.

Keeping one hand round the sheath of his gun, he reached out and tapped her shoulder. 'Excuse me, madam—'

'Excuse me—' faltered a male voice. Feeling the touch of a hand on her own shoulder at such a timely moment, Annie let out a small gasp and slammed shut her book. She looked up to see Michael Derwent, standing in the aisle clutching a newspaper and his leather jacket. Although it was her shoulder he had touched, he was addressing his words to her immediate neighbour.

'Excuse me, madam – I am so sorry to trouble you. Would you possibly consider exchanging places with me? I'm just four rows back, in a set of three empty seats next to a window. I know it's a frightful cheek, but it would not be exaggerating to tell you that it is because of a matter of the utmost urgency between your neighbour and myself . . . a matter of life and death, you could say.'

The woman needed no further encouragement. Casting a nervous glance at Annie, who was too amazed to offer anything beyond a head-nod, she scooped up her knitting bag and levered herself free. An operation that was greatly facilitated by the absence of the businessman, who had disappeared in the direction of the toilets, taking his laptop and sheaf of papers with him.

'Jesus Christ.'

'Nice to see you too.'

'Life and death?'

'I didn't want her to refuse. I am Foreign Relations' newest recruit. A desperate case, I'll admit myself, but then when you've reached my stage in life, with my history of personal disasters, quite frankly one is prepared to try anything.'

Annie buried her face in her hands. 'I don't believe this, I simply don't believe it.'

'That I'm desperate or that I'm here? Did you know your eyes change colour with what you wear? I've been making a detailed study of the phenomenon over the past few months – from grey to blue to green – and a sort of black too, when you're angry. It's really most impressive.'

'Michael, please tell me what exactly you want . . . I don't think I could bear anymore . . . games of any kind, you see—'

'What I want?' He drew in his breath sharply, turning to look at her. 'There are so many things, Annie, it's hard to know where to start. What I want right this instant is to kiss you, but with a whole two weeks in which to get to know each other I fear it might be imprudent. Besides which, we'd have something of an audience – a detail which I think I could probably over-look but which might well make you uncomfortable, especially given the fact that you turned ghostly white at the sight of me and don't appear yet to have recov—'

Annie prevented the completion of these sentiments by leaning across the arm rest and pressing her mouth against his. An action which caused her almost as much surprise as Michael, but which brought such a release of tension and pleasure that neither of them saw any reason to withdraw, until compelled to do so by a need for oxygen. 'So you don't think I'm an alco-holic with insurmountable personal hang-ups and an incapacity to face up to the truth?' she gasped, much to the bemusement of the stewardess parking her trolley of refreshments.

'Sir? Madam? Would you like a drink?'

'Two glasses of champagne please,' replied Michael quickly, not moving his eyes from Annie's. 'I think you're marvellous,' he murmured. 'I have from the start . . . but you had men swarming round you, like bees round a honey-pot—'

Annie threw back her head and laughed, so loudly that the

people in the next row threw reproving looks over their head-rests.

'The roses creep, the guy outside the café—'

'You mean Greg and Peter.' She was still laughing, incredulous and delighted to hear a version of events so far removed from her own perceptions.

'And the whole Jake business didn't exactly help,' continued Michael, ruefully, 'though the guy has certainly made up for it now.'

'What do you mean?'

'It's because of Jake that I'm here. We had a heated exchange of views on Saturday morning, during which I believe I communicated some of my feelings for you . . . I was sure I'd never hear from him again, but then he rang me last night full of details of your itinerary, insisting that I join you on the flight.'

'But . . . how did he—?' Annie blushed furiously, 'I mean, I never said – I never mentioned you to him at all.'

'I told him he was mad, that whenever I got within yards you turned hostile and suspected me of the most appalling things. He said being aggressive was your way of showing you cared and to take no notice. A drink?' Michael took the glasses from the steward and handed one to her.

'To take no notice?' Annie accepted the glass, pretending to look offended.

'And then there was the business of the keys – now I must admit that did give me a glimmer of hope, that in spite of your absurd pride and obstinacy you engineered a night in my company.'

'The keys?'

'That cock-and-bull story about the game on the gangplank, when they were in your handbag all along.'

Annie opened her mouth to give the correct, more complicated explanation of the truth, but closed it again. The two versions were not so dissimilar after all. 'So you knew all along . . . You looked in my handbag? I call that a bloody cheek.'

He leant across to her seat. 'And I undressed you too, don't forget that.'

Having returned with all the accoutrements of his mobile office, the businessman gave Michael a puzzled look and sat down.

Annie lowered her voice. 'Well, all I can say is, don't you forget that hordes of eligible bachelors will be flocking for my attention during the course of the next fourteen days—'

'You were going to ignore them all, if I remember correctly.'

'Well, I've changed my mind. Then there's the local talent – I've always had a thing about Italians – and of course I'll be working a lot of the time—' She swallowed and looked away. 'You realise that I am ranting because I am happy,' she faltered, 'that for me incoherence is a sign of deep emotion.'

'I rather hoped that might be the reason.' Michael smiled and took hold of her hand, pressing his fingertips against hers to form a perfect archway of their hands.

'Michael . . . I'm not sure I'm ready for this. I mean, I've only just made this massive mental leap towards realising that a life on my own is . . . OK . . . that I positively do not need someone else in order to be happy or successful.' She turned to look at him, puzzling over the phenomenon of stumbling across something the moment one had stopped hunting for it.

'That's been obvious to me from the start.' He smiled. 'Try thinking of me as an optional extra.'

'An optional extra . . . I like that.' She frowned suddenly, pulling her hand nervously onto her lap. 'But there are things you should know. I can look quite nice sometimes, but other times I'm unequivocally ugly – and sort of lopsided too – mostly when I'm sad I think – and sometimes in the mornings—'

'I've seen you in the mornings – on several occasions. You look . . . delicious.' He retrieved the hand and held it tightly.

'Oh God, so you have. But—' He'd seen the worst of her, she realised, not once but several times. 'We ought to toast Jake – my erstwhile rival for your affections,' Annie teased, chinking her glass against his, welcoming the elation that was welling up inside her, but distrusting it too. 'You ought to know that I don't believe in happy endings,' she added, slipping her thriller under the seat in front of her and turning to look out of the window, where the wall of cloud had given way to an expanse of violet blue.

'I'm not sure I do either. But happy beginnings are feasible enough, aren't they?' he whispered, putting an arm round her and leaning across to share her view of the sky.

A CAST OF SMILES

AMANDA BROOKFIELD

Veronica's group of friends are well-to-do professionals, intent on keeping up a charade of well-being and success. On the surface everything is fine: Julian and Veronica get married; Teddy tells good jokes; Gloria chases men. Trouble brews, however, when the sinister Katherine Vermont becomes obsessed with the deceitful activities of her ex-lover Julian. The tragedy that finally erupts shows the high price that can be paid for emotional dishonesty – to oneself as well as to others.

HODDER AND STOUGHTON PAPERBACKS

WALLS OF GLASS

AMANDA BROOKFIELD

While many regard her marriage with admiration and a trace of envy, Jane Lytton quietly reaches the shocking conclusion that her relationship with Michael, a successful banker with little time for the nitty-gritty of family life, has failed.

Jane's decision to leave a man who does not love her, but who has shown no obvious signs of abuse or neglect of her or their children, is greeted with a mixture of vitriol and measured, uncomprehending sympathy by family and friends. Mattie, Jane's needy younger sister is walking her own tightrope of depression. Even her oldest friend, while recognising the courage of Jane's action, becomes impatient with her difficulties in adjusting to a new life.

Sympathy and strength come from the most unlikely direction, but just as the seeds of trust have been sown, an unfortunate coincidence of events and human failing throws Jane off balance once more. When her vision at last clears to reveal her best chance of happiness, it seems she may have left it too late.

HODDER AND STOUGHTON PAPERBACKS